DEEPSTONE

A SAFEWELL MISSION: BOOK ONE

DEAN LAPPI

macroscian
books

ISBN-13: 978-0-9891726-8-4
Dean Lappi
macroscian books
Cover design by Dean Lappi

To the miners who currently work in the iron ore mines of northern Minnesota. You are keeping the United States strong.

And to the iron ore miners of the past. The iron you dug from the earth helped to build our country.

ACKNOWLEGEMENTS

A sincere thank you to **Erica Anderson** – Editor and proofreader extraordinaire. Your structural, story, and character improvements made this book better in every way. You have an amazing ability to see the story inside the story and help me drag it, kicking and screaming, into life.

To Jason Lappi: You helped me understand how modern open-pit iron mining operations in northern Minnesota work, especially how mine blasting is done.

To Leon Brown: Your input on military weaponry was invaluable.

To my beta readers: Keith Sweatt, Pam Talonen, and Wayne Lappi: Your feedback helped me improve the story.

Also by Dean Lappi

Black Numbers
The Aleph Null Chronicles: Book One

Blood Numbers
The Aleph Null Chronicles: Book Two

Broken Numbers
The Aleph Null Chronicles: Book Three

Beyond Numbers
The Aleph Null Chronicles: Book Four

Available on Amazon.com, BarnesandNoble.com, Apple Books, and other fine book sites

Prologue

Monday, **March 5, 1962**
Deepstone underground mine—Level forty-two
4223 feet underground
Angora Township, Minnesota

MILTON peered into the darkness in the tunnel ahead of him. He was down on Level forty-two of the Deepstone underground mine. 4223 feet of rock lay between him and the surface above. The small lamp on his helmet cast a pale glow that faded only a few feet ahead of him. The absolute blackness beyond the reach of his light told him to turn and run.

Every fiber of his being said to stop moving forward, to leave this god-forsaken tunnel.

Next to Milton, Jacob crept forward slowly, holding a Winchester 30-30 rifle. Marek and Jan followed behind.

Milton's forehead glistened with sweat. His hands trembled. His legs felt like rubber. He blinked sweat from his eyes, his breathing shallow and raspy. Yet from somewhere deep inside, he found the resolve to keep moving forward.

They must reach the hatch that led down to Level forty-three. They must bury it under tons of rock. It was up to the four of them to trap the seemingly unkillable monster that had slaughtered so many of the mining crew. The odds of making it out without being torn to pieces by the creature were against them. But when Howard, their mine boss, had asked for volunteers, Milton was the first to raise his hand. Too many of his friends, men who had been like brothers to him, had been killed by the unholy creature that hunted them in the darkness of these tunnels.

In the distance of the dark tunnel, Milton heard a faint roar. The sound turned his insides to jelly.

Jan whispered behind Milton, "Keep going. We have to finish this."

Milton lifted a shoulder and wiped sweat from the side of his neck, carefully cradling the large box of dynamite he held in his arms.

The roar came again from out of the darkness, this time closer.

Milton wanted to turn and run. The hatch was not far away, but he didn't know if they would make it.

Jacob clenched his teeth and lifted his rifle higher, aiming into the dark, his eyes hard and expressionless

Behind, Marek continued unrolling a spool of wire. Jan carried a fifteen-foot, wooden folding ladder.

Milton suddenly heard the sound of heavy feet pounding toward them. The monster was almost upon them.

A roar came from the dark just ahead, so loud that Milton almost dropped the explosives, a reflex to protect his ears.

Suddenly, a naked woman, her skin shifting with different colors and patterns, appeared as if from nowhere and darted past them. She glanced briefly at Milton as she passed, her large eyes haunted, yet determined.

The monster appeared out of the darkness into the small circle of light from their helmets. It was over seven feet tall, its eyes mirrored, mouth open, sharp teeth glistening.

The woman leapt into the air, covering at least a dozen feet, and sliced deeply into the creature's arm with a strange-looking knife.

Rage filled the monster's eyes. It swiped at her as she soared past, its long talons just missing her. Then it spun around and disappeared into the dark tunnel, chasing after the woman with an ear-splitting roar.

Her voice echoed back to them, "I'll lead the Vorgroth away. Blow that hatch, Milton!"

Milton stared into the darkness, completely shocked by what had just happened. Behind him, Jan shouted, "Get moving, now!"

Jacob sprinted forward and Milton ran down the tunnel after him, trying to keep the box of dynamite steady in his arms.

Sweat ran down Milton's face in rivulets, even though it was only fifty degrees in the tunnel. He couldn't see anything past the edge of his feeble light. He expected the monster to rise up out of the darkness at any moment.

Jacob ran hard ahead of him, holding his rifle steady.

The men Milton worked with were tough and feared little. Milton's friends Otto and Franc should have been here with him now, but they had been slaughtered by the monster. Milton had been with them at the time of the attack and had barely escaped with his life. He would never forgive himself for surviving when they hadn't.

Milton's light illuminated a curve in the tunnel just ahead. He ran fast around the bend and slid to a stop by the steel hatch in the floor. This was the end of the tunnel. Down below was Level forty-three.

Jacob whispered, his thick Finnish accent difficult to understand, "Do it, Milton. Blow that thing to hell."

Milton carefully placed the box of explosives on the rocky floor by the open hatch. He lifted his hands and was surprised to see they no longer trembled.

Marek set down the roll of connecting wire, unspooled another ten feet of it, then snipped it.

Jan quietly opened the folding ladder.

Jacob stood guard with his rifle. Milton knew the rifle wouldn't do any good against the monster, but it made them all feel better to have it down here with them.

4

Milton climbed four steps up the ladder and Marek handed bundles of dynamite up to him, detonation wires hanging from each bundle. Milton had prepared the bundles ahead of time. All he had to do was tape them to the walls and ceiling and connect the shorter wires to the main connector wire. With surprisingly steady hands, Milton attached the bundles to the ceiling using industrial-strength duct tape. The sound of the peeling tape echoed through the dark space and more sweat beaded on Milton's forehead. He soon finished with the ceiling, then attached two bundles of dynamite to each of the three walls. Milton expected the monstrous creature to rise through the hatch at any moment to pull him into the darkness below.

Milton descended the ladder and quickly spliced the wires from the dynamite bundles to the main wire that led down the tunnel. He stopped working at one point when he heard a roar in the cavern below the hatch. The hair on his neck stood up. They had to get out of here now. Milton twisted the final wire, then motioned everyone to retreat down the tunnel.

The four of them sprinted down the long, dark passageway to a large cavern. They crossed to the right until they reached the ladder that led up to Level forty-one. The main wire snaked up the side of the ladder and through the hatch. Milton quickly motioned for Jacob, Jan, and Marek to climb up, and as they did, Milton peered into the blackness behind him, hoping the strange woman would appear.

But she didn't.

Milton was disappointed, but knew time was running out. He quickly scaled the ladder. When he reached the top, he joined the mine boss Howard and four other miners who nervously waited, their eyes shifting anxiously from Milton to the darkness beneath the open hatch in the floor.

Milton knelt by the detonator box. He carefully connected the single wire to the box, giving it a soft pull to ensure it was securely attached.

Milton called out softly, "We are live. I repeat, we are live." He raised the plunger of the detonator box and rested his hands on the long handle. They still used this old-style detonator because the mine had not yet made the transition to the new electric blasting caps. Milton had been pushing for the changeover. Now it looked like it was too late, at least for this mine. No one would ever work down here again.

Milton waited for as long as he could to give the woman who had helped them a chance to escape from Level forty-three.

After thirty seconds had gone by, Howard cried out, "What are you waiting for? Blow that thing!"

Milton still hesitated.

Howard suddenly lunged forward, put his hands over Milton's, and roughly pushed the plunger down.

There was a two-second pause, then a rumble sounded below. The entire tunnel shook for twenty seconds, which felt like an eternity.

Then there was silence. The job was done. But had *she* survived?

Two men rushed forward, slammed the hatch closed, and immediately began welding it shut.

Milton cried out, "Wait! We must give her time to come up!"

The men ignored him, and two others pulled him away as he struggled to stop the welders.

Milton watched in despair until the last of the welders turned off their torch.

The hatch had a two-inch-thick weld around it.

It would never open again.

CHAPTER 1

*Sunday, **August 10, 2025***
Deepstone underground mine—Level forty-two
4223 feet underground
Angora Township, Minnesota

Team leader TALI MAYS made a short chopping motion with her left hand, her index finger pointing forward, and her team instantly moved toward the jagged hole in the tunnel floor thirty feet ahead. A solid wall of rocks blocked the tunnel just past the opening in the floor. This was the end of the Deepstone tunnel system, and down below was Level forty-three, the deepest point in the underground mine.

Peter, a tall man in his thirties with a thin handlebar mustache, who had once been a Pontifical Swiss Guard at the Vatican, stepped fearlessly to the three-foot-wide gaping hole in the floor and quickly peered over the edge. He spoke softly into his mike as he did. "The previous team must have detonated a large amount of high-density C4 explosives to clear away the collapsed rock, and blew a gaping hole where the hatch had been in the process." Peter scanned the area below the hatch through the night-vision device attached to his helmet. He remained completely still for a few seconds, then whispered into his mic, "The ladder has been severely damaged by the explosion, but it looks like they used a rope to descend into the hatch. The chamber below appears to be clear."

Casey, a tall Egyptian woman and former El-Sa'ka Egyptian Special Forces Marine Commando, carefully examined a rock climber's anchor bolt that had been driven into the floor ten feet from the opening. A climbing rope ran through the anchor. It trailed to, and disappeared into, the hole. She let the rope slide through her hand as she followed it back to the opening in the floor, then knelt to check where the rope lay against the edge to verify that it was not damaged. She stood and gave a quick nod to Tali that it was secure.

Terry, the final member of the team knelt on one knee, facing the dark tunnel behind them, his prototype SIG Sauer NGSW-R MCX Spear assault rifle held steady.

Tali had been ordered to determine the location

and status of the first military team that her employer, Thornlandon Holdings, had sent into the unused and deepest levels of the Deepstone mine four days earlier.

Deepstone was currently owned by the state of Minnesota, who operated a tourist attraction on Level thirty-two. The levels below thirty-two had been sealed off and forgotten since 1962.

Tali's team found no evidence that the first team had exfiltrated the mine. The answer to that team's disappearance was likely in Level forty-three below. There was nowhere else they could be.

Tali whispered into her mic, "Descend."

Casey pulled the rope up enough so she could step over the edge. She slid down to the floor of the chamber below, her gloves protecting her hands. She was quickly followed by Peter, then Terry. Tali followed last. In less than a minute, they all stood in the chamber below, rifles out, crouched low. They scanned the area through their night vision devices.

The chamber was no more than 200 feet across at its widest, roughly cut from the iron-rich rock. Piles of rock lay on the floor directly below the opening above, having fallen during the explosion that opened the hatch. The chamber itself had been created by the miners sixty years earlier to follow the iron-rich veins in the earth. It was not a perfect square of a room; it was shaped like a winding river, the chamber curving out of sight to the right. This had been the last level the miners had reached, and Tali could see the work down here had only just begun before the mining company had sealed this level. What had happened to cause the mining company to walk away from so much wealth was a mystery, and that mystery was beyond her pay grade. Her team was here to find their missing teammates. Tali could see four sets of boot tracks leading away to the right, so she whispered into her mic, "Follow the tracks on the ground."

Her team moved almost silently across the chamber, careful not to mess up the tracks they followed. The only noises in the cavern were the soft sounds of their steps. Each person covered a different section of the chamber with their rifle, their eyes missing nothing in the ghostly green light of their night vision.

Tali had never experienced darkness as absolute as the darkness down in this mine. She had briefly turned her night vision off in one of the tunnels above. She literally hadn't been able to see anything, not even the ghostly outlines one normally saw in the darkest rooms topside. The blackness around her felt like a heavy hand pushing against her eyes and she had quickly turned her night vision back on. If something catastrophic happened, such as their night vision devices being compromised and they lost their backup flashlights, they would likely never find their way back to the surface.

She brushed the thought aside and had taken two more steps when Peter, who was walking point ten feet ahead of the rest of the team, stopped with his left arm raised, fist closed, arm bent at the elbow. About thirty feet ahead, Tali saw a large pillar of stone that connected the floor and ceiling of the chamber.

They stood perfectly still, breathing softly, yet silently.

Peter stood for more than a minute, his head moving slowly from left to right. Finally, he knelt and reached out with a finger to touch the floor. He raised it to his face and studied it, then rubbed his finger and thumb together. He whispered into his mic, his voice flat yet tinged with suppressed emotion, "Blood. And more ahead. A lot more. And..." his voice faded without finishing his sentence.

Tali knew Peter well, having been his team leader for two years. Nothing flustered him. But just now, she had heard just a hint of fear in his tone. Tali whispered into her mic, "What do you see?"

Peter stared ahead, then softly replied, "There are other tracks here. They are..." he trailed off, his voice fading away to silence.

Tali interrupted, "Report what you see, now."

Shaking his head, Peter spoke more forcefully, "I...I see barefoot tracks, and they are huge. At least three times larger than my foot. They are all around me."

Tali felt a surge of adrenaline. *Giant footprints? Blood? What was going on down here?* She had seen no evidence of other hostile teams in the mine. Tali whispered into the mic again, but even her whisper seemed too loud, "Safeties off. Move slowly, eyes everywhere."

The team moved forward, and Tali now saw the blood. She came across one of the huge footprints. Only her years of training kept her from gasping out loud.

After another fifteen feet, Peter stopped again, only this time he didn't have to say anything. They all saw the body lying on the ground ahead of him. From the clothing, it was obviously a member of the first Thornlandon Holdings team.

Tali tried to swallow but couldn't, her mouth suddenly dry. The body had been torn in half. Not cut in half, as if by a large caliber automatic weapon, but torn in half; its organs strung out across the floor.

"What the fuck?" It was Casey, her voice tinged with panic.

"Quiet," Tali whispered. She approached the pillar of rock, and as she did, she saw two more bodies, ripped apart in the same way. Then, Tali saw the fourth body. Or at least she assumed it was the fourth body. A large pool of almost dried blood covered a section of the rocky floor, bits of gore interspersed within it. A hand, still gripping a rifle, lay on the ground not far away. Tali suppressed the urge to vomit when she bent over and saw teeth marks in the flesh.

Tali saw a helmet lying to her left. She stepped forward and nudged it with her boot. It tipped to its side and the face of team leader Kalim Amani stared back at her, his mouth twisted as if he had died screaming; his eyes open wide in horror.

Peter turned to Tali and said, "We need to get out of here. Now."

Straightening her shoulders, Tali suppressed her revulsion. "Negative. Search for their night vision units. We need to bring back the hard drives." The night vision devices recorded continuously, saving the footage to the 20 TB hard drives in each unit. They must bring them back to Thornlandon Holdings to find out what happened down here.

They quickly recovered two of the night vision devices. The other two units had been destroyed.

Tali motioned her head. "Peter, stow them in your pack. We are moving out now."

Not one member of the team needed to be told twice. They quickly retraced their route, their need to get out of the cavern so strong that it seemed to physically push them back to the rope that snaked up into the opening in the ceiling.

Peter had just swung his rifle over his shoulder and grabbed the rope when there was a growl behind them. It was so low that they felt it more than heard it. They all spun to face the chamber they had just come from.

A heavy thud reverberated through the chamber, followed by another.

Then another.

Something huge and heavy was walking toward them, hidden by the curve of the chamber.

Tali spoke harshly and turned to the team. "Peter, get up that rope. Then the rest of you. I will cover you."

Peter stood frozen to the spot, staring over Tali's shoulder.

Tali felt a shiver of fear, for in his eyes she saw madness. No matter how much she wanted to avoid turning around, she knew she must. Tali slowly turned her head and cried out involuntarily.

A dark form strode toward her. Through the grainy night vision, it looked like a demon from the depths of hell. Standing over seven feet tall, it glared at them malevolently, its eyes seeming to glow with a mirrored finish in the night vision. Its forehead curved inward and upward before sloping outward and down to its shoulders.

The creature opened its mouth to reveal a row of sharp front teeth, the incisors at least three inches long, glistening with saliva. Then it threw its head back and roared.

Casey stepped forward and fired her rifle on fully

automatic. Forty bullets struck the creature in the chest within five seconds, but they bounced away as if they were striking steel.

The creature strode quickly forward, and Casey looked up at its monstrous face in horror, her rifle clicking empty. The monster swung a giant fist down on her head. She crumpled to the ground, her body collapsing like a crushed soda can.

Hot blood sprayed across Tali's face.

The creature backhanded Terry, sending him flying across the room. He hit the floor and tumbled three times before coming to a stop, his head bent back at an unnatural angle.

Both had been killed in less than ten seconds.

Tali felt her mind clear. She raised her rifle and opened fire, emptying 40 rounds into the nightmare that stood before her. Tali's bullets bounced off the thing's skin. The creature turned and advanced on Tali. She stepped back as she replaced her magazine, and as she did her foot caught a rock. Tali fell backward just as the creature swung at her. The fist missed her head by inches as she landed on her back.

Peter screamed and began scrambling up the rope, his face contorted in horror.

The creature turned its head and took three long strides toward Peter. It reached out, plucked Peter from the rope, and took a bite from Peter's face as a human would an apple, the crunch almost identical.

Tali watched in horror, unable to believe what was happening. This couldn't be real. Her mind was blank, terror and adrenaline blotting out all thought. Then her training took over and she scrambled to her feet, took careful aim at the thing's back, and held the trigger of her rifle, emptying her magazine. The bullets bounced away in all directions. Tali felt one slam back into her leg. She ignored it, not feeling any pain.

The creature didn't even seem to notice the bullets as it took another bite from Peter's face, chewing loudly.

If bullets can't stop this thing, maybe my knife can, Tali thought. She tossed her rifle to the side and withdrew the twelve-inch Bowie knife from the sheath at her waist. It was her prized possession, having been made specially for her by one of the best bladesmiths in Texas.

Tali let out a blood-curdling scream and leapt at the creature, her eyes blazing in fury.

It turned its head in surprise at her attack and was too late to block her knife.

Tali stabbed the long blade of her Bowie knife into the monster's neck but the blade shattered upon impact.

The creature casually punched her in the chest.

Tali heard the bones shatter inside her body as she flew backward and struck the floor.

Heavy footsteps approached.

Tali turned her head and looked up defiantly at the monster.

The creature glared down at her for a moment, then stomped down on her head.

Chapter 2

Thursday, **August 14, 2025**
The Iron Range – Northern Minnesota

JOHN LUKKINEN ran a comb through his thick, black hair, then leaned closer to the mirror. The face that stared back at him still looked relatively young; no more than forty years old. Only the crow's feet crinkling at the corners of his eyes belied his true fifty-six years.

John reached up and moved his nose side-to-side. He had broken it badly in a fight when he was sixteen and it had never healed right. It remained slightly crooked, with a notch on the bridge. John had grown up an angry kid. He was proud of his Anishinaabe heritage, but he had been treated badly because of it. He had the darker skin and facial features of the Anishinaabe, but pale blue eyes from his Finnish heritage. He rarely fit in with the white kids at school, so he grew distant, avoiding any lasting friendships in school.

John's father was Finnish, his mother Anishinaabe. It had been quite the scandal in the small town of Virginia, Minnesota when they had married back in 1965. Some people had thrown rocks through their windows, while others had called his dad an "Indian lover" behind his back. The bigots who dared say it to his face often lowered their eyes and backed away without another word when they saw the look of compassion and sadness emanating from John's father.

Both of John's parents had passed away when he was in his forties.

John was six foot two; muscular without looking muscle bound; athletic, but not obviously so; handsome but often unnoticed by others. John had remained single his whole life; he'd never met a woman he wanted to settle down with.

John hurried down the stairs into the bright kitchen, the morning sun cheering up the thirty-year-old décor and cursed when he glanced at the clock on the microwave.

He was probably going to be late for work for the first time since he had taken the Deepstone job ten years earlier. As the lead tour guide, John loved his job at Angora Deepstone Underground Mine Tours. While it didn't pay that great, he made enough to live comfortably.

John lived in Virginia, which was normally a half-hour drive to the Deepstone mine. But he still needed to stop at the hardware store on Main Street to buy a few dozen batteries for the backup flashlights on Level thirty-two. *Damn,* John thought. *Why did I stay up so late watching Netflix last night?*

John locked his front door and quickly made his way to the twenty-year-old, dark green Subaru Outback parked on the street. The door protested loudly as he opened it. The seat creaked as he sat down. The car was old, but John loved it. He turned the key in the ignition and the engine started instantly, sputtering roughly for a couple of minutes before settling into a begrudging idle.

John put the car in gear, glanced in the side mirror, pulled out onto Fifth Street, and drove one block to Second Avenue. He sat at the stop sign until two cars had passed, then turned left. He didn't even have to think about the route, having driven it so many times over the years.

The Iron Range covered 10,000 square miles. When chatting with out-of-towners, John would often say he was from "The Range" instead of Virginia. He reflected that while many younger people complained about small-town life here and wanted to escape the first chance they could, people over forty tended to love it here. He sometimes heard people refer to the area as "God's country." They didn't mean it in a religious way, but more to describe the peacefulness and beauty of the area.

John fully agreed about the beauty of northern Minnesota. There was nowhere else he would want to live.

He stopped for a red light at Chestnut Street, which ran the length of the original downtown. The light turned green and John drove on, completely forgetting to turn and get batteries at the hardware store.

John kept the windows open as he drove. The fresh, warm air filled him with energy. It was the third week of August, and the area was experiencing a heatwave. It was already 80 degrees, and temperatures would likely surge to 95 by afternoon. It was tough sleeping last night without an air conditioner.

Even with the heat wave, John noticed the leaves already starting to lose their green color. By early October, the forests would turn bright red and gold. Then the temperatures would steadily drop, and snow could fall anytime.

John arrived at the underground mine at 8:45 on the nose, happy with the good time he had made. Multiple cars already filled the small gravel lot.

Tourists made their way up to the ticketing building. Most wore pants and sweaters, or held jackets in their hands, even in the early-morning heat. They had clearly read that the air temperature underground stayed a constant fifty degrees, completely unaffected by the temperature topside, and had planned accordingly.

John parked in a small area reserved for staff. He got out of the car and made his way to the staff building. He pulled the door open and stepped into the main room, smiling at Carl and Tammy, who sat at one of the tables drinking coffee and chatting quietly.

Carl gave a quick nod, not even bothering to look John in the eyes.

Tammy smiled widely, "Good morning, John." Her red hair seemed to float in the air briefly before falling back onto her shoulders as she turned her head. She was beautiful, young, and a truly nice person. Everyone loved Tammy.

Carl's eyes narrowed; the young man's crush on Tammy was still one-sided. She was friendly with Carl but had never reciprocated his romantic interest.

The fact that John had made Tammy his co-tour guide hadn't helped John's relationship with Carl. The young man was stuck operating the elevator every day. Carl always wore black T-shirts and faded jeans. Combined with his angular face and stormy eyes, he just didn't connect with others.

John smiled at Tammy as he stepped to the front of the room, then glanced over and nodded at Dennis, who operated the elevator mechanicals from the machinery building. Dennis was forty-three years old, with a stomach that pushed over his jeans. The elevator that brought tourists 3200 feet down to Level thirty-two was original, except for the new parts required to keep it operational. It was a feat of engineering simplicity and complexity at the same time. Dennis had to constantly adjust the cable speed and tension, as well as monitor the machine that powered the elevator. It was the most important job at the tour center, and the man's experience was invaluable. The team wouldn't dare take tourists 3200 feet into the earth in a steel cage without someone as trustworthy as Dennis at the helm.

John smiled. "Morning, Dennis. Is Sarah ready to go back to the U of M after her summer break?"

Dennis grunted. "She is. Though I hate the idea of her living in the Cities all by herself. She could have gone to Duluth or Bemidji State, but she just *had* to choose the U of M."

John grinned. "Minneapolis isn't *that* far away, Dennis."

Dennis shrugged. "I guess not. I just hate those

freeways. The people drive crazy down there."

John turned to Sherry, the ticketing agent, and said hello.

Sherry beamed at him, her eyes twinkling. "Hi, John. Another hot day today, hey?" At nineteen years old, she was the youngest employee. She worked for the summer months and went to the Mesabi Range College in Virginia during the school year.

Jim sat by himself at a small table, and John nodded hello to him. Jim was sixty-seven years old and the onsite safety inspector and mechanic. It was his responsibility to ensure everything ran smoothly. Jim was a quiet man who rarely spoke to anyone, preferring to keep to himself. He was good at his job and had been doing it for over twenty years. John didn't know much about him. The man preferred his own company and never voluntarily spoke to anyone.

The mine tours lasted an hour and operated four times a day starting at 9:30 a.m. The final tour started at 3 p.m. It was an easy schedule.

John turned to everyone. "Alright. We are pushing toward the end of the season; only two weeks left. I know you are all getting tour-fatigue from running the tours all summer, but those people out there are likely experiencing the mine for the first time. So let's make today a fun day for all our visiting friends. Tammy and I will lead the tours. Sherry, you are on tickets. Carl, you are our elevator operator. Dennis, you do your thing. And Jim, could you have a look at the air conditioner outside? It is forecast to stay hot like this for another week, so it would be nice to enjoy our breaks in a cool room."

Jim nodded, his face impassive.

Carl moodily asked, "Can I do one of the tours with you today, John? I'm sick of running the elevator day after day."

"I know you are, Carl. How about this. You can join Tammy and I for the second tour tomorrow. Jim, you wouldn't mind operating the elevator in Carl's place for that tour, would you?"

Jim shrugged. "Don't matter much to me."

Carl's face lit up. "Awesome! Thanks, John." He glanced at Tammy, obviously anxious to hang out with her for a tour.

John grabbed a thick sweater from his locker. As he pulled it over his head, a loud series of booms rattled the windows, shaking the ground beneath them.

Tammy jumped in her chair, cursing out loud, "God dammit! I hate that new Onamuni mine!"

Carl scowled, "They are too fucking close to us."

The Onamuni mine had recently received the environmental green light this summer to begin operations, and they had started to blast three weeks earlier. Blasting the iron-rich rock was performed through a series of controlled detonations massive enough to blow apart sections of ancient rock up to thirty feet deep and four hundred feet wide.

It was a huge concern when it came to the safety of the team and the tourists. John nodded to Tammy and Carl. "I will set up a meeting with the DNR to discuss it. In the meantime, Tammy and I will keep an eye out for any damage in the tunnel structure down on Level thirty-two." He looked around, then nodded. "Alright, let's get to work." He waited for everyone to exit the room before following them out.

A line of people already waited at the ticket gate.

John quickly got into the rhythm of the tours. Before he knew it, they had completed the third tour and were right on schedule for the final tour to begin at 3 p.m., in just a half an hour. The third tour had included a family of six. The children ranged in age from 3 to 15 years old. Upon returning topside, the family exited the elevator and each of the children formally shook John's hand and thanked him. The 3-year-old boy named Casey stopped in front of John, looked up through curly black hair that fell over his eyes, held his little hand out, and said in a sing-song voice, "Thank you for such a lovely tour, Mr. John."

John was still smiling when he entered the employee's office. Everyone was there except for Sherry, who would keep the next tour group busy until the final tour started in thirty minutes.

John's smile faded when he thought of the two-inch-wide crack he had just noticed in the back wall of the elevator room, however.

Jim looked at him curiously. "What's up John? You don't look happy all of a sudden."

Pulling a chair out and sitting down, John wondered how much he should say. Maybe he was worrying about nothing at all. *But what if the damage to the walls was something to worry about*? John felt the weight of his responsibility pressing upon him. *Was it safe to bring the final tour group down into the mine?* He put both elbows on the table, ran his hands through his hair, then sighed and looked up at his team. "I just saw another large crack in the wall down on thirty-two. I'm thinking we should consider stopping our tours until the stability of the mine can be reviewed by the DNR."

The Department of Natural Resources (DNR) of Minnesota was a sprawling government agency that controlled every aspect of the state's natural resources, as well as the outdoor recreation and commercial usage of those resources. The Deepstone

Underground Mine tours fell under their authority.

Carl groaned. "They'll shut this whole place down, won't they?"

John pulled open his desk drawer and rifled through the contents until he found a small black book. He glanced at Carl and said, "We don't know that, Carl. But it is better to run this issue up the chain, just to be safe."

John placed the book on his desk and opened the front cover where he had written down the mine-related phone numbers. He no longer memorized phone numbers. Who did anymore, with cellphones doing all the work now? He picked up the old-fashioned office phone and dialed the direct number for the assistant to the Director of Mining at the DNR main office, avoiding the dreaded automated phone system that took so long to get through.

A woman's voice answered, "Director's office, how may I assist you?"

John didn't recognize the voice. Maybe Bernice, the usual assistant to the Director, was out sick.

"Hello. This is John Lukkinen over at Deepstone Underground Mine Tours in Angora."

The voice replied coldly, "Yes?"

John rolled his eyes. Couldn't the DNR hire a temporary replacement with a personality? "Sorry to bother you, but I have a potential problem here at the mine and I need to speak with Director Mark immediately."

"What's the problem?"

"Well, as you might know, the Onamuni mine started blasting near us a few weeks ago. I noticed small cracks appearing in the tunnel ceiling down on Level thirty-two over the past week, and today I noticed another, larger crack running up the wall of the elevator room. It was about two inches wide. I am not sure if it is safe for us to be down there right now."

The line was silent for a few moments, then the woman replied, "Director Mark has moved on. I will patch you through to Director Meyers."

John felt the same feeling he always got when something didn't seem right. Companies changed employees all the time, but the DNR was old-school government and big changes at the top rarely happened there. If they did, those changes would be communicated quickly down the line. He hadn't heard anything about a change to the directorship.

He waited impatiently as some awful elevator music played a bland rendition of an 80s song he knew but couldn't remember the name of.

CHAPTER 3

HELEN POLSON put the tour guide on hold and immediately pushed the intercom for Director Judith Meyers' office.

"Yes?" The voice dripped with irritation.

"I have John Lukkinen, the tour guide at Deepstone, on the line. He said the Onamuni blasting has caused a large crack to appear in a wall down on Level thirty-two."

The door to Director Meyers' office opened, and her boss stuck her head out, "Get in here."

Helen hurried into Director Meyers' office. One didn't keep the director of Thornlandon Holdings waiting.

This was not the DNR headquarters. It was the inner sanctum of one of the most powerful corporations in the world. Thornlandon Holdings was secretly closing on the purchase of the Deepstone mine tomorrow morning. Not even the DNR knew about it.

Thornlandon Holdings had already determined the Deepstone mine may be at risk of being structurally compromised by the Onamuni mine blasting that had recently started. They had sent a recon team into the mine to verify its structural condition.

That first team didn't return, so they'd sent in a second team two days ago. The second team hadn't returned, either.

Worried, Director Meyers had ordered their tech department to reroute all calls from Deepstone directly to Helen's phone so no one at the DNR would know what was happening in the mine.

Director Meyers glared at Helen from behind a mahogany desk that was bare except for a modern desk phone and a laptop. "Tell me what he wants."

Helen remained standing. Not that she had a choice. There were no chairs in the room except for the one Director Meyers sat in.

"The tour guide says he is not sure if it is safe for the tours to continue. I think he wants to shut it down. And I doubt he'll keep the instability of the mine to himself."

Director Meyers asked, "Is that everything?"

Helen nodded.

Director Meyers shrugged. "If he wants the mine shut down, then we will shut it down." Her words carried a finality that made it clear her conversation with Helen was done. Director Meyers picked up the phone receiver and pressed the button for the waiting call. Her tone changed to that of a concerned boss, "Hello Mr. Lukkinen. How may I be of assistance?"

The man's rich, deep voice was pleasant. "Hello...Director Meyers?"

Director Meyers calmly asked, "You said you have some concerns about the tours?"

"Yes. I noticed a large crack in the stone wall down on Level thirty-two. I don't know if it is safe to continue the tours today. Can you send someone over to evaluate the damage?"

"Of course. We will send someone today. Do you know if any of the tourists noticed the issue?"

John replied, "No, the damaged wall is in the back corner of the chamber. The tourists didn't go back that far."

"Good. We don't want anyone spreading rumors. This would be bad for the mine tours and bad for your job, Mr. Lukkinen. Why don't you finish out the last tour today so as to not cause a scene, and then we will close the mine tomorrow? If you think it is safe enough for today, that is?"

There was a brief silence, then the man said, "Yes, it should be safe to do one more tour. I will tell the team not to come into work tomorrow. Thank you."

Director Meyers replied, "Of course, Mr. Lukkinen. Thank you for bringing this to our attention." She hung up before John could reply, sat back in her chair, and scowled at Helen, her second-in-command. "We cannot let the Deepstone employees leave that mine and tell anyone about the structural damage. If they do, that information could find its way to the media, or federal- and state-level government, and they could permanently shut the mine down. With less than twenty-four hours before we own it, we cannot let that happen. What's the latest intel on the mine?"

Standing even straighter than she had been, Helen said, "As you know, we have sensors placed on most of the levels of the Deepstone mine, and the data show considerable weakening in nine of the thirty-two levels. The two teams we sent in to investigate Levels thirty-three through forty-three have not returned. Those teams were equipped with low-frequency communication devices, yet both teams have gone radio silent. They have either been compromised by outside agencies, killed, or trapped by a cave-in. The latest blast from the Onamuni mine has compromised three more levels, so a cave-in is certainly possible." She felt a trickle of sweat roll down the small of her back as she continued, "I do not think it was wise to send in the team from SafeWell. We do not control them, and they are not cleared for any information they may gather down there."

Director Meyers eyed her coldly. "I did not authorize that team, and you damned well know it. It was that senator from Minnesota who did this without informing us."

Helen knew exactly who Director Meyers was talking about: Minnesota Senator Ronald Young. He had somehow found out about their proprietary DELIDR—Deep Earth Light Detection and Ranging—scanning technology that could determine the geological makeup of the ground up to ten miles deep, and specifically what those scans had revealed beneath the Deepstone mine, leaving them with no choice but to bring the senator into the organization.

The DELIDR scans had shown a vast network of tunnels and caverns more than 46,000 feet beneath Level forty-three of the Deepstone mine. The caverns yielded high readings of an element they could not identify, but which their top scientists believed may be some sort of unknown heavy metal with properties they had yet to understand. The scan also showed vast quantities of gold, Rhodium, Platinum, Iridium, and other rare metals. The potential value was estimated to be in excess of three trillion dollars. They had no idea what the unknown element might actually be worth, but Thornlandon Holdings intended to find out—and reap the rewards.

To make matters worse, over the past few months, Senator Young had grown more intrusive with his demands, becoming nearly impossible to control.

Coming out of her thoughts, Helen casually said, "We should get rid of Senator Young once and for all. He is a rodent, but a rodent with power. We need to get him out of our walls."

Director Meyers' eyes blazed. "Believe me, I would like nothing more than to kill Senator Young. But we both know you cannot 'get rid of'," she held her fingers in air quotes, "a senator, especially one like Senator Young. He is too powerful. And any investigation into his death would include all federal agencies. We do not know if he has saved documents about our involvement in Deepstone, or our discoveries below it. We cannot risk that."

Looking briefly at her nails, Helen asked, "Would you like me to send one of our kill teams to pay him a visit? Perhaps a night-time visit to his Washington D.C. hotel suite? We could gently impress upon him how important privacy is to us and him?"

Director Meyers shook her head. "No, that will not work on the senator. If we threaten him, he will dig in his heels and become even more dangerous to us." She sighed and leaned back in her chair. "It's too late, anyway. The SafeWell team arrived at

Deepstone this afternoon. They are likely already in the mine. As you know, we sent Renn Holder's team this morning to secure the mine for our takeover tomorrow. They are in the air and plan to arrive at Deepstone by 4 p.m. Call Renn right now and change his mission to full sanitation. But make sure he and his team arrive after the final tour is completed, and do not move in until all the tourists are gone. I do not want them harmed if we can help it, or more importantly, for them to see Renn's team arrive. I don't want a scene. The last thing we need is a news crew out there."

Helen nodded. Then, as calmly as if she were verifying a breakfast order, she asked, "Just to verify. You mean *full* sanitation, correct?"

Director Meyers' eyes flashed angrily, "Yes. I mean full sanitation. I want the onsite Deepstone employees and the SafeWell team sanitized. Clean out their homes. Get rid of their cars. Everything. If they live with any family, get rid of them as well. And if a missing person's report does get filed for any of them, we need to trigger a complete financial record indicating they are living somewhere else, so the police won't look any further into it."

Director Meyers calmly picked up her phone, but before she dialed, she said, "After the SafeWell team is terminated—including the CEO, Henry Skuggs—I want their company shut down. Permanently."

Helen briskly nodded. "Yes ma'am." She turned and strode from Judith's office, already dialing a number on her mobile.

The deep voice of Renn Holder answered, "Yes?"

"Mission change. Now Code Alpha...Zed. Authorization: 93772."

The voice on the other asked, "Details, please."

Helen explained the changed mission directive.

Renn was quiet for a few seconds, then said, "Affirmative" and ended the call.

Helen immediately began making additional calls.

CHAPTER 4

RENN HOLDER had his eyes closed, trying to catch a few hours of sleep as he lay back in the plush seat of the private Thornlandon Holdings jet. They had been in the air for almost 4 hours already and would be landing at the Range Regional Airport in Hibbing, Minnesota within the hour. Renn led three Thornlandon Holdings military teams. He was Navajo, forty-two-years-old, with a pockmarked, yet handsome, face, thick black hair, and piercing brown eyes. At 6'5", he had the build of a powerlifter but moved quickly and lightly on his feet.

Renn replayed the events that led him to being in this jet, about to start a military mission on American soil. His phone had rung at 9:15. a.m. When he answered the call, Helen Polson, assistant to Director Meyers, simply said, "Code Alpha: Garage. Authorization: 11000." Renn understood this was code for "report to central command."

Gathering his wallet and keys, Renn was out of his house in less than two minutes. He rode his BMW

1000RR motorcycle through San Bernardino, located on the far eastern edge of Los Angeles, and arrived at the headquarters of Thornlandon Holdings at 9:28 a.m. *Thirteen minutes,* he thought, as he rolled slowly into the underground parking structure. *Not bad.*

Somehow, Renn's entire team had beaten him there. All seventeen of them casually leaned against their vehicles.

Tess, a sniper on his team, looked at her watch as he dismounted, and said, "tsk, tsk," though her eyes danced with humor.

"If you 'tsk, tsk' me again, I'll put my boot up your ass," Renn growled.

She rolled her eyes, but quickly stood straight, her expression changing in an instant from playful to attentive when a door to the side of the garage opened and Director Meyers stepped through.

Renn stood at attention as Director Meyers approached. She was a short, Black woman in her sixties. Per usual, she wore thick, 1960s-era glasses, a drab grey blouse, black trousers, and white nursing-style shoes. He noticed she never wore any jewelry, and she clearly didn't spend much time styling her hair. If he didn't know her and passed her on the street, he wouldn't give her another look. This was exactly what Director Meyers was aiming for.

Director Meyers was followed by her assistant, Helen Polson, who looked the opposite of her boss.

Helen was in her thirties and wore a $5000-dollar suit impeccably tailored to fit her lean body. Her shoulder-length blond hair bounced with each step, providing glimpses of expensive diamond earrings. Helen carried a snakeskin briefcase in her left hand as she walked across the floor, her heels clicking loudly on the concrete.

Based on outward appearances, most people would have assumed Helen was in charge. She exuded a commanding presence combined with extraordinary beauty. She radiated power and he'd seen more than one person wither under a glare from her piercing blue eyes.

But it was Director Judith Meyers who commanded Thornlandon Holdings. And it was Director Meyers who struck fear into the hearts of all who came before her. Together, the two women wielded more power than the leaders of many countries.

Director Meyers came to a stop a few steps from Renn, her voice hard-edged as she directed Helen to open the briefcase.

Helen set the briefcase down hard onto the nearest car hood, then pulled it forward, the brass hinges of the case scraping loudly across the painted metal, leaving two, six-inch scratches in the paint.

It was the car of an Australian named Paul. The Aussie opened his mouth to say something but quickly thought the better of it. Although Paul had spent over $80,000 on the bespoke 2020 Mustang, he wisely ignored Helen purposely scratching the custom paint job.

Helen entered a code, and the latch of the briefcase clicked open. She removed a stack of papers and handed one to each of the team members as Director Meyers began to speak, her almost military-style cadence clipped and to the point.

"You will memorize the mission brief and leave the documents in the jet when you arrive at your destination. I will summarize. Thornlandon Holdings has located an ultra-rich iron ore deposit beneath the lowest level of the Deepstone underground mine in

Northern Minnesota. This iron deposit has an estimated value of almost ten billion dollars. We filed paperwork to acquire the Deepstone mine; the purchase will be finalized tomorrow. The iron ore mine operated until 1962, after which the mining company sealed eleven levels below Level thirty-two and closed down operations. The mine was donated to the State of Minnesota who have run it as a tourist attraction ever since. We sent two teams into Deepstone to map those lowest levels. They have not returned."

Before anyone could ask questions, she continued, "We verified the teams have not exfiltrated the mine. Their status is unknown. Your job is to verify the status of the two missing teams, verify the condition of Levels thirty-three through forty-three, then secure the mine until Thornlandon Holdings arrives in full force tomorrow after the purchase paperwork has been finalized."

Helen took out one more piece of paper and handed it to Judith, who scanned it silently before saying, "There is one complication. An open-pit mining company called Onamuni recently received approval to begin mining operations three miles from Deepstone and have started blasting. We have filed cease-and-desist paperwork, but this could take months to move through the courts, even with our connections. So, we have sent a demolitions team to orchestrate an 'accidental' explosion today. This will stop any further mining activity at Onamuni for months while investigations move through the necessary channels. However, the detonations that Onamuni have already set off have weakened the underground tunnel system in Deepstone. Do not use any explosives in the mine. I repeat, no explosives. If you come across a collapsed tunnel, you will mark its location and that is all. If that mine collapses because of your incompetence, you and everyone you know will be killed, whether or not you make it out alive yourselves. Do I make myself clear?"

None of the team members made a movement or sound. They knew it was not an idle threat.

Director Meyers handed the sheet of paper back to Helen and said, "A Thornlandon Holdings jet is waiting at our private hangar at Ontario airport with your equipment already loaded. Wheels up in an hour. I want you to arrive onsite at Deepstone at 4:45 p.m., after it closes for the day." She turned to leave but stopped and turned back. "I want no mistakes." She stared directly at Renn, her eyes hooded and emotionless.

Renn had been on multiple tours in Iraq and Afghanistan and had led his current team on dozens of missions in as many countries. He had personally killed eighteen hostiles. Yet Director Meyers' gaze sent a shiver down his spine. With one call, she could erase him and his team from existence.

Renn nodded curtly, knowing the Director didn't expect a reply from him.

Director Meyers turned and exited the garage, followed by Helen. As soon as the door closed, Renn turned to his team. "Meet at the airport in 30 minutes. I want our gear checked and double-checked before takeoff."

Light turbulence shook Renn out of his thoughts and he opened his eyes. He turned his head and glanced out the window, seeing nothing but blue sky with a few cumulus clouds below. Renn sighed and raised his seatback, then opened the intel report and reread it. The mission seemed straight forward. When he finished reading it, his phone pinged with an incoming text. It had no associated phone number. Renn hesitated to open it, aware of the complex cyber threats Thornlandon Holdings faced. But something told him to take the chance, so he opened the text. His heart rate increased as he read:

Thornlandon Holdings is lying to you. They located a massive deposit of rare-earth elements and precious metals 46,000 feet beneath the Deepstone underground iron-ore mine that has an estimated value in the trillions of dollars. Their scans show a potential way down to the minerals. They sent two teams to locate the access point on Level forty-three. Those teams have not returned. Director Meyers will have you and your team killed after this mission to keep that secret. Gather evidence in the mine, then quickly exfiltrate and disappear. I will make contact in one week. -R.

Renn saw movement out of the corner of his eye. He quickly turned to see the back of the flight attendant walking away down the aisle. The man passed through the curtains of the kitchen area without looking at him. Renn cursed softly. The attendant had not passed by him, which meant he had likely come up behind Renn, then turned around. Renn wondered if the man had read the text over his shoulder. He looked around, but most of his team were sleeping. Only Paul was awake, and he was busy reading a paperback.

Renn quickly deleted the text and slid the phone into one of his vest pockets. He sat back, remaining outwardly calm. That the text was true, he had no doubt. The message was too detailed. *Should he abort this mission and just disappear? Who could he trust on his team? All of them,* he answered himself. *He trusted them all. He had no idea who had sent the text, but whomever they were, they were powerful and obviously in Director Meyers' inner circle. Helen? No. That woman was dedicated to Director Meyers. Then who?*

Renn thought about this the rest of the way to Minnesota and just before they landed in Hibbing he received a call from Helen.

When he answered, she said, "Mission change. New Code: Alpha…Zed. Sanitize. Authorization: 93772."

Renn's heartbeat quickened. *The flight attendant, employed by Thornlandon Holdings, must have read the text over his shoulder and contacted Helen to relay the information.* He let none of his worry affect his normal quiet tone as he replied, "Details, please."

Helen explained the new mission parameters. "We have verified additional structural instability in the mine. We cannot let this information get out. If it does, Thornlandon Holdings will be wrapped up in red tape for a decade before we get approval to mine down there. You will eliminate a team that was sent into the mine this morning, as well as all mine employees on site. Wait until the mine closes today. After the last tourists leave, move in. We do not want any tourists harmed, nor do we want them to suspect anything is amiss. We need to keep this operation small."

Renn asked, "Who is the third team?"

"A three-person rescue team from SafeWell. They were sent into Deepstone today, without our knowledge, to 'rescue' the two teams we lost contact with." Helen's sarcastic tone led Renn to believe there was more to the story.

40

Renn was not even aware there might be someone in Thornlandon Holdings other than Director Meyers who could initiate a parallel operation without her permission. *Was it the same person who had written the note for his eyes only? Likely*, Renn thought.

Renn replied, "SafeWell teams are made up of ex-SEALs. They are all American citizens."

"You have your orders, soldier."

Renn seethed inside, but he simply said, "Understood."

Helen said, "Good. No evidence must be left behind." She paused, then said, "Oh, and Renn. Thornlandon Holdings' future rides on the discovery underneath Deepstone remaining a secret to all but a select few. You are now one of those few."

The phone call ended and Renn slowly put his phone on the small table in front of him, his mind replaying the nuances of the call. He gazed at the white puffy clouds below, considering the situation. His team had never been tasked with killing Americans on American soil. Helen's final statement made it obvious she knew about the warning text Renn had recently received. His team would be eliminated but he would live if he did as he was ordered.

Renn clenched the chair's armrests tightly. He would not kill innocent people. And he would not sacrifice his team. He pushed himself up, walked to the bathroom, closed the door, and called the Deepstone mine. When Jim answered, Renn pretended he was an FBI agent and ordered Jim to get everyone away from Deepstone. Ending the call, Renn used the bathroom for its intended purpose, then returned to his seat. He was disobeying a direct order from Thornlandon Holdings by telling the civilians to vacate the mine before his team's arrival instead of killing them all as the company had ordered. Renn hoped Jim would do as he was told.

Renn had worked for Thornlandon Holdings for nine years, but this was his first mission inside the US. He didn't intend to murder American citizens on American soil because his employer told him to. That was just not who he was. And from the debrief, there was an Anishinaabe tour guide on site as well. He especially had no wish to kill a fellow Indigenous person. This mission directive was a red line Renn would not cross.

Renn closed his eyes, but his mind raced. He needed to find a way out of this situation.

CHAPTER 5

JOHN returned to the ticketing building after his phone call with the DNR. He felt uneasy. As he walked, he saw two men and a young teenager standing next to their car. One of the men was trying to get the boy to take a thick sweater, but the boy kept turning away, his eyes glued to a hand-held video game.

John smiled as he remembered seeing similar situations play out every summer. Kids just had no interest in the mine tour—at first. But inevitably, their interest would be piqued during the elevator ride down and held during the train ride at the bottom. By the end of the tour, they usually had big smiles on their faces.

Seven people were already lined up for the next tour: a young, attractive couple in their thirties, an old couple who must be in their nineties, and three severe-looking people holding large packs. Anyone looking at them would immediately think, *military.* What they were doing here was another question.

John walked to the elevator gate and stood next to Carl and Tammy, who had gotten there before him because of his phone call with the DNR. As John turned to face the group, the two dads and teenager hurried up the path to the ticket office. Within three minutes, they exited the building and rushed over to join the group by the elevator.

It was the last tour of the day, and John just hoped it would go smoothly. He smiled widely and said, "Welcome to the Deepstone underground mine. You are all in for a treat today."

CHAPTER 6

At the back of the line, LARRY was already irritated with his thirteen-year-old son, Andy, and his husband, Ethan.

Ethan noticed Larry's exasperated look and bent over in front of Andy, who had his eyes glued to the Nintendo Switch in his hands. "Andy, I think it would be best if we left your Nintendo in the car. It might get broken during the tour."

Turning away, Andy never lifted his eyes from the screen as he mumbled, "I'll take good care of it, I promise."

Looking up at Larry with a shrug, Ethan stood up and said to Andy, "At least promise me you will put it into your backpack before we get into the elevator."

"Alright, dad." Andy twisted his body back and forth as he frantically tapped the buttons, trying to finish the level he was on before he had to stop playing.

Ethan always treated Andy like a child even though he had just turned thirteen. '*I think it would be best...*' Larry thought derisively. *Who talks like that to a teenager?* He had the firm belief that kids should be allowed to grow up. They should get hurt falling off a bike. They should be responsible for things, like putting a damn video game in their backpack without having to be asked nicely. Sometimes kids needed to learn things the hard way. But Ethan was always there, reminding Andy what to do and when to do it, but never backing his instructions up with real consequences. So, Andy didn't do anything the first time he was told because he knew he didn't have to. And when Larry spoke harshly to Andy, Ethan would usually take their son's side and Larry felt like he was in trouble instead of Andy.

Ethan misinterpreted Larry's expression as worry about the underground tour. He took Larry's hand and leaned close, whispering, "It will be fine down there, I promise."

Larry pasted on a smile, knowing now wasn't the time to pick a fight. "You know me, always the worrier."

Leaning closer, Ethan gave Larry a peck on the lips, then whispered, "Worrier."

Andy didn't even look up from his game as he said, "Yeah, worrier."

Larry couldn't help himself from grinning for real. As he did, the anger he had felt quickly drained away. At least for now. Larry studied the rest of the group. A young couple were first in line, who he immediately pegged as, "beautiful, outwardly interesting, but inwardly shallow." Larry liked to categorize people before he met them, then compare his categorization to what they were really like after he got to know them. He was rarely wrong.

Studying this couple now—well-worn hiking boots, flannel shirts, and well-used $500 adventure jackets, Larry guessed they had probably traveled to a lot of out-of-the-way places that looked great on their social media feeds. He looked at their faces and guessed they were about thirty years old—young, fit, and probably the type of couple that bragged to their friends at parties about their adventures in this or that country. Their names were probably something like Capri and Sage. The man looked nervous and unhappy, though. *Great*, Larry thought. *There always had to be one person who would make a scene.*

Behind them stood three solemn-looking people in their forties; two women and a man dressed in dark clothing. Each carried a large pack on their backs that looked to be full of heavy items. It was easy for Larry to categorize them: they were in the "stay the fuck away from us" category.

Just in front of Larry stood an older couple he guessed were in their nineties. The man had a curved back, bent by age or injury. But his eyes were sharp when he glanced back at Larry. *This man has seen some shit in his life,* Larry thought to himself. The woman was thin and athletic despite her white hair and wrinkled face. She had a kind face, but she also had eyes that showed her life had likely not always been easy. Larry thought they both fit into the "caring-but-no pushovers" category.

Larry, Andy, and Ethan were the final people in line. The group was quite small, maybe because summer was almost over and most tourists were spending every minute at the lake. No one wanted to waste time on a mine tour when they could be swimming, water skiing, or fishing.

The tour guide spoke loudly to get the group's attention, "Alright folks. We're almost ready to descend. My name is John, and I will be one of your tour guides today. That's Tammy over there. She'll be your other tour guide. We are going to show you some amazing things in the mine below, and we'll

47

answer any questions you have."

Larry liked John right away. He seemed like a man who got things done without complaining.

Tammy smiled, her face lighting up. She was young, maybe in her early twenties, and very pretty in a small-town, natural beauty kind of way. Tammy waved at the group, "Hi, everyone. If you have any questions during the tour, please, just ask me. And remember: There are no stupid questions, but not asking questions can make you look stupid."

The young couple chuckled, and the nervousness that had seemed so palpable in the young man earlier seemed to disappear a bit.

At the sound of Tammy's voice, Andy looked up from his game and stared at her, forgetting his Nintendo completely. Larry had to work to keep the grin off his face. *He is growing up so quickly*, thought Larry. *It seems like just yesterday we adopted him and now here he is, staring at a young woman with more than a passing interest.*

Larry and Ethan had been together for twenty-four years; married for five. They had met at university and had been together ever since. Larry had graduated from the University of Minnesota with a PhD in English Literature and gone on to teach English literature at Macalester University in Saint Paul. While teaching at the university he had written and published seven novels through one of the largest publishing houses in the world. After his eighth book had been published, he was making more from writing than teaching, so he quit the university to become a full-time writer. That was eight years ago.

Last week he had finished the first draft of his seventeenth book and to celebrate, the family had driven up from Saint Paul to spend two weeks at their cabin on Lake Vermillion before Andy had to return to school after Labor Day and summer was unofficially over. Andy was starting the eleventh grade even though he was only thirteen years old. Andy was special. The smartest in every grade since kindergarten. The school had recommended Andy test out of grades eight through ten, which he had done with ease. Ethan and Larry had been nervous for him starting eleventh grade with the older kids, but Andy was not only smart, he also made friends easily. Larry and Ethan hoped the eleventh graders would be kind to him.

Ethan was a tenured professor at the University of Minnesota, where he taught the history of the American Southwest, specializing in the Anasazi and Aztec influence in the region. Larry had learned long ago not to even mention the words 'potsherd' or 'kiva' unless he wanted a half-hour lecture on some interesting aspect of the two civilizations. That was one of the things that had caused Larry to fall in love with Ethan in the first place. He had an incredible mind with the ability to make even the most boring historical references interesting.

John walked down the line handing out red hard hats he took from a large box held by another, far younger man. "This is Carl. He runs the elevator, but please don't call him a doorman. He hates that."

Carl's eyes narrowed. The young man obviously didn't appreciate the bad joke, and when he rolled his eyes, it was clear to the group that John told the same joke about him every tour.

John continued, undaunted. "Please put these on and do not take them off for the remainder of the tour." When he tried to hand a hat to the first of the three tough-looking people, she dismissed him with a shake of her head. When John started to object, the woman impatiently held out an ID card. John eyed it carefully, then nodded and continued down the line. He stopped by Larry and held out a pink hard hat in his left hand and a red hard hat in his right. Initially defensive, Larry looked into John's eyes and saw nothing but kindness, so he took the pink hard hat with a good-natured grin. John smiled and continued.

Ethan chose a red hard hat instead of a pink one, and when John turned to hand one to Andy, Ethan good-naturedly elbowed Larry's side and grinned as he whispered, "Stop flirting. He's not your type."

Larry rolled his eyes at Ethan. "You are my one and only type and will be until the day I die."

Ethan turned serious, then softly kissed him, whispering, "As you are mine."

Andy turned his hard had in his hand, then looked up at John and quizzically asked, "Aren't these supposed to have lights on them?"

John smiled. "You are right, the miners had lights on theirs. At first, they strapped candles to their hard hats, and then later, flashlights. But we are just tourists, so we don't need them." John took a small LED flashlight from his pocket. "Plus, we carry these little things." He handed it to Andy, who immediately clicked on the light, shining it in his own face. It was bright, even outside in the daylight, and he immediately looked away, blinking his eyes.

John smiled. "I was just going to say these are powerful lights, so don't shine them in your eyes. They are much better than the lights the miners had when they worked at this mine."

Andy blinked, rubbed his eyes, and grinned as he handed the flashlight back. "Cool. It would be awesome to go back in time and give the miners a bunch of these."

John smiled. "That it would, young man."

Andy took off his backpack, slid his game console inside, and zipped it up tightly. Then he hoisted his pack over his back and grinned up at his dads.

Larry looked at Ethan, who shrugged, clearly surprised that he hadn't had to remind Andy to do that.

Carl dropped the box of hard hats on the ground and returned to the elevator. He yanked the accordion-style outer security door back, then slid open the elevator door and stepped inside without a word.

John started to say something to Carl, but instead, he picked up the box, carried it to the elevator entrance, and set it to the side before turning and pointing to the young couple. "Please, step inside."

The inside of the elevator was not impressive in any way. The floor, walls, and ceiling were made of steel, rusted to a dull brownish red. A small window sat about five feet up the door, the glass thick and grimy. The air inside the elevator held the faint smell of oil.

John stepped inside and Carl pulled the door shut with a clang, latching it securely.

John continued speaking, his experience and knowledge making the words flow naturally. "This elevator is an engineering marvel. The shaft does not drop straight down. Instead, it was cut at an eighty-two-degree angle." He held his hand vertically, then turned it just slightly to show the angle. "We will descend 3200 feet in four and a half minutes, which is about the same as going down four, 80-story skyscrapers that are stacked on top of each other."

At that statement, Andy said, "Whoa, that is a fast

elevator. But it is closer to three 80-story skyscrapers because each level of a building is not ten feet like is commonly thought. Each level is more like fourteen feet when you figure in the supporting concrete and mechanical systems between floors."

John smiled, "Well, now that you mention it, I think you may be right. I never thought of that."

Andy grinned, "Let's keep the story with four skyscrapers though, it sounds more impressive."

John laughed lightly. "That's a deal. Alright. Where was I. Oh yeah. The mine was dug thirty-two levels down. Each level takes up about 100 feet. We will be going all the way down to Level thirty-two."

The elevator jerked, then began to descend, moving much faster than Larry had expected a hundred-plus-year-old mining elevator to go.

The elevator was loud, rattling and shifting as it dropped.

To Larry, the descent seemed much longer than the promised four and a half minutes.

CHAPTER 7

BEN closed his eyes and put his hands against the side of the cage as it rattled and shook, every noise increasing his fear. He was filled with a feeling of impending doom. He was dropping into the bowels of the earth and nothing could stop it; he had no control over what was happening to him. Sweat broke out on his forehead. He knew he was going to die down here.

He felt a hand on his hip, then a soft brush of air against his ear as Fiona leaned in and kissed him. Her comforting gesture calmed Ben's fear just a little, and he took in a few deep, ragged breaths.

The noise of the cage seemed to grow even louder the lower it went, and Ben closed his eyes tightly.

Just when he didn't think he could take it anymore, he felt the elevator slow down, and then it bumped to a stop with a small shriek of steel-on-steel.

Carl slid open the door and Tammy stepped out. She motioned for the tourists to exit the elevator, and Ben quickly stepped out into a large cavern filled with light. He took a deep breath, then another as he gazed around the room. The temperature was indeed around fifty degrees, and the air was crisp and clean.

Fiona leaned close to him and asked, "Are you okay?"

Ben nodded, then forced a smile as he looked into her eyes. "I am fine now. It's not so bad down here."

"Just remember, this mine was carved from the strongest rock in the world. It is safe."

"I know. Honestly, I am fine." He held his hand out and was proud that it didn't tremble at all.

Fiona took his hand in hers and gave him a dazzling smile.

Ben and the other tourists studied the room. Directly in front of them was a rail track. A series of small carts sat on the tracks, each with two bench seats that held up to three people per side. It looked like a ride at an amusement park.

To their right was a garage-style door with a sign on it saying:

NUTRINOS PHYSICS LAB
Tours on Saturdays only
Buy your tickets online or in the ticket office

Andy ran up to the door, turned to his dads, and yelled out, "We *have* to come back for this tour! Can we, please?"

John pointed at the carts on the tracks, "Everyone, please, take a seat in one of the carts, starting with the one up front. We don't have a full tour today, so feel free to take your own cart if you like."

Ben turned and followed Fiona to the second cart. They took a seat, facing forward.

Fiona took Ben's arm. "Isn't this exciting?"

The tunnel that led from the room was lit by small lightbulbs that faded into the distance. Most of the tourists were settled in their seats, eagerly awaiting the start of the tour. Ben felt his palms begin to sweat, despite the cold air. He forced his shoulders back and took some breaths to relax his mind, repeating to himself: *We are safe down here. We are safe down here. We are safe down here.*

CHAPTER 8

MORGAN FISCHER cinched her backpack tighter and felt the weight of the tools and weapons inside. She glanced at the other two members of her SafeWell team, Karen and Jack, and they nodded. Morgan turned right as she exited the elevator and walked toward the back of the room. Her team followed her. When she reached the far end of the chamber, she turned and waited.

The old man in the tour group pointed at Morgan, Karen, and Jack and said something to John. John shook his head and said, "Don't worry, they are employees."

The old man glanced back at Morgan's team once more, then shrugged as he shuffled to one of the train carts.

Soon, the tour group were all aboard and the little train moved noisily into the tunnel.

When it was out of sight, Morgan turned and quietly said, "Gear up."

Morgan, Karen, and Jack all slid off their packs

and set them carefully onto the rock floor, before unzipping them in unison.

Morgan quickly put on her black, military-style helmet, already fitted with a night vision mount for her right eye and strapped it securely under her chin. She did not switch on the night vision yet as it would blind her with all of the lights on in the chamber, so she left the lens in the upward position to avoid obstructing her vision when she wasn't using it. Next, Morgan removed her Heckler & Koch GxX rifle, unfolded the stock, and set it carefully on the floor. Finally, she removed her Glock 19 pistol, checked the clip, and slid it into the holster at her side. Jack and Karen did the same, and the team was ready to go.

Morgan, Karen, and Jack zipped up their packs, slung them over their backs, and tightly cinched the straps. Morgan picked up her rifle and led her team silently into the tunnel the tour group had gone down only a few minutes earlier. They jogged quickly and quietly for a few hundred feet until they arrived at a narrow side-tunnel, a third of the width of the main tunnel, that led to the left. It was dark, and no light fixtures were attached to the ceiling. The team turned and entered it without hesitating and walked a dozen feet before switching on their night vision headsets. The tunnel turned from black to green, allowing the team to see perfectly in the darkness.

The tunnel had steel rails just like the one they'd just left, but these had not been used in decades. Morgan had memorized the map of Level thirty-two and knew the tunnel ran for 900 meters before entering a cavern that had been excavated sixty years earlier. But they weren't going that far. Their night vision was also equipped with a distance counter, and at the 520-meter mark, Morgan held her arm up, hand in a fist indicating she wanted her team to stop. Morgan walked slower now and soon came a small steel door on the left side of the tunnel wall. She motioned to Karen, who immediately stepped to the door and put her ear to the steel to listen. She then pulled the door handle down and opened the door, the un-oiled hinges screeching in the green glow of the tunnel.

They stepped to the side and stood perfectly still for a moment to ensure they hadn't surprised someone in the space beyond the door. Morgan and her team weren't sure if the teams they were sent to find were friendlies. The last thing they wanted was someone to start shooting at them. When she was sure no one was in the tunnel, Morgan led her team forward.

Jack pulled the door shut behind them, the clang of steel loud in the small space.

This tunnel did not have steel rails, the rock floor was dry, and the air was cool, but stale. The team noticed small rocks littering the floor, and after 300 meters, they came upon a small cave-in where larger rocks had fallen from the ceiling. They studied the ceiling and determined it still seemed structurally sound, so they proceeded carefully forward over the rubble. They saw no indication that the other teams had come this way. But the tunnel floor and ceiling were made from hard iron-bearing rock, so the small amount of rock that had fallen had not raised enough dust for someone to leave tracks.

Morgan and her team had received this assignment from their commander, Henry Skuggs, less than twenty-four hours earlier. Skuggs was an only child from a wealthy family in Connecticut. He had excelled in school and gone on to Harvard, graduating in the top 5% of his class. But he had chosen to go into the military after graduating instead of into the business world. Skuggs had joined Special Forces in 1988 and had risen quickly through the ranks. Skuggs had no children and lost his wife to cancer in 2003. He had never remarried and had lived a private life ever since.

And he was rich.

His father had died in 2001, his mother in 2012, leaving him their full estate. In total, he owned dozens of properties around the world and was worth more than four billion dollars. By age forty-eight, he had grown weary of the limitations of the military. He retired and formed a private, military-grade rescue company called SafeWell. While similar to the well-known Blackstone company that provided private security in some of the most dangerous places in the world, Skuggs created SafeWell as an investigatory and rescue group. Their missions centered around the rescue and recovery of people and equipment, usually scientists or corporate research teams who had gotten into some kind of trouble in some of the most inhospitable places around the world.

Skuggs provided the best equipment, the best weapons, and the best support for his teams. He created SafeWell to help people. That he made a good profit didn't matter to him. But he made sure his people were very highly paid; Morgan, for example, could have comfortably retired after just three years at SafeWell. But she hadn't. She loved her job too much to quit. Her SafeWell team had once rescued a group of scientists trapped in an ice tunnel 200 feet below the surface in Antarctica. And most recently they had rescued a small team of pharmaceutical researchers who had been captured and held prisoner by a drug warlord in a tunnel system deep in the jungles of Vietnam.

The SafeWell headquarters was situated on a 2400-acre estate in the Chihuahuan desert on the border of New Mexico and Mexico. The estate existed in both the US and Mexico, with 1200 acres on each side of the border.

At SafeWell, Morgan was making a difference in the world, while still getting to use her military training as a former Navy SEAL. She had retired from the SEALs at the age of forty-seven, well past the normal retirement age of thirty-eight. Morgan had worked for Skuggs for the past three years. She appreciated the freedom to perform missions that were not strictly military in nature. She had personally killed twenty-seven terrorists in her twenty years as a SEAL and while she did not regret those deaths, she had grown tired of the missions. Morgan began to feel like they were not making much of a difference anymore. No matter how many bad people they stopped, the world only seemed to be getting worse.

Morgan reflected on earlier this morning, when she got a text on her secure phone that simply read, "Priority One." That meant she needed to get to Skuggs' office ASAP. She arrived at Skuggs' office in three minutes. After standing respectfully at attention, Skuggs offered her a seat in front of his desk, which she declined, as she preferred to stand.

Morgan's commander shrugged as he leaned back in his chair. "You know you are not in the military anymore, Morgan?"

"Yes, sir." Morgan answered unironically.

"Suit yourself. Alright, down to business. Have you heard of the Angora Deepstone Underground

Mine in northern Minnesota?"

Morgan shook her head. "No, I haven't. In fact, I can't say I have ever been to Minnesota, sir."

"It's a nice state, if you like lakes and mosquitoes. This mine has been a tourist spot for over sixty years. A tour company takes people over 3200 feet to the bottom of the mine, which is at…" he looked down at his report before continuing, "Level thirty-two, where they get to see first-hand how iron ore was mined in the old days. There was also a dark-matter physics lab down there for thirty-five years, though it has been recently decommissioned. That is a separate tour."

Morgan remained silent, knowing Skuggs would get to the actual mission eventually.

Skuggs leaned forward and moved some folders around before pulling a thick blue folder out of the pile and opening it on his desk. He scanned the contents for a few moments, then nodded. "A new open-pit iron mine has begun operating not far from this old underground mine. They use controlled detonations to open up the ground." He leaned forward, then continued reading, "These detonations consist of a series of smaller explosions that are triggered one after the other. They can reduce up to a million tons of solid rock to rubble. Apparently, they can't use a single large detonation because one massive explosion would damage homes and businesses up to ten miles away." He looked up at Morgan and grinned. "That sounds like some fun stuff to play with!"

Morgan asked the question that had been on her mind since Skuggs had started speaking, "So what has happened that would require my team's services? Has there been an accident?"

Skuggs leaned back in his chair. "It seems these

blasts have weakened the underground mine used for tours. I was contacted by Senator Young to perform an investigatory, and possible rescue, mission below Level thirty-two, although he didn't go into many specifics." When Morgan raised an eyebrow, Skuggs held up his hands, saying, "Senator Young and I are old friends. This is a favor to him."

Morgan's mind quickly summarized the information she'd received. "I have two questions. First, you said Level thirty-two was the bottom of the mine, so how can we go below it? And second, why doesn't the senator send the military down to investigate?"

Skuggs nodded as if he'd expected her questions. "The *public* is told that Level thirty-two is the deepest the mine goes. But the senator confirmed there are eleven more levels below thirty-two. He said the mining company reached Level forty-three in the early 1960s, but something happened, and they used explosives to block access to those levels. They then welded the remaining hatches to seal off the entrances below Level thirty-two and closed the mine down shortly after."

"If they sealed off the last 11 levels, how will we get to them? Has someone found a way?"

Looking back down at the scattered paperwork on his desk, Skuggs eventually found the document he was looking for and read silently for a moment before addressing Morgan again. "There is an entrance point. I have the information here to lead you to it."

Nodding, Morgan asked, "Did the senator say what it was that caused the mining company to abandon the mine?"

"No, just that something happened, and several miners were killed. Believe me, I probed him with questions, but he would not reveal any more information. He told me most of the paperwork about that event is missing or has been destroyed."

Morgan felt a chill. Something felt wrong. A mining company would not abandon profits unless something really bad had happened. She couldn't even begin to guess what that could be, though. She pushed those thoughts to the back of her mind and asked, "Are there tourists trapped down there?"

Skuggs shook his head. "No, in fact tours are still operating."

"Then I ask again: why are *we* going down there?"

"Because someone, who that someone is I was not told, recently sent a team down to assess whether there had been any damage from the blasting being done in the mine next door to Deepstone. When that team didn't come back, they send a second one."

The slight chill she had felt earlier turned absolutely freezing, goose bumps standing out on her flesh. Morgan asked a question to which she was pretty sure she knew the answer, "And the second team?"

Skuggs fixed her with a steely gaze and said, "They haven't returned, either."

"So, this is a rescue operation, then."

"Maybe. I honestly don't know. Those teams were likely not equipped to handle the unknown. For all I know, they might have been groups of scientists who didn't plan correctly and just got lost." He looked at her, his expression turning deadly serious. "Or they may have been military teams and were ambushed. Either way, we are equipped to handle this type of mission. Your team will descend as deep as you need to go. Search for and rescue the other teams—or at least find out what happened to them."

Skuggs sat forward. "But Morgan. I want you to take a full weapons kit along with the normal rescue supplies."

Morgan tensed. While they always went in fully armed when performing missions in other countries, they had never used full weapon kits for missions in the United States. In-country, they usually just equipped themselves with handguns for personal protection. Morgan shifted the weight on her feet subconsciously and asked, "Sir? Why would we need a FWK on a mission into an old mine in Minnesota?" She pronounced FWK as "fuck," although the acronym meant Full Weapons Kit.

Skuggs looked contemplative. "I just have a feeling about this one. Something's not sitting well with me. Two teams go missing in a tourist mine. It doesn't make sense. I want you to treat this as a hostile mission. I hope it turns out to just be a simple rescue, but I want you prepared for anything. While Senator Young is my friend, he may not have told me everything."

Morgan nodded to Skuggs and said, "Yes, sir. We will operate as a hostile mission. When do we leave?"

Skuggs stood up and handed her the thick blue folder. "Here is your briefing. It includes a full background on the Deepstone mine and an overview of the teams that are missing," he cocked his head and continued, "though I wouldn't put too much faith into the intel, especially as it pertains to the teams. I get the feeling it is a cover story. Regardless, there are also details about where the teams entered the lower levels and their last reported locations. Be prepared to depart in an hour."

Morgan nodded as she accepted the folder, then

turned to leave before Skuggs stopped her.

"Morgan?"

She turned her head to look at him, and he said, "Please, be careful on this one." She nodded once, then left his office.

Morgan shivered as she came out of her thoughts, which she was sure was from more than just the cold air in the tunnel. These tunnels put her on edge, and she wasn't sure why. Morgan and her team had completed dozens of dangerous missions and never before had she felt such a sense of impending danger.

Morgan suddenly saw a unique type of darkness appear about thirty meters ahead that not even the night-vision could penetrate. The dark mass blocked part of the tunnel. She put up her hand and the team stopped. They all listened, making no sound. The darkness confused Morgan. It looked like it was a solid mass, but her night-vision registered nothing. She whispered into her headset, "Can you tell what that is about thirty meters ahead?"

Karen and Jack stepped silently forward until they were even with her and stared intently forward.

Karen whispered, "I can't make it out. Stay here, I will check it out."

Morgan put her hand out. "Negative. I will investigate."

Karen stepped back, clicking off the safety of her rifle. Skuggs had an old friend who was CEO of Heckler & Koch and was able to get advanced weaponry from them before anyone else. These rifles were not even in production yet.

Jack did the same with his weapon.

Flicking off the safety of her own GxX, Morgan moved forward, stepping slowly and deliberately, her gaze fixed on the dark mass ahead. She was twenty meters away when the darkness seemed to move. Then it was just gone. Morgan knelt and raised her rifle, staring through the sight. She didn't move for over a minute. She saw no sign of the dark mass. *What the hell was that? And where did it go?* Morgan wondered to herself.

Morgan whispered into her mike, "It's no longer there." She stood, and moved forward slowly in a crouch, weapon never wavering until she arrived at the spot where the darkness had been. She listened for a few moments while staring down the tunnel, but neither heard, nor saw anything more. Lowering her weapon, Morgan studied the floor for any signs of what it could have been but saw nothing. Whatever it was had vanished without a trace.

Karen and Jack joined her, and Karen asked quietly, "Did you identify the target?"

"No. I saw only…darkness."

Under his breath, Jack said, "I saw it fucking move."

Morgan said, "Me too, Jack. But we don't know what it was. It might have been a malfunction of our night-vision in this zero-light environment." Morgan and her team knew this was unlikely, as they were using special night-vision devices with advanced technology designed to work in zero-light areas. Most night vision was used above ground where there was almost always some source of ambient light even if it seemed dark to the naked eye, such as star light or light from a distant town. But down here underground, there was absolutely no light source, so they had to use special night vision technology that didn't rely on ambient light sources. Morgan continued, "Or maybe the magnetite is messing with our night vision." She had read about the composition of the rocks in the mine, and magnetite, which is naturally magnetic, was one of the most common minerals down here.

"Maybe," Jack whispered, although he didn't sound convinced.

Then Morgan cursed, "Shit, why didn't I switch to thermal imaging mode on my night vision?"

Both Jack and Karen both swore, realizing they'd forgotten as well.

"Alright, let's keep moving. Stay alert. Karen, you have our six." Morgan started forward, Jack to her left, and Karen behind.

After 140 meters, they came to another steel door in the wall. Morgan tried the handle, and with some effort was able to pull the door open.

Jack immediately moved forward, sweeping his rifle right and left.

Morgan followed him through into a small chamber of no more than ten square feet.

Karen was last through the door, but stayed in position, facing behind them to look for any threats.

Morgan quickly surveyed the room. It appeared to be empty, with walls roughly carved out of the rock. In the far-left corner, she saw a smooth hole where a large steel hatch had been cut free, likely with a Metal Vapor Torch. This tool was essentially a blade of flame so powerful it cut steel as cleanly as a hot knife though butter. The hatch had been set to the side of the hole. Due to the lack of circulating air, the smell of melted metal was still strong. Morgan didn't think the two teams they were trailing would go through this much effort just to check the structural integrity of these lower levels. Something else was going on here. Something big. And her team had not been given the full story, which meant they just might be expendable if shit went south. Morgan only hoped Skuggs knew what he had gotten them all into with this mission.

Morgan crossed over to the hole and knelt to examine it. When she did, her expectations were confirmed: it was an access point to the next level down. A ladder descended about fifteen meters through a chute cut out of the rock until it reached a tunnel below. The miners had dug small stone rooms for each hatch in these lower levels. For Levels thirty-two and above, the hatches were in alcoves. Why the miners changed to enclosed hatches below Level thirty-two, Morgan didn't know. She spoke quietly to her team, "Alright. We are going down to Level thirty-three. Jack, you take point."

Jack nodded briskly as Morgan held up three fingers and counted down to one, then he leaned forward and pointed his gun down the hole. Satisfied all was clear, he swung his rifle over his shoulder and started down the ladder.

Morgan watched him descend until he reached the tunnel floor of the next level. As soon as his boots hit the ground, he swung his rifle from his back, slowly rotated 360 degrees, then said into the mic, "All clear."

Karen's voice broke in, "The darkness is back in the tunnel, and it is moving toward us." Her voice was calm but held a slight edge of uncertainty. Karen was not easily spooked, but she seemed to be confused by what she was seeing in the tunnel.

Stepping to the doorway, Morgan saw the black mass moving toward the room they were standing in. It was only about twenty meters away. She still couldn't make out any discernable shape to it.

Morgan pressed the button on her headset to change from night vision to thermal imaging. The dark mass changed to a cool green with a red and orange interior. It had four legs with a long tail stretched out behind it. Her heartbeat quickened as she thought, *Is that a fucking dog?*

Whatever it was, it shouldn't be down in this tunnel system. Morgan pulled Karen back a step and pulled the door closed with all her strength. It slammed shut with a loud bang. There was no locking mechanism.

Morgan and Karen moved back a couple of steps, staring at the door, weapons raised.

The room was silent.

They waited. They couldn't hear any sound on the other side of the door. Morgan stepped tentatively forward and pressed her ear to the steel. At first, she heard nothing. She was just about to pull away from the door when she thought she heard a noise. She pressed her ear harder against the door, holding her breath. Then she heard movement against the other side of the door, as if a hand was sliding against it.

Keeping her ear pressed hard against the steel, Morgan's blood ran cold when she heard what sounded like a sigh. Morgan gripped her rifle and backed away from the door.

"What did you hear?" Karen asked in a whisper.

Morgan turned and rushed over to the opening in the floor. "Come on, let's get out of here. Quickly."

Karen didn't hesitate, quickly scurrying down the ladder.

Morgan glanced at the door one last time before descending to the level below.

What have we gotten ourselves into?

She shivered.

And more importantly, how are we going to get back out with that...thing up there blocking our way?

CHAPTER 9

JOHN pulled the brake lever, and the little train of carts screeched to a stop at a small alcove. He pointed to a steel ladder in the alcove that rose into an opening in the rock ceiling. "This is one of the access points between levels. These were built as a safety system for miners to escape a level if the power went out or the elevator stopped working. Every level has an access and exit point. Some levels extend two miles through networks of tunnels like the one we are in. While the tunnel roofs are only around fifteen feet high, those ladders go up seventy-five or more feet, cutting through solid rock to the next level."

He watched as most of the tourists glanced at the ladder with polite interest before facing forward. But Andy studied it carefully. John smiled as the boy faced him again, surprised to see so much interest from a teenager. John guessed he was probably thirteen years old, or so.

Andy pointed at the ladder, "They remind me of

the ladder systems of the Anasazi cliff dwellings."

Surprised, John said, "You are right, they are similar in that they are very long ladder systems that help people move between levels of the earth." He winked and said, "Except down here in the tunnel, you don't have to deal with 120-degree heat."

Andy laughed, and his dads seemed genuinely surprised by their son's interaction with John.

John faced forward again and released the brake, pushing the acceleration lever forward slowly to start the train of carts moving again. After moving forward only twenty feet, he suddenly pulled the brake lever, which is something he hadn't done in all his years of leading these tours. "No worries, folks. I just have to clear a couple small rocks from the track ahead."

Ben spoke in a tremulous voice, "Is there a cave in? Do we need to get out of here?"

"No, it's just a couple of small rocks. These tunnels are cut through some of the oldest and strongest rock in the world. In fact, that is why this is one of only a handful of *underground* iron ore mines in the world: because the composition of the rock is very rare, yet very stable."

"Then why are there rocks on the track?" Ben asked, frowning.

John cursed silently, knowing full well it was because of the blasting from the Onamuni mine. But he didn't want to worry the group, so he just smiled and said, "Sometimes, maybe once every twenty years, a rock or two will crack off because of the dampness. It is nothing to worry about." Ben didn't look convinced, but John continued before he could ask another question, "They used to set off explosives down here, yet there has never been a cave-in, which shows you how strong these tunnels really are. Now, I will be right back. Please stay in your seats."

John stepped from the lead cart and walked down the track, stopping by the small pile of rocks. He looked up at the ceiling and saw a large crack running across it. *Shit*, he thought to himself. *This isn't good.* He picked up the largest rock, which was maybe ten pounds, and set it to the side of the tunnel. Then he kicked the smaller rocks to spread them out and get them off the tracks. John returned to the train and forced a smile. "There, we are good to go! Next, we will arrive at the main cavern where the core mining was done on this level." He released the brake and moved slowly past the spot before increasing the speed. Within a few minutes, they exited the tunnel into a large cavern, and the group's incredulous exclamations filled the air.

John had been running this tour for so many years that he could do it with his eyes closed. But he never tired of the sight in front of him. He spoke clearly, "If you would get out of the carts now and follow me, Tammy and I will show you some of the cool things about this mining cavern. Watch your step, please. We don't want anyone twisting an ankle." John moved over to the old couple, Claire and Milton, and said with a warm smile, "You can stay in the cart if you prefer."

Claire shook her head. "We need to do this." Her tone hinted they had a reason for coming down here other than recreation, but she didn't volunteer any more information.

"Ok, just be careful." John stepped to the front of the group and spread out his arms. "This cavern is 297 feet wide, 722 feet long, and the ceiling rises seventy-seven feet at its highest point. Though it isn't a single, wide-open space, as you can see. The width extends the full 297 feet in some areas, but narrows to thirty feet in others, kind of like if you slowly poured water onto a mirror and watched it spread out. The miners followed the richest iron-bearing veins in the ceiling, and those veins never led in a straight line."

He pointed to the group's immediate right, "Spaced throughout, you will see these solid stone pillars connecting the floor and ceiling. The miners left these to support the ceiling." John pointed to the left. "See that pile of rocks over there? Those are leftover magnetite tailings from the blasting that was done down here. Miners drilled holes into the ceiling of the cavern and slid bundles of dynamite into them. The resulting explosions caused huge sections of the ceiling to fall to the floor. They gathered the rich, iron-bearing rock and carted it out, and they piled the worthless magnetite over there. They blasted upward at least seventy feet without danger. It was a great system."

The old man, Milton, spoke up from the back, his voice hushed. "It wasn't a great system."

Andy asked, "Why do you say that?"

"Well, young man, because a great many men died down here."

Excitement filled Andy's eyes. "Really? How many?"

Milton whispered as he looked around, "Too many. Just too many."

Milton's comments and tone made it clear he had worked in these mines. John felt nothing but respect for him, knowing how hard Milton had worked down here, as well as just how bad the conditions really had been in the early days. But he didn't want the mood to darken within the group, so he hurriedly said, "Milton is right. There were accidents from time to time. This was one of the most dangerous jobs in the world. If you will follow me over here and gather in a circle, please?" John led them to an area farther away from the tunnel entrance that was flat and free from debris.

When the group had all gathered in the spot he'd requested, John said, "How many here have been camping in the woods before?"

Everyone raised their hands. Ben and Fiona smiled knowingly to each other; they clearly thought they were experts on the subject.

John continued, "You've probably had to leave your tent in the middle of the night to go to the bathroom. It was really dark, right?"

Everyone nodded and smiled.

John smiled back. "I know I've been bitten by mosquitoes while trying to relieve myself in the dark." He mimicked swatting at mosquitoes and the group chuckled. "But the darkness down here? It's like nothing you've ever experienced before."

The group grew quiet, suspecting something interesting was going to happen. John loved this part of the tour the most.

He stepped to a small post rising from the floor that had a red and green button on it. "This post has a button on it that will turn off all the lights. Now don't be scared, I will only leave them off for a few moments. But you will experience the absolute absence of light. Please, put your phones into your pockets."

Andy grinned and looked up at his dads. "Cool, hey?"

Larry's dour expression showed he didn't share his son's excitement.

"On the count of three, I will shut the lights off. I want you all to look around and tell me what you see." John put his hand on the switch and smiled, "Okay. One. Two. And... three."

John pushed the red button, and the group was enveloped by total darkness.

CHAPTER 10

Deep within the tunnel on Level thirty-three, BAUWEN sniffed the air. She had been following Morgan and her team since Level thirty-two and had shown herself briefly to them a few times to test how they would react. She could sense they were hunters, yet they had not fired their weapons, which intrigued her.

She needed to eat something soon, now that she had awakened from her decades-long slumber. While she had slept, her body had shut down most of its physical functions. Even her heart had only beaten once a minute, just enough to keep blood coursing through her veins and feed oxygen to her brain.

She made the decision to see if there was any food on Level thirty-two, so she ran lightly down the tunnel, climbed up the ladder to the next level, and ran down the side-tunnel. She carefully opened the steel door that led to the main tunnel of Level thirty-two and silently made her way to the main chamber where the elevator was, listening carefully for any voices or movement.

Sensing the chamber was empty, Bauwen crept forward toward a cabinet. She inhaled deeply and smelled food inside of it. She opened the small cabinet door and found a box of candy bars. She took four of them and a bottle of water, then sprinted back to the side-tunnel. Only when the door was closed did she tear off the wrapper and eat one of the candy bars. The sweet flavor of the bar shocked Bauwen, as she had never tasted chocolate before. She ate all four of them; she needed energy. She took a long drink from the bottle of water and sighed. It had been a long time since she had eaten.

Bauwen sat down with her back to the wall of the tunnel, feeling the energy fill her body. Bauwen had been trapped in this mine for so long that she had found it more and more difficult to remember details of her home. She thought back now to how she had found this mine so long ago.

*   *   *

In the human year of 1962, Bauwen had come across a fissure inside the great boundary wall in her world far below the mine. This was the wall that kept the Vorgroth imprisoned. Despite her people's warnings to the contrary, she had investigated and come face-to-face with a Vorgroth. Cornered, Bauwen's only way of escape was to scramble upward inside of the fissure. With the Vorgroth giving chase, Bauwen had climbed relentlessly for more than ten days, eventually reaching the lowest level of this mine.

She explored the tunnels until she came across

three men in a small cavern. They sat around a crude table with a dim light in the middle, playing cards and talking as they ate. As Bauwen listened, she found that she innately understood the language the men were speaking. Her brain processed the sounds into words without effort, regardless of the language, and she listened in wonder.

"Milton, what'd your old lady send for lunch today?"

Milton grunted, "None of your damned business, Franc."

Franc reached over and grabbed Milton's lunch box and opened it. Inside he took out a sandwich wrapped in paper. Unwrapping it, he lifted the top piece of bread and laughed. "Ha! You went and spent your paycheck over at Frankie's bar, again, didn't you? And your old lady was pissed, so she sent you a raw potato sandwich for lunch."

"I said it's none of your business." Milton grabbed the sandwich from Franc's hand. "I happen to like raw potato sandwiches."

Otto sighed as he bit into his own beef sandwich. He chewed and swallowed, then quietly said, "Milton, I've told you before. You need to cash your check, bring it home to Claire, 'cept for $5, *then* go to Frankie's. And don't go buying rounds. That's how you go broke and end up getting raw potato sandwiches in your lunch box."

Milton looked down, embarrassed. "You're right, Otto. I'll do better next time."

Otto gently patted Milton's shoulder, "I know you will."

The men finished their meal and rose, brushing their hands on their clothing.

Milton cracked his back and murmured, "These

breaks are never long enough. We didn't even finish our game. I have five cents riding on it, and I was winning."

"Quit your complaining, Milton. These tunnels won't dig themselves," Franc said as he slid a few coins off the table and into his pocket. "Grab your pennies and leave the cards where they are. We'll finish this game tomorrow."

Three days after she arrived in the mine, the Vorgroth emerged from the crevasse and slaughtered Franc and Otto. Only Milton had been able to escape.

Milton and his fellow miners decided to trap the Vorgroth on the lowest level. Bauwen, her skin mimicking the walls of the tunnel, had secretly followed them down the levels until they reached Level forty-two, when the Vorgroth suddenly attacked.

Without thinking, Bauwen had leapt forward, slicing deeply into the Vorgroth's arm with her *Forss* knife. She sprinted down the tunnel hoping it would follow her. The Vorgroth roared in rage and gave chase. She went down to the lowest level as quickly as she could. She hoped it would be enough of a distraction for the miners to set the explosives and trap the creature down there.

The Vorgroth hunted Bauwen. She had hoped to escape back down to her world, but the Vorgroth guarded the fissure, as if it knew her plan.

Bauwen eventually managed to slip unseen past the Vorgroth and climb back up to Level forty-two. Seeing bundles of explosives taped to the walls and ceiling, Bauwen hurried down the tunnel, making it a few hundred feet before the explosives went off. She had been thrown to the ground from the concussion of the blast but had been uninjured. When the dust finally cleared, tons of rock covered the hatch leading to Level forty-three.

Bauwen didn't know it then, but the blast had also blocked the opening to the fissure that led back down to her own world. The Vorgroth was imprisoned below her on Level forty-three.

When she tried to climb up to the next level, she found the humans had permanently welded the hatch shut.

Bauwen was trapped on Level forty-two.

*   *   *

Bauwen's memories of that awful time so long ago clarified her course of action now. She decided to initiate contact with Morgan's team. *They deserve to know about the Vorgroth*, she thought to herself. *After all, it is my fault it is here in this mine.*

Bauwen turned and retraced her route back down to find Morgan's team.

CHAPTER 11

JIM knelt by the air conditioner unit near the wall outside of the break room, grunting as he turned his wrench. He broke a bolt loose and ratcheted it quickly out of the air conditioner's housing. His work was suddenly interrupted by laughter, and he turned to see a car pull into the parking lot and disgorge a group of four rowdy people. Jim grimaced when one of the guys drained the last of a beer and tossed the empty can into a cooler. Before he closed the cooler, he stuffed a new beer can into his coat pocket and slammed the car door shut.

Jim hated this type of tourist: rude, loud, drunk, and a pain in the ass. His thoughts turned again to retirement; maybe this was the year. The money he made from this job was less than he would make from Social Security once he decided to start collecting it. As with many other people of his generation, he had worked since he was fifteen years old and the idea of not working was just too foreign a concept for him to easily accept. What would he do with his time if he retired?

The man who had pocketed the beer laughed loudly and pushed his friend hard.

Jim grunted again. *At least if I retired,* he thought, *I wouldn't have to spend my days dealing with bozos like that.* He stood up and walked down the short path to the parking lot. He yelled to the tourists, "Hey, the mine tours are done for the day. Come back tomorrow."

The drunk man started walking toward Jim with an ugly look on his face, but a skinny woman pulled his arm and whined, "Come on, Darryl, forget about this stupid tour. Let's go back to the campsite."

The drunk let himself be pulled back to the car, but not before giving Jim the middle finger as he got behind the wheel.

The car tires shot gravel everywhere as the car spun in a circle and accelerated out of the parking lot.

Jim glared after the retreating vehicle, then sighed and returned to the air conditioning unit. He considered reporting the drunk driver to the police, but he knew they would probably never bother looking for the car this far from town. He loosened the final three bolts on the air conditioning unit and carefully set his wrench into its spot inside of his pristinely organized toolbox. He then dropped the four bolts into a small plastic Tupperware container so he didn't lose track of them.

As he started to wrestle the housing from the air conditioner unit, he felt a mosquito land on his neck. He felt the sting and pushed his neck backward, trying to kill it, but it was no use, so he continued lifting the housing unit until it was free. He carefully set it off to the side, his back protesting with a twinge of pain. As soon as he set it down, he slapped his neck, killing the mosquito. He looked at his hand and saw a bloody smear.

Jim absently wiped the blood on his pants as he stared at the internals of the central air compressor unit. The machine was probably installed in the late 80s or early 90s. But it still pumped out cool air, so the DNR had never approved a replacement unit. Jim had to repair it at least once a summer. Some repairs were easy, while others took him weeks to get the right parts delivered for such an old machine. A few years ago, the office had gone the entire summer without an air conditioner because they couldn't get a new air compressor delivered. The DNR could have sent a brand-new air conditioner unit to them in just a few days for not much more money than that air compressor had cost. *That was government bureaucracy for you*, Jim mused.

Jim got lucky this time, though. He immediately saw a missing bolt for the air compressor. Luckily, he found it lying on the steel plate, so he picked it up and examined it. The bolt was a little rusty, but the threads were still good. The rubber mount was also sitting on the steel plate, but it was in two pieces. Jim picked each piece up and saw they were dried out and unusable. The mount had cracked and fallen away, which had caused the bolt to loosen over time until it had eventually vibrated off, which was causing the current problem with the air compressor unit. It was a simple fix Jim could make without spending a dime. He went into the tool shed, opened a drawer in the floor-standing toolbox, and took out a small baggie of extra rubber mounts. He removed one, put the baggie back, closed the drawer, and returned to the air conditioning unit.

Within 10 minutes, he had the housing bolted

back together and had turned the power back on. He entered the office and turned the thermostat to "Cool". The air conditioner's compressor hummed quietly, and he smiled as cool air filled the office, happy it had been an easy repair job.

The office phone rang. Jim considered letting it go to voicemail and letting John deal with it when he came back topside. But not one to leave work for others to do, Jim picked up the green handle of the old 1970s phone and said, "Angora Deepstone Mine Tours."

The voice on the other end of the phone was deep, male, and had a slight Native American accent. "Who am I speaking to?"

"This is Jim."

"Listen, Jim. I am Special Agent Smith of the FBI. Please call John Lukkinen on the intercom and tell him to return topside with the tour group immediately. Then send everyone home and close the tour site for the day."

Jim replied, "Why do we need to close the tours down for the day?"

His voice gruff, the FBI agent said, "Just do as I say."

Jim wondered if this was a prank, but the man sure sounded like an agent. "Listen. I can't contact John. The intercom system has been out of service for two weeks." He looked at his watch, then said, "John will return topside in thirty minutes. It's the final tour. Can't this wait until he returns?"

The line was silent for a few moments, then Agent Smith said, "This is confidential, do you understand? There has been a bomb threat against the Oramuni mine not far from you. We must shut the mine tours down as a precaution. An FBI team is on the way with an estimated time of arrival of thirty minutes."

Jim started to speak, but Agent Smith cut him off. "You must tell all remaining tourists and tour employees to leave the premises right now; do not tell them why. We do not want a panic. Then go down and quickly get John and the tourists topside." He continued, his voice hard and authoritative, "If you say anything about the bomb threat, or call anyone, you will be arrested, do you understand?"

Jim's mind reeled. *Bomb threat at Onamuni? Fucking terrorists! I hope they kill them all*, he thought. He stood straight and said, "Yes, sir. Consider it done."

"You have twenty-five minutes. Move it!" The line went dead.

Jim replaced the receiver in its cradle and left the building in a hurry. He slowed from a run to a fast walk as he entered the ticketing building. Sherry stood by the counter, looking at her phone and giggling. Jim said, "Sherry, pack up your stuff and get out of here for the day."

She looked up, then glanced at the clock. "But we don't close for another thirty minutes."

Jim forced a smile. "Well, you're off early today. Don't look a gift horse in the mouth."

Sherry shrugged. "Okay. See you tomorrow." She grabbed her purse, put her phone in it, then asked, "What about the till?"

"Don't worry, John will close it out."

Smiling brightly, Sherry quickly left the building.

Jim followed her out, then turned and made his way toward the elevator building. Carl was there, looking bored and antsy for his shift to end. "Hey, Carl. Why don't you go ahead and leave for the day? I'll man the elevator for John and Tammy's return."

Carl looked at him suspiciously. "You trying to get me fired?"

"No, I just feel like operating the elevator. I miss it."

"Whatever, old man. I'm not letting you run my elevator. If John sees that I left before the final tour group came up, I'm out of a job."

Jim was going to argue, but knew how stubborn and angry Carl could be, so he gave up. "Alright, wait here a few minutes."

Jim turned and jogged over to the mechanical building, where Dennis sat at his station, reading an old *National Geographic* magazine. An entire stack of the old, faded yellow periodicals leaned against his desk.

"Hey, Jim. What's up?" Dennis asked.

"Not much. Hey, we just have the final elevator ascent, so why don't you head out? The old lady might like to see you home a little early for once."

Dennis glanced at the clock. "I don't know. I should stay till John and Tammy return topside."

"Bah, this machine would run itself for decades without you, and you know it. Now go ahead."

Dennis yawned, cracked his back, and said, "I guess you're right." He checked the gauges once, then grabbed his lunch box. Before leaving, he turned to Jim and asked, "What about you?"

"I've got no one to get home to. I'll stick around to run the elevator."

"You're a good man, Jim. See ya tomorrow."

"Sure thing. Have a good one."

Jim followed Dennis out and watched him amble slowly to his car and leave.

That left John and Tammy and the tour group.

Jim walked back to the elevator building and

stepped inside the elevator.

"What are you doing?" Carl asked.

"Listen, I got a call from corporate. They want us to shut down early today. I need to go down and get John and the group back up here."

Carl shrugged. "Fine, let's go. The sooner we get them topside, the sooner I can go home." He shut the gate and pushed the button for Level thirty-two.

The elevator descended fast. Jim smiled with enjoyment at the rattling and shuddering of the cage, and soon they had arrived at the bottom. He opened the cage doors and stepped out, then cursed when he didn't see any motorized carts. He would have to walk to the cavern.

He turned to Carl. "Wait here. I will be back shortly."

"Whatever."

Jim gritted his teeth, then started down the tunnel, careful not to twist an ankle on the cross boards.

He was about 300 feet down the tunnel when the lights went out.

Chapter 12

MILTON felt every one of his ninety-four years as he stood in the unlit cavern on Level thirty-two of Deepstone. He turned in a circle, careful not to lose his balance. The blackness was so complete that Milton wondered if this was what death would be like. He touched his abdomen with a shaking hand and could feel the stage-four pancreatic cancer pulsing inside of him. The pain was growing worse by the hour. *I guess I'll find out soon enough*, he thought.

Milton had received his cancer diagnosis six months earlier. At that time, his doctor had told him he had six months to live. Like clockwork, Milton had felt his body start to shut down three days ago. This morning, he had heard a little voice inside of him whisper that the cancer had broken through. At first, he was confused by the message, but eventually he understood. He was in the final stage. Milton had watched one of his oldest friends die from pancreatic cancer a year earlier. If her illness and how he was feeling now were any indication, Milton likely had two or three days left before he would be unable to walk, and then a day or so after that he would be unable to communicate. Then he would fade away. That was why this morning he had told Claire his final wish was to come back down into Deepstone and say goodbye to his friends Otto and Franc, who had died down here more than sixty years earlier.

Milton hadn't really been upset by his diagnosis. He'd been more surprised that he had reached ninety-four years on this earth, especially after working for the mining company his whole career. He'd spent sixteen years working down in this very underground mine where he had seen so many people either killed on the job or die later of lung diseases.

Milton had been unprepared for the surge of emotion that had filled him when John had turned off all the lights. Memories rushed back through the darkness around him—how he and his crew had worked their way ever deeper into the depths of the earth, often talking over lunch breaks about how far down they thought they could go. Milton had been satisfied with the $220 he earned each week. This job had paid for a beautiful house in the country, a cabin on Lake Vermillion, a boat, multiple cars, and college for his kids. He squeezed Claire's hand. She had been there with him the entire time. They had lived a good life because of this job.

Milton's fondest memory was the comradery between him and his fellow miners. Many of the old-timers had worked for thirty years or longer down here, right up to 1962 when the mine had closed. They had taught Milton how to do things the right way. They had all followed strict rules meant to keep each other alive. Milton had learned a lot from them.

90

But they hadn't been able to keep everyone alive, had they? he thought sadly. A tear spilled out of Milton's eye and ran down his right cheek as he realized he could no longer remember all the names of the 185 men who had died down here while he had worked at the mine. But his best friends, Otto and Franc, lived in his memory and he still spoke to them almost every day.

The number of reported deaths in the mine had always been much lower than the actual total, especially back in the 1800s when there were fewer safety standards. The mine company purposely kept many of the deaths secret, which had been especially easy, since most of the workers were recent immigrants from Finland, Sweden, Poland, Russia, and a dozen other countries. Back then, no one would miss them when they died, or know anything about them, other than their names. Few people back then spoke English in the mines, and people tended to work alongside others from their home countries.

Things had gotten better in the 1900s, and by the time Milton had started working at the mine in 1946, working conditions had improved, and most people spoke English. But it was still a dangerous business, and four or five men had died every year. Most of the deaths had been on the Scraper crews, the men who entered a cavern after a blast to pry loose rocks from the ceiling that hadn't fallen in the initial explosion. Many times, a single loose rock could cause a small collapse of the ceiling, killing the man instantly. It had been one of the highest-paid positions in the mine due to the danger. There had been a waiting list for those jobs, with no shortage of men willing to risk death for a few extra dollars a week.

Light filled the cavern once again, and the

exclamations from the other tourists brought Milton back to the present day. He felt tired and drained, and the pain in his stomach was almost unbearable. Milton didn't take his morphine pill this morning. He wanted to be fully alert for this final visit to the mine. But right now, Milton wanted nothing more than to lie down and close his eyes. He took a deep breath, squared his shoulders, and patted Claire's hand upon seeing her look of concern.

Claire leaned into him, not saying a word but offering her presence and warmth to comfort him.

John smiled at everyone. "So, what did you all think? Have you ever experienced darkness like that before?"

Andy raised his hand and said, "Can you do that again? It was awesome!"

Smiling, John looked at his watch and said, "Sorry, little man, but we have to get back to the elevator."

The boy looked crestfallen, so John grinned and said, "Alright, one more time. But just a quick one. Everybody ready?" When everyone nodded, John reached for the post, but before he touched it, there was a loud boom, almost like thunder, and the whole place shook violently.

The lights went out before John could press the red button again.

CHAPTER 13

JIM listened carefully while standing in the tunnel in the purest darkness anyone could experience. John's voice echoed faintly in the distance. The cavern where John and the tourists gathered was about 600 feet ahead of him, too far for Jim to try and make his way in the dark. Jim carried an old clamshell cellphone, but it didn't have a built-in flashlight. So, he continued to wait, every second of darkness seeming like an eternity.

The lights flickered back on and partially lit the tunnel as it stretched ahead of Jim. He moved forward again but had only made it about thirty feet when a powerful explosion shook the tunnel. Pieces of rock fell to the floor. Jim put a hand on the nearest wall to steady himself. Then there was a loud cracking sound followed by a long series of crashes behind him. Jim cursed the Onamuni mine under his breath as the rumble faded away. *That sounded like a massive cave-in*, he thought.

Jim was unsure whether he should move forward

to get John and the tourists or go back to see if Carl was alright. Before he could make his decision, the lights flickered, then went out. Jim thought John may have turned off the lights for the tourists again and waited for him to turn them back on. But he also didn't think John would turn the lights off after the intense blast from the Onamuni mine. Something was seriously wrong.

Jim calculated the distance he had traveled already and knew he was closer to the cavern where the tour group was than he was to the elevator. He continued forward. It was so dark that he literally couldn't see anything; darker than closing your eyes in a dark room. Jim shuffled forward, raising each foot no more than an inch off the ground, while keeping one hand on the wall. It was slow going, but it was the safest way for him to move forward. The confused and frightened voices of the tourists echoed in the tunnel. Jim trusted John's ability to calm them down and keep them that way.

At his current slow pace, Jim figured it would take him ten or fifteen minutes to reach the cavern. He didn't dare move faster, though, for his own safety. Even so, it was agonizing, and it took everything Jim had not to try and go faster. After what seemed like an hour but had likely only been ten more minutes, Jim heard the tourists' voices more clearly, and he yelled out, "John! It's me, Jim!"

A cacophony of voices erupted into the silence. John yelled out, "Please, be quiet. I said, QUIET!" John never raised his voice, but he did now, and the tour group shut up.

John called out tentatively, "Is that you, Jim?"

Cupping his hands to his mouth, Jim yelled out, "Yes. I don't have a flashlight."

"Hang tight. We will come to you."

Jim leaned against the wall; thankful he didn't have to walk in the total darkness any longer. Only a minute or two passed before a light appeared ahead of him. John must still be at least a hundred feet away, but in the total absence of light he had been in, even a flashlight in the distance seemed bright.

Within another two minutes, Jim saw the flashlight beam, the light bouncing slightly as John walked. Jim yelled out, "I see you now!"

Soon, John and the tour group were standing in front of him.

John looked worried, his eyes looking past Jim to survey the tunnel behind him. He looked at Jim again and asked. "Jim, are you alright? What are you doing here?"

"I need to talk to you in private," Jim said, looking over John's shoulder at the seven tourists, with Tammy in the rear.

Milton shook his head and said, "No. You will not speak in private. We deserve to hear what's going on."

John glanced back at Milton as if he was going to argue, but then nodded and turned back to Jim. "Go ahead, they need to know what happened."

Grimacing as he wiped a sleeve against his forehead, Jim said, "That's the thing. I don't know what happened."

"Then why are you down here?"

"I was ordered to send everyone away from the mine."

John looked shocked. "Ordered? By who?"

Jim shrugged, "Some FBI agent. He asked me to bring you up and close the mine down."

Ben, who was tightly holding Fiona's hand spoke

up, his voice quivering as he asked, "Are we trapped down here? We are trapped, aren't we? We're going to die down here." He looked like he was going to completely lose control, his eyes wide and glassy.

Fiona turned and stared into his eyes in the meager light from the flashlight beam. "Ben, look at me. We are going to be alright. Do you understand me?"

Jim had seen that same panicked look on a soldier's face in Vietnam during a firefight in the jungle, and he knew Ben was close to losing it. If he did, the whole group might follow suit. Stepping past John, Jim stopped in front of Ben and leaned in close so that all Ben could see was Jim's face. "We just briefly lost power. But the lights will come back on. We will be alright."

Ben tried to look past him, but Jim moved to keep himself in front of Ben's eyes.

Fiona leaned in close to Ben and said, "Ben. Just take a breath. Good, and now another. And another."

Ben did as she asked, and he soon looked a little calmer. He finally sighed and lowered his eyes. "Sorry. I don't do well in enclosed spaces."

Jim nodded to him and then to Fiona before turning back to John. "I have the elevator waiting for us. I'm sure the power company is working on the power issue. We should be able to go back up shortly."

Professional and calm to the core, John smiled at the group. "Alright, folks. I'm sorry, but no power means we don't have the train available, so we are going to have to walk back to the elevator." He smiled, "But hey, just think of this as how the old timers used to work down here." John stepped over to Milton and Claire. "What are your names?"

The old woman immediately said, "My name is Claire, and this cranky old man is Milton."

Milton huffed indignantly and said, "At my age, I have the right to be cranky."

John smiled. "Nice to meet you both. Will you be able to walk back?"

Milton squared his shoulders, his eyes flashing in the meager light. "Of course, I can. I may be ninety-four, but I bet I can still do more pushups than most of you young fellas!"

John grinned, then turned and pressed a button on the side of his flashlight, replacing the beam with a soft glow that filled their immediate area with LED light. Tammy did the same with her flashlight and the tunnel lit up brightly.

Jim had recommended these types of flashlights down here because they could be set either as a tight beam of light, a lantern, or even a strobe light with speed settings from slow to fast. He and John had fought over the purchases, as John hadn't thought they were necessary. Jim had convinced John of the light's benefits if there was ever a power outage and they were stuck in the dark with a tour group, so John had eventually agreed to the purchase.

John continued speaking, "Before we begin, I think it would be helpful for the rest of you to briefly introduce yourselves."

Fiona was first, calling out, "My name is Fiona, and this is my husband, Ben. We are from Ohio, but love to travel the world."

Larry quietly said, "I am Larry, this is my husband Ethan, and our son Andy. We are from Saint Paul."

John nodded to each of them. "Nice to meet you all. Now, before we continue, I want you to stay close together and watch your step. I don't want anyone to get injured. We should make it back to the elevator in 10 minutes or so. We have more flashlights, bottles of water, and even some snacks for us there."

Andy, the growing thirteen-year-old that he was, grinned and exclaimed, "Cool! What kind of snacks?"

"Oh, you know, things like pickled pigs' feet and herring," John leaned down with a grin, "and there might even be a jar of lutefisk in gelatin."

Andy scrunched up his face and said, "Eww…"

The entire group, including Ben, laughed. Jim was amazed how quickly John was able to put people at ease.

Claire grinned at Andy, "Lutefisk is the best food in the world, young man."

Andy shook his head violently, "No it isn't. It's disgusting."

"Disgusting? What's disgusting about fish soaked in salt and lye for days until it turns to gelatin? Add some butter to it and you have a dish fit for a king."

"That's so gross." But Andy was grinning as he looked up at his dads. "You haven't eaten lutefisk before, have you?"

Ethan put his hand to his chest and dramatically said, "Andy. Son. All adults in Minnesota eat lutefisk in secret every Thanksgiving and Christmas until their children turn thirteen. When a child becomes a teenager, they are required to attend a secret lutefisk ceremony. After that, they must eat lutefisk at Thanksgiving and Christmas. It is the way."

Andy rolled his eyes. "*It is the way*? Oh, dad. A Mandalorian quote? Please."

Ethan tousled Andy's hair with a smile.

Ready to move the group along, John asked, "Tammy, are you alright bringing up the rear?"

"Of course, boss. Lead the way."

John nodded, then said, "Okay, let's get moving. Remember, take it slow and watch your step. We don't have far to go." He led the way, with the group sandwiched between him and Tammy.

Jim walked next to Claire and Milton. They smiled at him but didn't say anything as they turned their gazes back toward the floor. Milton stumbled, but Claire held his arm to steady him.

Jim studied the tunnel as they walked and was dismayed when they came across a one-inch crack running the entire length of the ceiling, snaking across its surface for almost twenty feet. The closer they got to the main entrance of the mine where the elevator was, the more the air filled with dust.

The air soon became difficult to breathe, so John called out, "Cover your nose and mouth with a shirt or sleeve. We're almost to the elevator."

Jim could now tell there had been a cave-in. He just hoped that Carl and the elevator had been spared. The group could make their way to the surface by climbing ladders to each level, but Milton and Claire might not make it even four or five levels. *Hell*, Jim thought, *I don't even know if I would make it topside*. Each of the ladders stretched at least seventy-five feet straight up; some of them were probably over a hundred feet in height. They were set in a tight shaft in solid rock, which meant that sometimes there was barely enough room to hold your elbows away from your body. And there were thirty-two levels in this mine, which would be like climbing inside a tube up three Empire State Buildings stacked on top of each other.

Jim pressed his sleeve harder against his nose and squinted into the dusty darkness ahead and wondered if this day could get any worse.

CHAPTER 14

MORGAN studied the rusty door in front of her. For the first time since entering the Deepstone mine, she wasn't sure what to do. They were in an old shaft that hadn't been used for over sixty years. Her team had been making their way carefully down this tunnel for more than fifteen minutes and hadn't seen any exits. The rough-cut walls glistened with moisture and the dark grey stone was sharp-edged and dangerous. Morgan bent down and picked up a rock from the floor and studied it, turning it over in her hand. It was heavy and the edges were almost as sharp as the flint or obsidian that Indigenous people used to craft their arrowheads. Morgan couldn't imagine how the miners had worked with this material every day without shredding their bodies.

Morgan glanced at her watch, then said, "Let's stop here. I need to send a report to Skuggs. Karen, keep your night vision on. We still cannot be sure whether or not the hostile is following us. Jack, turn yours off to conserve batteries. While we all have spare batteries and flashlights, we do not know how long we will be down here."

Karen nodded solemnly, removed her pack, and set it down against the wall before stretching her back, the cracking and popping echoing loudly through the tunnel. She sighed quietly, then removed her canteen and an energy bar from her pack and sat down, her weapon laid across her legs.

Jack followed suit, as did Morgan. It felt good to get the packs off their backs. They were heavy with equipment, weapons, ammunition, food, and water.

Jack reached up and deactivated his night vision.

Morgan carefully removed the MATCOM communication device from her pack and turned it on. The device was a new ground-penetrating communication technology that SafeWell had developed in conjunction with a high-tech startup company. It was not available to the public—or even the military—yet, as it was still in the testing phase. Since the team's job was to rescue scientists from underground locations, having reliable communication was often the difference between success and failure. The MATCOM device seemed like it was going to be a game-changer.

Morgan slipped an ear bud into her ear and pressed a button on the device. "Saint Bernard to base…do you copy?" Jack had picked the name for their team because he loved the old cartoons with the St. Bernard carrying a small barrel of liquor hanging from its collar while saving people on snowy mountain tops. Karen had rolled her eyes at the suggestion, but a small smile had lifted the corner of her mouth, so Morgan had agreed to the name.

There was no static over the MATCOM, as it didn't use radio waves. Instead, it used an experimental form of matter waves that penetrated solid materials. Morgan had helped test the device in caves 200 feet below the surface of the earth and it had worked flawlessly. The only issue was its speed. During testing, it had taken the reply from topside more than six seconds to return to her.

Morgan suspected there was a good chance the matter wave technology used by the device would not work under the more than 3200 feet of solid, dense, iron-rich rock of this mine. She waited for two minutes, then tried again, "St. Bernard to base…do you copy?" She waited two more minutes, then said, "St. Bernard to base. We are not receiving you. The MATCOM may not work this far underground. If you are receiving us, we are in Level thirty-three. We found evidence that the previous two teams passed this way, but we haven't made contact. We had a potential hostile encounter with an unknown bogey on Level thirty-two. Repeat: Potential hostile encounter with unknown bogey on Level thirty-two. Not human. I repeat, not human. We will continue the mission down to Level forty-three in search of the missing teams. Next communication in two hours. St. Bernard, out."

Morgan placed the device back into her pack, removed her canteen and an energy bar, then deactivated her night vision.

She closed her eyes as she tore open the package and took a bite from the tasteless energy bar. It had been a long day already, and nothing so far had gone according to plan. Morgan snorted as she thought, *when has any operation gone the way it was planned*? Per their training, as soon as her team took their first step, they would adjust their plan based on the evolving situation.

Morgan let her mind wander. Soon, memories of her late husband Oba filled her thoughts. She had met him in Navy Recruit Training, and they had an instant connection. They hadn't acted on it at the time, though, as fraternization had been frowned upon at that level of the military. Then, they had met by accident—or fate—at a Navy function six years later and their relationship had moved quickly. They were married within a year.

Oba's grandparents had moved from Nigeria to Alabama in the 1940s. He had been the first in their family to join the military; a source of pride to them all.

Morgan felt tears of happiness well up as she thought of their wedding day ten years earlier. It had been a perfect autumn day. The sky was blue, and the maple trees were blazing orange and yellow along the boulevard next to the courthouse. Both sets of parents, as well as Oba's grandparents, had been in attendance for their simple ceremony. Afterward, she and Oba had flown to Fiji for two weeks of sun-filled days and steamy nights. Life had felt perfect for them.

Morgan's skin went cold as the happy memory darkened. She thought of the phone call she had received from the hospital three and a half years ago. Oba had been hit and killed by a semi-truck while cycling on a back-country road. For three months after that, Morgan had buried herself in her service, going on three missions back-to-back. But she had eventually reached her emotional limit and had broken down. She retired from the Navy and two months later, Skuggs had called her with a job offer at SafeWell.

Shaking the past from her thoughts, Morgan raised her wrist and pressed a button on her watch.

The light emitting from the small device seemed to light up the entire tunnel. It was 4:13 p.m. They had been down here for almost forty-five minutes already. Despite seeing occasional disturbances, such as a scuff mark on the stone floor, Morgan and her team had no idea what may have happened to either of the two teams they had been sent to rescue. The intel said the two teams had planned to make their way down to Level forty-three. According to the maps of the mine Skuggs' contact had obtained, the route Morgan and her team had taken to Level thirty-two was the only entrance point to the lower levels. *So where were the other teams?* Morgan wondered. Morgan's team had also seen no indications that the teams had returned. This meant one of two possibilities: either they had used an unmarked exfiltration route, or they were still down here. Morgan ran through the possible scenarios in her mind. Had they been killed in a cave-in? Were they trapped somewhere down below? Or had they met with the same potentially hostile force Morgan and her team had seen just a short while ago in this very tunnel?

Morgan and her team had a lot of firepower. But while she didn't worry about her team defending themselves, she didn't necessarily want to kill something she knew nothing about.

Morgan turned her night vision back on and the green and black images of Karen and Jack almost startled her after sitting in the complete darkness of the tunnel for so long.

Suddenly, the tunnel shook. Pieces of rock fell from the ceiling as a massive blast echoed around them. The team wore Kevlar helmets, so they hunkered down as a group into as small of a target as possible until the rumbling stopped.

The tunnel soon became quiet.

"What the hell was that?" Jack asked, clearly rattled.

Morgan looked down the tunnel trying to see if there was any damage. "I think it was a blast from the Onamuni mine. It was in the report that they had begun blasting not far from here."

Jack reached up and activated his night vision, saying, "That didn't sound like an ordinary fucking blast. It was bigger than anything I've even felt in combat. I think it may have collapsed a tunnel above us."

Morgan pointed back the way they had come, "Karen, go back and investigate this level for stability. If you see any sign of the potential hostile, do not engage; return here as quickly as you can."

Karen immediately set out, her rifle held steady as she moved swiftly down the tunnel. Within fifteen minutes, she returned. "Some rocks fell from the ceiling in various spots, but the tunnel is passable. I noticed large cracks in the ceiling, though, which didn't look good."

Jack swore. "I don't like this shit."

Morgan quickly considered their options before addressing her team, "We came down here to either rescue two teams or find out what happened to them."

Jack and Karen agreed in unison. "Affirmative."

Morgan continued, "So we can keep going down until we reach Level forty-three, or we can abandon this mission due to the unsafe situation. It's possible the other two teams were trapped or killed by a cave-in from the Onamuni blasting, but right now we have no way of knowing where or even if that is true. The problem I see is two-fold. First, this mine has miles of tunnels across forty-three levels. It could take days to search all of the tunnels for alternative ingress and egress points. According to the report, the Onamuni mine performs blasts once or twice a day, and today there have been two. So, I think we are good for another twenty hours or so. Second, and most importantly, I don't think this tunnel system will survive many more blasts, and I won't risk us getting trapped down here."

Karen nodded her head. "Plus, we didn't plan for an extended mission."

Jack nodded and readjusted his pack to make it more comfortable. "This whole mission smells bad," he muttered.

Morgan agreed with both of them; she felt unsettled, as well. Normally, her team had a clear mission objective. People went missing, and her team rescued them. One way in and out. But this situation felt different to her. They didn't even know who the teams were they were sent to rescue. They didn't know if they were military, scientific, or something else, perhaps even something dangerous? Morgan adjusted her night vision strap and slid her pack on her back. "Let's go down a few more levels. If we do not find either team in the next four hours, then we will end our mission and return topside." Morgan set a timer on her watch. She had been given the code to unlock the elevator controls, so they should have no problem going back up after the mine closed.

Both Karen and Jack nodded in agreement, so Morgan motioned to Jack. He stepped forward and tried the rusted handle on the iron door, but it wouldn't budge.

"Boss? We have movement behind us," Karen whispered.

A chill ran through Morgan's body as she turned.

CHAPTER 15

JOHN pressed his sleeve to his mouth. The dust that clouded the air as they got closer to the elevator room meant only one thing: there had been a cave-in, likely near the elevator shaft. With the loss of power, this meant the way they would normally take tourists out of the mine may not be an option anymore. John mentally crossed his fingers that all would be OK as he led the tour group the final distance toward the elevator.

The light from John's LED flashlight could not penetrate very far through the dust, so he had to keep the group moving at a slow pace. The dark tunnel with its irregular walls chiseled into the earth, seemed to stretch endlessly in front of them. The flashlight batteries would supposedly last for 10 hours of continual use. And there was always a cabinet of spare flashlights and batteries in the elevator room. But John didn't know if the food and water there would still be fresh. *Dammit*, John cursed to himself.

I should have been more careful with my daily safety checks down here! John had gotten a little blasé with everything after doing this for so many years. And now, the lives of everyone in the group may depend on the contents of that cabinet.

The tunnel turned to the left up ahead, and John's experience told him the elevator would only be thirty or forty feet past that. The group continued at a slow pace, and when they finally made the turn, they saw the shadowy opening of the cavern illuminated by John's flashlight beam.

John sighed with relief when they finally entered the main elevator room, but this was short lived, and his mouth fell open in shock. The room was originally thirty feet wide by 120 feet long, and, although the elevator still stood relatively untouched, that was where the room now ended. Most of the room was now blocked by collapsed rock.

The tourists gasped at the mountain of rock in front of them. Jim moved forward to the elevator and yelled, "John, bring your flashlight here!"

John snapped out of his shock and made his way over to Jim, who was bent over something. Then he realized it was Carl lying on the ground covered in dust.

Jim put a finger to the young man's neck to check for a pulse, and when he did, Carl opened his eyes and screamed.

Jim made a soft shushing sound, "It's alright, Carl. We're here. Are you hurt?"

John knelt and moved his light over Carl's body. He didn't see any visible injuries.

Carl pushed himself up to a sitting position and shook his head, his eyes haunted. "I'm fine, I think. I…" he looked at the faces of the tour group, and when he saw Tammy, his eyes cleared, and his face filled with embarrassment. He pushed Jim's hand away and stood up, brushing dust from his shirt and pants. "I'm fine. I just didn't have a flashlight, so I couldn't see anything and the elevator..." His voice trailed off as he stepped into the elevator cage and pressed the darkened buttons on the control panel for the floors above. He turned to the group, his eyes looking wild. "The elevator. There's no power. It doesn't work." He pressed the buttons repeatedly to prove his point.

John stepped forward and pulled Carl's hand off the control panel. "I think that last blast cut the power supply."

"What the hell does that mean? They're fixing it, right? Jim's fixing it, right?" Then Carl turned to Jim as if seeing him for the first time and said, "Shit."

Ben called out, his voice wavering with emotion, "We *are* stuck down here, aren't we? We're trapped and we are going to die."

"No, we are not trapped," John said calmly, hoping to keep the rest of the group from panicking. He quickly ran through their options in his head. They could wait for help here by the elevator, but it might take days for someone to restore the power. And what if they couldn't repair the power connection? While a rescue team could repel down, how would the group get back up?

The air was quickly clearing of dust, which appeared to be pulled up the elevator shaft. John aimed his flashlight at the cabinet next to the elevator and smiled. At least that had been left undamaged. When he looked closer, however, he noticed the door was slightly ajar. John walked over and opened the door. He counted ten bottles of water and a box of candy bars, though it looked like some bars were missing. The flashlights were all there, but there weren't any extra packs of batteries. Then he remembered taking the batteries topside to recycle them yesterday, since they had been expired for two years. He swore to himself, just now realizing he had completely forgotten to get more batteries on the way to work this morning.

Even though they always stored the flashlights without batteries for safety reasons, John checked each of the flashlights anyway, half-heartedly hoping at least one would be full. They were all empty. The group would have no light except for John's and Tammy's flashlights. The one minor saving grace was the tourists' cellphones, which had small flashlights built in. These would only provide a weak, undirected amount of light, but hopefully between the phones and two flashlights, they would have enough light until they could get topside.

But how they would get topside was another matter entirely.

The only other way to get out of the mine was to climb to each level via the ladder system.

John cursed under his breath again. He had never been to any of the other levels. He had no idea where each of the access points were on the other thirty-one levels above them. And, he had no idea if there had been additional cave-ins on the other levels, but logic suggested a grim reality. Since the blasting at the Onamuni mine was done on the surface, the closer they got to the surface, the more damage there should be.

John looked at the group. It would take a miracle to get them all topside safely. Nevertheless, he put on a professional, optimistic expression and said, "It looks like our tour is going to take you to areas of the mine that you normally wouldn't see."

Jim's face grew determined, and he asked, "We are going up, then?"

John nodded. "It's the only real option. It may take the authorities days to restore the main power or find a way to connect backup power that can handle the large electrical load of the elevator. And it is not safe to stay down here if the Onamuni mine does more blasting again tomorrow. There are access points to each level that we can reach by ladder. We can climb out that way." He looked at Milton and Claire. "It will be hard work. But we are here to help you."

Milton looked determined. "I worked down here over sixty years ago. I know this mine better than anyone. We are wasting time standing around talking. Let's go."

Milton's assurance seemed to calm the group down. Even Ben, who was obviously terrified, nodded.

John spoke loudly, "Alright, listen up. We need to take the water and candy bars." He pointed to Ben and Fiona. "Can we use your backpack to carry the water and food? I will be happy to carry one of them, as it will be heavy."

Fiona immediately nodded, "Of course. And we can take turns carrying it. My husband and I hike with much heavier packs than this." She looked at her husband, who seemed to be getting his color back. Having a task that would help the group get out of the mine seemed to buoy Ben's spirits. Fiona took her pack off and unzipped it.

"Thank you both," John said, as he handed Fiona water bottles and candy bars.

Andy stepped forward, "I can take some in my pack, too. It's probably better to split up the food and water anyway."

Ethan put a hand on his son's shoulder. "Are you sure, Andy? That will be heavy."

Andy spoke with a serious voice, "Dad, I can handle this."

Ethan stared into his son's eyes, then nodded and stood up straight. "Alright, son."

After distributing the food and water, John led the small group of people into the tunnel, walking confidently. But inside, he worried for them all. He had no idea of the condition of the 31 tunnels or escape hatches above them, or if the hatch that opened onto the surface was even still operational. For all he knew, it could be rusted shut after 60 years of non-use, or a fallen tree could be laying across it. He pushed those negative thoughts aside and concentrated on just getting them up to the next level. One step at a time.

CHAPTER 16

JOHN aimed his flashlight upward and looked at the hatch seventy-five feet above him. Sixty feet of the distance was contained within a forty-two-inch-wide hole bored through the rock of the ceiling. He grabbed the steel ladder leading up to the hole and shook it. It didn't move, as solid today as it had been when it was built many years ago. He turned to face the small tour group. "Alright, this is the way up to Level thirty-one. It's a long way to the hatch, so I want you to go slow and make sure your feet are secure before you even reach up to the next rung." He looked at Andy, whose eyes were shining brightly in anticipation of the climb. With a stern voice, he said, "Andy, I know this looks like fun to you, but please remember one thing: if you slip and fall from seventy-five feet, you will likely die and possibly kill someone below you."

Ethan opened his mouth to protest at John speaking to his son in such a way, but when Larry put his hand gently on Ethan's arm and shook his head almost imperceptibly, Ethan thought the better of it and remained quiet.

John continued, "I know that sounds harsh, but it's the truth. This is not a game. I'm not going to sugar coat it: we are in a serious situation here. But, if you climb slowly and carefully, you'll be just fine." He turned to Milton and Claire. "Do you think you can climb these ladders?"

Claire looked concerned, but Milton straightened his back proudly and said, "Of course. No need to worry about us."

John nodded, then continued, "OK, I'll make the first climb to make sure everything is safe and to open the hatch. I'll yell down when it's OK for the rest of you to start climbing. Claire and Milton, I would like the two of you to go up first, followed by the rest of you in any order." He turned without another word and climbed the ladder. Each foot- and handhold was solid and true. John reached the hatch in a couple minutes and studied the lock mechanism for a few moments.

It was a simple latch system, so John reached up with one hand to twist the handle. At first the latch didn't move, so he tapped on it with the palm of his hand, hoping to free any rust that had built up over the years. He didn't know if anyone had used the hatch in sixty years. After hitting it five times, John tried pulling the steel latch again, and this time it slid free from its housing with a screech.

Breathing hard from the effort, John put his hand back on the ladder and closed his eyes to catch his breath. He glanced down and quickly realized his mistake when he saw the floor so far below. John looked back up at the hatch, holding the rung of the ladder tightly. Once his breathing slowed, he climbed to the next rung and bowed his head so he could place his shoulder against the hatch. With a heave, he used his shoulders to push the steel plate upward. It wasn't as heavy as he had expected, its hinge squealing as the hatch opened and slammed to the floor above with a loud bang. The tourists exclaimed below, so John called out to reassure them. "Everything is fine. That was just the hatch hitting the floor when it opened."

John stuck his head above the rim. It was pitch black. John's flashlight was in his pocket because he had needed to hold the ladder with both his hands when opening the hatch. Earlier, when Andy had asked why their helmets didn't have built-in lights like the miners did, John had said they weren't needed anymore. He had to admit a helmet like that would be very useful in his current situation. John reached through the hatch opening, pulled himself into the darkness, and climbed the last few rungs of the ladder with his feet until he could pull himself over the edge and sit.

The air in this level smelled stale and damp. John quickly took out his flashlight and switched it on. He was in a small alcove set off from a tunnel, similar to the one they'd been in below. John swung his legs up to the floor and stood up. He took a few steps and aimed his flashlight down the tunnel to his left, then his right. He couldn't see anything beyond the beam of his flashlight. A chill went down his spine as he realized he was probably the first person to have been up here in decades. A rusty steel rail track ran the length of the tunnel. The floor was rough-hewn from the stone, not flattened from use like the level below was.

John heard a drip of water in the distance, but

116

nothing more. Tammy called up to him, her voice lacking its normal cheerfulness. "John, is everything alright?"

He stepped back to the hatch and leaned over it. "Yep, it's all good. Send Claire up first, then Milton. I will be here to help them through the opening at the top." He changed his flashlight's setting to lantern mode and set it on the ground. The alcove lit up with soft light.

Milton leaned forward and kissed Claire on the cheek, then put his mouth to her ear and whispered something the rest of the group couldn't hear. She smiled and patted his cheek, then turned and started up the ladder. She moved quicker than John had expected, so he reminded her, "Claire, please slow down."

She looked up at him and nodded, taking extra time with each rung. Soon, she was right below him.

John knelt and reached down, saying, "Go up one more rung, then take my hand," he tapped a spot on the edge of the hatch and continued, "and place your other hand here, then climb the remaining two rungs using your feet."

She did as he said, and he pulled her up until she was through the hatch.

She was only slightly out of breath, her flushed cheeks the only indication she had just climbed up a seventy-five-foot ladder.

"Thank you, John. Please pull more gently with my husband, his bones are brittle."

John nodded, "Of course." He led her to the tunnel. "Sit here and be careful, the floor is uneven."

Claire nodded silently.

When he returned to the hatch, John saw Milton had already started up the ladder. He moved slowly, his hands trembling as he reached for each rung. After a few rungs he stopped to catch his breath, then climbed a few more before resting again. He repeated this cadence until he was just below John.

Repeating the same commands he had used with Claire, John gently helped the old man through the opening in the floor, using extra caution to not pull his arm too hard. Soon Milton stood next to him, breathing hard, his face pale in the lantern light. Leaning forward, John asked, "Are you alright, Milton?"

After a dozen more breaths, Milton nodded. "I'm…fine. Thank you. Where is Claire?"

Claire's voice came from the darkness to reassure her husband. "I'm here, dear."

John took Milton's arm and helped him walk over to Claire.

She took his other hand and said, "Sit down here, against the wall."

Milton nodded, slowly lowered himself to the ground, and leaned his head against the stone.

John turned and went back to the hatch, to find Andy climbing through the opening.

Grinning, Andy said, "That was fun. But I was careful, like you said, Mr. John."

John clapped him on the shoulder. "Good man. You can call me John. I don't like the 'mister' part. Can you do me a favor?"

Andy immediately nodded. "Sure."

"Good, I knew I could count on you. When each person arrives up here, would you help them over to the tunnel, making sure they don't stumble or fall, and tell them to wait there, out of the way?" John gestured to where Claire and Milton were sitting.

Andy's eyes shone with the importance of his

task, and he nodded.

John held out his hand and said, "Thank you, Andy."

Andy looked at John's hand, then shook it, a serious expression on his face.

John returned to the hatch and helped each person through, directing them to Andy who led them to the tunnel, telling them where to stand or sit. When Ethan climbed through, Andy stood a little straighter and taller. John told Ethan, "Andy is in charge of helping everyone safely into the tunnel. Take his hand and let him lead you. The ground is uneven."

Andy stepped forward and held his hand out, a look of pride on his face.

Ethan took his son's hand, and Andy led him down the tunnel to a spot where he could wait.

Soon, Tammy came through the hatch, which meant everyone had made it safely. John slowly closed the hatch cover, picked up his flashlight, and entered the tunnel where everyone was waiting. He didn't want to alarm the tour group, but he also didn't want to lie to them. "I have to be honest. I don't know where the next ladder is located. None of us have been in these levels before."

A few members of the group looked around with wide eyes, but they all remained respectfully quiet. He continued, "But the good news is, we all made it up here with no problem. We have food and water, and we should make it topside in a day or so."

Ben looked around and raised his hand.

"Yes, Ben?"

Ben swallowed hard before asking, "We are going to stay together, right? I don't want to get lost down here."

"First of all, you won't get lost down here. It isn't

a maze. The tunnels pretty much just lead in two directions." He shined his light down the tunnel in each direction to underscore his words. "But you raise a good point: How should we search the tunnel for the entrance to the next level? I think those of you in the tour group should remain here with Jim and Carl. Tammy and I will explore each direction to look for the next ladder."

When the group started protesting, John raised his hand and loudly said, "Quiet, please!" When the group was quiet again, he continued, "Tammy and I can cover ground much quicker if we are alone. And it will reduce the risk of one of you stumbling and getting hurt."

Carl looked like he was going to disagree, but he lowered his eyes and remained silent. When no one else spoke up, John said, "Good. You all probably have cell phones. I want you to power them all off except for one, which you can use as a flashlight. We need to conserve the batteries."

Andy raised an arm.

John asked, "Yes, Andy?"

Andy said, "I think we should all turn off our Wi-Fi and Bluetooth settings as well. If we leave those on, they will drain the phone batteries faster because the phones will constantly search for signals."

"Good point, Andy. Thank you. Everyone, please do as Andy says."

When everyone did as requested, John said, "Good. Andy. You will be in charge of the light, OK?"

Jim scowled, "I think that's a bad idea. I should be the one with the light."

John shook his head. "Sorry, Jim. But Andy's young, and if he happens to trip, he will catch himself quickly and have less chance of dropping the phone. No offense to you."

After some grumbling, Jim finally nodded in agreement.

John put a hand on Andy's shoulder. "Stay here and don't go exploring, alright?"

Andy nodded solemnly.

"Tammy, are you ready?" When she nodded, John said, "If you find the hatch, memorize its location, then return to the group. I will do the same. Sound good? You should come across the elevator shaft in that direction so be careful. I have never been down here so I can't guarantee all the levels have gates across the elevator shaft opening like at the surface. You don't want to step into an open shaft by accident."

She nodded again.

John leaned close to Tammy, quietly warning her, "Be careful and watch each step. The ground is rougher up here. There's not a nice, even floor like on Level thirty-two."

"You too, John. Be safe." The concern in Tammy's eyes was real.

"I promise. See you soon." He held his flashlight high so it cast light in a larger circle, then turned and made his way into the tunnel at a fast walk.

After a short while John turned back to look at the group. The light from Andy's camera looked like a pinprick in the darkness. After a few more paces, the tunnel curved to the left and John lost sight of the group. The tunnel was cool and damp, just like Level thirty-two, but somehow, it seemed more oppressive to John. He hadn't realized the DNR had done so much work to make Level thirty-two suitable for tourists. They had even leveled and smoothed the tunnel floors.

John also felt uncomfortable on this level because no one had been here in many years. It was like an abandoned house that has lost its feeling of being lived in; the absence of people removes the soul that makes a house a home. John had the same sense on this level. More disturbing to him, it felt like humans were not meant to be here.

Suddenly, John thought he saw movement just out of range of his light. He stopped, remaining still and holding his breath. He stared hard into the darkness but saw nothing. He chuckled without humor, *I'm already seeing things that aren't there*, he chastised himself.

Releasing his breath, John started forward again. He soon came to a large cavern where mining had been done. It had an uneven floor filled with both small rocks and boulders that were larger than him. He raised his flashlight as high as he could but couldn't see the other side of the cavern. He tried switching the flashlight to a concentrated beam but still couldn't see the cavern's far walls. He moved the light left and right and estimated the space was about 400 feet wide. He couldn't tell how long it was, though.

John whistled softly to himself. The cavern on Level thirty-two was much smaller than this. He hadn't realized the miners had made such large caverns. John cautiously walked into the vast area, casting his light around, but saw no exit tunnels. He kept walking, careful with his footing, until finally, in the distance, he caught sight of the far wall. He estimated the cavern must be about 1500 feet long.

He approached the wall and shined his light all around but saw no exit tunnels or ladders. It was a dead end.

John turned and made his way back across the cavern, then back into the tunnel, returning the way he had come as quickly as he could. As he made his way, he turned to look back one last time and thought he caught movement again just out of reach of his light. Logic told him there couldn't be anyone down here, but he soon found himself running, his breath coming in ragged gasps. The darkness around him felt like a heavy blanket pushing him down.

John stumbled and caught his balance in time to save himself from falling to the ground. He forced himself to stop and slow his breathing down, scolding himself for almost causing himself a serious injury.

John started forward but refused to look behind him again. He carefully made it back the way he came and eventually saw the light from the group in the distance. They saw his light as well and Andy called out his name. When John arrived back at the group, he noticed Tammy had already returned and was looking at him with concern.

She stepped close to him. "John, are you okay? You were gone a long time!"

Nodding, John said, "Sorry, I didn't see any ladders, but I did come to a cavern that must have been five times larger than the one on Level thirty-two. I crossed it just in case there was an access point to the next level on the other side. It took me longer than I had expected. What did you find, Tammy?"

She frowned. "You scared us. We were debating whether we should come find you, in case you had injured yourself."

John realized they were right to be worried. "I am sorry about that. Maybe it would be a good idea to go in teams of two next time."

Tammy nodded, then said, "There's a ladder leading to Level thirty about 500 feet down the tunnel. It looks identical to the one we just came up."

"Excellent. Let's go then. You lead the way, and I'll go last."

The group moved down the tunnel, and John followed, glad that Tammy had found the way up to the next level.

He couldn't shake the feeling that they were being followed, but time was of the essence if he wanted to get the tour group out safely. Or at least that's what he told himself when he refused to look behind them to confirm his fears.

CHAPTER 17

At precisely 4:45 p.m., six black SUVs pulled into the Deepstone mine parking lot, leaving a large dust cloud in their wake. RENN immediately exited the lead vehicle and surveyed the parking lot.

The doors to the other five vehicles opened in unison, and seventeen black-clad soldiers exited the vehicles and fanned out, assessing the area with alert eyes and stoney expressions. Most of them held prototype SIG Sauer NGSW-R MCX Spear assault rifles with specially designed, forty-round magazines. A few of the team members carried specialized weapons like sniper rifles and shotguns. Each team member also had a Sig Sauer M17 pistol in a holster at their side.

They all wore sleek, black military helmets. Each helmet was outfitted with a night-vision scope and side-mounted LED flashlight. Their Kevlar tactical vests were heavily loaded with ammunition for their weapons. The vests had been designed to hold seven magazines and eight pistol clips. All team members carried at least one bandolier in their packs that held six spare magazines; most had two or three. Half the spare magazines were filled with soft-point rounds, designed to inflict as much damage to flesh as possible, and the other half contained armor-piercing rounds able to penetrate even the most sophisticated Kevlar vests. They would all rather carry extra weight and be slightly less comfortable, than go lighter but run out of ammo.

Renn stretched his back. He had been sitting for most of the past six hours, first in a plane from California to Hibbing, then in the SUV for the final hour drive from Hibbing to the Deepstone underground mine.

Renn looked over his team as they gathered around him. His main team was divided into three sub-teams of six members each. He was the overall commander, as well as leader of Team One, which included a tracker, Ficks; Paul, who, although not a specialist in any one area, was a skilled jack-of-all-trades; an electronics expert, Greg; and two expert sharpshooters, Lucy and Millie, each of whom could hit any target with any rifle. Lucy radiated a cold callousness, like a coiled viper ready to strike out at any moment, which made most people give her a wide berth. Millie was the opposite of Lucy: always smiling, yet giving off a little sister vibe that endeared her to the entire team.

Team Two was led by Sally, an ex-Army Major. She commanded Karl, an ex-KGB soldier, and four ex-Marines: Jillian, Charlie, Johan, and Jason.

Team Three was responsible for site security and was led by Tess. Her team secured an active site against enemies and locals. Her team included sniper

Terryl, ex-FBI agents Gwen and Monique, and two men codenamed Sills and Roberts; not even Renn knew their real names.

Renn motioned Team Three to deploy.

Tess gave her team the signal to disperse. She was dressed in brown camouflage and carried a standard M24 SWS US Army sniper rifle and a large pack. She nodded once to Renn and then melted into the woods and ran fifty feet parallel to the road before stopping next to a tall Norway pine tree. She removed a specially designed tree stand from her pack, swung its strap over her back, and slipped a pair of spikes designed for tree climbing over her shoes. She climbed twenty feet up the tree before deftly securing the stand. Tess had designed the tree stand herself. It had a carbon-fiber platform that allowed her to lay forward and rest her rifle on a mini-tripod. This way, she could view a 270-degree range of fire that covered the entrance to the mine from almost all directions. From her post, Tess would watch for any incoming hostiles and offer fire support to Gwen and Monique if things turned violent.

Renn and Tess had become good friends over the years, and he had once asked her why she used such a common sniper rifle when she could have her pick from any of the high-tech models on the market. Tess held up the rifle, examining it carefully before looking back at him and answering, "Because it works."

Renn couldn't argue with her logic. He remembered watching her repeatedly hit stationary targets from 900 yards one day, until he'd decided to challenge her, "You can hit nice, immobile targets, but can you hit a moving target?"

Tess stood up without a word, reached into her

pack and took out a deck of playing cards. She opened the card case and pulled out the cards, fanning them out before offering them to Renn, who chuckled and drew one. It was the queen of hearts.

Tess put the deck of cards back in her pack, took the queen of hearts from his hand and walked down range to a tree. When she returned, she handed him her spotter monocular and pointed. Then she laid down and looked through her scope, adjusting it to her target.

Renn lifted the high-tech 30x100 monocular to his eye and zoomed in on the tree, the image clear and still thanks to the auto-stabilizer. It gave a readout of 834 yards. At first Renn didn't see the playing card. Then, movement caught his eye, and he zoomed in a little more to the left until the monocular focused on the queen of hearts. The card was tied to a string and dangled from a tree branch. It swiveled in the wind, swinging in random arcs. He scoffed as he looked back at Tess and said, "If you hit that card on the first shot, I'll buy you a new motorcycle."

She murmured, "Panigale" as she sighted down range.

"What?"

"I will take a Ducati Panigale V4 S." She said, "A red one."

Renn chuckled as Tess looked back through the scope. She remained still for almost a minute. Then she took a deeper breath, released it slowly, took another, shorter, breath and as she released it, gently squeezed the trigger. The rifle report was loud, and the weapon kicked hard against her shoulder. Tess switched the safety on and sat up smiling, then said, "I've always wanted a Panigale."

Renn lifted his monocular, zoomed in on the tree

and then the card. It still spun wildly in the wind. Just as he was about to comment sarcastically on her effort, the card stopped rotating and he saw a perfect hole right through the middle.

Renn had made good on his promise and bought her a Panigale, even though it had cost him $35,000. A bet was a bet, and he learned to never underestimate anyone on his team again.

Gwen, an Irish woman, and Monique, a Black woman from Alabama, were both dressed as FBI agents, their T-shirts and baseball caps prominently displaying the FBI logo. They removed large, plastic, sandwich board signs that read 'CLOSED' from the back of an SUV, propped them up to block the entrance to the parking lot of the mine, then ran yellow crime scene tape between them. They took positions on either side of the roadblock, each holding standard, FBI-issued Heckler & Koch MP5 SD 9x19mm submachine guns. They would remain there for the entirety of the mission, ensuring no one entered, not even the police. If any law enforcement did arrive, they would see Gwen and Monique's uniforms and likely defer to their authority.

Terryl was a slim, Black man from Queens, New York. He carried a next-gen MK-22 US Army sniper rifle, which he had named Nia in honor of his late wife, who had been a teacher killed in a school shooting. After the trial, as the murderer had been walking to his transport bus to be brought to prison, Terryl had shot him in the head from 1200 yards. The young man who had killed his wife toppled to the ground, a hole in his forehead and the back of his head missing. Terryl knew he would be the first suspect, so he had gone underground. Somehow, Thornlandon Holdings had found him and offered him a job, which he had gladly accepted.

Renn wasn't sure who was the better shot, Terryl or Tess. He just knew he wouldn't want either one as an enemy.

Terryl ran 300 yards to the back of the mine property and climbed onto a flat-roofed supply shed with a direct-line of sight to the mine entrance to the south as well as the woods to the north. He carefully spread out a heat-resistant blanket on the hot sheet metal, then laid down on his stomach, propping his weapon on a short tripod.

Renn nodded to Sally, Team Two leader, and pointed with two fingers toward the three buildings. He hoped the mine tour employees had, indeed, gone home after his call.

Sally motioned to her team to check out each of the buildings. All five team members quickly returned. None were accompanied by any of the mine employees.

Jillian was the last to return. "Sir. The elevator is at the bottom of the shaft. And sir? The power is out."

Renn had hoped the place would be empty, but he hadn't expected the power to be out. "Greg, see if you can find out why the power is out."

Greg eyed the power lines above them and followed them into the woods.

Sally leaned against one of the SUVs. She was short and squat and walked with a bad limp. From looking at her, no one would guess she was one of the deadliest people in the unit. She was blessed with a cool, calm demeanor that never wavered, no matter what was happening around her. She had been with Renn in some of the worst shitshows in Iraq and Afghanistan and he knew firsthand that she was unflappable no matter the chaos that surrounded her.

In March of 2013, Renn and his squad were on patrol in Kabul when a firefight broke out, bullets flying from the flat rooftops on both sides of the street. Three soldiers were cut down in the first five seconds. Some tried running to the closest open doorways but were shot to pieces by insurgents before they could make it. But Sally stayed where she was, calmly shooting hostiles off rooftops, a single shot at a time, picking them off like ducks in a carnival game, all while bullets whizzed past her head and struck the ground all around her. In the end, Sally killed seven of the men attacking them and took two bullets to her left leg and two to her left arm. Incredibly, she finished off the final two insurgents while lying in the dirt, bleeding from her wounds. She had been retired by the Marines with multiple medals of honor.

When Renn joined Thornlandon Holdings, Sally had been the first person he had personally recruited. Even the toughest, biggest, nastiest men in the unit treated her with the utmost respect.

The second person Renn recruited had been Paul. He was a large Australian with a wicked sense of humor. Thornlandon Holdings had found him in South Africa, where he had been facing twenty-seven charges of first-degree murder. One day, while watching TV in Australia, Paul saw a documentary about the extensive poaching problem in South Africa. He had gotten on a plane to South Africa the next day. Once there, he purchased a rifle and hundreds of rounds of ammunition on the black market and went into the bush for a little safari hunt of his own. He had killed twenty-seven poachers before he was finally apprehended.

Paul smiled for the cameras as he was brought to

the courthouse for his trial and even winked at an attractive reporter covering his story. Thornlandon Holdings arranged for him to disappear one morning as he was being transported to the courthouse and Paul had enthusiastically joined Thornlandon Holdings.

Renn scanned the Deepstone parking lot. Satisfied the perimeter was secure, he strode toward the elevator building, his face devoid of emotion. Except for Greg, who was scouting the power lines, the remainder of Team One, all of Team Two, and Sills and Roberts from Team Three followed Renn, fanning out as they did.

Renn knew he must make a decision soon, both for himself and his team. He had initially considered telling his team about the text he had received on the plane and ordering them to go off grid and stay off grid to avoid being hunted down by Thornlandon Holdings. But now, with the power out, there were people trapped down in the mine. Innocent people. Renn couldn't leave them trapped down there at the mercy of Thornlandon Holdings. With a sigh, Renn knew his decision was made for himself. But he would give his team the option to either stay and help the people below or disappear into the wind.

CHAPTER 18

MORGAN and Jack swung around to stare down the tunnel.

Karen whispered, "It's gone. Just gone."

"What did you see?"

At first Karen didn't answer, she just stared intently down the tunnel. Morgan repeated her question, a bit louder this time, "What did you see?"

As if startled out of a dream, Karen jerked her head around. Her face appeared haunted in Morgan's grainy night vision. "I…I don't know for sure. I saw someone…no, some*thing* peek around the corner of the tunnel ahead, but…"

Morgan touched her shoulder, "Karen, take a deep breath."

Karen did as Morgan suggested.

"Good, now another."

The deep breaths helped Karen calm down and her shoulders lowered as the tension released from her body. Her voice, when she spoke, had a hint of shame in it. "Sorry, these tunnels are getting to me."

"They're getting to all of us," Jack whispered from behind Morgan.

Facing forward again, she said, "I saw a…darkness glide along the wall, then it seemed to retreat from view. I don't know what it was, but it could not have been a trick of shadows, because there is no light source down here to cast a shadow. And it was not a person. It did not walk upright."

A chill ran down Morgan's spine. *What could it be*? she wondered to herself.

Karen calmly continued, "Therefore, we will consider it a bogey of unknown origin. It has not attacked us, so I cannot conclude its intent."

Jack asked, "What the hell can it be, though? I mean, we are almost a mile underground in a man-made tunnel system. It's not like we are in a natural cave system animals can get into."

Morgan wondered the same thing. This was for all intents and purposes a hermetically-sealed environment. The only way down here was via the elevator, or using the ladders and hatches. There was no way an animal could open a hatch, and she was pretty sure people would know if an animal rode down the elevator with them. She gasped as she realized what this likely meant.

Hearing Morgan gasp, Jack and Karen quickly turned to stare down the tunnel, clicking off the safeties on their weapons. Karen whispered, "What is it? Do you see something?"

"No, sorry. I was just thinking that no animal could find its way *down* here, since the elevator or hatch system requires a human to get through. So," Morgan paused a few moments, knowing how crazy her next thought was going to sound out loud, "that leaves only one other option. What if whatever we've been encountering came *up*?"

Both Karen and Jack turned to look at her, and Jack asked, "Up? Like from…" he gestured to the floor with his H&K.

"That is the only other option as I see it. What if, back in 1962, the miners stumbled upon a system of naturally-formed caves that were populated by an unknown species? What if that species was hostile? That might account for the sudden closure of these levels and the abandonment of the mine." Morgan let her statement breathe for a bit. She knew how unbelievable her idea sounded, but she couldn't think of any other explanation.

"That sounds as logical as anything," Jack said. "We've all seen the thing that is tracking us down here, and it sure as hell isn't human. Which begs the question: what do we do now? Do we engage?"

Morgan shook her head. "Not unless we are attacked. So far, whatever it is has kept its distance from us." She squared her shoulders. "Our mission was to find the two missing teams sent down here. We will continue searching for them."

Karen and Jack nodded without saying a word, their expressions grim, their eyes sharp and focused.

Morgan opened the rusty door, and they moved into another chamber with a hole in the floor where the hatch had again been cut out by a metal vapor torch. She noticed what looked like a scuff mark on the floor, which she guessed was caused by a boot twisting as someone turned. It must have been made by a member of one of the two teams they had been following. Morgan knelt and touched it with her finger. "This is freshly made—no more than a few days ago."

She motioned to Jack and after a quick look down the hatch, he swung his legs into the hole and disappeared down the ladder.

Karen closed the door behind her, and they both followed Jack down to Level thirty-four.

As Morgan descended the ladder, she knew they were definitely on the trail of the two missing teams. But she wondered what exactly it was that was on *their* trail.

CHAPTER 19

RENN pulled the gate of the Deepstone elevator open and leaned forward to look down the shaft. He could only see about twenty feet down. After that, there was nothing but complete blackness. The elevator cable was set about three feet from the side of the shaft unlike an elevator in a building, where the cable is positioned in the middle of the shaft. It was designed this way to reduce stress on the cable. He pressed the button to recall the elevator, but nothing happened.

Greg jogged up to Renn. He sounded a little winded. "The blasting appears to have knocked down a few large basswood trees, which took out the power lines. There is no way to restore power quickly. It will probably take the power company days to clear the downed lines and add new ones."

"Verify there is no power to the elevator."

Greg set his bag of tools down and opened it, exposing several common, everyday tools and some high-tech items provided by Thornlandon Holdings. He grabbed a simple screwdriver and used it to open the elevator's control box. He then took out a voltage tester, placing the black and red connectors on two wires within the box. He glanced at the readout then at Renn and said, "Nothing. No power at all."

Renn cursed under his breath. "Is there a backup generator?"

"There is…or was one in the mechanical building. I was able to briefly start it, but it caught fire almost immediately and burned out the engine before I could extinguish the flames. I don't think it had run in decades, and my guess is the tour company had not serviced it in as long." Anticipating Renn's next question, Greg continued, "The generator we brought was intended to power a lighting system, or a small bivouac. It does not have the capacity to run the massive elevator pullies."

Renn didn't have time to dwell on this setback. "We will descend the shaft using the elevator cable."

Renn stepped away from the elevator building, pulled his phone out of his pocket, and dialed a number.

Helen Polson answered immediately, "Yes?"

"We have an issue. The mine is empty of personnel, but the power is out, and the elevator is at the bottom of the shaft. It is likely the tour guides and tourists are stranded down on Level thirty-two."

The line went silent for some time before Helen came back and said, "We have verified no law enforcement agencies, nor the power company, have been notified. Descend and take out all targets below as planned."

Helen disconnected before Renn could reply.

Renn put his phone away and spoke loudly,

"Everyone, gather round."

All thirteen members of the squad quickly approached and stood at ease, facing him. Renn lifted his radio and pressed the button, "Team Three, do you copy?"

The members of Team Three, who were positioned elsewhere around the site, confirmed one after another.

"Listen in. I have the entire team with me. As you know, our orders were to verify the status of the two teams previously sent here, then secure the mine until the rest of Thornlandon Holdings' personnel arrive tomorrow. On the plane ride here, I received a text from an unknown source."

Paul grinned and said, "From an unknown source?" He turned to Ficks, a thin Hispanic man with a scar on his chin that divided his scraggly beard down the middle. "Just like in the spy movies, hey mate?"

Ficks and the rest of the team remained silent, waiting for Renn to continue.

"We have been lied to about why we are here." At the questioning expressions of his team, Renn recited the text from memory. When he finished, murmurs of anger filled the air, and Paul cursed violently.

Renn held up a hand. "There is more." He explained Helen's phone call and her not-so-subtle implication that if he kept the information that he received a secret he would live.

Most of the team's expressions hardened, and some members put hands on their pistols. None of them missed the nuance in the last statement: they, as a team, would not make it out of this mission alive.

Renn softly said, "I will not sacrifice any of you so I can stay alive. We will all get out of this together." Their faces seemed to relax a little, but they remained tense.

"We have been ordered to kill all the mine employees onsite, as well as any tourists stuck below. A three-person team from SafeWell is also in the mine. They were sent in this morning to find our missing teams. We are to take them out as well."

Sally cursed. "Renn, this is bullshit! Our job is to protect Thornlandon Holdings from terrorists, cartels, or any number of hostile entities around the world. We do not kill innocent people."

Renn nodded. "I agree with you. But Thornlandon Holdings can't let any of this information get out. If it does, they will never be able to use the mine to extract the precious metals below it. They want to keep their multi-trillion-dollar discovery a secret from everyone. You know what will happen to Thornlandon Holdings if it ever gets out that they had Americans killed on US soil? They would be finished."

Paul, who normally found the humor in everything, spat to his side and growled, "They're gonna kill us all, mate, so why don't we just bug out of here now?"

Everyone started talking at once, some in agreement with Paul, others arguing that they must not run.

Renn put up his hands and yelled out, "Quiet!"

In the instant silence that followed, Renn said, "If we leave now, the company will send in more teams to kill everyone below. We cannot let innocent people die."

Sally asked the obvious question, "So where does that leave us?"

"Fucked. That's where it leaves us," Paul said.

Tess spoke quietly and calmly over the radio. "We need to rescue everyone down below, get them all to the FBI, and tell the media what happened. It is the only option. And after that, I am gone. I won't stick around for Director Meyers to take me out."

Everyone but Lucy nodded in agreement. She eyed Renn coldly and said, "Why should we risk our lives for these people? I say we leave. Disappear."

Renn said, "You can leave if you like, Lucy." He turned to the rest of the team. "That goes for all of you. I will not stop you. But I am going to help those people down there."

No one moved.

Lucy glanced around, then said, "Alright. Fuck it. I'm in."

Renn felt the tension leave his body. His team were truly the best of the best. He quietly said, "Tess was correct. If we commit to saving everyone below, we will all have to go silent after the mission—to disappear into the ether. Thornlandon Holdings will hunt us all down, and with their resources, they may find some of us. But at least we will have a chance to survive if we can get the civilians and the SafeWell team to the authorities. We might even take down Thornlandon Holdings." Renn motioned to the tracker, Ficks, "Descend the shaft and gather intel. We will follow in ten minutes and meet you at the elevator down below."

Ficks walked to the empty elevator shaft, connected his rappelling harness to the cable, and dropped down the shaft in a controlled descent.

Renn continued giving orders, "Sills and Roberts: descend to Level thirty-two as well and remain by the elevator. If any civilians, or the SafeWell team arrive there before we find them, I want you to help them get topside. Take down a half-dozen extra MADs. We can bring up the civilians and SafeWell team in shifts using the extras." The MADs—motorized ascent drives—were powerful electric motors that could carry a person back up the cable. The MADs were equipped with compact, solid-state batteries that held enough energy to make at least three full ascents up the 3200-foot shaft.

Renn continued, "Terryl and Tess, guard the site from any additional intrusions by Thornlandon Holdings until we can get everyone topside and out of here. Gwen and Monique, as our 'FBI agents,' your job will still be to keep any civilians or local police from entering the parking lot."

Millie spoke up. "Sir, why don't we call the FBI, Homeland Security, the State Sheriff's office, and the media to explain what is happening here?"

Shaking his head, Renn said, "We can't do that. Our phones are almost certainly monitored. And Director Meyers has people within those agencies, as well as in the media. If we make those calls now, Thornlandon Holdings would send more teams here before we had the chance to rescue everyone below. In fact, I would bet that they already have kill teams in the air who will probably be here within hours. Our only chance to successfully rescue everyone is to not give Thornlandon Holdings any indication of our plans. We might just have enough time to get everyone safely away before Director Meyers or Helen figure out what we've done."

Renn looked at each team member. "Lean and mean is our goal. In and out quickly. I'll lead Team One and Sally will lead Team Two. We will descend into the mine. As you know from the intel report, this elevator shaft runs at an eighty-two-degree angle, so you will descend by hanging horizontally, using your legs to rappel down like you would going down the side of a large dam. I want tight, ten-second separations between us on the way down. Any questions?"

Paul looked around, then asked, "Can't we just use the MADs to descend? It would save us some time."

"No. We must keep them fully charged. We will have to make multiple ascents to bring up everyone."

When the team's questions were done, Renn looked at his watch, then said, "We descend in five minutes. Harnesses on. Team Two goes down first, followed by Team One."

The teams geared up, checking their weapons, ammunition, and other supplies. The specialists all carried the essential tools of their trade. In addition, Johan brought a flame thrower with a compressed fuel tank and Jason brought a semi-automatic shotgun and exploding shells. Renn was going to remind Jason about the 'no explosives' rule given to them by Director Meyers, but he decided against it. Exploding shells were not explosives, per se. *Besides*, thought Renn, *fuck Director Meyers*. The exploding shells would be a last resort anyway. If they were needed, it meant they were likely at the end of a firefight they weren't going to survive, anyhow. Causing a possible tunnel collapse would be the least of their worries at that point.

The teams separated into the order in which they would be descending, strapped into rappelling harnesses, and double-checked each other's equipment.

When everything had checked out, the teams stood in line, ready to move out at Renn's signal.

Some took quick sips of water, but most stood still, their faces blank as they waited for the order to descend.

Johan was the only one not on his feet. He sat cross-legged on the ground and chewed absently on an energy bar with his face raised to the sun, eyes closed. Were it not for his tactical gear, he would look like a young college student on campus without a care in the world.

Renn's watch beeped and he turned off the alarm before giving the order, "Team Two, descend."

Johan stuffed the remainder of the energy bar into his mouth and jumped up, all business.

Each team member took turns hooking onto the cable and stepping off the platform, each doing so as calmly as if they were walking into a room of a house, disappearing down the shaft with a swish of air.

When his whole team had entered the shaft, Renn closed his right eye to avoid being blinded and switched on his night vision, the rubber-mounted eyepiece covering his right eye only. Then he stepped off the platform. He dropped fast, his feet only occasionally encountering the wall of the shaft as he rappelled down. He used the harness brake to keep him at a controlled descent. After a few seconds, the shaft became pitch dark, so he opened his right eye and looked down through the night vision.

The shaft seemed to stretch out endlessly beneath him, highlighted in the artificial light of his night vision.

The ten-second separation between team members worked out to about fifteen meters, a good, safe distance. The digital readout in Renn's night vision counted every meter he dropped, the numbers rolling quickly by: 100, 160, 220, 300, 500. When Renn approached the 700-meter mark, he began applying the harness brake harder to slow him down even more.

By the time Renn reached 950 meters, he could see the bottom of the shaft. The elevator's roof hatch was open and as each team member landed on it, they disconnected from the cable, grabbed the edge of the hatch and dropped to the floor of the elevator. When Renn reached the roof of the elevator, he disconnected from the cable and dropped through the hatch to the interior. The readout in his night-vision indicated it had taken him just over twelve minutes to descend the shaft.

His team had secured the immediate area, but it was obvious that a worst-case scenario had already happened: the walls had caved-in, filling most of the room outside the elevator with rubble piled to the ceiling. The tunnel seemed passable, though.

With the power still out and no lights working, the area looked like a war zone.

Everyone had removed their repelling gear immediately upon entering the elevator room, including their MADs.

Ficks strode forward and stopped in front of Renn. "Sir, the tunnel is intact. I believe eleven people climbed up to Level thirty-one." He motioned down the tunnel and continued, "The three-member SafeWell team went down the tunnel about 500 meters and entered a tunnel on the left side." His expression changed, and he looked like he was going to say something more, but he stopped himself.

"Out with it, Ficks," Renn said, "Never hold anything back from me."

Hesitating for a few seconds, Ficks scratched the

scar on his chin, then shrugged. "I saw a faint imprint of a footprint that doesn't make sense. It is not...human." He looked around as if expecting others to mock him.

Goosebumps broke out on Renn's arms. "What do you mean, 'not human'? Maybe there's a dog down here with the tour group?"

"No sir. It is not a dog. I have never seen a track like this in my life. It is huge."

The team members looked into the dark tunnel with narrowed eyes, their hands gripping their weapons tighter. Renn knew that even hardened soldiers such as themselves could still get jittery around the unknown.

In a calm tone, Renn said, "OK, there is a potential hostile down here. Remain on extra alert. As I said earlier, Team One is with me to track the SafeWell team. Sally, you lead Team Two to rescue the tour group. You know the procedure."

Sally nodded briskly.

"Everyone, prepare to move out."

Paul glanced down the dark tunnel, then turned back with a grin and asked in his thick Australian accent, "And what about the thing that made that track? Are we allowed to do a little sport hunting if we see it?"

Some of the team members chuckled.

Ficks shook his head. "You don't hunt animals, Paul, just poachers."

Paul clapped Ficks on the back and leaned down, "Well, if whatever made that track hunts us, then I will hunt it back. Don't worry, I'll protect ya from the big, bad monster."

Ficks rolled his eyes and turned away.

Paul chuckled and grinned at the rest of the team.

Ficks and Paul were unlikely friends; Ficks calm and quiet, and Paul loud and boisterous.

Renn spoke sternly. "Sally, once we separate, our radios will no longer work. The rock is too thick between levels. So, follow your orders and meet topside when you complete your mission. If anything goes wrong, you and your team are responsible for fixing it. Alright, move out."

As Renn entered the tunnel, he thought of the footprint that Ficks had found.

What the hell could make a print that big? And more importantly, was it hostile?

CHAPTER 20

JOHN pushed against the hatch to Level thirty with his shoulder and let it slam open against the floor, revealing a similar alcove to the one on Level thirty-one. He climbed through, looked briefly around, then called down, "Just like before, OK? Andy, I'd like you to come up first and continue being my assistant, if that is alright with you, Ethan and Larry?"

Larry called upward, "Of course, John." He looked down at Andy and took him by the shoulders. His expression was serious as he said, "Andy, you listen to Mr. John and do what he says. He knows what he is doing. I know you will be careful."

Andy nodded solemnly, then turned and scrambled up the ladder as only a teenager could, before rising through the opening to stand next to John, a grin on his face.

John didn't smile back. "Andy, I want you to listen to me carefully."

The boy looked up at him, his face flushed from the climb.

"I asked you to climb slowly and carefully. I mean it when I say that if you can't do what I ask, I cannot continue having you as my number two."

Andy's grin disappeared, and he lowered his eyes. "I'm sorry, Mr. John. I promise I will be more careful next time."

John held out his hand and Andy hesitantly shook it. "Good man. I will hold you to that, because I need your help, and I need you to be safe."

Andy nodded, then turned back to the hatch opening, leaned carefully forward and called down, "Good job, Mr. Milton." After a few more minutes, Andy called down again, "OK, you only have a few more rungs to go. You're doing great, Mr. Milton. Give me your hand when you get to me."

John smiled in the darkness. He was pleased at how Andy seemed to handle his new role like an adult. John knew teenagers didn't like being treated like kids; at least he hadn't when he was that age.

Milton's trembling hand reached up and Andy grasped it, gently helping Milton the rest of the way through the hatch opening. Milton stood unsteadily, his face white. He seemed more out of breath than he had been before. Andy slowly guided him to the tunnel, then helped him sit on the floor.

Milton nodded, still struggling for breath. "Thank you, young man. Now, go and help the others."

Andy nodded and made his way back to John.

The tour group made it up the ladder and through the hatch easier than they had with Level thirty-one, and soon everyone had gathered in the tunnel, waiting for John to speak.

John did a quick count and frowned. Fiona and

Ben were missing. He strode to the hatch and looked down but saw no one below. He turned his head and asked, "Andy, did you help Fiona and Ben through the hatch?"

The boy shook his head. "No, sorry, I didn't even notice they were missing."

John went back to the tunnel and shined his light in each direction, but they weren't with the rest of the tour group. He returned to the hatch opening and climbed onto the ladder, looking at Andy and Jim. "I am going back to look for them. Wait here." Then he put his head down and descended back to Level thirty-one. Just as he set his feet on the ground, Fiona appeared from the darkness. John shined the light past her but didn't see Ben. "Fiona? What's going on? Where's Ben?"

She looked behind her once, then sighed. "He needs a few minutes alone. He's scared, John. He is more afraid of enclosed spaces than he let on to everyone. I thought he would do fine once he got used to things down here. He's so brave in everything else that I just thought…" Fiona trailed off and went silent.

John touched her shoulder. "It's alright. It's just bad, dumb luck that we're stuck down here. We've been doing these tours without incident for decades, and Ben happened to be here the one time we have a problem." He glanced down the tunnel. "Do you want me to go get him?"

Fiona shook her head, then pointed up the ladder and said, "No, he wants us to wait for him up there. He doesn't want any of us to see him struggle. He is ashamed."

John resisted a sigh and forced himself to calmly say, "I understand. If he doesn't go far, he should be fine. Let's go up and we'll wait right by the hatch opening for him if he needs any help."

Fiona nodded. She glanced back down the tunnel, then turned to the ladder. She climbed slowly until she reached the hatch opening.

John considered going after Ben, but he decided to respect the man's wishes—for now. They needed to reach each of the hatch access points as quickly as possible, though. They had to get out of this mine before the Onamuni site began blasting tomorrow. If there was more damage to the mine, they risked being trapped down here forever. They couldn't wait for Ben to compose himself on every level. As soon as Fiona reached the top, John started up the ladder, vowing to go back down to find Ben if he didn't come back in a few minutes.

CHAPTER 21

BEN was finally alone and could clear his thoughts without feeling like everyone was judging him. The tunnel ahead was a wall of pure darkness that the light from his phone couldn't penetrate. Fear welled up within him, heavy and oppressive. Ben had once read an article about the human fear response to the dark. Millions of years of evolution had built the fight-or-flight response to darkness directly into the brain to ensure survival against predators. Ben was 3200 feet underground. He didn't have to worry about predators down here. The darkness was just darkness. But despite this, Ben could not shake the sense of doom that filled him.

Ben soon entered a mining cavern. He held his phone out, moving it around. Ben could feel the vastness of the space but could see nothing past the few feet that his feeble light reached. He heard the sound of dripping water from somewhere in the distance. *Drip. Drip. Drip.* The sound was ominous, as if the cavern demanded silence as well as darkness.

Ben had no desire to go far into the cavern. It would be easy to lose his way in such a large space. And what if his phone battery died? Just the thought of that happening made Ben gulp. He took a few hesitant steps into the space and realized that was as far as he would go. As far as he *could* go.

Ben closed his eyes. He took a few deep breaths, trying to center his thoughts and prepare for the climb to the next level, where Fiona waited. Ben felt ashamed by his weakness. He needed to be strong. He needed Fiona to know he could beat his phobia. Ben took a few more deep breaths, then let them out slowly, feeling a little better after each one. After a few minutes, he squared his shoulders, ready to return to the ladder.

Ben suddenly heard movement nearby and held his breath, listening intently. He shifted his phone to the left, then the right, but couldn't see anything in the inadequate light.

A rock skittered across the floor and a low growl floated across the darkness.

The hair on Ben's arms stood up. There couldn't be anything down here with him. *The brain was always trying to trick you into believing strange things when under stress—wasn't it?* he thought nervously.

Be that as it may, Ben turned to go back to the ladder, but as he did, his foot caught the edge of a stone and he stumbled forward. He lost his balance and fell to the ground hard, dropping his phone as he hit. Pain flared in his hands from the sharp rocks on the stone floor.

He lay there cursing, then struggled first to his knees, then back to his feet. His phone had landed on its back, the flashlight emitting only a faint ring of light around the edges of the case to indicate where it had landed. Before he could take a step toward it, he heard—or, rather, felt—another deep growl. It was almost more of a vibration in the air than a sound.

Ben whipped his head around in the pitch blackness of the open space, unable to see anything. The wall of darkness pushed back against him.

He began to shake. That had been real, not his imagination. Was someone from the tour group playing a prank on him? *It was probably that young guy, Carl*, Ben thought angrily. *He seemed like someone who would do that.* Ben took a deep breath and forced himself to calm down. He and Fiona had traveled to some of the most remote and highly paranormal places on the planet. They had experienced things that had no explanation.

In Romania, they had come across a long-abandoned village. In one of the buildings, they saw a doll lying on a bed. The evil that radiated from it made them run away before they even knew what they were doing.

They had enjoyed the adrenaline rush of exploring an abandoned insane asylum in up-state New York, sensing the presences of those who had died in the building, many of whom had been tortured to death in hideous experiments.

And they had spent two nights in the Aokigahara forest in Japan where more than 500 Japanese people had committed suicide over the past two centuries. He and Fiona had wanted to fully experience the reported malevolence that made most visitors leave after only minutes.

They had purposely searched out areas that filled them with dread and excitement, but never once, in

154

all those experiences, had they felt they could ever truly be harmed.

Now, in this mine, and for the first time in his life, Ben felt a mortal threat to his existence. That growl had been real. Something was down here with him, its malevolence palpable.

Ben carefully made his way to his phone and picked it up, but as he looked down to make sure it wasn't damaged, he heard the growl again, this time right behind him. The hair on his neck rose as he slowly turned, holding up his phone with a shaking hand.

An impossibly tall figure leaned forward from the darkness.

Ben froze, unable to process what he was seeing.

The creature's mouth slowly opened, its teeth glistening in the meager beam of Ben's light. As Ben moved the light upward, the monster quickly turned its head and stepped back into the darkness.

This was enough to unfreeze Ben from his frightened paralysis. He sprinted back the way he had come, his mind blank except for one thought: to run as fast as he could.

His phone's light bounced up and down in front of him as he pumped his legs. He was back in the tunnel in five strides. The alcove and ladder to the next level was no more than thirty feet ahead. He ran even faster.

Behind him, Ben heard a roar, the sound so loud it caused him to stumble. He took a few awkward steps, flailing his arms before he got his footing under him again and was able to continue running. Ben heard pounding feet behind him, growing ever closer. He wasn't going to make it. The alcove was only ten feet ahead, visible in the diffused light of his phone, but it might as well have been a hundred feet away.

His mind would not let him look back. Ben simply could not gaze upon the horror again.

The alcove was right there in front of him, no more than five feet away. Ben dove forward and scrambled on his stomach, the sharp rocks cutting into his hands and knees. His phone tumbled away, and struck the alcove wall by the ladder, its pale white light facing upward. Ben reached for the ladder and grabbed the first steel rung, pulling himself forward, briefly hopeful he might escape.

Ben pulled himself up and strained to reach the next run of the ladder when pain exploded in his back. He was slammed back to the ground from a blow that felt like a sledgehammer hitting his spine, the sound of breaking bones loud in the alcove.

A roar bellowed behind Ben, full of rage.

Ben tried to cry out from the pain. He could not breathe. His vision began to fade. Knowing this was the end, Ben twisted his head to look up at the hatch above him. He saw Fiona peering over the side of the hole, her face ghostly illuminated by the flashlight in her hand, her face twisted in horror.

Ben was lifted from the floor like a rag doll and more pain exploded within him.

The monster turned Ben's head until he was forced to look directly into its silver eyes. Jaws opened impossibly wide, teeth glistening with saliva in the semi-darkness. It slowly leaned forward.

Ben's last thought was of profound sadness that he would never be with Fiona again. Then, an image of her floated into his mind. She smiled at him, her eyes brimming with love and tenderness.

Ben felt at peace.

Then pain, worse than any he could have

imagined, engulfed him, and in a flash of light, Fiona's image was gone.

And so was Ben.

CHAPTER 22

RENN raised his hand, arm bent, fist closed, and his team froze in unison. No one made a sound. Then he motioned with two fingers pointing ahead.

Ficks moved forward, knees bent, weapon held steady as he glided down the tunnel.

Renn and his team had been tracking the SafeWell team for twenty minutes through narrow, unused tunnels until they came upon a door ahead of them. From the intel report, the ingress and egress points down in these lower levels were located inside small stone rooms with doors. On Level thirty-two and above they were in alcoves.

Ficks slowly approached the door, put his ear to the steel, then tried to peer through the thin space between the door and the wall. It was too narrow to see through. He stood up and faced Renn, saying, "It is thick, at least two inches of solid steel. I am going to use the Inchworm to see inside so we don't get any surprises. The SafeWell team may have booby trapped it."

The Inchworm was a high-tech camera on the head of a six-inch, string-like rubber body that, when activated, used micro-motors inside to pull itself forward using inchworm-like movements. He opened his pack and dug around briefly before removing the small case that contained the Inchworm device. He opened the lid and removed the Inchworm. He pressed a small button on the end to power it on and fed the tip of it into the small space between the door and the floor.

Ficks then removed a small, hand-held controller with a two-inch screen and two mini-joysticks and activated it. He cycled through the camera settings until he found the night vision view. The image on the screen changed from black to glowing green. He put his thumbs on the joysticks and pushed the right one forward. The Inchworm began pulling itself into the crack. Ficks stared at the small screen until he got a view of the room beyond. He studied the image for a few seconds, moving the left joystick in a circle to see every part of the room, including the inside of the door. He pulled back on the right joystick to reverse the Inchworm until he could pull it free. Ficks turned both devices off and put them back in the case. He quietly said, "The room is empty. No devices set on the door. There is hole in the floor in the far north corner. Nothing else."

Renn nodded and said, "Open the door. Paul, you have point."

The big Aussie stepped forward, pulled the handle down, and opened the door just enough to slip through the opening. He swept the room with his rifle, his movements quick and efficient. He whispered, "Clear," before moving to the hole in the floor where the hatch had been.

He was soon joined by Ficks, who moved forward and stuck his gun barrel down the hole, staring through the sight. He held that position for ten seconds, then twenty.

Renn felt his adrenaline spike. It should not be taking this long to clear the hole. Renn whispered, "Ficks?"

When the man didn't respond, Renn stepped forward and whispered directly in his ear. "Ficks!"

Ficks started as if he had been zapped by a taser and quickly stepped back. He looked at Renn, his eyes like dark pits when seen through Renn's night-vision lens.

"What did you see?"

Ficks hesitated briefly, then whispered, "I...don't know. I saw...blackness?"

Renn narrowed his eyes. "That's all there is down here."

Ficks whispered, "This blackness was darker than everything around it. And it moved."

"It moved? What do you mean? Did your night vision flicker?"

"No, I mean it moved. And I swear I saw it turn and look up at me before dropping to the floor and disappearing down the tunnel."

Renn growled, growing impatient. "Enough of this shit, Ficks. Was it a SafeWell soldier?"

Ficks thought for a moment, then shook his head. "No. It was not human."

Ficks was not a superstitious man, so Renn took his report deadly seriously.

Renn straightened and softly commanded, "Local bogey." It was code for potential hostile nearby, so the team needed to be on extra alert for action.

The soldiers all lifted their guns a little higher and spread out, eyes shining with anticipation in the night vision.

"Descend, cover top," Renn commanded, which meant one person covered from the above position while the first soldier descended the shaft. This way, if the soldier descending was attacked, at least the one covering could have a chance to kill the attacker. Renn continued, "Standard order. Move now."

Lucy swung her rifle on her back, gripped the sides of the ladder and slid down the shaft. As soon as she reached the bottom, she immediately crouched, covering the area while Ficks, Paul, Millie, and Greg followed.

Renn brought up the rear. When he stepped onto the floor of the next tunnel, he immediately saw a disturbance that might have been caused by a boot, indicating the previous teams were indeed down here.

Ficks came trotting up from the opposite direction and motioned over his shoulder, "Nothing that way."

Renn nodded, motioned to the left.

The team moved down the tunnel, weapons held steady, the only sound the occasional swish of fabric or crunch of a boot on a small rock.

They were hot on the SafeWell trail. Renn hoped they could establish communication and avoid a firefight. But he worried more about what Ficks had seen.

Just what in the hell was down here with them?

CHAPTER 23

BAUWEN peered down the long corridor, water dripping slowly on her head from a crack in the rough rock ceiling. She stayed still, her skin constantly transforming to reflect the darkness and texture of the rock surfaces around her. She did this subconsciously, like how some octopuses can change their color to blend in with their surroundings.

No human could see her unless she wanted them to, not even with night vision or infrared devices. When Bauwen revealed herself to Morgan's team earlier to gauge their reactions, they had shown restraint by not immediately firing their weapons. But Renn's team, who she had been observing for the past half hour, seemed different to her. She did not sense evil from them, but she could feel their aggressive nature even from a distance. And even though the small tracker had not fired his weapon when she showed herself to him, she was still not convinced the rest of the team wouldn't try to kill her. Bauwen could tell they were hunters of hunters.

Bauwen turned and ran silently down the tunnel until she reached an iron door. She grasped the handle and slowly turned it, trying not to make a sound. But when she pulled it open, its rusty hinges squealed loudly. In the distance, she heard Renn's team instantly stop moving and whisper fervently amongst themselves. There was nothing she could do but open the door wide enough for her to slip through, then quickly close it. She would not have much time before they found her, now that she had given away her location.

Bauwen must warn Morgan's team below. Bauwen was a scientist in her world, not a hunter. She would be no match against the more aggressive humans. She had heard Renn's team mention something about chasing the tourists. *Would they slaughter innocent members of their own kind?*

So far, there had been nothing Bauwen could do but gather as much information as possible about what was happening in the mine. She feared the Vorgroth most of all, especially since she did not know where it was located at the moment. She worried the Vorgroth was moving upward toward the tourists, who seemed to Bauwen to be hunted by both the Vorgroth and Renn's team.

A tear fell from her eye at the prospect of the tourists being brutally killed. She couldn't do much herself to help them. Her only option was to make contact with Morgan's team and hope they could help.

Bauwen thought about Renn's team close behind her. She wondered how Morgan's team of three could match up against Renn's six. Or, worse, against the Vorgroth?

Bauwen was quickly losing hope, but knew she had to at least try to help.

She ran as fast and quietly as she could down the tunnel, the walls slipping past her in a blur. If she could gain some distance from Renn's team, she felt she may be able to warn Morgan's team in enough time for them to be prepared.

Bauwen saw a small room with a hatch and ladder far ahead of her, and she ran even harder, her breathing becoming labored with the effort. She had not eaten anything except for the candy bars, and her energy was fading. But she pushed on until she arrived at the door. Pulling it open as quietly as she could, she slipped inside and shut it. She then slid down the ladder to the next level, not even bothering to use the rungs. She was now in the large mining cavern on Level forty-two where she had been trapped since 1962.

Bauwen sniffed the air and caught the scent of Morgan's team. She turned left and ran fast through the cavern; she knew the layout very well. She entered the tunnel at the far end and ran for some distance until she heard movement ahead of her. Bauwen stopped to catch her breath and let her heart rate slow down. When she had recovered, she glided slowly forward until she reached a bend in the tunnel.

Turning the corner, she saw Morgan's team directly ahead of her.

Bauwen stopped. She remained camouflaged with her surroundings as she considered how she should make contact with this group of humans.

CHAPTER 24

JOHN pulled Fiona back from the hatch.

She struggled against him, screaming Ben's name, and soon Jim appeared, helping to hold her back. He snarled at John, "Close that damned hatch!"

John let go of Fiona and lunged forward, pulling the hatch up from the floor and letting it slam shut, though not before he caught a glimpse of the Vorgroth staring up at him with blood and flesh dripping from its jaws. *Not blood and flesh*, John thought. *This was a person from our group. It was what remained of Ben.*

John jumped away from the hatch and turned to the group.

Fiona screamed and struggled in Jim's embrace as he held her. She soon quieted to a soft sobbing, before finally going limp in his arms.

Larry and Ethan held Andy protectively, their eyes wide.

Carl called out, his eyes full of worry, "What's

going on?"

Still trying to process his own thoughts, John merely stared at them all for a few seconds. Then, his prior military training took over and he squared his shoulders. "Something is down there. It…it killed Ben."

They all gasped in unison, and Fiona began sobbing again.

Then they heard it. The heavy creaking of the ladder through the closed hatch.

John felt a shiver move through his whole body.

The Vorgroth was climbing the ladder. *Could it open the hatch?* John wondered. He had to assume it could. He bent down and studied the steel structure of the hatch, but there was no locking mechanism. John felt helpless. In the caves of Afghanistan, he and his team had guns to fight the enemy. Now, he had no weapons but his bare hands, he was in charge of a group of civilians, and they were facing an unknown evil hell-bent on killing them.

The image of the monster swam in John's mind—the sloped, black head, the mirrored eyes of a demon, and bloody teeth as long as his hand.

It slammed into the hatch from below. The steel buckled upward, cracking along the top.

John backed away, his arms spread out to push everyone behind him, as if he could somehow protect them if the Vorgroth made it through.

Carl whimpered, and Tammy shushed him.

The Vorgroth hit the hatch again, causing the bolts to break loose.

Carl turned and ran down the tunnel into the dark, away from where the group was standing.

Tammy raised her flashlight to use as a weapon, even though it was just a small piece of plastic. John did the same, knowing it was like using a stick to fight a grizzly, but it was all they had available to them. John thought of trying to lead the group to the next ladder, but he knew it was no use. The Vorgroth would be through the hatch in seconds.

The group stood, rooted to the spot, waiting for the creature to burst through the hatch. John heard Ethan saying a quiet prayer.

Then, to John's surprise, he heard the Vorgroth climb back down the ladder, the creak of the metal fading away. After a few moments, John let his shoulders slump from the pent-up tension he had been holding at bay.

He couldn't believe the Vorgroth hadn't broken through the steel. One more blow would have probably done it. Something must have drawn it away.

Then John heard the distant sound of gunfire from below.

CHAPTER 25

SALLY thought she had heard a distant scream, though it was muffled, so she wondered if it was her imagination. She raised her arm, her fist closed. All five members of her team stopped, squinting as they peered down the tunnel of Level thirty-one.

Thornlandon Holdings had built her team from the toughest warriors she had ever known. Karl was ex-Russian KGB, and Jillian, Charlie, Johan, and Jason were all ex-US Marines. They were trained to always keep a finger on the safeties of their weapons so they could flick the switch off in a tenth of a second and fire at an enemy before their minds had even registered what they were doing. But right now, Sally had a bad feeling, as if that tenth-of-a-second delay might mean the difference between life and death.

Sally whispered, "Safeties off," and was just about to motion her team forward when they heard another scream, this time louder. It was a sound filled with terror and pain that made the hair on Sally's neck stand up.

Her team moved slowly forward until they came to an alcove. A ladder led up ninety-seven feet to a hatch, according to the electronic readout on her night-vision screen. She motioned to her scout, Jason.

The lithe young man looked like he was a still a teenager, but had been a ten-year Marine veteran before joining Thornlandon Holdings. He put his gun over his shoulder and raced up the ladder to the hatch. He opened it and disappeared through the opening. A few seconds later, he stuck his head down through the hatch opening and gave the all-clear signal.

The team quickly ascended the ladder and gathered in the tunnel of Level thirty.

Jason motioned down the tunnel and Sally nodded. He glided forward ten meters, then the rest of the team followed.

The sides of the tunnel were roughly hewn from solid rock, jagged and sharp to the touch. Sally kept her senses just as sharp as she moved across the floor, staying away from the steel rails the old miners had used to push carts full of iron-bearing rock. She had researched the mine during their trip there.

Each level had an elevator stop, the shaft blocked by a steel accordion-style gate. The miners would push a cart into the elevator, where another miner would operate the controls to bring it topside. The full cart would then be pushed a short distance down the track, where it would be dumped, then the empty cart pushed back into the elevator. Sally had marveled at the inefficient means of mining and how much labor had been needed at every stage of the process.

After only fifty meters, Jason halted and raised a

fist.

Sally stopped mid-step and slowly lowered her boot to the floor. Then she heard it. In the distance, the sound of a hatch slammed shut, followed by the percussive sound of something striking steel.

They all stood in silence, listening. Up ahead, Charlie stepped on a loose rock, causing it to grind against the stone floor, loudly breaking the otherwise complete silence. Charlie carefully lifted his boot and placed it slowly back on a clean patch of the floor.

Sally was about to motion her team forward when she heard something heavy hit the ground ahead, just past the gradual turn in the tunnel.

Up ahead, Jason stepped out of view around the curve in the tunnel, only to come sprinting back toward them, his eyes wide.

Sally and the rest of the team instantly crouched lower and aimed their weapons just past Jason's running form, waiting for whatever had spooked him. She couldn't figure out what could have made the young scout run away. Jason was fearless, which made him a good tracker. He wasn't afraid to go into dangerous situations before anyone else on the team. The fact that he was now running in terror sent a cold chill down Sally's spine.

Jason yelled out as he approached them, "Go fully automatic!"

The team all calmly switched their rifles to full-auto mode. But when they saw the Vorgroth come around the corner not more than twenty paces behind Jason, they froze in horror as they tried to comprehend what they were seeing.

Sally saw the Vorgroth materialize from the inky blackness and move fast toward her team. She could see it was humanoid in shape, at least seven feet in height, and massively built. It was like the worst demon she had ever seen in a horror movie.

She forced herself to remain calm as she called out, "Fire when Jason passes."

Jason ran past them, slid to a stop, and quickly turned back the way he had come.

The team's six next-gen SIG Sauer NGSW-R MCX Spear assault rifles instantly spat out hybrid 6.8x51 armor-piercing rounds at the rate of 1000 rounds per minute.

The team replaced their specially designed, forty-round magazines so quickly that the gunfire never stopped. Over 700 rounds hit the Vorgroth within the first fifteen seconds. No living thing could survive that barrage and Sally watched with satisfaction as the Vorgroth was pushed violently backward until it disappeared back around the bend in the tunnel.

Sally raised her arm. The team instantly stopped firing and replaced their magazines as they crouched, their rifle barrels glowing hotly in the darkness. They waited patiently, peering down the sights of their rifles, fingers flat against their trigger guards.

Sally rose to a standing position and motioned Jason and Charlie to investigate. The two men crouched low as they glided forward, slowing down when they came to the turn in the tunnel. They had just disappeared around it when Sally heard a muffled scream. Then Jason came running back into view, firing backward as he sprinted toward them, yelling, "To the hatch! Now!"

Just past Jason, the top part of Charlie's torso flopped to the ground, then was pulled back out of sight.

Sally calmly, but firmly, called out, "Retreat to Level thirty-one!"

Her team backed up, rifles aimed down the tunnel, covering Jason until he ran past them without slowing down.

Jillian and Johan, two of the most senior members of the team, stopped and covered their retreat, while Sally, Jason, and Karl double-timed it back to the hatch. Sally motioned Karl and Jason toward the opening, "Get below, now."

The two men glanced once back down the tunnel, then quickly descended to the level below.

Sally called out to Johan and Jillian, "Move it, now!"

The two soldiers turned and sprinted back to the hatch as the Vorgroth came around the curve in the tunnel, holding what looked like Charlie's head. It roared and threw it toward them with great force. The head struck Jillian in the back, knocking her down. The Vorgroth charged down the tunnel.

Jillian scrambled to her feet and spun, firing point-blank at the creature's head on full auto. Forty rounds struck it in the face and bounced away as if they had struck solid steel.

The Vorgroth reached down and grabbed Jillian by the head, popping it from her body as easily as one would separate a flower from its stem. Jillian's headless body fell to the ground. The Vorgroth growled at Sally, holding Jillian's head at its side. They glared at each other across the 10-meter distance until Johan arrived at the hatch, his eyes wide and face pinched tight in horror. He ejected a spent magazine and loaded another, then turned and fired at the Vorgroth.

The monster roared and charged forward.

With a guttural cry, Johan dropped his rifle, pulled a Benelli M4 shotgun from his back, and fired down the tunnel in quick succession, the impact from the blasts driving the Vorgroth backward, yet not appearing to do any damage to its body. He yelled out to Sally, "Get down to the next level!"

The Vorgroth roared and bent to the floor, digging its claws into the stone to stop itself from sliding backward. It raised its head and glared at Johan, murderous intent flashing in its eyes.

Johan dropped his empty shotgun and lifted a nozzle from his side. It was attached to a hose that led to a separate pack on his back. He clicked a button and flame ignited at the tip of the nozzle. He looked up at the Vorgroth standing in front of him, his face twisted in a feral grin. "Time to BBQ, motherfucker!" He pulled the trigger and liquid fire shot forward. The flames engulfed the Vorgroth completely, roiling and undulating as if they were alive.

The creature lifted its head and roared, and as it did, Johan lifted the nozzle and shot a stream of liquid fire directly into its mouth. The Vorgroth shook its head, then crouched down, putting a hand up against the flames.

Johan laughed as he walked forward, one slow step at a time, keeping the flames shooting from the nozzle like water from a firehose.

Then the flow of liquid flames slowed to a dribble. The pack of liquid accelerant was empty.

The Vorgroth knelt, its body undulating with blue and red flames. It looked up at Johan and seemed to smile through the flames. With a roar, it sprang forward, a demon of fire. Before Johan could move, the Vorgroth brought both fists down on his head. Johan's body collapsed to the floor in a pile of gore, organs and flesh bursting outward from the sheer force of the impact.

Sally watched the Vorgroth step forward, the flames around its body dying away until it stood still, glaring at her through narrowed eyes. Sally couldn't believe the Vorgroth was still alive. No organic being could survive a sustained dousing of liquid fire from a flamethrower, yet the Vorgroth didn't even seem injured.

With a final gulp of breath, Sally calmly climbed down the ladder, grabbed the hatch and pulled it closed. She then put her feet on each side of the ladder and slid down to the ground.

She looked at Karl and Jason, the remaining two members of her team.

They nodded in silent understanding, their eyes flashing murderous rage mixed with resignation.

Sally motioned back down the tunnel in the direction from which they had just come.

She tried to block out the images of the Vorgroth and what it had done to her team, but those images would stay with her until the day she died—perhaps at the hands of this seemingly unkillable creature.

CHAPTER 26

MORGAN stopped walking. In the distance, in the furthest reaches of her night-vision, she saw a steel door. Jack was on point and Karen was guarding their six, both stayed vigilant. She didn't yet know who or what they had seen earlier, which worried her. Morgan understood hostile humans. Their motivations were usually based on money, power, politics, or religion. When she and her team had entered this abandoned mine, Morgan had suspected the mission fell into the politics and money category. But the unknown entity that seemed to be following them was something Morgan had never dealt with before. And her team's survival could be at stake.

They passed quickly through Levels thirty-four to forty-one. According to the intel, these lower passageways were not as extensive as those on Levels thirty-two and above.

For the past fifteen minutes, they had been making their way first through a large cavern, then down the tunnel of Level forty-two.

The team came across what looked like another boot mark on the floor, which confirmed they were still on the trail of the two missing Thornlandon teams. These lower tunnel systems had several cross tunnels, some of which had been only roughly cut and wide enough for a single person to fit into at a time.

Morgan and her team were in a long-forgotten area of the mine, and the sense of elapsed time hung heavily in the air.

Jack suddenly halted. He put up an arm for her and Karen to stop and remain silent.

Morgan could just make out what looked like a hole in the floor of the tunnel.

Jack moved slowly forward and stopped next to a steel anchor that had been driven into the stone floor. A carabiner was fastened to the anchor, with a rope attached and leading to, and over the edge of, the hole in the floor, which was less than four feet in diameter.

Jack motioned for Morgan and Karen to join him.

They both crept forward and stopped by Jack, who knelt and carefully examined the opening in the floor. Jack leaned over the edge, feeling with his hand. He then looked up to study the gouged-out ceiling. Finally, he looked back to Morgan and Karen and quietly said, "As the intel report mentioned, the ceiling above this access point to Level forty-three was purposely collapsed back in 1962. It looks like the teams that we are tracking set charges to clear away the rubble around this hatch access point. I suspect the hatch was too severely damaged to cut open like the others, so they used more explosives to blow it apart."

What Jack didn't say, but Morgan assumed they were all thinking, was, why would the miners of old block this access point to Level forty-three? Was it to keep people from accessing the level below, or to keep *something* from accessing the levels above?

Morgan pushed conjecture aside to focus on the mission. She was about to speak when Jack continued, "There is something else. The rope has blood on it." He leaned closer to the edge of the hole and said, "And there are marks in the stone right here." He pointed to a set of gouges next to him, then pointed to the other side of the hole. "More are over there. They are deep and do not appear to be made by tools. It is almost as if something with claws grabbed the stone around the edge and pulled itself up from below. But that's stupid, right? I mean, not even a grizzly could make gouges in solid stone with its claws. Or, for that matter, even get down here in the first place."

Morgan knelt on one knee and ran a finger along each of the four gouges in the stone. They were large and deep, each at least three times larger than her own fingers. She had no idea what could have made them. She stood up and said, "I don't like this at all."

Jack looked back the way they had come and said, "I think whatever made those marks went down the tunnels we just came from. Maybe that was the darkness we saw?"

When neither Morgan nor Karen replied, he shrugged and peered down the hole again. "I see a cavern floor sixty feet below. The ladder is too badly damaged to use, hence the rope. I can see something down there, it looks like…"

When Jack didn't continue, Morgan asked, "What is it, Jack?"

He gasped and quickly pulled back, looking at them both with a horrified expression, his eyes wide and mouth hanging open. He moved his mouth as if to speak but couldn't seem to get any words to come out. Finally, he motioned for Morgan to look.

Morgan leaned forward to look down at the floor of another cavern below. She saw something strange, so she increased the magnification of her night vision unit and gasped at what she saw.

Karen whispered, "What is it, Morgan?"

Below, Morgan could make out the scattered and bloody remains of what she assumed were the missing teams. It was difficult to tell because all that remained was mostly blood spatter, sprayed in all directions. It looked like a slaughterhouse, with a few limbs scattered about as if they had been casually discarded. The blood appeared black in the night vision.

Sitting back on her heels, Morgan looked up, her face grim. "We found the missing teams."

A new voice spoke from behind them, soft and melodious, "And we will all die like them unless we can stop the Vorgroth."

They all spun around, rifles raised, safeties clicked off.

Morgan called out, "Hold your fire!"

Bauwen stepped out from the darkness, her strangely beautiful face creased with worry. "I am Bauwen. I have been following you. You are all in danger!"

CHAPTER 27

JOHN'S flashlight went dead. The alcove plunged into complete darkness and frightened cries erupted from the group of tourists. John cursed himself again for not getting batteries from the hardware store on the way to work this morning.

"What's going on? Turn the light back on!" Carl, who had rejoined the group, yelled loudly. Tammy switched on her flashlight, bathing the group in a ghostly light once more.

Ethan looked at the hatch. "What if that thing comes back? It...it killed Ben. We have to get out of here!"

Andy touched his father's arm and said, "Dad, calm down. Mr. John knows what he's doing. And you're upsetting Fiona."

Ethan looked guiltily at Fiona. "I am sorry, I didn't mean that to come out so badly. I am so sorry for your loss, Fiona."

Fiona didn't even acknowledge him. She was in a bad state, and it was too early to tell if she would ever recover.

John felt a moment of self-doubt. Ben had been torn to pieces by a monster, and there had been nothing that John could do about it. He felt unworthy of Andy's trust.

John forced himself to clear his mind, something his mother had taught him how to do. Everyone's survival depended on him, and he must take charge. He felt his heart rate slow down and his mind clear itself of his self-doubt. He took one breath, then another. Then he turned to Tammy and nodded thanks to her before saying, "Folks, it seems my battery's dead. We still have Tammy's flashlight, as well as your phones as a last resort. We'll be fine. We need to find the next hatch up to Level twenty-nine. If it's like Level thirty, the hatch should be just down there." He pointed down the corridor to his left, and Tammy shined her flashlight in the same direction.

"We will go as a group," John continued. "Tammy, you lead the way with the flashlight, I will bring up the rear." He took out his cell phone and powered it on, then activated the flashlight feature. Here in the depths of the tunnels, the light that came from it only lit up a few feet of space. In combination with Tammy's more powerful flashlight, however, it was enough to provide light for the group to walk without stumbling on any hidden objects.

John said, "Let's move quickly, but safely. Milton, Claire, do your best. We will be here to help you if necessary."

Milton looked up and mumbled, "Don't go slow on our account. We will keep up."

Claire took his hand and held it tightly, her face worried.

Raising her flashlight, Tammy led the way into

the tunnel and within ten minutes, they had arrived at an alcove with a ladder, just like on the previous level.

John stepped around the group and shined his phone upward, then put the phone between his teeth. It wasn't ideal, but it provided enough light for him to see the rungs of the ladder. He climbed upwards and soon reached the hatch. He opened it and climbed through into Level twenty-nine's alcove. It smelled dusty up here. He had smelled the same thing after the collapse on Level thirty-two. There must have been a cave-in somewhere on this level from the last blast at the Onamuni mine. John vowed to think about it after everyone got up here safely. One thing at a time. Besides, there was no other way they could go but up.

He turned back to the opening just as Andy climbed through. He wasn't even out of breath.

Leaning into the opening, John called down. "Alright, just like before. Be careful!"

Milton had to stop to rest every third or fourth rung during his climb. He had been slowing down over the past hour. His eyes often looked glassy and vacant when he stopped to catch his breath, and John worried about him. He was obviously very ill, and his advanced age was a problem despite his protestations to the contrary.

John decided that it was time for a break once everyone had made it up. They didn't know if the monster could make it through the hatches, but the group needed to rest. The creature had been lured away by something, so John hoped for the best. The gunfire that had erupted in Level thirty-one had been both a frightening and encouraging sign. Maybe there was a search party looking for them. *But why would they have been armed?* John asked himself. Something didn't seem right.

As Milton arrived at the hatch, he reached up a trembling hand and Andy carefully grasped it, gently helping Milton up until he was able to sit on the edge of the opening. Milton then stood up on shaky legs and said, "Thank you, Andy. I will be just fine. That was just a longer climb than before."

As Andy led the old man away, John worried even more. That ladder had been shorter than the previous few they had climbed.

Claire came up next, followed by Ethan, Larry, Jim and Tammy. Carl and Fiona were last. John had wanted Fiona to rest for as long as possible before they asked her to climb. He didn't want her to fall because she was distracted or in shock.

When Carl and Fiona didn't appear on the ladder, John peered over the side. Far below, Carl stood next to Fiona, urging her to climb, but she wouldn't even stand up from her seat against the wall.

Carl looked up with a worried expression, shaking his head. John swung his legs over the edge and carefully descended the ladder until he was standing on the floor of the level below. "Carl, you go on up, I will take it from here."

The young man nodded, relieved, and began climbing.

John sat down. He didn't touch Fiona. He just sat there for a few moments in silence. Finally, he whispered, "Fiona? I am sorry about Ben."

Fiona gave no indication she had heard John. She just stared vacantly into the darkness of the tunnel.

John wasn't sure if she would be able to go on. She was in shock.

But he had to try and reach her.

"Fiona, can you look at me?"

She didn't respond or even blink.

John slid around until he sat in front of her. "Fiona, please, answer me." He waved his hand in front of her eyes but saw no reaction from her.

John sighed, unsure how to proceed. Suddenly, he heard a heavy footstep in the darkness of the tunnel, followed by another. Fear coursed through him, and his adrenaline spiked. Bending down, he urgently whispered, "Fiona, we must go now. That…thing is coming!"

Fiona's eyes focused for the first time since Ben had been killed, and she turned to look into the blackness of the tunnel.

John sighed, glad she seemed to be functioning again. He stood and held his hand out. She took it and stood.

John whispered, "You climb first. I will follow."

Fiona turned and began walking into the darkness of the tunnel—*toward* the footsteps they had just heard.

John took three steps and grabbed her arm, whispering, "What are you doing? We must climb up to the next level!"

Fiona yanked her arm away and when she faced him, he didn't recognize her. Her face was twisted in a fierce contortion of violence, her eyes flashing in the meager light of John's phone. She spun away and ran down the tunnel, disappearing into the total darkness.

John took a few steps after her but stopped when he heard Fiona scream in rage. Then the scream was abruptly cut off.

John sprinted back to the ladder, his fear pushing him rapidly forward. He scaled the ladder three rungs at a time and almost tumbled through the opening, twisting to slam the hatch shut before falling back, out of breath.

Jim and Carl approached. "Where is Fiona?"

John gulped in lungfuls of air until he could speak. "She is...gone."

Carl leaned in, "What do you mean?"

John motioned toward the hatch and said, "We heard that...thing approaching, and when we did, Fiona pulled away from me and ran toward it. I tried to go after her, but she had a head start. Then I heard her scream and..." He couldn't finish.

Jim helped him to his feet, his eyes hard. "I'm sorry to be blunt, but Fiona's gone; there's nothing we can do about that now." He held up a steel bar and continued, "I found this old crowbar in the tunnel. The recent blasting created a crack along the whole wall above the hatch. I think I can use this to create a small rock-fall over the hatch and hopefully seal it up tight."

John nodded and Jim went to work, jamming the end of the crowbar into the two-inch crack in the stone wall and pulling it to the side. There was a cracking sound, but nothing moved. Jim jammed the crowbar further into the crack and pulled but still nothing happened.

From below the hatch, the ladder shuddered, as if something massive had stepped onto it.

With a fierce look, Jim said, "John, help me pull!"

John stepped forward and gripped the crowbar right below Jim's hands. They both pulled, their faces turning red from the effort.

They could hear the ladder shaking below them.

In a panic, their strength boosted by adrenaline, Jim and John pulled until the rock wall and ceiling above the hatch collapsed. They both jumped back, stumbling to the ground and scrambling backward.

The air filled with thick dust, and they coughed, putting their arms over their mouths and noses. The dust billowed out into the tunnel, then quickly dissipated. When it cleared, the alcove was nothing more than a pile of jagged rocks.

The access point to Level thirty was blocked.

John signed with relief as he helped Jim to his feet. "Are you alright?"

Jim coughed once more, then nodded. "Nothing broken. Just a few bruises. You?"

John ran his hands down his body but felt no injuries. "I'm fine, as well. I sure didn't expect that big of a cave-in! Thank you, Jim. Your idea may have saved our lives."

The older man shrugged and turned away to join the group a little further down the tunnel. "Who has the water?" he asked, as if nothing had happened.

Andy dug a bottle of water from his pack, unscrewed the cap, and handed it to Jim, who nodded his thanks before taking a big swig from it. Wiping his mouth, Jim passed it over to John.

John took a large mouthful, swished it around, then swallowed and passed the bottle back to Andy, saying, "Let everyone have a drink, but only a swallow. We don't know how long we will be down here and need to conserve the water."

Andy passed the water to Larry, who drank and passed it to Ethan, who then passed it to Milton and Claire.

John looked down the tunnel that led toward the elevator shaft. "Stay here," he said to the group. "I am going to scout ahead. I will be right back."

John walked about 800 feet down the tunnel and

came to the ladder leading up to Level twenty-eight. Or what was left of the ladder. It had collapsed into a pile of rock. The tunnel was still passable, with maybe two feet of space where they could get past the rock fall, but it just led to the unusable elevator shaft. There was no way up to the next level. They were trapped.

John returned to the group, unsure what to say. They needed time to recuperate, so he said, "Let's move down this tunnel and get some distance from the caved-in hatch in case more of the roof comes down."

Tammy lifted the flashlight over her head and asked, "But the next alcove should be in that direction."

John shook his head.

To Tammy's credit, she resisted the urge to question him. She quickly turned and with a voice much more cheerful than she felt, said, "Come on, let's see if there is a nice cavern this way where we can rest for a bit." The group followed her, and they soon entered a cavern. It was so vast that the other side was not visible in Tammy's beam of light.

John called a halt, "Let's break here. Andy, can you dig out four of those candy bars and hand them out? Everyone gets a half of a bar."

Andy seemed to be thinking, then he said, "But that doesn't leave any for you, Mr. John."

"That's alright. I'm not hungry."

"It's *not* alright! You need to eat, too." Andy dug out a fifth bar, broke it in half, slid half the bar out of the wrapper, and handed it to John.

John smiled as he accepted it. "Thanks, Andy."

The teenager twisted the wrapper over the remaining half and put it back in his pack.

After everyone had eaten and had another drink of water, Milton spoke up. "I have faced that monster before. It is called a Vorgroth." His voice sounded small and faded quickly in the large cavern. But everyone turned to listen to him.

John asked, "How do you know what it is called?"

Milton stared at the ground for a few moments as if collecting his thoughts, then said, "I worked in this mine from 1945 until the day it closed in 1962. One day…oh, it must have been April 4th, 1962, I…"

Claire leaned down and whispered in his ear. He nodded and continued, "It was March 4th, sorry. My wife never forgets a date. Why, she can remember the…"

Claire whispered again and he grumbled, "Alright, alright, I'll get to the story. It was March 4th, 1962. I had just started the night shift when word came through the ranks that Steve Jalkanen had not punched out from his day shift. The mine boss told us all to search for him. You see, there were always accidents back then, and we had a death every few months. So, we searched for Steve, but never found him."

Ethan spoke up, "Milton. Andy is only thirteen. He shouldn't be hearing this."

Before Milton could say anything, Andy turned to his dad. "Two of our friends just got killed by a monster, dad. Mr. Milton's story may help us survive this."

Ethan opened, then closed his mouth without saying anything; he couldn't argue with his son's logic.

Milton continued. "We searched all the way down to Level forty-three."

John turned to Milton. "You mean Level thirty-two. There is no Level forty-three."

Milton shook his head. "I meant Level forty-three. You see, we had dug down forty-three levels by the summer of 1962."

John was astonished by this bit of information. He had been working in this mine for a decade and had never once even heard a whisper that Level thirty-two wasn't the deepest level. He nodded to cover his surprise and said, "Please, continue."

Milton rubbed the stubble on his chin. "Rumors immediately started swirling amongst the crew that there was a monster down here who had killed poor Steve Jalkanen. No one wanted to go to work the next day, and the mining company called a meeting. They forced us to return to work or be fired. We didn't have a union, so we had no bargaining power. We all went back to work. Then, a day later, my best friends Franc and Otto and I were attacked." Milton paused, then asked, "Can I get another sip of water?"

Andy handed him the water bottle, and Milton took a small sip then handed the bottle back to the boy. Milton was quiet for some time, his face showing fresh anguish at the memories.

Claire leaned close to him and whispered, "Tell them the whole story, dear. They deserve to know."

Milton smiled wanly. "My apologies. Even though it's been more than sixty years, it seems like yesterday to me, and the emotions are hitting me hard." He patted Claire's hand, then took a breath and continued.

"My closest friends, Otto and Franc, and I were the next to be attacked. The three of us were having our lunch break in a small grotto when we heard movement out in the tunnel. We thought it was someone from the crew coming to tell us to get back to work, so we stayed quiet, hoping to get a few more minutes to finish our sandwiches and card game. That's when we heard a low growl. It was like nothing we had ever heard before. We dropped our cards and leapt to our feet. Franc and Otto each grabbed a large rock and raised it, ready to strike whatever was in the tunnel. We listened for a few seconds but didn't hear it again, so Franc stepped out of the grotto into the tunnel to investigate and was jerked away, screaming. Otto and I ran after him. And that is when we saw the Vorgroth for the first time. It almost blocked the entire tunnel with its size. It held Franc in its hands, then tore him in half as easily as we would tear a piece of bread off an unsliced loaf." A sob escaped Milton, and he closed his eyes at the memory.

Claire held his hands tightly in her own.

The gesture must have helped, for Milton took a ragged breath, then whispered, "I only escaped because Otto led the thing away from me. He screamed and ran past the monster, yelling for it to chase him. Which it did. The last thing I heard was Otto scream out, 'Run, Milt! Get out of...'"

Milton sat quietly for a while; his eyes closed. Finally, he continued, his voice choked with emotion. "Otto never finished what he was saying because the Vorgroth caught him and..." Milton's voice broke and he sobbed silently, his shoulders trembling. Finally, he whispered, "I'm ashamed to say I ran away."

Milton turned to look at John, and asked in a rising tone, "You saw this same creature when it killed Ben and Fiona, didn't you?"

John's mind raced as the image of the Vorgroth swam through his mind. He gulped, then whispered,

"Yes, I did."

Carl spoke before anyone, "So there is a literal monster down here with us?"

Milton nodded, "Yes, son, there is. You see, the mining company realized we must have dug too deep, that we had released the devil upon the world." He chuckled humorlessly. "They were a religious lot back then. But they weren't entirely wrong. That thing is not of this earth."

John asked, "How do you know that?"

Pausing, Milton sighed, then said, "Because I saw *her*, at least for a second, and she was not human, either. You see, when I escaped to the surface, I quickly met with the mine boss and my fellow miners, and I explained what had happened to Otto and Franc. We quickly decided to bring explosives down to try and trap the Vorgroth. I volunteered to lead the team who would do it. I set up the detonator on Level forty-one by the hatch leading to Level forty-two. Howard and some welders stayed there while Marek, Jan, Jacob, and I climbed down to Level forty-two. We were trying to make our way to the hatch that led down to Level forty-three when we suddenly heard the Vorgroth coming toward us. I am not ashamed to admit that we all froze, knowing we were all going to die. But then *she* ran past us from out of nowhere and attacked the monster. Her image is etched in my memory. Her skin was like nothing I had ever seen before, it changed color as she passed us. She lured the creature away from us, but not before faintly calling out, telling us she would lead the Vorgroth to Level forty-three so we could blow the hatch. We quickly set up the explosives, then returned to Level forty-one and blew the tunnel, trapping the creature down there forever." Milton

190

paused for a few moments, then whispered, "Unfortunately, I don't think she survived. Even if she had, we were ordered to seal all the levels up to thirty-two. It is my greatest shame that I was unable to save her, whoever or whatever she was. She saved us all."

John was astonished by the story, and by Milton's bravery. Not many people would have volunteered to do what he and his fellow miners had done. Then he asked, "I wonder how the Vorgroth escaped?"

Milton shrugged. "Maybe the blasting from the Onamuni mine has somehow opened access to Level forty-three which allowed it to come back up here?"

Jim asked, "But how could it still be alive after 60-something years stuck in a mine with no food or water?"

Milton looked at him and shrugged, "Who knows? I don't think it's of our world, so maybe it isn't governed by our laws of life and death."

Tammy quietly asked, "Do you think the woman survived?"

Milton sighed wistfully. "If the Vorgroth is free, maybe she is as well?" He looked at Claire and asked wistfully, "Wouldn't that be something, Claire? I sure would like to thank her for what she did."

Claire smiled and said, "She knows how you feel, Milt. She knows."

John sat back against a large rock, digesting this information. It was an amazing story, and after what he had seen, he didn't doubt that every word of it was true.

Even so, it didn't really help them at all. They still had to find a way out of the mine. This reminded him it was time to tell everyone the truth about their circumstances. He cleared his throat. "Thank you for sharing this with us, Milton. I wish it helped us but unfortunately, I discovered there's been a cave-in at the access point up to Level twenty-eight. There is no way for us to get up to the next level."

Milton smiled. "I know another way up."

CHAPTER 28

MORGAN lowered her rifle slightly so she could look at the intruder. She saw what looked to her like a young woman in her twenties with black hair and an angular, yet gentle, face with large eyes. Morgan saw she was naked, but her skin was almost translucent and seemed to change patterns and colors so quickly that Morgan couldn't be sure of what she was seeing. Most importantly, the woman did not project any ill intent.

Smiling, Bauwen nodded, as if reading her mind. "I am no threat to you."

Morgan lowered her rifle, knowing that Jack and Karen would stay as they were, rifles aimed directly at Bauwen's chest until Morgan told them to lower their weapons.

Her voice neutral, Morgan said, "Stay where you are and don't move."

Bauwen nodded and remained where she stood.

"Good. Now, what do you mean we are in danger?" Morgan had more questions, namely who this woman was, but as a soldier, her first order of business was always to ascertain any threats.

Bauwen didn't waste any words and pointed behind her. "There is a team of six soldiers approaching behind me, one level up. I think they may be hunting you, but it seems they may not mean you harm."

Morgan asked, "How do you know this? Who are you?"

"I have been following you for some time. I heard the other people coming behind me, so I investigated them. I heard them speaking. They appear to want to initiate contact with you, but they have weapons like yours and they are hunters, like you are. I do not know if we can trust them."

Jack spoke up from Morgan's right. "You are the darkness we saw in the tunnels, aren't you? You can disappear into thin air!"

Bauwen cocked her head and looked at him with a small smile. "No, I cannot disappear into thin air, as you mean it. I do have the ability to change the molecular structure of my skin so that you cannot see me, even with your strange eye-device, it appears. The 'darkness' that you described seeing is merely my skin *mimicking* the darkness."

Morgan brought the conversation back to the other team. "You said this team is hunting us. Why are you warning us about them?"

Bauwen pursed her lips into a flat line, her eyes hardening. "Because I think you are good people. I knew people like you when this place was being mined. I helped them to trap the Vorgroth in that level down there." She motioned to the hole in the floor, then she scowled and continued. "Not long ago, there was a cave-in on Level thirty-two that damaged the elevator. It also damaged the lighting system."

Karen swore, then asked, "You mean the power is out?"

Bauwen nodded.

Jack said, "Great. That's just great."

Bauwen softly said, "There is more. There is also a team of hunters following a group of innocent people up the levels above the elevator."

Morgan nodded, "You must mean the tourists?"

Bauwen considered this as if she were unfamiliar with the term, then nodded and continued, "They were trapped down here when the rocks fell. They are trying to escape by traveling up through each level of this mine. I followed them for a short distance, but then I smelled the Vorgroth and came back down here."

Karen asked, "Vorgroth? What is that?"

Bauwen shivered, her face set in a hard look. "It is a creature from my world far below us. Its only desire is to kill. And it cannot be killed by human weapons, for it is made from a heavy mineral called *Forss* that makes its skin stronger than steel. Bullets will not harm it." She slid a knife from the sheath at her waist and held it up. It reflected brightly in the night-vision, seeming to undulate as it changed colors. "This is made from *Forss*, which is the only thing that can penetrate the Vorgroth's skin." She must have noticed the look of interest on Morgan's face because she quickly said, "You could never get close enough to the Vorgroth to use it before it tore you apart."

Morgan pointed at the hole in the floor. "We saw a scene of slaughter down there. Was that done by the Vorgroth?"

Bauwen nodded sadly. "Yes. It killed them all a few days ago."

Morgan had many more questions, but knew she didn't have time to ask them right now. They must prepare for the coming threat. She had feared there was more going on with this mission than just a simple rescue effort. There seemed to be multiple human forces at play in this mine, as well as the strange woman standing in front of her and the Vorgroth she had just mentioned. The fact that another team had been sent down here, most likely to eliminate both the tourists and her SafeWell team, meant that someone wanted this mine for themselves and were willing to make everyone disappear. Permanently.

She turned to Jack and Karen, "Lower your weapons, Bauwen is not a threat. While we will give the team that is following us a chance to initiate a peaceful meeting, we must be prepared for a potential firefight."

Bauwen stepped forward. "There may be time for us to leave this place before they arrive. I know a secret alcove in the cavern you passed through back that way." She pointed down the tunnel. "We can hide there until they pass, then go back up to the elevator. If we run, we can make it to that cavern before the ones hunting you reach it."

Morgan knew that was the best plan. While the other military team might be trying to make contact with Morgan and her team, they could just as easily be down here to eliminate them. Morgan had not received any intel from Skuggs about other forces at play down here. It was a tough situation for her team to be in. They needed to prepare for the worst-case scenario.

Morgan nodded once. "Ok, let's go. You lead the way and move fast. We will be right behind you."

196

Bauwen didn't wait. She turned and sprinted away.

Morgan called out to her team, "Move out!"

The three of them took off after Bauwen, their legs pumping hard to keep up with her. They could sustain a flat-out run for over a mile, and the cavern was less than a half mile away.

As she ran, Morgan wondered if she would die down here in this god-forsaken mine.

The odds for survival didn't look good.

CHAPTER 29

LARRY was last in the line, the rest of the group ahead of him. His leg muscles protested as they crossed the cavern on Level twenty-nine, and he wanted nothing more than to take a break and sit down. But he forced himself to keep going. He had not exercised much over the past decade, and his body was telling him he would pay for it when they got out of here.

If *they got out of here*, he thought.

His only goal right now was to protect Andy and Ethan and get them safely to the surface. But he was just a writer who had grown soft from years of sitting in front of his laptop. He and Ethan and Andy would often go for short walks around their neighborhood over the weekends. But that was the extent of his exercise. He had never learned a martial art, or taken a gun class or any other form of self-defense. He was useless.

Larry glanced at Ethan ahead of him and noticed that he was doing much better physically. Ethan would most likely give him a hard time if they got out of this alive. He would probably say something like, '*See how much better you would have done if you had joined me at the gym three nights a week like I have always pestered you to do?*'

Larry grunted. Maybe he *would* join him at the gym after this. But for now, they just had to survive.

Andy had to survive.

Larry would fight the Vorgroth bare-handed if it meant his son would be safe.

He stumbled on a rock in the near-dark and caught his balance just in time to avoid falling.

Ethan turned back and whispered, "Be careful, hon."

Larry nodded. The light from Tammy's flashlight was at least fifteen feet in front of him, so the light had diffused to almost nothing where he walked. Normally, John was in the back with his phone's flashlight on, but he had moved forward to talk quietly with Tammy. Larry glanced back and shuddered at the absolute blackness that seemed to be closing in behind him. He pictured the monster lunging out of that darkness, grabbing him with long-taloned hands and dragging him into the black void without anyone even knowing. He fell a bit further behind the group, lost in his thoughts, and quickened his step until he was right behind Ethan and Andy again. As he did, he grew light-headed, and his left arm seemed to throb a bit. He shook his head to clear the dizziness.

As if sensing Larry's discomfort, Andy turned and asked, "Everything alright, dad?"

Larry smiled. "Of course, bud. Now turn back around and watch your step."

Andy nodded and turned back.

Larry couldn't believe the transformation that had taken place in his son over the past few hours. Andy did what was asked of him and didn't need to be told twice to do anything. He also seemed to like their tour guide, John. Part of Larry felt jealous, wishing Andy looked up to him the same way. But overall, Larry was just happy his son seemed to be growing into a responsible young man.

Andy had been a prodigy all his life and had been spoiled by everyone because of it. Now it seemed like Andy no longer wanted to be treated specially—or like a child. A few minutes earlier, Andy had tripped on the uneven surface and fallen. He had scraped his palm bloody, but when Ethan had tried to put his arm around Andy to coddle him, Andy had twisted away saying, "I'm alright, dad."

Ahead, Milton stopped and gave a short whistle, then listened intently. After a few seconds he raised his arm and pointed a shaky finger to their left. The group changed course to walk across the cavern.

They had been moving steadily for twenty minutes already with no end to the cavern in sight. Of course, with such a small radius of light, Larry had no way of knowing how much further they had to go. At least Milton seemed to know his way, which was a blessing. How Milton could get any sense of direction in the dark cavern was a mystery to Larry. But he trusted the old man.

Milton suddenly moaned in pain. He stopped and put a shaky hand to his stomach, his eyes closed, his face twisted in agony.

Everyone halted, and Claire immediately leaned close to Milton, supporting him with both hands. They whispered to each other and Claire hugged him tightly.

After a few moments, Milton straightened up, patted Claire's hand and said something into her ear. They hugged each other for a few moments and when they separated, tears streamed down Claire's face.

Milton started walking forward again, still holding his stomach. Claire kept one arm around his waist, walking closely by his side.

The group continued their march forward, but Larry noticed that Milton's steps had grown less steady, and his back seemed to stoop forward more, as if he were ready to collapse to the floor at any moment.

Milton gave occasional directions and his voice seemed fainter each time he spoke.

They made their way across the cavern for another fifteen minutes, when suddenly they saw a stone wall appear out of the dark about ten feet from them.

Milton pointed a trembling arm to the left and asked, "Tammy, can you adjust the flashlight to have a focused beam and point it over that way?"

Tammy clicked the switch and shined the beam of light to her left. It was earie watching the small circle of light move around the rock wall.

Larry had no idea what Milton was looking for. To him, the rock wall looked the same as every other wall they had seen.

Milton weakly exclaimed in a tremulous voice, "There! Go back to the right just a little bit."

Tammy did as she was instructed and the beam of light illuminated a small fissure in the rock, no more than a few feet wide—but wide enough, it looked, for a person to fit through.

Milton started to shuffle forward in the darkness, when John put his arm out to stop him.

"Hold up, Milton. Let's get some more light so you don't fall." He dug out his cellphone and powered it on. Within half a minute, the screen illuminated, and John activated the flashlight. The area lit up in a soft white light, though it still only reached a few feet in front of them. John took Milton's arm and carefully led him across the rocky floor to the fissure in the wall.

Milton pointed, "If you don't mind, can you see if that crack opens up when you enter it?"

John nodded, let go of Milton's arm, and stepped forward. He extended his phone into the fissure, then squeezed inside and disappeared for a few seconds. When he reappeared, he confirmed, "Yep, it is a small cave. And it looks like there is an opening in the ceiling with a makeshift wooden ladder leading up to it."

Milton smiled. "That's the way up to Level Twenty-Eight. My friends and I discovered this natural fissure back in 1958. It leads up to a small grotto with a short narrow tunnel that connects to the main tunnel system of Level twenty-eight. We built the ladder through the fissure so we could have a short-cut down here." His voice grew wistful. "The grotto up there is the place I mentioned earlier where Otto, Franc and I often had our lunch and played cards. It was nice and private, like our own picnic spot." His eyes welled up with tears as he said, "It is also the spot where we were attacked by the Vorgroth."

John put a hand on Milton's shoulder compassionately, "Thank you for showing us, Milton." He removed his hand and turned to the group and pointed to the small opening in the wall. "Tammy, can you go in first with the light?"

Tammy nodded and entered the opening.

John said, "Alright. Andy, will you lead Milton through? We will all follow you."

Larry stepped through the fissure and saw that the chamber was small, no more than ten feet by ten feet. It was crowded with all nine of them inside. A wooden ladder led up the far wall and into another fissure in the ceiling. The ladder was crudely nailed together from what looked like scrap pieces of two-by-fours and didn't look very sturdy. Larry wasn't sure it would hold anyone's weight after sitting there for sixty-plus years so far underground. He voiced his concern, and Milton glanced at him and rasped, "It will be sturdy as a rock. Trust me, we built things to last back then."

Looking up, John said, "I will go up first and test it."

Before he even knew what he was doing, Larry stepped forward and said, "No, let me go. You don't need to always put yourself at risk. We are no longer tourists under your protection. We are all in this together. It's time for the rest of us to share in the risks."

John opened his mouth to protest, but Larry had already stepped forward and put his hands on the ladder, shaking it slightly to test its sturdiness.

John put a hand on Larry's shoulder and offered his cellphone with the flashlight on. "Go slowly and test each rung before putting your full weight on it. When you get to the top, shine the light down for the rest of us."

Larry nodded, put the edge of the cellphone in his mouth and clamped it between his teeth, tasting the salty tang of sweat but ignoring it. He set his foot on the first rung and put his full weight on it. The rung felt solid, so he reached up, grabbed the next rung, then stepped up with his other foot. The ladder creaked but seemed solid.

Larry quickly found his rhythm. Grip the next rung, step up, plant both feet, repeat.

He probably looked pathetic, but he didn't care. He cared more about safety than how he looked to everyone else. He had entered the fissure in the ceiling and had probably climbed forty more feet when he put his weight on a rung and it snapped beneath him, falling away to the ground. Without thinking, he screamed, dropping the phone from his mouth. It fell down the shaft, the precious light spinning away from him as it fell. He hung on with his hands and scrambled to find his footing on the previous rung to steady himself before his hands could slip.

There was a shout from below and Larry yelled down, "Is everyone alright? Andy, Ethan?"

John called up, "Everyone is fine. No one was hit. But are you OK? What happened?"

Larry realized they couldn't see anything in the sudden blackness, so he yelled out, "One of the rungs snapped free when I put my weight on it." He looked down, trying to remember how many rungs he had climbed. "Be careful when you get about forty feet up. The place where it broke is very sharp and jagged."

Ethan's voice drifted up, "Be careful the rest of the way, Larry."

Larry heard John say, "Everyone back up a few steps in case anything else drops down. Tammy, can you give me the flashlight?"

Faint light reached up the shaft and Larry sighed with relief when he could see the ladder again, even if it was more shadow than anything. He called down, "Thanks, John. That helps a lot."

Larry reached up to the rung above the broken one and grabbed it, pulling to test it without letting go of the one he was holding. It felt solid, so he continued climbing, stretching to cover the gap in rungs. He breathed a sigh of relief when he finally reached the top and pulled himself over the edge. He lay on his back in the blackness, able to see only the barest hint of light from the flashlight down below. He gulped air, his heart hammering as he released the stress he been holding in during the climb. Eventually, he rolled over and crawled to the opening.

Larry cupped his hands and called down, "I made it. The rest of the ladder is solid. Just be careful at the broken spot."

Andy came up next, the cellphone held in his teeth, and he was not even out of breath when he reached the opening. He took the cellphone from his mouth and grinned when he saw his dad. Then he surprised Larry by stepping forward and hugging him tightly. Andy whispered into his chest, "I'm glad you are OK, dad. What you did was awesome!"

Larry smiled, "Right back at you, bud."

Andy let go, stepped to the hole and shined the light down.

Carl climbed up, grimly nodding to Andy and Larry before he crawled away from the opening to give the next person room.

Ethan came next, followed by Jim and Tammy.

Just Claire, Milton, and John remained below.

Larry leaned over the edge of the fissure and saw Claire start up the ladder. When she approached the broken part, he called down, "Claire, be careful."

After a few minutes, the elegant woman's head

appeared and she grimaced before asking, "Larry, could you please help me this last little bit?"

Larry leaned down, took her hand, and helped pull her up until she was sitting on the floor, her legs dangling over the hole.

Andy helped her stand up and Claire turned to Larry. "I don't think Milton will be able to make it up here." Her eyes were filled with fear.

Larry nodded grimly. "I will go down part of the way and help him." But when he leaned over the hole and shined the light down the ladder, he cursed under his breath when he saw that Milton was hanging onto the wooden rung just below the broken part of the ladder, unable to get past the gap in rungs. He yelled down, "Milton, please wait for me! I am coming down to help you."

John called up, "Larry, I am right beneath Milton, helping to hold him. I don't think he has the strength to get past the broken rung."

Larry handed the phone to Andy. "Shine this down."

Taking the phone with a worried expression, Andy nodded and pointed the phone's light downward as Larry swung his legs over the opening. Before he could take a step down, Milton's voice floated up in gasping, quivering breaths. "Larry? Can…you…hurry?"

Larry climbed down the ladder as quickly as he could. He didn't know how he and John could help Milton past the missing rung.

When Larry stopped just above the broken rung, he felt fear jolt through him. Milton's face was sunken in, his eyes were barely open, and both arms trembled as he held onto the rung of the ladder. Milton was going to lose his grip at any moment.

John called out, "I'm here, just below Milton. I have hold of his waist. Can you grab Milton's jacket and on the count of three, lift while I push?"

Larry looked at Milton's face and saw it go slack. With a surge of strength, Larry gripped the rung above him tighter with his left hand and quickly reached down to grab Milton's jacket with his right hand just as the old man's arms slipped from the rung. Larry grunted and called out, "I've got him."

John groaned from the sudden weight, "Can you lift him up as I push?"

Larry gritted his teeth and pulled, and as he did, Milton cried out in pain. It was a long, drawn-out mournful sound.

Larry couldn't see what had happened, but he felt tears fall from his eyes at the sound of pure agony coming from Milton. Larry pulled up as hard as he could to get Milton past the broken rung.

John grunted out from below, "Keep going. Don't stop climbing."

Larry stepped up onto the next rung, put one foot against the opposite wall of the fissure and quickly grabbed the next rung above him. He felt like his shoulder was going to pop out of its socket, but he ignored the pain and kept pulling Milton up.

Milton cried out again, this time louder.

Larry and John continued this way until Larry was right below the opening at the top of the ladder.

Carl leaned over the edge and put a hand under Milton's right armpit. Jim leaned down and grabbed Milton's other armpit.

Jim said, "Larry, you can climb out. We have him."

Larry used the last of his strength to climb up the final rung of the ladder and onto the floor, wheezing, and feeling like he might pass out.

Jim and Carl pulled Milton up as soon as Larry was clear of the ladder and gently laid him onto the floor.

Milton was no longer making any sounds. His eyes were tightly closed, his face drawn in agony.

John climbed over the edge and stood up shakily.

The group gasped as one when Andy moved the light directly over Milton and they saw a sharp and jagged piece of wood from the broken rung of the ladder protruding from Milton's stomach. Blood welled around it, but the wood kept the wound from bleeding too much.

Larry pushed himself into a sitting position and felt a sickness in the pit of his stomach. The wood must have pierced Milton's stomach as they lifted him up past the broken rung.

Claire cried out as she knelt by Milton's side.

Milton's body suddenly arched, one final cry of pain erupted from him, then he fell back and lay still. His face in the light of the phone was white, blotchy, and slack.

John pulled his sweater off, folded it, then knelt and gently placed it under Milton's head.

Claire took her husband's hand, crying softly. She leaned down and whispered something into his ear that the rest of the group couldn't hear.

Milton cracked open his eyes, his expression suddenly relaxed and peaceful. He smiled up at Claire and softly whispered, "I love you, too, dearest." His eyes suddenly grew wide as he looked up into the darkness past Claire. He smiled wider and softly said, "Oh, hey Otto! Hey, Franc!"

Milton didn't take another breath.

Claire leaned forward, tears streaming down her

face. She whispered into his ear, then touched her lips to his before gently closing his eyes with two fingers. With a sob, she laid her head on his chest and closed her eyes, holding him tightly.

Larry felt tears falling down his cheeks, and he caught a brief glimpse of Andy's stricken face before his son turned and stepped into the darkness.

Larry and the rest of the group all moved away a few steps, giving Claire her privacy.

After a few minutes, Claire lifted her head and, smiling sadly through her tears, addressed the group. "This was Milton's favorite spot. He and his best friends Otto and Franc spent many years coming here for lunch breaks. She pointed to a small wooden table and three stools sitting in the corner, looking like they belonged in the small space. An old deck of playing cards rested in the middle of the table, with three hands of cards hastily dropped on the table.

Claire smiled wistfully. "The three of them played cards at that table over their breaks. They were playing a game of Gin Rummy in 1962 when the monster attacked them, and Otto and Franc were killed. Milton never came back here after that day, and the mine closed soon after." Her voice cracked, "Now the three of them are together again and they can finally finish their game."

She looked around in the meager light. "Milton only had a few days left to live. End-stage pancreatic cancer. He had been in home hospice care for the past three months." She wiped a tear from her cheek and then continued, "Milton's body started to shut down yesterday. He knew he didn't have much time left, so he forced himself from his bed this morning and told me he had to come down into the mine one final time. Milton put on a brave face for everyone here today,

209

but every moment he was down here was an extraordinary effort for him. I don't know how he was able to climb all those ladders and walk down so many tunnels. But that is Milton. When he set his mind to something, he would do it, no matter what."

Claire smiled even as more tears fell down her cheeks. "It was a gift for him to die in this special place."

Andy appeared from the darkness and knelt by Claire. He took her hand and said through his tears, "I am glad Mr. Milton came down here. I am honored to have known him. I will never forget him."

Claire gently touched Andy's cheek. "You remind me of him, you know. Fearless and always caring for others."

Andy stood and stepped a few paces back, holding his clasped hands in front of him, his head lowered in reverence.

John knelt. "Claire, when we reach topside, I will send a recovery crew back down here to bring Milton to the surface for a proper burial."

Claire shook her head. "That is kind of you, but Milton will stay right here. It is where he wanted to be, so I think he should remain here forever."

John looked like he was going to protest, but then nodded, obviously realizing it wasn't his decision to make.

They stayed in the small alcove for a while longer, giving Claire the time that she needed. Finally, she bent down and kissed Milton on the cheek, then stood up and said, "I am ready to leave."

Putting a hand on her shoulder, John asked, "Are you sure? We can stay longer."

"No, I am at peace. It is time we all got out of here." Claire bent down, gently lifted Milton's head, and removed John's sweater. She handed it to John and said, "You need this more than Milt does."

John nodded as he took the sweater from her and slipped it over his head. He then turned and said, "Tammy, will you lead us?"

Tammy, normally happy and bubbly, somberly turned and passed through the small passageway that led into the main tunnel. She shined the light left and they saw the opening to a mining cavern only a few feet away. The tunnel led away to the right.

Larry took Ethan's hand and squeezed it.

Ethan returned the gesture with the same combination of relief, gratitude and apprehension, and they followed the rest of the group, who were now more like family to Larry, than the complete strangers they had been only hours earlier.

CHAPTER 30

SALLY called a halt when they reached the exfiltration point leading down to Level thirty-one. Before she, Jason, and Karl descended, she needed to think. They had run all out through Level thirty after the firefight with the creature that killed Charlie, Jillian, and Johan, and so far, they heard no pursuit.

She had never run from danger in her life and felt slightly ashamed for doing so now. Though, to be fair, she had never faced an unkillable demon before, either. She didn't know if it actually was a demon, but that was the only word she could think of to describe the thing they had gone up against.

Sally whispered into the mic, "Let's rest here. Jason, guard our six."

Jason nodded, his face no longer showing the fear and shock of the initial encounter with the Vorgroth. He quickly moved back into the darkness of the tunnel.

Sally indicated Karl's pack and said, "Karl, take out the map of this mine."

Karl dug into his pack and removed a folded map. He knelt on the rocky ground and unfolded it, lifted it briefly to sweep some rocks clear, and then let it settle to the floor. He had a digital 3-D map of the mine layout on his phone, but he always preferred physical maps. A phone could break on a mission. Maps were easy to tuck into a pocket or backpack. Karl studied the 2-D cross-sectional layout of the mine for a few moments, then pointed a dirty index finger to a spot on the map. In a thick Russian accent, he said, "We are here."

Sally knelt and studied the map, then pointed to a small square one level down from their current location. "This is the exfiltration point on Level thirty-one, right?" She then slid her finger down one level and to the right. "And this is the elevator shaft on Level thirty-two?"

Karl said, "Affirmative."

"We will descend to Level thirty-two and sync up with Sills and Roberts from team three, who are guarding the elevator. Using the MADs, we'll ascend back up the elevator shaft to Level twenty-seven and locate the exfiltration point from twenty-six." As Sally spoke, she traced her finger up the elevator shaft on the map to Level twenty-seven, then followed the tunnel to the square on the map that indicated the access location between Levels twenty-six and twenty-seven. She tapped her finger on the spot. "We'll wait for the tourist group to come to us right here."

Sally stood and Karl folded and secured the map in his pack. Sally opened the hatch and peered down the opening. She quietly said into her mic, "Clear. Jason, return to our location."

Karl was already halfway down the ladder when

213

Jason came jogging back to Sally.

Sally indicated the hatch opening and Jason immediately started climbing down into the hole. His head was at floor level when a deep roar echoed down the tunnel. Jason paused, staring down the tunnel.

Another roar filled the tunnel, much closer now.

Sally quietly said, "Jason, please continue down with caution."

Jason hurried down the ladder.

Sally calmly climbed into the hatch opening, put her feet on the ladder, climbed down a few rungs, and pulled the hatch closed above her. She quickly descended to the ground below.

As she stepped away from the ladder, she heard the hatch being ripped away above her. Then the ladder shook as the Vorgroth began to descend it. She called out, "To the next exfiltration point!"

The three of them sprinted away in a flat-out run. They reached the next hatch within three minutes, quickly descended to Level thirty-two, and ran back to the elevator room.

They immediately came across the remains of Sills and Roberts; both had been torn to pieces. Hundreds of empty shell casings littered the floor. The two soldiers had obviously gone up against the Vorgroth and given it everything they had.

Sally coolly said, "Suit up. There is nothing we can do for them."

Jason, Karl, and Sally immediately began strapping themselves into their MADs harnesses.

In the distance, they heard another roar as the Vorgroth approached.

Karl pulled himself up through the elevator hatch and connected his MAD to the cable. He quickly went up the cable via the motorized ascender.

Sally pulled her MAD harness tight, then jumped up, grabbed the edge of the elevator hatch and pulled herself up through the opening. She started to hook the MAD onto the cable when she realized that Jason had not climbed onto the top of the elevator behind her. She knelt and stuck her head back through the opening in time to see Jason unbuckle and drop his MAD.

Sally called out, "Jason, strap back into the MAD and climb up here now!"

But he didn't seem to hear her as the sound of heavy feet pounded toward them.

"Jason, that is an order!"

The Vorgroth entered the elevator chamber from the tunnel and stopped to survey the room, its head sweeping left to right. It roared when it saw Jason and charged forward, its eyes reflecting brightly in Sally's night vision.

Jason tossed aside his rifle and pulled a semi-automatic shotgun from its strap on his back. He walked forward, holding the gun at his hip, firing a round per second, his face calm as the Vorgroth charged toward him. The shotgun shells held high-density explosive cartridges that could blow a two-foot hole in a concrete wall with a single blast.

Explosions roared in the tunnel as Jason walked toward the Vorgroth, firing until his shotgun magazine was empty. He slapped a second magazine in without stopping, and continued firing.

The Vorgroth was blown backward with each explosive impact but kept climbing to its feet and advancing.

Sally watched the scene in fascination, unable to look away from Jason's unbelievable heroics. It took every ounce of her willpower to not climb back down

215

and join him. Sally had fired hundreds of rounds of armor-piercing bullets at the Vorgroth up on Level thirty and had not harmed the thing in the slightest. She knew she could not help Jason now.

Sally took one last, helpless look.

The Vorgroth reached out, picked Jason up, and squeezed his back and spine between its two massive hands. As it crushed his body, Jason lifted the shotgun and pulled the trigger, but it clicked on empty. Jason reversed it and smashed the stock directly into the Vorgroth's face with three hard blows, knocking its head back.

The Vorgroth dropped Jason by reflex, its eyes looking astonished.

Jason fell to the floor, unmoving.

Sally connected her MAD to the elevator cable, feeling sick to her stomach. As she shot upward into the shaft, she heard Jason laugh. The sound filled the chamber briefly, then was cut off.

Sally arrived at Level twenty-seven and was helped into the tunnel opening by Karl. He squinted down the shaft, then up at Sally and calmy asked, "Jason?"

She shook her head, her face grim.

Karl sighed, then stepped back, all business. "Ready when you are."

Sally nodded as she unbuckled herself from the harness and lowered her MAD to the floor.

The two of them jogged down the tunnel toward the next exfiltration point.

In the distance far below, she heard another rage-filled roar.

Chapter 31

RENN raised his arm, bent at a 90-degree angle, fist closed.

His team immediately stopped their forward progress, their bodies motionless, completely silent. They were in Level forty-two. The tunnel ended ahead in a pile of rocks. In front of the rocks, he could just make out the outline of a jagged hole in the floor, which looked grainy in his night vision. His intel indicated that Level forty-three had been sealed shut by explosives back in 1962. This was the end of the line. The SafeWell team was likely in the chamber below. He didn't want to surprise them and risk a firefight in this stone tunnel. He spoke softly into his mic, "Remember: do not engage with the SafeWell team."

They slowly moved forward, each foot carefully placed to avoid stepping on stones or gravel which could be loud enough to give away their position.

Renn slowly and carefully leaned forward until he could peer down into the hole, ready to pull back if any shots were fired from below. The chamber floor below was covered with rubble.

Renn saw something else, as well. He magnified his night vision by two times. When he did, Renn saw it looked like a slaughterhouse below him. Black blood spatter covered the rocks and floor. Discarded limbs and pieces of torn clothing were scattered about. Renn stared for a long time, analyzing every aspect of the scene below. He couldn't ascertain if he was seeing the remains of the SafeWell team or that of the two missing teams.

Renn turned to his tracker, Ficks. "Investigate below. Tell me who was killed and how. Report back in three minutes."

Ficks gave a curt nod and slid down the rope to the chamber below. Within two minutes, he climbed back up and pulled himself over the edge of the hole, not even out of breath after the 60-foot rope climb. But his expression was pinched and subdued. "Sir. Eight soldiers were killed below. They were Thornlandon Holdings teams. Not much remains of their bodies. A few miscellaneous limbs, and a helmet with Kalim Amani's head still in it."

Renn felt his body go cold. *So, they had found the two missing teams. Or what was left of them.* He pushed away his growing fear and asked, "What about the SafeWell team? Are they down there?"

Ficks shook his head. "No. I saw no evidence they were ever down below."

Paul spoke quietly from behind Renn, his normal joviality replaced by barely controlled anger. "What the fuck killed 'em all down there, mate?"

Looking at his friend, Ficks said, "I saw the same footprints below that I found up on Level thirty-two. Whatever it is, it is huge. Probably seven or eight feet tall. Hundreds of shell casings are scattered around the area, but I saw no evidence that the bullets injured whatever they were shooting at." Ficks pointed to the marks on the stone around the jagged hole in the floor, and then at the rope. "Whatever killed those teams climbed out through this hole. You can see where it gripped the rock and gouged it with what appear to be claws. There is blood on the rope, so it must have had blood all over its hands as well, most likely from the slaughter below."

Paul let out a string of expletives, his eyes looking both frightened and angry. He ended with, "We need to kill this motherfucker."

Renn had been furiously thinking while Ficks and Paul had been talking. *If the SafeWell team was not below, and he and his team had not seen them on the way down here, then where the hell were they?* Realization hit him. *The cavern! They must have been hiding in the cavern while Renn and his team walked right past them.*

Renn stood straight and said, "We will not hunt whatever killed the teams below. I know you want revenge, but those soldiers used all the firepower they had against whatever it was that attacked them and they were still slaughtered. If we encounter this thing, we will fight it, but until that time, we will continue our mission and search for the SafeWell team."

Paul opened his mouth to say something but closed it when Renn glared at him.

Renn continued, "We did not see the SafeWell team on the way down here. Which means they likely came here, saw the carnage below, and got the hell out of here." He pointed down the tunnel with his rifle. "My bet is they went back to the cavern we passed through, heard us coming, hid, and let us pass by before escaping up to Level forty-one."

Paul looked back down the tunnel and spat on the floor. His eyes flashed in anger, his Aussie accent thick as he said, "They hid from us like a bunch of pussies."

Renn turned and looked at Paul disapprovingly. "The SafeWell team did the right thing, Paul. They do not know our intentions, so why should they risk a firefight? They also likely saw what happened to the other teams down there," he pointed with his rifle barrel down toward the hole, "and understood gun fire might draw the thing that killed them back here to all of us."

Renn suddenly cursed, remembering he had left Lucy Miller to guard the exfiltration point in the cavern right where the SafeWell team was likely hiding.

Lucy was known as 'Miller the Killer' to the team. She was always on a hair trigger, almost too ready to kill. Lucy had been the weak link in his plan to attempt to make contact with the SafeWell team instead of killing them as they had been ordered to do. She was the one person who Renn didn't completely trust.

About a year ago, Renn had quietly put in a request to his superiors to remove Lucy from his team, but the request had been denied. She was very good at her job and that was that. So, Renn had learned to put her into situations where she had less of a chance to shoot first and ask questions later. On this part of the mission, he had left her to guard their exfiltration point, hoping to keep her out of the way when they initiated contact with the SafeWell team. Renn hadn't expected the SafeWell team to get past them. He felt a sense of dread and quietly called out,

"Double-time it back to the cavern. We can't let Lucy start a firefight with the SafeWell team."

Ficks sprinted down the tunnel and the rest of them followed the tracker at a run.

CHAPTER 32

MORGAN crouched just inside a narrow fissure at the back of the cavern on Level forty-two. Jack stood behind her, and Karen lay on the ground. All three looked through their rifle scopes toward the exfiltration point on the other side of the open space. Bauwen stood outside of the fissure to Morgan's left, out of the way in case they had to fire. Or Morgan *thought* Bauwen was to her left. One moment Morgan glanced over and saw Bauwen calmly standing a few feet away, but when Morgan looked a moment later, she appeared to be gone.

Bauwen's soft voice floated to Morgan, more of a whisper than anything, "I am still here, Morgan. I just changed my molecular structure to blend with the rock wall."

Ten minutes earlier, they had reached the huge mining cavern on Level forty-two, pushing themselves to their limits trying to keep up with Bauwen as she had sprinted down the tunnel.

Bauwen had led them unerringly through the dark,

but even using their night-vision, it had still been a dangerous run. The floor was uneven, so they had to constantly look down as they ran to avoid injury.

When they reached the cavern, Bauwen whispered, "Follow me, quickly and quietly. I can hear the other team approaching. They are not far away from the opening to this level." She led them to a narrow fissure in the stone wall on the back side of the cavern.

Now, Morgan peered ahead as Renn's team climbed down the ladder across the cavern. In her night vision, Morgan could tell they were well trained. They moved in unison and each member covered a different area of the cavern.

Morgan, Jack, and Karen were among the most highly trained soldiers in the world. They didn't twitch a muscle or take too deep of a breath. Even the smallest sounds could carry across the cavern. Morgan felt an itch on her neck. She wanted nothing more than to scratch it, but she pushed the thought from her mind.

Morgan followed Renn's team's progress through her scope. She heard only the faintest whisper of clothing rubbing together as they glided through the cavern, and their boots made the barest of sounds on the rocky ground. Morgan was impressed. These were obviously elite soldiers, probably a mixture of ex-SEALs, Israeli Mossad, British SAS, and Russian Spetsnaz. She had no interest in going up against them.

After the other team disappeared down the tunnel, Morgan waited another minute before whispering, "Move out."

Bauwen rematerialized next to Morgan, causing her to flinch in surprise.

Bauwen quietly said, "Sorry, I should have warned you I was going to do that."

"It's alright. I am still getting used to what you can do. Follow us. We do not want you to be in the way if we must return weapons fire."

Morgan, Karen, and Jack started across the uneven floor of the cavern, with Bauwen a few paces behind them. They were halfway across when Morgan cursed silently to herself. She stopped suddenly and crouched. Karen and Jack immediately did the same.

Morgan had just realized that six soldiers had descended the ladder, but only five left the cavern. One of them had stayed behind to guard their exfiltration point.

Bauwen spoke almost directly into Morgan's ear, her voice so soft it was more like a disturbance in the air, than words, "There is someone ahead by the ladder. She is armed and just turned our way, but I do not think she has seen us yet."

Morgan nodded. She didn't want to kill this person, especially if the other team was down here to help. But, from experience, Morgan knew it was extremely risky to try and make contact with an unknown shooter in a strange environment. Morgan weighed their options and finally said, "Stay here."

Karen whispered, "Morgan, it is too dangerous to approach this person."

"Rules of engagement say we cannot kill someone who hasn't yet threatened us. And we must keep moving so we can save the tourists and the mine employees from the Vorgroth."

"Then let me go."

Morgan whispered, "No."

Karen wasn't happy, but nodded assent anyway,

deferring to her leader.

In Morgan's night vision, she saw that Lucy was also wearing night-vision gear and was constantly rotating her field of view. Morgan crouched low and slowly made her way across the cavern, moving only when Lucy's head had rotated away from her.

Knowing she could be dead in the next few seconds, Morgan took a deep but quiet breath to calm her nerves, knelt down on one knee, and softly but clearly called out, "Hello. We come in peace."

Lucy spun toward Morgan and raised her gun, sighting through the scope. Her cold voice called out, "Do not move or I will fire."

Morgan replied, "I will not move. I am not here to harm you or your team."

"Place your weapon on the ground and stand up with your hands up."

Morgan shook her head. "I will not do that. Listen, there is a creature down in these tunnels that is hunting all of us. It killed the two previous teams who were sent down here. We found their bodies, or what is left of them, down on Level forty-three. The creature could be anywhere right now."

Lucy spoke in a mocking tone, "Yeah, right. Nice story. Now, place your weapon on the ground or I will shoot you."

Morgan remained as she was. "No, I will not do that. If I had wanted to kill you, I could have shot you instead of initiating contact. Now, I'm going to approach you so we can speak quietly and not risk drawing the creature to us."

"I said remain where you are and place your weapon on the ground." Lucy's voice turned even colder as she said, "I will shoot if you do not obey my command right now." Morgan heard the distinct click

225

of a safety being switched off.

If Morgan lowered her weapon to the ground, she would be defenseless. But if she didn't lower it, she would be killed. As she was weighing her options, Morgan heard the soft report from the woman's gun and a bullet ricocheted from the stone floor not more than two inches from her left foot.

Lucy's voice floated over to Morgan, "Tell the rest of your team to put their weapons down and approach. I can see them a hundred meters behind you aiming their guns at me. On the count of three, I will put a bullet through your head if they do not place their guns on the ground. One. Two. Three…"

Lucy's head snapped back, and she dropped to the ground.

Karen and Jack sprinted forward. Jack slid to a stop by Morgan, and Karen continued past them toward the fallen woman.

Bauwen cautiously joined them, her eyes troubled by the violence.

Karen quickly returned, whispering, "All clear."

Morgan sighed, then nodded. Karen had done the right thing shooting the woman. Morgan had no doubt that the soldier would have made good on her promise to shoot on the count of three.

They approached the dead woman. Jack stepped forward and nudged Lucy's body over with his foot to reveal a bullet hole between her eyes. Blood and brain matter radiated out and across the floor behind her.

Jack looked up at Karen. "Nice shot, but it looks to be a millimeter off to the left."

Karen knelt to examine the bullet entry point, then stood up and whispered, "Damn, you're right."

Jack grinned and they touched closed fists in a gesture of obvious affection and respect.

Bauwen looked at them both in confusion, then shook her head, her eyes sad. She stepped forward and scaled the rope using only her hands, reaching the next level in a matter of moments.

Morgan followed, and soon all of them stood in the tunnel of Level forty-one. Morgan took a few steps when her night vision flickered and went out. "Damn. My night vision batteries died." She turned to her team. "Check your batteries as well and replace them now. We don't want them going dead when we encounter the other team or the Vorgroth."

Morgan took a spare battery out of her pack. She removed her night vision unit, popped open the battery compartment and replaced the battery by touch alone, the entire operation taking no more than thirty seconds. When she powered her night vision back on, the speckled view of the empty cave was a welcome sight.

They all continued down the tunnel, following Bauwen at a fast run, staying vigilant for any sign of the Vorgroth or other hostiles. They backtracked up toward Level thirty-two, going more quickly now that they knew their way.

Morgan, Jack, and Karen followed Bauwen through the doorway into the main tunnel of Level thirty-two, then stopped to listen for a few moments. The area was empty. They carefully moved down the tunnel, the smell of dust and gunpowder growing thicker as they approached the room with the elevator.

About thirty feet from the entrance to the room, they slowed even further when they saw the remains of a human torso. Morgan motioned with two fingers and Jack moved ahead while they covered him.

Jack stopped when he reached the dead body, then

he crouched and rotated in a 360-degree turn, looking through his rifle sight. He finally motioned the team forward.

Morgan stopped at the body, aghast by what she saw. A soldier's upper torso lay on its side, still gripping a shotgun. Gleaming stainless steel shotgun shells littered the ground in a trail from the elevator all the way to his body, indicating he had walked toward whatever had killed him, firing the shotgun the whole way. The remains of his lower torso lay ten feet away, one leg twisted and crumpled like paper. The man had clearly been torn apart, his entrails lying strewn over the ground.

Bauwen whispered, "The Vorgroth did this."

Karen bent down and picked up a shotgun shell, turning it in her hands before saying, "Explosive shells. Next-gen casings. Not much could stand against such firepower in close combat."

Morgan could almost recreate the battle scene in her head. The soldier had approached the Vorgroth, firing at least thirty of these exploding rounds at it, only to be picked up and torn in half. If the Vorgroth could do this with its bare hands without being injured by exploding shotgun shells, there was absolutely nothing they could do to stop it.

Morgan motioned her team and Bauwen forward until they reached the elevator room. Most of it was caved in, rubble lying everywhere. Two more soldiers had been slaughtered here. But the elevator stood intact, with twelve pieces of equipment next to it.

Jack stepped forward and bent down to examine one of them, then stood up. "MADs: motorized ascent devices. Battery powered. These can carry a person with full gear up the elevator cable almost as quickly as the elevator would."

Morgan asked, "Bauwen, you said there is a team following the tourists. I assume there are six of them as well?"

Bauwen nodded that Morgan was correct.

Morgan continued, "Operational procedure would be to have a third team protecting the entrance and exfiltration points to the mine. I think these two bodies by the elevator were soldiers protecting the exfiltration point down here. These two were in a completely different firefight from the one the soldier with the exploding shotgun shells engaged in. Which means there are probably four soldiers guarding the exit point topside. So, eighteen soldiers in total. We have confirmed that four of them are dead. That means we face a minimum of fourteen members of the unknown team. Not good odds. Let's hope they are, as Bauwen suspects, not hostile."

Morgan entered the elevator car and pulled herself up through the hatch in the ceiling. She stood on the roof and peered up the shaft, listening for any sign of those above her. Just then, a long roar echoed down to her from somewhere far above, the sound raising goosebumps over Morgan's whole body.

Morgan lowered herself back through the hatch and dropped to the ground, her face looking grave.

Bauwen seemed to shrink into herself at hearing the Vorgroth's roar, her eyes wide and haunted.

Morgan double-checked her magazine and spoke quietly, "The Vorgroth is likely using the elevator shaft to move between levels. That roar clearly came from within the shaft itself. I don't think the tourists are moving too quickly, as I saw an old couple in their 80s or 90s on the elevator ride down. So, I estimate they haven't made it any further than Level twenty-eight or twenty-nine. The second military team must be close behind the civilians by now. The Vorgroth may have gone to a level above them to wait for them to come to it. The thing seems smart."

Jack muttered darkly, "Let's suit up with these MADs. We can catch up to the tourists more quickly that way."

Morgan nodded. "Agreed. Let's go."

Morgan strapped on a MAD and climbed up through the elevator hatch.

Jack and Karen both followed, with Bauwen coming up last.

Bauwen timidly asked, "Morgan, can I hold on to you as you go up? I do not know how to use one of these machines."

"Sure. Hold on tightly."

Bauwen stepped forward and wrapped her arms around Morgan's shoulders.

Morgan activated the MAD, and they quickly ascended the shaft.

Above, she heard another faint roar, the sound reaching deep into the fear center of her mind where, as children, all people feared the dark and the monsters that existed there. She never dreamed those monsters were real.

CHAPTER 33

JOHN tried to keep sadness from overtaking him. Three of the tourists had already died and they were only on Level twenty-eight. *How many of those left would reach the surface?*

All of them, he thought with determination. *He would not let another person die.*

There were eight of them left. They could all make it. They *would* all make it.

The tunnel of Level twenty-eight stretched out ahead of them, the light from Tracy's flashlight revealing a well-traveled corridor. This level must have been one of the biggest of the entire mine. Milton had mentioned they had mined this level for six years.

John was about to call for a break to rest when Tracy's flashlight flickered, then went out.

They were plunged into total darkness.

Cries from the group rang out, and someone fell, cursing.

John called out, "Tracy, what happened?"

"The flashlight just died."

"Alright, everyone, stay where you are. Don't move. Andy, can you turn on one of the cell phones?"

"Sure. Give me a sec."

John could hear Andy opening his pack. The seconds seemed to stretch on interminably.

In the total blackness of the tunnel, John's imagination started running wild. *Was the Vorgroth down here with them now? Was it standing right in front of him, its jaws dripping saliva as it reached out its clawed hands...*

Andy's face suddenly appeared as he turned on a cell phone, the light from the home screen bright in the otherwise complete darkness. After about fifteen seconds, Andy called out, "Who has the Google Pixel?"

Carl answered, "I do. That's mine."

"What's your pass code?"

"I'm not giving you my code. Give it to me, I will log in."

Jim called out in an exasperated voice, "Oh for God's sake, Carl. Just give him the passcode and stop being an ass."

Carl grumbled under his breath, then said, "Fine. Its 123456."

Andy raised his eyes and said, "Really? That's your passcode?"

"Shut up, kid."

Andy logged in and activated the flashlight feature, before handing the phone to John. "Here you go, Mr. John."

"Thanks Andy. Can you get one more phone out and activate the flashlight? These cellphone lights are not great, so I think we need two, one in the front and back of the group."

"Sure thing. One sec." He dug into the bag, now that he could see and pulled one out with a smile. "This is yours, dad." Andy booted it up and turned on the flashlight.

Ethan looked at him quizzically, "How did you know the passcode?"

"Oh dad, please. My birthday is so obvious."

Ethan arched an eyebrow at Larry and challenged him, "What? Yours is the same."

Despite being in a dark mine and chased by a monster out of his worst nightmare, Larry managed to grin and say, "Guilty as charged."

John held the phone above his head, but the diffused light only reached a few feet in front of him. He strained to see further, but the inky blackness pressed back like a wall of nothingness, daring him to step into it. "Alright. The next exit point to Level twenty-seven should be a fifteen to twenty-minute walk down this tunnel. So far, each level has been relatively the same. Just a single tunnel with a mined-out cavern at the end. So, let's get going."

Jim stepped forward and asked, "What about that thing chasing us? Do you think it can find a way up here?"

"No, we blocked the exit point to the last level. We are safe."

Jim looked troubled, so John asked, "What is it, Jim? If you are worried about something, tell me."

"Well, the exit point is covered. But what about the elevator shaft?"

John felt like he had been punched in the gut. He couldn't believe he hadn't thought of the shaft. He must not have been doing a very good job hiding his feelings of guilt, because Jim reached out and touched his arm, something he never did normally. "It's alright, John. It's not your fault. I didn't think of it till just now, either. The question is, 'can that…that…'"

Jim struggled to find the right word, so John said, "Monster. Let's call it what it is."

Jim nodded. "Can that *monster* climb the shaft? The shaft is not vertical; it runs at an eighty-two-degree angle."

The rest of the group crowded around to listen, and Carl asked, "What is an eighty-two-degree angle? I knew the elevator didn't drop straight down but was never sure what that meant."

Jim knelt and said, "Ninety-degrees is straight up and down. Every degree that is added or subtracted tilts that line one way or the other." He drew a line straight up and down in the dust of the floor. "This is a ninety-degree angle."

|

He then drew a line below it at a slight angle. "And this is approximately an eighty-two-degree angle."

|

/

"The mining engineers designed the elevator shaft like this so they could put in a sort of rail system for the elevator to attach to, which allowed the pully to more efficiently lift the heavy loads of iron ore. If they had tried to pull the elevator via the normal free-hanging cable system that other elevators used, it would have been too much weight and stress on the cable and the boom, leading to a risk of catastrophic failure."

Andy nodded enthusiastically. "It's all about

weight distribution and applied thermodynamics, reducing the pull of gravity and heat against the motor and cable. Quite simple, really, isn't it?"

John and Jim stared at Andy with surprised looks.

Larry put a hand on Andy's shoulder, pride on his face. "Andy is a prodigy."

The boy pulled away, his face red with embarrassment. "Dad, please, stop."

Larry grinned at Jim and John. "He hates when we call him that in public."

Jim turned to Andy and said, "It's alright to be smart, Andy. And yes, you are correct. It is all about weight distribution and thermodynamics."

Andy looked thoughtful for a moment, then his face turned white. "So, you are saying because of the angle, the monster could find enough grip to climb up the shaft? I heard the thing roar earlier and it sounded like it came from above us."

Nodding, Jim said, "It is theoretically possible, though the elevator shaft is sixteen feet across and the steel walls are fairly smooth. I don't think it could climb the shaft." He turned to John, "I thought I heard the roar above us as well, though. I don't know if it was a trick of acoustics or not, but I think we should be extra careful, just in case."

John nodded. "Alright, everyone. Let's get going. Be as quiet as you can." He turned back toward the tunnel and started forward, calling back softly, "Follow me and watch your step. You can't see the ground as easily with these phones as we could with the flashlights, and we don't want anyone twisting an ankle."

They moved slowly down the tunnel, huddled closely together to be near the meager light. No one spoke. All John could hear were soft footsteps and even softer breathing. He peered ahead as he walked, thinking of the darkness around them. A memory of his grandmother came to him.

As a child, John often hunted deer with his grandmother, Wenona. Her name meant 'First born daughter' in Anishinaabe. She was an elder in the Anishinaabe council; respected by everyone and feared by many because of her sharp eyes and even sharper tongue. John never used her name. He always referred to her as 'Nookomis,' which meant 'grandmother.' He would often say things like, "What is this plant called, Nookomis?" Or he would tug at her sleeve and ask, "Nookomis, can we go hunting today?"

His grandmother taught him how to move silently through the forest. Even at the age of three he was already mimicking her every movement as they made their way through the deep woods, eyes always moving back and forth, never focusing too long on any one tree. The key to moving through the forest quietly was to not move in a straight line, but to weave in a meandering route across the forest floor, always looking for the path of least resistance. This usually meant following animal trails.

She had told him once, when he had asked her why the animals made trails, "The animals do not want to be heard, John. They do not wish to be seen. They are always aware of predators. So, they created the best paths through the woods, paths that let them pass silently through the forest."

He had always been inquisitive, so he remembered asking her, "But if the prey animals follow those paths to avoid predators, then don't the predators follow them, as well, to catch the prey?"

She had nodded, her eyes gleaming. "Yes. It is a

game of survival, and sometimes sticking to the same routines all the time lead animals to their deaths."

John came out of his thoughts with a start. He was leading these people along the same kind of trail. John stopped walking as a thought struck him: *If the creature was able to climb the elevator shaft, it could be waiting in a tunnel ahead of or above them, ready to pounce upon its prey: the group of people he now led.*

The rest of the group stopped behind him.

Jim asked if he was OK.

Scratching behind his ear, John turned and said, "I am, but I just thought of something. If the Vorgroth can climb the elevator shaft, then it could be quietly waiting up ahead for us. When I was a boy, my grandmother taught me how predators often hunt by lying in wait by an animal trail, ready to kill unsuspecting prey. We need to think of a way to outsmart the Vorgroth instead of walking into its trap."

Tammy stepped forward. "What if we find another way up, kinda like how we got to this level?"

Carl nodded immediately. "Tammy is right. I vote we go back and try and find another way up."

Ethan and Larry stayed quiet, though they were nodding.

It was Andy who cleared his throat to get everyone's attention. He looked unsure of himself when all eyes turned to him. "Um, what if we like, try to lure it back down to the level below us. Then we can continue upward."

Carl snorted. "Yeah, sure. Why don't we just throw a stick and say, 'Go get it, boy!'"

Andy surprised everyone when he said, "That is almost exactly what I mean."

Carl rolled his eyes, but John knew Andy was smart, so he stepped close to the boy and asked, "Can you explain what you have in mind?"

Andy nodded as he slid his backpack to the floor and opened it. He rooted around for a second, then pulled out his Nintendo Switch and held it up to show the group.

Carl laughed contemptuously. "You are going to give it your video game to keep it busy?"

Jim scowled at Carl. "Would you just shut up? That boy has more sense than you do. Maybe you could learn something from him."

Carl's eyes flashed angrily. He stepped forward, his fists clenched at his sides.

John stepped between them and hissed. "Cut it out. Both of you. For all we know that creature can hear us right now."

Andy nodded, his eyes showing his excitement as he whispered, "Exactly! I will go back to where Mr. Milton is, climb back down to the previous level, and go about halfway into the cavern." He held up the Switch. "I will turn this on with the volume at its highest level, then start the Super Mario game and put it on the floor. I will run back up here, and we can hide until the monster passes us by. Once it does, we can get out of this mine as fast as we can." He looked at everyone, his eyes shining with excitement. "Easy as can be!"

Ethan and Larry immediately shook their heads. "No way. You are not doing that, Andy. It's too dangerous."

Andy was about to protest, but John raised his voice a little, "This is an excellent plan, Andy. But your dads are right. We can't let you do this." He put his hands on Andy's shoulders and kindly said, "I know you *could* do it. Probably better than any of us. But I am responsible for everyone here. I will do it."

Carl saw the look of adoration on Tammy's face as she looked at John, so he stepped forward. "No, I will do it. You need someone young who can move fast. I can scale that ladder in thirty seconds. It would take you a couple of minutes at least, John. By then, the monster could already be on you, and we will all be dead."

John was about to disagree, but he realized that Carl was right. He was the youngest and fittest one here, aside from Andy. "Alright, Carl. Thank you for being so brave."

Carl stood straighter when Tammy glanced at him and smiled. Then, Tammy stepped next to Carl and said, "I will go with Carl and wait for him at the top of the ladder with a light. I used to run Track in high school. I am fast in case we need to run."

John nodded kindly. "Thank you, both. The rest of us will hide in the mining cavern. You two get back as fast as you can. If the Vorgroth is above us right now, it will hopefully go directly to the Nintendo, which should give us enough time to get up to the next level. The distraction might confuse the creature long enough for us to get a good lead on it."

Then Ethan asked the question John had hoped no one would ask. "Even if we do slip past it and get up to Level twenty-seven, won't that thing just double back and catch us on a higher level?"

John didn't really have an answer for that. "All we can do is keep trying to get topside as quickly as we can. We have no other choice."

Everyone was silent for a few moments, then Carl held out his hand to Andy. "Give me the game system. I want to get this over with."

Andy set up the game and pointed to the volume button. "Crank up the volume with this button, and when you set it down, press Play."

Carl took the Nintendo Switch.

They all backtracked to the opening in the wall that led to the grotto.

John pointed, "The cavern is only a few feet further. We will be just inside the cavern to the right."

Carl and Tammy nodded, then entered the narrow opening and disappeared from view.

John led the rest of the group into the cavern, where they found a pile of tailings large enough to hide behind.

He hoped Carl and Tammy would be safe. He hoped they all would be.

CHAPTER 34

MORGAN exited the elevator shaft into the tunnel on Level twenty-nine.

Bauwen stepped free from her and moved away to give her room to remove the MAD. As they ascended the shaft, they noticed the gates for each level were closed except for Level twenty-seven, indicating the second team had entered there. Morgan had directed her team to drop down to Level twenty-nine so they could catch up to the civilians from behind.

Jack and Karen were a few paces away, crouched on one knee, rifles pointed down the tunnel.

Bauwen sniffed the air and pointed. "The tourist group has been in this tunnel."

Morgan whispered, "Ok, before we move out, I need to check in with headquarters." She slid her pack to the floor and removed the MATCOM device. Morgan put in the ear bud and switched on the machine. "Saint Bernard to base…do you copy?" Morgan waited a few seconds, then said again, "Saint Bernard to base…do you copy?"

After a minute, she began to give her report, though she was unsure if it was being received. "Saint Bernard to base. We are not receiving you. We are on Level twenty-nine. We found the two missing teams. They were killed by a creature called the Vorgroth. It came up to the mine from far below the surface. The creature is indestructible. I repeat: indestructible. We have also made contact with another human-based lifeform from far below the mine who is a friendly. Her name is Bauwen. I repeat: She is a friendly. There are also two potentially hostile teams down here. I repeat: At least two potentially hostile teams are in the mine, with one more team likely topside. There was a power outage, so the elevator does not work. There was also a partial cave-in due to blasting at Onamuni mine. We will continue searching for the tourists and mine employees and make our way topside via the ladder systems between levels. We will initiate contact in two hours if we can. Saint Bernard, out."

Morgan waited two minutes but did not receive a reply, so she packed the MATCOM away and slid her pack over her back. "I do not know if our message reached base. We must proceed as if we are on our own. Let's move out. Karen, you have point. Jack, you have our six."

Bauwen whispered, "I should go first. I will smell the other humans and the Vorgroth before you will ever see them. I can also see better than you, even with your special seeing devices."

Morgan didn't argue. One thing the SEALs never did was ignore an option that could assist in the completion of a mission. "Alright. Karen will be right behind you. Jack and I have the rear."

Without another word, Bauwen melted into the

darkness, and they followed her.

This tunnel was wider than the other tunnels had been, the rails for the ore carts barely rusted and gleaming as if they were still well-used.

The team made their way silently through the darkness, the night vision allowing them to move quickly. Within a few minutes they came to a partial collapse of the tunnel, but they had enough room to get past it. Then they came to the egress point leading down to Level thirty. It had been buried under rocks.

Morgan looked around, then asked, "Karen, what happened here?"

Karen stepped forward and surveyed the scene for about fifteen seconds before turning to face them. "There is no evidence of blasting. Nor is there evidence of a widespread natural cave in. The tourist group most likely collapsed the ceiling to block access from below. Probably to stop the Vorgroth from coming up. It seems there are some people in the group who know what they are doing down here, which means they might be able to stay alive until we can reach them."

Morgan half smiled. This was good news, indeed. She turned to Bauwen. "Did the tourists move forward from here?"

The woman motioned down the tunnel. "The tourists went this way a short time ago."

"Any signs of the other team or the Vorgroth?"

Bauwen shook her head. "No, they have not set foot in this tunnel."

"Good. Let's move, and fast."

They set off at a quicker run than before.

Morgan was surprised by how quickly she had been able to put her trust in the strange woman from an even stranger world, whom they had just met.

Normally, Morgan would not trust anyone but her team. But in this case, she somehow innately trusted Bauwen.

The tunnel constantly shifted direction. Apparently, the iron veins that the miners followed didn't run in a straight line. Under normal circumstances, Morgan's team would slow down and carefully approach each turn in case an enemy was lying in wait. But Bauwen never slowed down, and time was short. So, they ran until they reached the entrance to the mining cavern.

Jack removed a laser device. He pointed it across the cavern, the narrow green beam disappearing into the darkness. He looked up and said, "One thousand and fifty meters across."

Bauwen knelt and touched the floor with a finger, then studied the area a few meters ahead before turning her head and whispering, "They went right across the middle, but I no longer see them in this cavern. I wonder...," her voice trailed off and she seemed lost in thought.

Jack cursed under his breath, and Karen followed suit.

"Bauwen, do you sense the Vorgroth or any other humans here?"

Bauwen seemed startled from her thoughts by Morgan's question, and said, "What? Oh. No. Only the tourist group have been here."

Morgan looked around with her night vision, seeing no one. "Could there be a hidden way out of this cavern?"

Bauwen nodded. "Possibly. I was just thinking about this. When I first arrived in this mine, I secretly observed three miners named Milton, Otto, and Franc who often spent time in a small grotto in the level just above this one. I remembered seeing a ladder leading down from that space, but I never explored it back then. It must have led down to this level though. We can follow the tourists to see if they found it."

They set off, moving slower now in the cavern because of all the loose rocks scattered about, making the route treacherous. They were halfway across when Bauwen stopped and whispered, "I hear someone ahead."

They all lowered down into a crouch and slowly moved forward. They were approaching the far wall when Bauwen pointed to their left.

Morgan turned and saw a young man exit a crack in the rock. He held a cell phone up high, its weak flashlight only showing a few feet of illuminated ground. Since he was unarmed and wore jeans and a somewhat tattered jacket, Morgan assumed he must be one of the tourists or tour employees. But why was he coming back here alone?

Morgan motioned and her team moved forward even more slowly, completely silent, until they were thirty feet in front of the man.

Morgan could now see his face. He was the elevator operator, Carl, and he seemed terrified, constantly looking all around him as he made his way forward. He carried a small device in his right hand that she couldn't identify. He held the cellphone high in the air with his left hand.

Carl suddenly stopped and quickly knelt to place the device on the ground.

Morgan couldn't tell if he had an explosive device, and she didn't want to be here if he set it off. She crept forward until she was only ten feet away from Carl, raised her night vision scope to avoid being blinded by the cellphone light, and asked,

"What are you doing, Carl?"

Carl screamed and jumped up, spinning around in a crouch, his eyes wide in terror.

Morgan stepped into his ring of light and put her hand up. "I mean you no harm."

Carl looked ready to bolt, but her words seemed to sink into his mind enough for him to ask in a tremulous voice, "Who are you?"

"We are a rescue team, and we are here to help."

At these words, Carl seemed to relax a bit. He nodded. "I remember you and two others came down in the elevator with the final tour group."

Morgan smiled and stepped forward, extending her hand. "My name is Morgan, and these are my teammates."

Jack and Karen stepped forward into the light. Bauwen stayed back, just out of sight.

Morgan quietly asked, "Are you with the tour group?"

He nodded, then grew agitated, as if remembering why he was there, and held out his hand. "They are waiting for me to plant this and meet them up on the next level."

Morgan glanced down and saw he was holding a video game device. "What are you planning to do with that?"

"I am going to turn it on at max volume. There is a monster somewhere around here." He looked embarrassed when he said '*monster*,' but continued in a rush, "We think it might be on the level above us and didn't want to walk right into it, so we thought we could use this game system to lure it down here so we can get past it up to the next level." His face colored slightly. "I know you probably think I'm lying, but there really is a monster in this mine."

"Don't worry, we believe you. How do you get up to the next level from here? Is there a secret way in that opening in the wall back there?"

Carl looked over his shoulder but of course, all he could see was blackness. He turned back and nodded. "There is a small chamber back there, with a ladder leading up to the next level." He looked at the night vision scope covering her right eye. "That's night vision, isn't it? Can you see everything down here?"

Morgan nodded. "We can. Why don't you show us the way up? Karen here will stay back and turn on the video game after we all climb to the next level, then she'll join us. Sound good?"

Carl glanced nervously over at Karen. He quickly nodded and handed her the game device. He seemed to be glad he was no longer required to do the job anymore. He pointed at a series of buttons, "Press this to power it on. Press this to turn the volume way up. And press 'Play' when the game is ready."

Karen distastefully took the Switch, then arched a questioning eyebrow at Morgan.

Morgan nodded to Karen, then turned back to Carl. "Please turn off your light so we can use our night vision. We don't want to make ourselves visible if the Vorgroth is already down here."

Carl glanced quickly into the darkness of the cavern at the mention of the Vorgroth.

Touching Carl's shoulder, Morgan said, "Don't worry, we can see everything with our night vision. You will be safe."

Carl gulped, then turned the phone's flashlight off with a shaky finger. He whimpered in the sudden darkness.

Morgan powered her night vision back on and whispered. "Carl, you are fine. I am right here. I am reaching out to take your hand, okay?"

Carl nodded, so she reached out and grasped his hand.

Carl flinched when she touched him, then quickly tightened his grip on her hand.

Bauwen had already made her way across the cavern and stood by the narrow crack in the wall.

"Alright, Carl. I am going to lead you. I won't let you step on any rocks or bump into anything." She turned to Jack and Karen. "Jack, follow me. Karen, wait here and be ready to turn on the gaming device when Jack gives you the signal."

Karen nodded.

The three of them moved slowly, and Morgan thought of just carrying Carl, but she decided against it, not wanting to tire herself out unnecessarily. They made their way to the fissure in the wall one careful step at a tim. "Alright, Carl. We are here. Can you turn on the phone's flashlight again?"

He nodded vigorously.

Morgan and Jack turned off their night vision just as Carl turned on the phone, illuminating the opening in front of them.

Carl sighed in relief when he could see again. He pointed, "It's only a little way to the room inside."

Morgan turned to Jack and said, "Wait on the outside of this entrance and in two minutes, motion to Karen to start the music. Wait here for her so she knows exactly where to go. She will be moving fast. Then climb up to the next level as quickly as possible. We likely won't have much time before the Vorgroth comes to investigate."

Jack gave a curt nod of agreement.

Morgan turned to Carl. "Where are you supposed to go now?"

Carl pointed up the ladder. "Tammy is waiting for me up there. There is a small room with an opening to the main tunnel. Once in the tunnel, there is a large cavern not far to the left. Everyone else is waiting there for us to return."

Morgan turned to Jack. "Got that?"

Jack nodded and looked at his watch. "Two minutes, starting now."

Carl held the light up and led Morgan through the opening until they stepped into a room. There, Bauwen stood at the base of a wooden ladder and shielded her eyes from the light.

Worried, Morgan asked, "Bauwen, are you in pain? Does the light hurt you?"

"No, I am fine. It will just take me a few moments to adjust."

Carl gasped when he saw Bauwen in the light, his eyes growing wide at seeing her naked body and her strange skin. "Who is she?"

Morgan introduced them, finishing with, "She is from the same place the Vorgroth is from. They are mortal enemies."

At this, Carl relaxed, though he still didn't take his eyes from Bauwen, completely transfixed.

A voice called down from the opening in the ceiling. "Carl? Are you OK?"

Morgan glanced upward, then at Carl. She quietly asked, "Tammy?"

Carl nodded. "She is one of the tour guides."

Morgan had read the Deepstone tour employee files and remembered the young woman from the elevator. "Go ahead and climb up. Stay quiet, though."

Carl didn't need any more urging. He grabbed the first rung of the ladder and quickly climbed up.

"Bauwen, you go next," Morgan said. "I will follow you."

Bauwen scaled the ladder as if she were unaffected by gravity.

Morgan started up after her and got halfway when she heard the familiar song of Super Mario Bros start playing in the distance, incredibly loud in the cavern. She continued climbing, carefully moving past a broken rung with blood on it, and as she reached the top, she felt the ladder twitch, indicating Jack and Karen were already climbing below her.

Morgan pulled herself up into a small grotto. Tammy stood holding Carl's hand, her eyes frightened. His whole demeanor had changed now that he was with her. He was obviously trying to project confidence and strength.

Bauwen was off to the side, kneeling next to an old man who lay on the stone.

Morgan stepped closer and started slightly when she realized it was Milton from the tourist group.

Bauwen looked up and whispered, "This is Milton. He is the one who trapped the Vorgroth all those years ago. He was such a young man back then. How can he be this old after just 63 years?"

Morgan got down on one knee. "Humans age quickly, Bauwen. But we must go, now."

Bauwen leaned forward and kissed the old man's forehead. When she stood up, Morgan was surprised to see tears in Bauwen's eyes.

Morgan stood, as well, and when she did, she noticed Tammy staring at Bauwen, her eyes as wide as Carl's.

Then Jack rose up through the opening, followed immediately by Karen.

"Carl, Tammy, lead us to the others. Quickly."

Tammy started as if she'd been electrocuted, then turned away from Bauwen.

Carl led the way, holding Tammy's hand, and they soon entered a tunnel. They turned left and within a few steps were inside a cavern.

A voice hissed out of the darkness, "Over here. Turn off that light. We don't know when the Vorgroth will arrive."

Carl and Tammy turned off their lights and Morgan immediately switched her night vision on. She saw John Lukkinen, the tour guide, standing next to a pile of old tailings about ten feet away, whispering for her group to follow his voice. She had seen his military record. A decorated US Army Special Forces recon specialist. He had done three tours in Iraq and Afghanistan. The tourists couldn't have had a better person leading them through these tunnels.

Morgan motioned for Jack and Karen to hang back and keep an eye down the tunnel for the Vorgroth's approach. Then she followed Carl and Tammy until they reached the rest of the group, who were hiding behind the pile of rocks. Morgan counted only eight people, including John, Carl and Tammy. When she and her team had come down into the mine, there had been seven tourists. She was surprised to see the mechanic, Jim, here as well. That meant that along with Milton, the young adventure couple had not made it this far, either. She would ask John about them when things were safer for them all.

The civilians all stood in the dark, waiting for the Vorgroth to arrive, their faces masked in terror and anxiety. She couldn't imagine the fear they must be feeling as they stood in the pitch dark, unable to see anything.

Morgan thought of the Vorgroth and her own fear rose. She had no idea if this plan would work, but all of their lives depended on it, so Morgan took a deep breath and let it slowly out. Feeling her heart beat slowing down, Morgan lifted her rifle a little higher, ready for whatever happened next.

CHAPTER 35

HENRY SKUGGS, CEO of SafeWell, removed his earpiece and dropped it onto his desk, then switched off the MATCOM device. He had just listened to Morgan's latest report. He had been able to receive her transmission, even though she could not hear him respond.

He picked up the cigar from the ashtray on his desk and put it between his lips. It had gone out, but he didn't bother to relight it as he digested the SITREP that Morgan had just sent. She had reported making contact with a friendly being named Bauwen who was from a world deep below the mine. It was incredible, if it was true. What that discovery could mean for scientific knowledge was beyond priceless. But she had also mentioned an indestructible creature called a Vorgroth who was hunting them all, apparently also from the world below the mine. And there were three other military teams in the mine as well. Something big was happening. Skuggs bet that Senator Young, who had asked for a SafeWell team to be sent down into Deepstone in the first place, knew more than he was letting on. Skuggs did not trust any politicians, and his history with Senator Young caused him to trust him even less.

First things first. Skuggs picked up his secure desk phone and pressed *7.

His assistant answered immediately. "Yes, sir?"

"Get McBride in my office right now. And I mean *now*."

"Yes, sir."

Skuggs only had to wait thirty seconds before he heard a hard rap on his door. "Enter," he said with a gravelly voice.

McBride, a large man with red hair and a crooked nose, pushed the door open and strode forward, coming to a stop in front of Skuggs' desk.

McBride was the SafeWell fixer. He had contacts with almost every law enforcement agency in the world and could get things done that no one else could.

Skuggs didn't waste time with pleasantries. "Our team is in trouble on the Deepstone mission." He gave a quick recap of Morgan's last transmission, omitting the mention of Bauwen and the Vorgroth. "Call up the sheriff's office in Virginia, Minnesota; they are the closest available law enforcement to the mine. Tell them to get a large contingent of law enforcement out to Deepstone now. Then, contact your source in the FBI and tell them what is happening. I also need you to find out who is behind the Deepstone incursion. My bet is on Thornlandon Holdings. I have heard rumblings they may have an interest in Deepstone. Now, go."

McBride nodded, not saying a word, and left the office in a measured hurry.

Skuggs called his assistant again. "Get me Senator Ronald Young on the line."

"Yes sir. One moment."

Skuggs and Senator Young had known each other for two decades, well before Senator Young had become a senator and Skuggs had formed SafeWell. Both of their families were wealthy and traveled in the same circles. Skuggs and Senator Young had, at one time, been good friends. But, until this week, when Senator Young had come to SafeWell for help, they had not spoken in at least a decade.

Within a minute, a light blinked on Skuggs' phone. He pressed the button and said, "Ronald, you have some explaining to do."

The smooth-as-butter voice of Senator Young on the other end said, "Why Skuggs, how good to hear from you. I take it you have some news about the two teams in Deepstone?"

"What I have is a total clusterfuck, Ronald."

"Oh? And why is that?"

"My SafeWell team found your two missing teams. They have been slaughtered." When the senator didn't respond, Skuggs continued, "There was a power outage at the mine and a possible collapse of some tunnels. My team is trapped down there and now face a number of hostile teams who were also sent into the mine, most likely to eliminate them and the civilians who also happen to be trapped."

Senator Young inhaled sharply at the report.

Skuggs almost smiled. "I take it you had no idea about that?"

Senator Young calmly said, "Skuggs, I assure you. I have no knowledge of these teams being sent in. And let's not be too hasty about saying there is structural damage to the mine."

"Who are you working for, Ronald? Is it Thornlandon Holdings? They are some bad people. Murderers, thieves, and worse."

"Skuggs, I like what SafeWell represents. You and your company have done some fine work protecting people. But if you accuse me of something, you better be able to back it up with facts."

Skuggs smiled. The senator might as well have come out and said he was involved with whomever sent the teams in, even if he had no direct knowledge of the teams themselves. "Senator, I am sure you are innocent in all of this. Frankly, I don't care. All I want is to keep my team and those civilians safe. You hired my company to investigate the two missing teams in Deepstone. That means you must have an interest in the mine. And the fact that someone sent additional military teams into the mine means that you may not, strictly speaking, be in the inner circle of what is happening down there."

Senator Young sighed, feigning boredom. "What are you trying to say, Skuggs? I don't have all day."

"I suggest you make some calls to find out what's going on. The shit is hitting the proverbial fan at Deepstone, and I know you would prefer not to be implicated if this becomes public. So, any help you can provide would be appreciated." Skuggs knew that the senator was smart and canny, which was confirmed a moment later when Senator Young took the bait Skuggs had laid out for him.

"I will be in touch shortly, Skuggs." Senator Young ended the call before Skuggs could respond.

Skuggs tossed his phone onto his desk and sat back in his chair, thinking about the situation. He pressed the Enter key on his laptop and replayed both of Morgan's transmissions. Then Skuggs picked up his phone again and made a call to his Director of operations. It was time for him to go to Minnesota.

CHAPTER 36

SENATOR RONALD YOUNG ended the call with Henry Skuggs and set his phone down. He had been careful not to incriminate himself in any way, but he knew Skuggs was no dummy.

Senator Young had tried calling Director Meyers and Helen Polson several times over the past week but had been unable to get through to either of them. After his initial discussion with Director Meyers regarding Deepstone two months ago, he was appointed as a silent board member of Thornlandon Holdings. As such, he received regular updates on the project.

Until recently.

Senator Young had clandestinely purchased over $77 million in stock in Thornlandon Holdings over the past two months. He was already worth more than $6 billion but, like all billionaires, he wanted even more money. Once news of the multi-trillion-dollar discovery beneath Deepstone became public knowledge, Thornlandon Holdings' stock would likely increase twenty-fold—or more. Senator Young's investment could be worth as much as 2 billion dollars.

Since the status reports from Director Meyers had all but stopped, Senator Young had provided a three-million-dollar payment in Bitcoin to Spencer Radcliffe, an old friend from his Harvard days, to hack Director Meyers' and Helen Polson's phones. Spencer, Harvard educated and brilliant, was one of the best dark-web hackers in the world. Senator Young and Spencer had used each other's services many times over the past two decades. He paid Spencer a retainer worth a small fortune to dig up information on political opponents, and Spencer used Senator Young to keep investigations far away from his hacking activities.

It had taken Spencer almost a week to crack Thornlandon Holding's security. But as of last night, Senator Young had access to both Director Meyers' and Helen Polson's phones. Always thorough, Spencer hadn't just hacked their phone calls. He had hacked their phone's microphones, as well, which allowed Senator Young to listen to their conversations whether the phones were on or not. The technology was already used by the largest online and social media corporations to tailor ads to users based on keywords picked up while actively listening to conversations through the phone's microphone. When Senator Young expressed concern to Spencer about this tactic, Spencer told him that using the technology for tailored ads was only the tip of the iceberg. If Senator Young really knew what the companies were doing with such technology and data, he would throw his phone away and never use another again. Senator Young took this under advisement and vowed to be careful with what he said when near his phone in the future.

What Senator Young had heard Director Meyers and Helen discussing early this morning turned him cold. While Senator Young didn't mind bending the rules to get his way in the Senate or in his business dealings, he had never crossed the line into murder. And he didn't intend to start now.

Spencer had performed a full background check on Renn Holder, the leader of the Thornlandon Holdings paramilitary team dispatched to Deepstone. By all accounts, Renn Holder was an honest, honorable man. Based on that report, Senator Young had asked Spencer to send an encrypted text to Renn this morning to provide full details about the Deepstone situation. With the SafeWell team in Deepstone, and the information he had provided him, Senator Young hoped Renn might disobey Director Meyers' kill order.

It was time for Senator Young to get out of this mess, so he dialed the personal number of Kelly Chan at his investment firm.

Her soft voice filled his phone, "Yes, Senator? What can I do for you?"

"Kelly. I want you to immediately sell all of my stock in Thornlandon Holdings. And sell my stock in Meta, Google, Apple, and Amazon as well."

"Yes sir. It may take a few days to complete transactions of this size, but it will be done."

"Thank you. I don't care if I take a loss. Do you understand? Time is of the essence."

"Understood, sir."

Senator Young understood the stock market enough to know that Kelly Chan would call her contacts and offer to sell for less than market share if it came to it. This was common when trying to quickly dump a large amount of shares. She just had to be sure they wouldn't run afoul of insider trading laws. Senator Young was selling his stock in Meta, Google, Apple, and Amazon to hopefully avoid this. No matter what happened to Thornlandon Holdings stock, his involvement would not be questioned.

Senator Young opened his wall safe and removed a large binder. It contained all of the intel Spencer had collected on Thornlandon Holdings over the past few months, including the data he had unearthed about Deepstone. This data is what had prompted Senator Young to approach Director Meyers in the first place. He had seen an opportunity to make billions, and he had taken it. Now Senator Young not only wanted out, he also wanted to bring to light what Director Meyers and Helen were doing in Deepstone. Senator Young couldn't do anything personally, since he had signed a Non-Disclosure Agreement with Thornlandon Holdings upon joining their board. But his friend Skuggs at SafeWell had deep contacts in the government and would know what to do with the information he and Spencer had gathered. Senator Young had printed multiple copies of all the information he had received, to create a literal paper trail leading to Thornlandon Holdings.

Senator Young wrote a short note to Skuggs but didn't sign it before slipping it into the binder. Then he buzzed his assistant, Don, who was still working even though it was so late at night.

The voice immediately answered, "Yes, sir?"

"Get me a FedEx box." His assistant immediately knocked on his door and entered, handing Senator Young a box. "Thank you, Don. Please wait."

Senator Young put the binder in the FedEx box,

sealed and addressed it to SafeWell headquarters, then handed it to Don. "Please go down to a FedEx facility in person tomorrow morning and mail this for same day delivery. Take a few other packages to mail, I don't care what they are. Just make it look like you are performing your normal duties."

"Of course, sir." Don had been with Senator Young for almost ten years and never asked questions. He took the package and left the office.

Senator Young dialed Skuggs' number. His old friend answered on the first ring.

"Skuggs. I sent you your birthday card. You should get it tomorrow. Sorry it is late."

Skuggs' voice didn't skip a beat as he replied, "Thank you, Ronald. You are a good friend. Talk soon."

The call ended and Senator Young stared at the screen for a moment, then put his phone down.

What happened now was out of his hands.

CHAPTER 37

SALLY backed down the passage of Level twenty-seven, eyes sharply focused, weapon raised with the safety off.

Karl mirrored her movements to her left, his eyes peering down the tunnel, gun held steady and level.

She and Karl were the only two people remaining on her team. Jillian, Charlie, Johan, and Jason had all been killed by the Vorgroth as if it was a human stepping on ants. These were four good people whom she had called friends. Now they would never see the light of day again. Sally pushed her grief aside and concentrated on surviving. There would be time enough later to grieve.

They had found the alcove with the ladder leading down to Level twenty-eight. If the tourists were still alive, they would have to come up this way.

Sally's team had heard no sign of the Vorgroth's pursuit since they entered the tunnel on this level. It may be able to climb the elevator shaft, but Sally didn't think this was likely.

This whole mission was a clusterfuck. They had been sent down here to kill the tourists and the SafeWell team. The fact that they were trying to save everyone felt like the right thing to do. Sally was under no illusions regarding who she worked for and what Thornlandon Holdings was willing to do for money, especially with trillions of dollars on the line. The problem was, even if they were able to get the tourists and SafeWell team safely out of the mine, what then? Thornlandon Holdings would know they were still alive when they didn't find their bodies in the mine—Sally knew they would send a reconnaissance team to confirm this. When it was clear the tourists had survived, they would be silenced, one at a time. The SafeWell team, and probably the whole SafeWell company, would be eliminated, as well.

Sally also didn't harbor any doubts that Thornlandon Holdings would eliminate their own team, as well—her, Renn, and all the other team members would disappear.

As if things hadn't been fucked up enough, now they were fighting a monster they couldn't kill.

They were in a no-win situation. If the Vorgroth didn't kill them all, then Thornlandon Holdings would. It would only take a day or two, a week at most. But Sally knew with unfailing certainty they would all meet their end from a blade flashing out in the dark or an untraceable bullet to the back of the head. They could not run anywhere that would be out of the reach of Thornlandon Holdings.

Sally would rather die on her own terms, with a gun in her hands and a full magazine of bullets. Even if they were useless against the Vorgroth, she intended to go down fighting, like a warrior.

Karl suddenly turned his head to look down the tunnel behind them.

Sally felt the hair on her arms rise. Karl was like a goddamned bloodhound. He could sense danger before anyone else. She turned to follow his gaze, whispering softly, "What is it?"

He stared as if not hearing her.

She waited, then asked again, "Karl. What do you hear?"

The man whispered from the corner of his mouth, his Russian accent thick and guttural, "It comes."

Sally turned and motioned to the hatch and urgently whispered. "Get down to Level twenty-eight. Now!"

Karl lifted the hatch, causing a metallic screech. In mere seconds, they heard a roar from down the tunnel, followed by the ground shaking as the Vorgroth started to run toward them.

Karl slid down the ladder, not even bothering to use the rungs.

Sally climbed down three rungs and pulled the hatch closed over her before sliding to the ground. They ran down the tunnel toward the elevator shaft. Behind them, Sally heard the hatch being torn from its hinges. The ladder groaned from the weight of the Vorgroth as it descended. Sally had no idea how it could fit through the hole. Maybe it could reform its body somehow? There was no doubt that it made it through and was coming for them.

Sally's mind worked quickly, and an idea came to her; one that might give them a way out of this whole mess. The Vorgroth was the key. If she could get topside and make a call to Thornlandon Holdings to give a SITREP about the Vorgroth, she could say it killed everyone in Deepstone. Then, just maybe, they could get everyone out of the mine and hidden safely away until they could blow the lid on what exactly Thornlandon Holdings was doing down in Deepstone.

It was the only option they had.

But first, they had to reach the elevator, put on their MADs, and get topside before the Vorgroth could kill them.

Sally and Karl reached the elevator shaft and immediately started strapping into their MADs. The Vorgroth was not far away and charging fast.

They were not going to make it.

Sally felt death coming toward her. She was determined not to die at the hands of the Vorgroth. She decided to empty her magazines, backing up as she fired, and then step into the shaft at the final moment and fall to her death. She would die on her own terms.

The Vorgroth rounded the final turn in the tunnel and roared as it entered the small room where they stood. Karl and Sally immediately opened fire, emptying their magazines in a couple seconds, then reloading over and over again.

The bullets bounced off the Vorgroth, not harming it in the slightest. The Vorgroth slowed down to a walk as it approached its prey, confident in its upcoming kill. Its mirrored eyes reflected soullessly in the night vision as it glared at them.

Sally stepped back, firing until her fourth magazine clicked empty. She pulled it out, dropped it, and slapped another in. She sensed she was only a couple steps from the open shaft.

Then, the Vorgroth stopped and cocked its head slightly, as if listening to something. It inhaled deeply, lifting its nose up as it did. Its eyes dilated, then it turned and charged back into the tunnel. as if Sally's team didn't even exist.

They stopped firing, their hot rifle barrels glowing in their night vision.

Karl looked at Sally, an eyebrow raised as he whispered, "What the hell just happened? I thought we were dead!"

All Sally could do was shrug. She was too full of adrenaline to form any words.

Karl slid his rifle over his shoulder and continued strapping into the MAD, ignoring the hissing and smoke rising from his back where the hot gun barrel was burning through his outer layers of clothing, right down to his Kevlar vest.

Sally also strapped into her MAD.

They both ascended to the next level. Karl started to slow down when Sally called up, "Keep going to the surface! I need to call Thornlandon Holdings. I have a plan."

Karl nodded and continued upward.

Sally didn't look forward to calling Helen Polson or Director Meyers, but she had no choice. It was a gamble, but would be worth it if it helped them get out of this mess alive.

At the top of the shaft, Sally climbed onto the floor of the elevator building and stepped outside. She inhaled deeply. Fresh air had never smelled so good.

Sally took out her cellphone and powered it on. She had kept it powered off while in the mine to save the battery. It would not have received a signal that far underground, anyway. She dialed the director's number from memory; she didn't save any numbers in her phone, even though it was encrypted.

Helen answered on the first ring, "Yes?"

"This is Sally from Renn's team."

"Is it done?"

Sally hesitated only a fraction of a second, just enough to cause Helen to sigh and ask, "What happened?"

Sally gave her report in concise details, telling Helen about the Vorgroth and how it had killed most of her team. She hesitated a second, then said, "The Vorgroth has killed all of the mine employees and tourists who were trapped below." She finished by saying she didn't know the status of Renn's team, but that the Vorgroth had gone down deeper into the mine after Sally and Karl had escaped topside, she assumed to hunt Renn and his team.

Helen put her on hold for over a minute, then came back on. "We are sending ten more teams, equipped with every weapon we have short of explosives. The teams will arrive in three hours. Until then, take Team Three back down with you to assist Renn and his team."

The line went dead.

Sally grimly powered her phone back down. Helen had not even bothered to question her about the Vorgroth; it was as if she had already known about it. By ordering Sally's team back into the mine, Helen was obviously planning for them to all be killed by the creature. Sally had no idea if Helen believed her about the civilians being killed, which meant they still had a chance to escape. If they could, the civilians may have the time they needed to go to the FBI and tell their stories. Three hours wasn't long. But it might be just enough time to get back underground and get everyone out of the mine.

If they could avoid the Vorgroth, that is.

Sally activated her comms now that she was topside. "Team Three. Copy." When each team member had confirmed, Sally provided a SITREP of what had happened below. To everyone's credit, no one wasted time asking questions. Sally finished by saying, "Monique, you'll remain topside. Ten more teams from Thornlandon Holdings have been dispatched to this location. They will arrive in three hours. Our plan is to get everyone out of here before those teams arrive. Until then, keep the site secure. If we do not return before they arrive, I want you to disappear. The rest of you, assemble at the elevator right now."

Within two minutes, Gwen, Tess, and Terryl from Team One joined her and Karl by the elevator shaft. Terryl looked around and asked, "So you have no idea what happened to Renn and his team?"

"No. We have had no contact with Renn. Karl and I are all that is left of Team Two."

Terryl smirked. "You really expect me to believe some kind of monster killed everyone on your team?"

Before he could react, Karl stepped forward and put his face to Terryl's, their noses touching. "One more remark, and I will gut you."

Terryl leaned back and glanced down to see Karl's knife pressing into his stomach where the Kevlar vest had a gap.

Karl's Russian accent deepened as he snarled, "We emptied a thousand rounds into that fucker down there and it didn't even flinch. It tore everyone to pieces with its bare hands."

Terryl immediately held up his hands and said, "I shouldn't have questioned you two."

Karl glared at Terryl a moment longer before slipping his knife away back into the sheath.

Terryl grimly said, "I'm sorry, brother."

Sally stepped forward. "I'm not going to lie. We

will all likely die down there. But we have to try and rescue those people."

The four of them stood firm, their eyes not flinching at what she said. They would all die for their team, no questions asked.

Sally went into a full tactical description of the Vorgroth: how fast it moved, how strong it was, which weapons and ammunition types they had tried against it, and the effects their weapons had on it. They needed a full picture of what they were facing.

When Sally finished, Terryl ejected the bullet from his sniper rifle and removed the magazine. He slid his pack from his back, reached into a side pocket, and removed a half-dozen magazines. He checked the loads of each, then held one of the magazines up and said, "These bullets are made from a Tungsten/Chromium/Iron/Uranium alloy, designed by the Weapons Division of Thornlandon Holdings. This bullet was created to penetrate steel plates up to three inches thick—specifically on armored vehicles. Let's see if that thing down below can withstand these."

Tess eyed the magazine and glanced up at Terryl with a questioning look.

Terryl nodded. "They are the same caliber as your rifle. You will have to load them into your own magazine, though, as our rifle magazines are not compatible."

Terryl handed Tess three of his magazines and she smiled as she accepted them.

Tess immediately emptied three of her magazines and refilled them with the special armor-piercing bullets. Tess slapped one of the magazines into her rifle with a loud snick and placed the other magazines into two of her now empty vest pockets.

Sally nodded, impressed. She had had no idea bullets like this existed. "Alright, strap into your MADs. We are going down to Level twenty-five. Our mission is to rescue the civilians. If we come up against the Vorgroth, we will try to escape. If we are unable to do so, fire everything you've got at it."

She stepped to the edge of the shaft, hooked onto the cable, then stepped over the side and descended into the darkness.

As she went down, Sally glanced up at the square of light at the top of the shaft.

It was probably the last time she would ever see sunlight again.

CHAPTER 38

JOHN kneeled on one knee in the absolute darkness of Level twenty-eight. It was terrifying to wait like this, without being able to see anything, yet knowing that the Vorgroth could be anywhere. Then he heard the music from the game start playing from far below them. While John was familiar with the Mario Bros song from the game, it sounded eerie in the pitch blackness, like it was coming from another world.

This was it. John would likely know within a matter of minutes whether or not their idea would work.

He soon saw a light approaching, so John stepped away from the rock pile and quietly called out, "Over here. Turn off that light and follow my voice. We don't know when the Vorgroth will arrive."

Carl and Tammy did as he said and soon stood next to him.

John whispered, "Good job, both of you."

As John said this, he sensed there were more people in the darkness than just Carl and Tammy. His grandmother had often taken him into the woods when there was no moon and taught him to learn to use senses other than sight to move around in the dark. He could sense, now, that there were at least three new people standing with Carl and Tammy, even though they made no sound. He also didn't feel any hostility coming from them. Only a sense of calm.

John spoke softly and evenly, "You may join us, friends."

He heard a soft chuckle, followed by Morgan's quiet voice saying, "We come in peace, John, and are here to help you."

The fact that they knew his name probably meant they were government special ops. They also, most likely, wore night vision and were studying him now. So, John smiled and whispered, "Please, step over here. We probably don't have much time before the Vorgroth comes."

John heard soft footfalls as the people stepped up next to him. Although they were likely wary and curious, no one reacted to the new people, though John heard Carl whisper, "I am the one who brought the people here. They are here to rescue us."

Jim shushed him. "Be quiet before you get us killed."

They waited in silence. John heard automatic gun fire erupt somewhere farther down the tunnel. It went on for a full two minutes and sounded like hundreds of rounds were being fired. Then silence filled the area.

John heard a woman whisper to Morgan, "It approaches now."

In the sudden silence, John heard a low, rhythmic rumble in the floor.

As the Vorgroth approached, the rumble turned to pounding and grew in volume. The Vorgroth soon passed right outside the cave entrance and entered the grotto.

John heard the creak of the ladder as it struggled with the weight of the creature. There was a loud splintering of wood, then a crash as more wood burst apart. The ladder must have broken under the weight of the Vorgroth. There were a couple of seconds of silence, then they heard the impact of the Vorgroth striking the ground sixty feet below.

John grinned despite the situation.

Bauwen's voice softly whispered, "It was not harmed from the fall. I can hear it running toward the music. Come, we must go now."

John called out softly. Turn on your cellphone lights. Move as quickly and quietly as you can."

Light filled the small space and John heard his group gasp when they saw the newcomers. Then John saw Bauwen, her skin pulsing with color and shapes. Without thinking, he asked, "You are the one who saved Milton all those years ago, aren't you?"

Bauwen cocked her head to the side as she studied him, then she nodded. "Yes, it was my honor to help them back then. My name is Bauwen."

Morgan motioned urgently. "We must go now."

Jack motioned them forward, whispering, "That's Karen; follow her. Groups of two, side-by-side. Quickly now."

They were soon in the corridor, each trying to be quiet, though John still heard footsteps that were louder than he'd have liked them to be. Hopefully the loud music below would mask any sounds they made.

The group made it twenty feet down the tunnel when they heard a roar. Then the music stopped.

The group halted, afraid to move.

Morgan whispered calmly, "Keep going. Slower now, and quieter."

They moved down the tunnel and soon found themselves at the alcove with the ladder leading up to Level twenty-seven.

Jack scaled the ladder and quickly came back down, whispering, "The hatch has been torn away. Climb. Quickly. Be careful of the sharp metal at the top. As soon as the person in front of you is high enough, you start up right behind them. We don't have time to go one at a time."

Jack scaled the ladder again, followed by Claire, then Andy, Ethan, Larry, Tammy, Carl, and Jim.

Morgan motioned to John that it was his turn, so he climbed the ladder as quickly as he could. In the distance, he heard a faint roar of anger. Then he was through the hatch.

Morgan, Karen, and Bauwen quickly joined them.

Morgan motioned with an arm toward the tunnel to the right. "Follow Karen and Jack. Go single file—and quietly—to the next exit point."

They rushed down the tunnel to the next alcove. Jack was already up the ladder and opening the hatch before the last of the group arrived. They ascended to Level twenty-six without incident.

By the time they reached Level twenty-five, Claire and Ethan were panting heavily and moving much slower than they had been. Larry stopped and bent with hands on his knees, gasping.

John whispered to Morgan, "We need to take a short break."

Morgan looked like she was going to disagree but

nodded to John instead.

Karen and Jack went down the tunnel about twenty meters in opposite directions, weapons pointed forward. John knew this was standard procedure for soldiers. They always guarded ingress and egress routes while the other team members rested.

John turned to Bauwen and smiled. "Milton told us how you helped him to trap the Vorgroth."

Bauwen gave a small nod of acknowledgement. "I saw Milton laying in the …" She paused, as if searching for the right words, before continuing, "chamber, below. He has now joined Otto and Franc in the afterlife."

John smiled sadly. "Milton saved us all today by showing us the secret way up to Level twenty-eight. If it weren't for him, we would have all been killed by the Vorgroth."

At this, Bauwen closed her eyes for a few moments. When she opened them again, they glittered with fear and sorrow. "I only hope his sacrifice was enough. I sense the Vorgroth is close again."

A distant roar seemed to confirm this.

Morgan leaned down and put her ear to the closed hatch. She lifted her head and whispered, "It has broken through the hatch one level down. It will be here in minutes. We must leave now."

John nodded as he stood.

Larry struggled to his feet, his face pale.

John didn't know how much Andy's dad had left in his tank. But there was nothing they could do. They had to leave now if they had any hope of staying ahead of the Vorgroth.

Ethan put his arm around Larry's waist and

helped support him as they went.

Andy held his other side.

They half-ran for at least ten minutes before they came to the ladder leading up to Level twenty-four. This one wasn't situated in an alcove like the others. It just ran up the side of the tunnel wall and into a large opening cut into the stone ceiling eighteen feet up.

Larry collapsed to his knees, gasping for air. His face was sweaty and white.

Suddenly he gasped and fell to his side, his eyes closed in agony.

John leapt into action, suspecting right away that Larry was having a heart attack.

Larry cried out and arched his back, before falling back to the floor, where he remained still.

Ethan cried out as he fell to Larry's side, taking his hand.

Andy had tears in his eyes as he sank to Larry's other side. "Dad? Dad! Talk to me!"

John reached out and felt Larry's carotid artery.

Larry was gone.

CHAPTER 39

RENN knelt and examined Lucy's corpse on Level forty-two. A bullet had entered her forehead dead center. He didn't need to turn her over to know the entire back of her head would be missing. She had been shot by a long gun, and from the intel report he had read, the SafeWell team carried Heckler & Koch GxX rifles, weapons so advanced that none were even out in the wild yet. He had seen the specs, though. They were deadly and accurate.

Some of the team growled in anger at seeing Lucy's dead body. She had been feared by everyone on the team, and while they didn't like the idea that someone had been able to kill her, their respect for the SafeWell team begrudgingly went up a notch.

Renn motioned to Ficks. "Tell me what happened here."

Ficks studied the ground, then moved off into the cavern, bending low to the floor as he went. He soon returned and said, "A SafeWell operative stood about a hundred feet away. Two more operatives stayed further back. I also saw an indentation in dust that could have been a bare foot mark, though much smaller than the other ones we found."

"What does it all add up to?" Renn asked, though he already suspected what had happened.

The tracker spoke calmly, "One of the SafeWell operatives advanced within one hundred feet of Lucy and stood in the same position for some time. Her boot marks are deeper there than elsewhere. I suspect she approached Lucy to make contact, which we all know is one of the most dangerous maneuvers you can make in a potentially hostile situation. I found one empty casing further back in the cavern where the other two SafeWell operatives had waited. Since there is an empty casing next to Lucy's body, as well, I suspect she fired her weapon and one of the SafeWell operatives returned fire, killing her."

Renn nodded. He needed to diffuse any possible anger within the team at Lucy's death. While few here considered her a friend, they had all respected her as a teammate. "We all know Lucy. She was hot tempered and not one to parlay. I understand she was our teammate, but I believe the SafeWell team went above and beyond to avoid bloodshed. No one will take retribution against them when we make contact. Is that clear?"

Everyone nodded in agreement, though Paul still showed resentment and anger.

Renn continued, "Unfortunately, we will have to leave Lucy here. We cannot carry her out of the mine. Take her weapons and distribute her ammo."

It took the team only a minute to remove Lucy's ammunition from her pack and gather her weapons.

Renn took one final look at Lucy's corpse, then

reluctantly said, "Let's go."

The teams climbed up to Level forty-one and moved down the tunnel at a half-run. They continued like this up the next eight levels, moving quickly now that they understood the layout, yet exercising caution, knowing the SafeWell team could be lying in wait to ambush them at any turn.

They soon exited into the main tunnel system of Level thirty-two, right back where they had started.

Renn turned to his right and smelled the unmistakable after-effects of discharged weapons from the direction of the elevator shaft.

Ficks caught his eye and nodded, whispering, "Smells like there was a firefight by the elevator. Want to me investigate?"

Renn nodded, and Ficks took off at a run, soon disappearing around the bend in the tunnel. He returned in a few minutes, his face white.

"Report."

Ficks ran a finger along the scar on his chin and said, "Sills and Roberts of Team Three are dead, as is Jason from Team Two. But..."

"Spit it out, Ficks."

"They were...they were torn apart, sir."

Paul stepped forward, his eyes glittering. "You mean, just like the two teams on Level forty-three?"

Ficks nodded. "Yes. They didn't go down without a fight though. Especially Jason. He is surrounded by dozens of shotgun shells, with a trail of them leading *from* the elevator."

Paul smiled. "He walked toward the motherfucker while firing, didn't he?"

Ficks half-smiled. "It appears so."

Renn gruffly said, "Alright, let's follow the SafeWell team. Whatever happened by the elevator is out of our purview now. Move out."

Ficks interrupted, "Sir, the SafeWell team did not go to the ladder that leads up to the next level. I believe they used our MADs to go up the elevator shaft."

Renn swore. "Did they kill Sills and Roberts?"

"No sir. The creature killed them. The SafeWell team arrived here after the fact, just like us. There are five MADs missing. If the SafeWell team used three of them, that means only two members of Sally's team escaped up the elevator."

Renn felt his body tense up with shock as he thought, *All that is left of Team Two are two members?* Forcing his voice to remain calm, Renn said, "Let's get topside and link up with Team's Two and Three. We need intelligence."

They quickly returned to the elevator room and strapped into the remaining MADs. Renn took the lead, pulled himself through the hatch in the elevator ceiling, and attached his MAD to the cable. He ascended first, followed by the rest of his team. He had risen 500 meters when he saw movement above him. He slowed down and then braked to a stop, pulling his handgun from his holster and pointing it upward. His team almost bumped into him, only stopping at the last moment.

Five people descended quickly from above.

Renn exhaled the tension that had been building up inside him when he recognized Sally, who braked to a stop just above him. Above her, he could see Karl, as well as Terryl, Tess, and Gwen from Team Three.

Sally, slightly out of breath, whispered, "Did you find the SafeWell team?"

Renn shook his head. "Negative. They escaped up

this shaft not long ago."

"No, they never came topside. They must have exited into one of the tunnels."

"Shit. I didn't even look at the levels as I came up. They could be anywhere."

Ficks whispered from below. "I think they entered on Level twenty-nine."

Sally nodded. "That makes sense. Let's get down there and I will provide a SITREP on what we encountered."

Renn motioned below him and called out, "Back down to Level twenty-nine. SafeWell could be lying in wait, so stay frosty. Remember, they do not know we are here to help them. They will most likely assume we are here to kill them."

His team immediately dropped downward, and Renn followed. The gates for each level had large numbers printed on them. They stopped at '29' and took turns climbing onto the landing. Renn was glad, again, that the elevator cable ran down the side of the shaft. If it had been like a normal elevator and run down the middle of the shaft, it would have been much more difficult to dismount.

Ficks jogged down the tunnel system to scout ahead.

Renn turned to Sally, "Tell me what happened."

Sally gave a brief but detailed report, ending with the message from Thornlandon Holdings, that they were sending ten more teams down here.

Renn swore. There was no way they could hold their own against ten teams. They needed to escape before the additional Thornlandon Holdings teams arrived. Then he shuddered in both disbelief and anger at the description of the Vorgroth and the battles Sally's teams had fought against it.

Sally said, "Now it's your turn to report."

Renn told her about going down to Level forty-three, and how they had found the remains of the two teams who had been sent down previously. He explained how the SafeWell team had gotten past them by killing Lucy Miller. At this, Sally's eyes narrowed, but she didn't speak. Renn finished by talking about their recent ascent to where they'd met Sally's team. He stretched his shoulders, hearing them pop loudly in the silence of the tunnel. "There are only ten of us left now. Let's see if we can make friends with the SafeWell team. I have a feeling we are going to need them to get everyone out of here alive."

Ficks returned, a worried expression on his face.

Renn said, "Report."

"There is a partial cave-in not too far down the tunnel where the ladder leading up to Level twenty-eight is supposed to be. The ladder is gone."

"Shit. What about the tourists?" Renn asked.

"It looks like they collapsed the area around the hatch leading down to Level thirty. Probably to protect themselves from the Vorgroth coming up. I saw tracks leading away, further into the tunnel. I only followed a few hundred meters to make sure, then returned."

Renn let out a breath. "Everyone, check your weapons. Let's go find the others."

They all silently glided down the tunnel, following Ficks like a ghost in the shadows.

After ten minutes, Renn heard faint music playing in the distance.

They all halted, listening.

Paul turned with an incredulous look on his face. He cocked his head, listening, then asked, "It that

Super Mario Bros?"

Renn recognized it now as the music from the famous video game. The simple tune floated down the tunnel, repeating on a loop. It brought back memories from when he had been a kid on the reservation playing the game on a beaten-up, decades-old Nintendo machine. The song sounded eerie down here in the blackness of these tunnels, almost ethereal. This mission kept getting weirder and weirder.

Then he froze. *If that music is playing*, he realized, *it is to get someone's—or some* thing's *attention.* He whispered, "Ficks, go ahead, but be silent. We will follow. It is likely a trap."

Ficks glided forward and soon disappeared around a bend.

Renn motioned forward with two fingers, and the rest of the team followed, carefully avoiding any loose rocks or gravel. As they made their way down the tunnel, the music grew louder.

Then Ficks approached, moving quickly, motioning for them to retreat.

Renn and his team turned and made their way back down the tunnel toward the elevator shaft. As they retreated, the music suddenly ended, and a loud roar echoed down the tunnel. They all froze in place, not daring to make a sound. Then the roar sounded again, but seemed to be moving away from them.

They continued forward and soon arrived at the elevator opening.

Renn whispered to Sally, "Was that the…?"

Sally nodded. She pressed her lips tightly together and glanced away from Renn to gaze down the tunnel.

Sally was the calmest person in a firefight that Renn had ever known. He had never seen her afraid of anything. Seeing the fear on her face now sent a chill through his body.

Ficks motioned to the elevator shaft. "The tourists and SafeWell team must have found a way up to Level twenty-eight. I bet they used the music to draw the creature to it so they could move past it. At least that's what I would have done. We should use the MADs to go up two or three levels to get ahead of them."

Renn agreed and motioned to the MADs. "Quickly. Let's get up to Level twenty-four to be sure we are ahead of them. It's time we stopped following them and started waiting *for* them."

The team geared up and had soon made it to Level twenty-four. It was dusty up here, and Ficks went to scout ahead, only to return within a minute. "There's a cave-in ahead. We need to go up one more level."

Renn asked, "What about the access point? Will the tourists and SafeWell team be able to get up to the next level?"

Ficks nodded. "I don't think it affected the exfiltration point further down the tunnel."

"Ok, back in the shaft and up to Level twenty-three."

There was some grumbling, but everyone strapped back into the MADs and ascended another level.

This time, as they exited onto the platform, Renn didn't smell any dust, so there likely had not been any cave-ins on this level.

Ficks ran down the corridor and quickly returned, confirming that all was clear.

Renn lowered his MAD unit to the floor and stepped free of the apparatus. He raised his gun, checked that the safety was on, then whispered,

"Alright. Ficks, find where the next entrance-point is back down to Level twenty-four. We will wait for them there and say hello when they come up."

Ficks gave a curt nod, then sprinted down the tunnel.

The rest of them moved out at a slower pace. This tunnel was a little narrower than the previous tunnels they had been in. But it still had steel rails leading down the center for the iron ore carts. They carefully made their way and within fifteen minutes, Ficks rejoined them.

"The entrance is thirty meters ahead."

Renn nodded. "We will open the hatch so we can better hear when they approach from below us. Then we will call down to them and ask for a parlay."

Everyone nodded. It was a good plan.

They moved forward again, many of the team members walking with a lightness that had not been there before.

They quickly arrived at the alcove containing the hatch. Renn leaned forward and quietly opened it. He pulled back when he heard voices below. They had gotten lucky. The SafeWell team and civilians were directly below them. He was about to call out when a roar echoed from inside their own tunnel. His team swung around and raised their weapons, clicking off the safeties.

Ficks whispered urgently, "It's coming fast!"

Renn leaned furtively over the hatch and started in shock when he saw a beautiful woman looking up at him from below.

CHAPTER 40

A few minutes earlier, MORGAN glanced over at Andy. He was distraught, his face wet with tears. His dad, Ethan, sat with his deceased husband's head in his lap, stroking his hair.

John knelt by Ethan; his head bowed.

Ethan looked up at John, his face stricken with grief and pain. "I don't understand. Larry was healthy. Sure, he was a bit overweight, and didn't exercise, but he was healthy. How could this happen?"

John looked up and put a hand on Ethan's shoulder. "I am truly sorry, Ethan. Larry was a good man."

"I can't leave him down here, especially with that…thing down here. I won't let it desecrate his body."

John looked questioningly at Morgan, who shook her head. John turned back to Ethan. "I am so sorry. But there is no way we can carry him up those ladders. We will have to leave Larry and send the authorities back for him after we get to the surface."

Ethan looked at him incredulously. "We can't leave him!"

John felt a tear fall down his cheek. "I am sorry. We have no choice."

Morgan stepped forward, "Ethan. With the Vorgroth chasing us, we need to move quickly. John is correct. We cannot possibly carry Larry up those ladders."

John squeezed Ethan's shoulder. "We must go. The Vorgroth will be here soon."

Ethan moaned in despair.

Morgan waited a few moments out of respect for Ethan and Andy, but they needed to get moving. Just as she was about to tell Ethan that they must go, Ethan let his shoulders slump in resignation. He leaned forward and kissed Larry's forehead, then smoothed his husband's hair. Finally, he sat back and carefully set Larry's head onto the stone floor. He walked over to his son and the boy practically leapt into his dad's embrace. They hugged tightly, Ethan caressing Andy's head.

Morgan liked what she saw in John. He was a man who cared for others. She studied his face. It radiated fortitude and kindness, compassion and a deep strength of character. He was a man she would like to know better. But for now, she had to get them all out of this mine alive. She spoke into her mic that Karen and Jack should return from their positions down the corridor.

Karen's soft voice in her headset said, "The next exfiltration point is only fifty meters away."

Morgan turned to the group of civilians and quietly said, "Alright, everyone. Let's get going. The

288

next ladder is not far away."

As they approached the next alcove, Morgan spoke to her team through her mic as she jogged, "I will go up the ladder first."

A distant shriek of the Vorgroth echoed from an unknown location within the tunnels.

Morgan reached the ladder and shined her flashlight upwards, then leapt away when she saw a man looking down at her from the open hatch. She swore out loud and immediately sprang away from the ladder.

Karen stepped toward Morgan, keeping her rifle pointed down the tunnel. "What is it?"

Morgan moved further back, pulling Karen along. "There is a person up there."

Renn's strong voice called urgently down to them, "Hello, SafeWell team. We are friendlies and would like to descend. And quickly, if you don't mind. Something is approaching us that we have no desire to face."

A loud roar underscored the urgency of Renn's request. The Vorgroth was getting closer.

Morgan turned to her team, "We can't let the Vorgroth kill them. Keep your weapons trained on them. Safeties off." Then she turned to John, "John, take everyone back down the tunnel. If bullets fly, I don't want any of you near here."

John immediately helped guide the group of civilians down the tunnel.

When they were out of sight, Morgan turned and called up, "Come on down. Do not touch your weapons when you get to the bottom."

"Roger that. We are coming down now."

CHAPTER 41

RENN cursed silently to himself as the roar of the Vorgroth echoed from the direction of the elevator shaft on Level twenty-three. He broke out into a sweat.

Back on the Navajo Reservation in Utah, he had heard stories of the Skinwalkers. It was said they roared like this out in the deepest parts of the desert in the dark of night. Renn had never experienced a close encounter with a Skinwalker, but his cousin Tokala had encountered one while seeking isolation and spiritual guidance in the desert. Tokala had come back a changed man: skittish, with a haunted look in his eyes that never went away. He had stayed holed up in his house for years after his experience.

The Vorgroth roared again as it drew closer.

Renn quickly motioned to the hatch. "Do as she says. Keep your hands off your weapons when you get to the bottom. Go now, as fast as you can."

His team quickly scaled down the ladder, leaving

Renn remaining above. Renn heard the shaking of the floor as the creature approached. He swung his rifle to his back and climbed onto the ladder, stepped down a few rungs, and pulled the hatch closed. This was one of only a few hatches he had seen with a locking mechanism. Renn wasn't sure why this was so, but he wasn't going to question it. Renn placed his feet on the outside of the ladder and slid down to the bottom.

Renn's team faced the SafeWell team, who had guns trained on them.

Above, they heard the Vorgroth slam into the hatch twice, followed by a roar.

Everyone glanced upward in worry. No one moved.

When no more sound came from above, Renn put both hands up and took three steps forward. He briefly considered telling the SafeWell team that he and his team were sent down to get everyone to safety, but Renn thought honesty would serve him better in this case. He calmly stated, "I am team leader Renn Holder. We were sent down here by Thornlandon Holdings to kill you all."

At this, the SafeWell team narrowed their eyes and gripped their rifles tighter.

Renn continued, his voice quiet, "We have decided to disobey those orders."

In response to Morgan's questioning look, Renn grimaced and said, "We don't have much time with that thing up above. But I will summarize quickly. It is about money. Thornlandon Holdings, who we work for, found a multi-trillion-dollar deposit of heavy metals far beneath this mine, including some strange new element they desperately want their hands on. Thornlandon Holdings will take ownership of this mine tomorrow. They do not want anyone to know about the structural damage down here, as that would likely keep them wrapped up in legal red tape for years. The company, run by Director Judith Meyers, wants you all erased from existence. So, we have collectively decided that Thornlandon Holdings, and specifically Judith Meyers, can go fuck themselves."

Morgan studied Renn for only a moment, then said, "I kind of figured it was something like that. What do you want from us?"

Paul called out, before Renn could answer, "I *want* to get the motherfuck away from this monster and out of this mine!"

Renn glanced at Paul and grinned despite their dire circumstances, then faced the SafeWell team again in time to see the group of civilians come jogging around the corner.

Renn continued, "We were supposed to kill the mine tour employees who were topside, then come down here and kill all of you. But I made a call to one of the mine employees instead, and gave a story designed to ensure they would all leave the premises before we arrived."

Slightly out of breath from his recent run, Jim stepped forward. "That was you I talked to on the phone?"

"You must be Jim. Yes, it was me. You got everyone topside to leave. You are a good man. Unfortunately, Thornlandon Holdings has sent ten more teams to take us all out, including my team. They, apparently, don't like us making decisions for ourselves. If you will have us, we would like to help you get everyone to safety."

After a few beats of silence, Morgan stepped forward and held out her hand, introducing herself. "I am Morgan, SafeWell team leader."

Renn shook her hand. "Renn. Previous team leader for Thornlandon Holdings. Now, I suggest we get the hell away from this access point, and that monster."

As if on cue, they heard another crash and an angry roar.

Morgan motioned upward with her index finger, "That monster is called a Vorgroth."

Renn cocked his head in surprise. "How do you know what it is?"

Bauwen stepped forward for the first time, and in a light melodious voice said, "Because I am also from the world of the Vorgroth. My name is Bauwen."

Renn heard a collective intake of breath from his team members. None of them had noticed the woman until now. She was unlike anything Renn had ever seen before. Her skin constantly shifted colors and patterns, she was nude, and she was quite beautiful. Most importantly, if she was with the SafeWell team, she was a friendly. Renn stepped forward and held out his hand, "It is nice to meet you, Bauwen."

Bauwen looked at his outstretched hand with her head slightly tilted, as if she was unsure what he meant by the gesture.

Renn hesitantly dropped his hand.

Bauwen studied his face for a moment, then stared directly into his eyes. Unexpectedly, she smiled at him, and as she did, her face radiated such warmth and kindness that Renn almost leaned forward to hug her, something he had not done with anyone in many years. She had a powerful peace about her.

Renn broke eye contact with Bauwen when Morgan said, "With the Vorgroth above us, I think the only way out of here is via the elevator shaft. We have not used the shaft to get to the surface up to this point because we assumed there would be a team there waiting to take us out." She arched an eyebrow at Renn.

Turning away from Bauwen, Renn said, "You are right. Although now we just have Monique stationed up top. Tess, Terryl, and Gwen have joined us down here."

Sally stepped forward. "Renn, the ten kill teams will arrive in only a couple of hours. Whatever we are going to do, I suggest we do it now."

Renn nodded and said, "We need to exfiltrate this mine before they arrive or they will hunt us down and kill us." He glanced back toward the ladder. "That is, if the Vorgroth doesn't get us first."

Morgan hesitantly spoke to Renn. "We are sorry for killing your soldier. It was not our first choice."

Renn reassured Morgan, "That is the way it went down, and we are to blame, not you. We know you likely tried to negotiate with Lucy."

Morgan nodded solemnly. "You are very perceptive. But I am still sorry. Now, let's get back to the elevator shaft and get out of here."

They all turned and fled down the tunnel back the way they had come. Behind them, they heard…nothing.

This worried Renn more than if the Vorgroth had been right behind them.

Where had it gone?

CHAPTER 42

JOHN helped guide Andy, Ethan, Claire, Jim, and Carl down the dark tunnel of Level twenty-four.

The tourists' final cell phone battery had died not long before Renn's team had joined them. Fortunately, the SafeWell team had powerful flashlights, which they didn't hesitate to use now that speed was more important than stealth.

Tammy stumbled but kept her balance. She had been a source of strength for everyone, but the stress and exertion seemed to be catching up with her. John put a hand on her arm as they jogged down the corridor and said, "Tammy, we will get out of here."

Tammy nodded and seemed to find strength from his words. She picked up her pace. Her resilience amazed John.

Just a few moments earlier, Karen from the SafeWell team and Millie from Renn's team sprinted ahead of everyone and disappeared into the darkness of the tunnel ahead.

John studied Renn, who was just ahead of him. He was a huge Navajo and as dangerous looking as any man John had ever met. But Renn also projected a strong intelligence combined with kindness and honesty. The military leader intrigued John. He put his musings aside when Bauwen raised her arm up ahead. The group stopped and John made his way forward so he could hear what Bauwen was saying to Morgan and Renn, who seemed to have naturally taken over the job of leading everyone out of the mine, which John was honestly quite relieved about.

Bauwen spoke quietly, "The Vorgroth is ahead. I can sense it." She looked frightened, and she pointed back down the tunnel. "The Vorgroth is smart. It has gone back to the elevator shaft. We must return the way we have come and climb to the next level."

That explains where it went. The Vorgroth was like a cat hunting its prey, guiding us exactly where it wants us before leaping in for the kill, John thought to himself.

Morgan spoke into her mic, "Karen, return immediately. Repeat. Return immediately."

Renn gave the same instructions to Millie through his own mic.

A few seconds later, gunfire erupted in the distance. John noticed the guns were firing on full auto, punctuated only by brief silences as the team members exchanged their magazines. Then Karen and Millie came running out of the darkness, motioning them to run, as well.

John immediately said, "Go! Go! Go!" as he pushed the backs of the tour group to get them moving. The tourists and soldiers were soon running full speed back down the tunnel, Karen and Millie following behind them. The light from the flashlights bounced up and down, making it difficult to see their footing.

Claire stumbled and fell hard to the ground with a cry of pain.

John was surprised when Carl stopped, pulled her to her feet, and put an arm around her waist to help her start running again.

Claire didn't complain and limped along as quickly as she could with Carl's assistance.

John had a sinking feeling that the Vorgroth had them this time.

CHAPTER 43

MORGAN slid to a stop by the ladder that led up to Level twenty-three. Sally had already climbed up the ladder to open the hatch.

Morgan helped Claire onto the ladder, followed by Andy. The Vorgroth couldn't be more than two hundred meters away. There was no way to get everyone up the ladder in time. She called out urgently, "Hurry, everyone!"

Ethan, Carl, and Tammy had terrified expressions on their faces as they glanced backward. Morgan sternly commanded, "Don't look back. Move, move, move!"

Renn turned to Tess and Terryl. "It is about sixty meters from here to the curve in the tunnel. Slow that thing down to give us time to get everyone up this ladder."

Tess and Terryl nodded, removed their sniper rifles from their shoulders, walked about five feet down the tunnel and knelt on one knee. They both calmly removed the clips from their rifles, double-checked that they were the special armor-piercing bullets Terryl had brought, and clicked the clips back into place. They chambered a round and flicked off their safeties in perfect unison. The entire process took no more than three seconds.

From around the distant turn of the tunnel, the Vorgroth appeared at a full run, all seven feet of it pounding heavily toward them, its nightmarish visage highlighted by Tess and Terryl's powerful military helmet flashlights.

Renn murmured quietly, disbelief filling his words, "What the hell?"

Next to Renn, Paul added his own, less eloquent, but nevertheless appropriate, commentary, "Holy shit fuck, what the fucking fuck is that fucking thing?"

Tess and Terryl calmly sighted through their scopes and fired at the same time. Their rifles thundered in the enclosed space and both bullets struck the Vorgroth in the chest. They didn't ricochet away like the other bullets had. Each bullet penetrated about an eighth of an inch into the Vorgroth's skin, completely flattening out. Not enough to harm the creature, but enough to surprise it.

The Vorgroth slid to a stop and looked down at its chest. It reached down and picked one of the bullets from its skin with two giant fingers and held the flattened piece of metal up to its eyes, studying it with surprise and curiosity. Its surprise quickly turned to rage as two more bullets struck it in the face, throwing its head back as if it had been punched.

Tess calmly told Terryl. "Aim for the same spots. Let's see if we can fully puncture its skin."

Morgan had turned to watch, guiding Jim and the rest of the teams up the ladder as if on autopilot. She was amazed by how calm Tess and Terryl were. It was as if they were just shooting rounds at the range.

Tess and Terryl fired three more rounds each, their bullets striking almost identical spots on the Vorgroth's chest, making it stumble backward with each hit.

The Vorgroth raised its head and roared at the ceiling, shaking its head in rage. Then it lowered its head and charged, its eyes wide open and radiating malignant, murderous intent.

Everyone had made it up the ladder. Tess and Terryl had bought them the time they had needed.

Renn called out, "Tess, Terryl, up the ladder, now."

Tess and Terryl stood and ran back, slinging their rifles over their shoulders and climbing up the ladder without pausing.

The Vorgroth was no more than forty meters away and closing fast.

Without waiting, Morgan hurried up the ladder right behind Tess.

She lost count of how many rungs she had climbed before the ladder shuddered violently, as if a car had smashed into it. She heard huffing right below her, and Renn spoke urgently, "Hurry up, Morgan. Faster!"

Morgan increased her speed, hoping she wouldn't miss a rung and fall, taking out Renn on the way down. If the fall didn't kill them, the Vorgroth certainly would. Her hand slapped against the floor at the top and she almost cried in relief as she climbed over the side and fell flat on the ground.

Renn climbed over the top right behind her and said, "Close that hatch, now!" His voice was calm, but his command was edged in panic.

Sally slammed the hatch closed.

Within seconds, the Vorgroth hit the closed hatch…hard. The steel would not hold long against the power of the creature.

Morgan called out, "Karen, Jack, get these people to the next exfiltration point! Renn's team, follow and help them."

Karen and Jack nodded and guided John and his group down the tunnel at a run, followed by the rest of Renn's team. Bauwen held back, a worried look on her face as she stared at the hatch. She fingered her small *Forss* knife reflexively.

Morgan put a hand on Paul's chest to stop him as he began to follow the rest, "I see a portable arc welder tied to your belt. Weld that hatch shut, now!"

The big Aussie nodded, not even bothering to get verification from Renn, and returned to the hatch. He unclipped the portable arc welder from his belt. It was no bigger than a hand-held drill. Paul then reached inside his pack and took out a bundle of thick grey sticks. He knelt by the hatch and the tip of the welder crackled as he quickly and efficiently added an ugly, but solid, half-inch-thick weld around the hatch, all while the Vorgroth was smashing into it from below.

Morgan was impressed. Not many people could have accomplished something like that, especially with the added pressure of knowing the Vorgroth could crash through it at any moment.

When Paul was finished, he stood and clipped the small arc welder back to his belt. He looked up and grinned, "I suggest we get the fuck outta here. This probably won't hold back that big fella for long, and when he does break through, he'll be mad as a cut snake."

Morgan nodded. "Let's go." She, Paul, Renn, and

Bauwen sprinted down the corridor. Thirty feet down the tunnel, Morgan heard the banging beneath the hatch stop.

All three of them slowed to a stop and looked back down the tunnel toward the hatch, listening.

Paul spoke quietly, "That fucker didn't give up already, did it?"

Renn grunted. "Maybe it went back to the elevator shaft to get ahead of us. That bastard is smart."

Bauwen shook her head. "No, it is probably weakened after expending so much energy. It will most likely go back to the lower levels to feed on what is left of your fallen friends. It does not have the *Forss* metal to keep it strong, like I do."

Renn, his eyes hard, opened his mouth to respond, before deciding against it. He realized he couldn't do anything to keep their fallen comrades from being eaten by the Vorgroth.

Morgan thought about what Bauwen had just said and how she had reflexively touched her *Forss* knife when the Vorgroth had been trying to break through the hatch. Morgan was sure their luck would run out if they kept trying to stay ahead of the Vorgroth. At some point, they were just going to be heading into an ambush.

They needed to stop acting like prey and start acting like hunters.

An idea came to Morgan. She motioned for the group to follow her and sped down the tunnel. They caught up with John and his group just as Jack started to climb the ladder up to Level twenty-two. Morgan called out, "Stop!"

Jack halted, one foot raised halfway to the next rung, and looked down at her.

Morgan regarded the people around her, a mix of hardened soldiers and frightened civilians—twenty people in total, plus Bauwen. Renn had told Morgan that his team had started with eighteen soldiers but was down to ten now, plus Monique, who was still topside. Renn had lost a lot of good people today. Too many. Morgan didn't want to lose anyone else.

Realizing she was gripping her rifle tighter than she needed to, Morgan forced herself to relax. "Listen. We have spent all our time and energy running *from* the Vorgroth; just reacting to it in an effort to get topside. It has controlled the entire situation. It is time for us to change that."

John looked up at the hatch, then back to her. "You mean we need to treat it like prey."

Morgan smiled grimly and nodded, appreciating John's quick mind. "That's right, John. We need to figure out a way to kill it. Or at least trap it down here."

Bauwen shook her head. "Morgan, I already told you. The Vorgroth cannot be killed by your weapons."

Tess grinned at Terryl and said, "I think *we* hurt it a bit back there."

Morgan nodded to Tess and Terryl. "Thank you for what both of you did. You bought us enough time to save everyone. But unfortunately, you didn't seriously injure it." Morgan turned to Bauwen. "You said only the substance you call *Forss*, can fully penetrate its skin."

Bauwen stared at Morgan, her face unreadable. "That's right. But it is all down below this mine, in my world."

Morgan gestured to the knife in the sheath tied to Bauwen's waist. "You have that knife. And your arm

303

bands."

Bauwen glanced down. "This is a little blade. It is used for digging vegetables from the dirt or cutting fruit from trees. My people have not faced a Vorgroth in generations, so now we use the *Forss* to make blades like this for menial tasks. You couldn't get close enough to use it against the Vorgroth, and even if you did, it would be like poking it with a small stick."

Renn calmly said, "You can kill a grizzly with a stick if you use it correctly. And that knife is sharper than a stick. Plus, it is at least four inches long. While I am not sure of the Vorgroth's body structure, I think if we stab it at the base of its skull," he reached up and touched his head in the spot he was talking about, "or under its armpit, I think we might be able to inflict serious damage. Maybe even kill it."

Morgan nodded and held out her hand. "Bauwen. May I see the knife?"

Bauwen slid the blade free and handed it to her, handle first. "Be very careful. It is sharper than any blade you carry. And it never loses its edge."

Turning the knife in the beam of her flashlight, Morgan was awed by the way the colors seemed to flow through it, shifting like it had an electric current. She looked up and asked, "How did you forge it?"

"While it is indestructible in normal situations, if you apply a great enough heat to it, it will soften enough to work with. We use machines to heat the *Forss* to temperatures more than twenty times that of molten magma. Then we forge it using *Forss* hammers when it is white hot. With great effort, we are able create what you see."

Renn leaned forward and held out his hand, "May I?"

Morgan handed him the blade.

Its colors changed quickly in the direct beam of light that Renn shined over it. He raised his eyes to Bauwen. "Your skin looks just like this. Are you made from this *Forss*?"

Bauwen nodded. "In a way, yes. My people consume it in small quantities our whole lives. We heat it until it is white-hot, then use a powerful machine to pound it flat until it is so thin it almost floats in the air. Then we use another machine to chop it into a powder. When done, we form it into capsules. We swallow a capsule once per month. The *Forss* combines with our bodies' chemistry, giving us many abilities. I had *Forss* capsules on me when I was chased up to this mine by the Vorgroth. I keep them in the handle of the knife."

John asked, "Is that how you survived being trapped the past 63 years?"

Bauwen nodded. "Yes. I swallowed a capsule once every year. It was not enough to fully sustain me, so for the rest of the time I put my body into a sort of stasis to slow down my metabolism. This is how I survived. I still have three capsules left, which the Vorgroth can sense from a great distance."

Renn's eyes seemed to bore into her as he asked, "What abilities do you have?"

Bauwen's skin cycled through colors and patterns at a faster rate. Then her arms and legs extended out and her torso changed shape into something resembling a dog. After a moment, Bauwen reformed back to her normal form.

Morgan heard exclamations and curses around her, and some of Renn's team raised their weapons.

Renn commanded, "Lower your weapons."

His team immediately complied, although Ficks

continued to eye Bauwen suspiciously.

Wiping a hand through his thick hair, Renn whispered, "I wonder…"

Morgan raised a questioning eyebrow. "What is it, Renn?"

"I am from the Navajo Nation in the southwest. Stories have been passed down for generations about creatures called Skinwalkers. They are evil spirits who haunt the deserts at night. We are told they are malevolent men and women who change into wolves, mountain lions, bears, and other predators. Our oral histories say these Skinwalkers come from the underworld. I wonder if they could somehow be from your world, Bauwen."

Bauwen looked at him curiously. "What you describe sound like Wyngren. They are members of my people who go insane from the effects of *Forss*. They use their abilities to cause harm. We imprison them for everyone's safety, but some escape across the great boundary between our land and that of the Vorgroth; a place we are never meant to go to. Perhaps, over the years, some have found a way up to your world like I have?"

Renn handed the *Forss* blade back to Bauwen. "I think my people and your people have a lot in common. I would like to visit your land someday."

"You would be welcome."

Morgan had listened to their conversation in amazement before bringing the conversation back to their present problem. "I think that *Forss* knife is our only chance to kill the Vorgroth. We need a plan to ambush it, though. Maybe we can place one of our phones next to a hatch and trigger a ringtone to play at full volume. When the Vorgroth climbs up through the hatch, we can stab it in the base of its neck like

Renn mentioned and drive the blade up into its brain, assuming its anatomy is similar to ours."

It was Andy who immediately saw the flaw in the plan. He raised his hand and timidly said, "I'm sorry, but I don't think that will work."

Renn smiled, "And why is that, little man?"

"Well, our phones are all dead. Do you have phones with a charge?"

Renn nodded. "We do. We left them powered down, so they are fully charged."

Andy nodded. "Good. But I wouldn't set an alarm because they only last like fifteen minutes at the most. Then you would have to fiddle around trying to set another alarm, which would distract you. I would use a music playlist."

Renn nodded and said, "Good point." He turned to say something to the group, but Andy interrupted him.

"Sorry, but that's not all."

Renn turned back toward Andy, his face showing slight irritation at being interrupted again.

Andy swallowed, obviously not comfortable speaking to such hardened soldiers as Renn and his team. But he squared his shoulders and continued, his voice gaining confidence as he spoke, "That Vorgroth is smart. It seems to be learning, changing its tactics to try and catch us. When we were trapped on a lower level, we set my Nintendo to play music from a game and left it in a cavern to draw the Vorgroth away from us, which worked. But I don't think it will come towards a stationary device playing music again. It might suspect it is a trap and try to circle around to come at us from a different direction, like down this tunnel, while we're waiting by the hatch with the music playing. If that happens, we would all be killed."

Andy looked thoughtful, "We need to trigger its attack response. Predators may ignore a stationary prey animal but give chase when it tries to escape. We need to do something similar. We need to make the Vorgroth think one or all of us is desperately trying to escape but are helpless, causing its attack response to kick in and chase after us. But it must be in a location where it can't easily attack us or defend itself."

Renn's smile disappeared. He turned to Morgan. "The kid's right. The Vorgroth might be ugly, but it's smart. I like Andy's idea, but I have no idea how we could do something like that without all of us being instantly killed by the Vorgroth."

Ficks sighed and quietly said, "I know a way."

Everyone turned toward the small man.

Ficks looked directly at Renn and said, "It is likely a suicide mission for one of us, but it may be the only way to kill the Vorgroth."

Renn was already shaking his head. "Whatever you are thinking, Ficks, one of us offering ourselves as bait is not the answer."

Ficks ignored him and turned to the stone wall and pointed to a long crack leading upward to the ceiling. "Imagine this is the elevator shaft." He traced the crack upward with his finger. "What if one of us uses a MAD to slowly ascend the elevator shaft, using the music to lure the Vorgroth after them? Even if the Vorgroth thinks it is a trap, like the kid mentioned, it probably won't be able to resist chasing a person up the shaft if it thinks they are trying to escape. This Vorgroth will either climb up after the person and the music, or if it is already above us, it will wait by an opening to try and grab them. Either way, it will put us on relatively even ground, so to speak. The Vorgroth will either be busy climbing, or it will have to reach out over the shaft opening to grab us; it will be at least partially preoccupied. It may be the only chance we have to distract it long enough to try killing it with that *Forss* knife."

Everyone stood silently, digesting the plan.

Renn sighed. "It will be almost certain death to try that, but I think you are right. It is the best option we have. I will not sacrifice any of you. I will do this."

Paul stepped forward and put a hand on Renn's shoulder, completely serious for one of the only times since Renn had known him. "No, mate. The team needs your leadership. Even if we kill this big bad monster thing, we still need to escape from the ten teams the company has sent to kill us. I am the only choice. I used to hunt crocodiles back home. This fella is just like a really big croc."

Ficks snorted, "Paul, you're not Crocodile Dundee. You've never killed a croc in your life. You jumped out of boats to subdue the smaller ones so the wildlife service could chip them."

Paul shrugged. "Well, I'm not going to chip the damned Vorgroth. I'm going to kill the fucker."

Before Renn could say anything, Paul held his hand out to Bauwen.

She handed him the *Forss* knife.

Paul grinned down at Ficks. "Crocodile Dundee's knife looked more impressive, but this will do."

Ficks held out his hand and Paul grasped it forearm to forearm. "Kill the bastard, Paul. But you'd better come back alive. You owe me a hundred dollars."

"Mate, I'm from Australia, where everything tries to kill you. I'm not about to die in a hole in

Minnesota." Paul turned toward the assembled group and grinned. "See ya on the other side, mates." He jogged down the tunnel and disappeared around a turn, his flashlight beam quickly swallowed up by the dark.

CHAPTER 44

PAUL turned on his helmet-mounted flashlight. He needed both hands free for what he was about to do. He turned off the larger handheld flashlight, spinning it like a cowboy with a gun in the movies before sliding it into a loop on his vest. He strapped on the MAD, cinching it tightly and checking the battery readout, thankful when he saw it still had an 87% charge; enough juice to go all the way up the 3200-foot shaft at least twice.

The rest of the group soon joined Paul by the elevator shaft.

Renn stepped forward and held out his hand. "I'll buy you a case of Foster's when we get out of here."

It was an inside joke because, like many Aussies, Paul hated that beer. He leaned forward and squeezed Renn's hand a little harder. "Mate, that thing is as good as dead. It just doesn't know it yet. And if you bring me a case of that piss water, you might be, too."

Renn laughed quietly, but his face was drawn and

heavy with sadness.

Letting go of Renn's hand, Paul took out his cell phone. He opened up his music app and scrolled through a number of playlists from his music library. He had downloaded thousands of songs to his phone a long time back because many of the places they were sent to didn't have cell service. He could not be without his music. He kept scrolling, searching for a playlist that was right for the moment.

Then he stopped scrolling and chuckled as he found the perfect one.

Paul put the phone into his pocket, then reached out, connected the MAD to the elevator cable, and swung out. He hung over the thousand-foot shaft as calmly as if he was standing in someone's living room. Before departing, he grinned at everyone and said, "See ya 'round like a rissole." He lowered himself a few levels first, just in case the monster was lurking farther below. He then switched the MAD control to automatically ascend the shaft at a slow rate.

He didn't need his hands now, so he took out his phone and pressed "Play." He turned the volume up as far as it would go before placing the phone back in his pocket.

Wagner's "Ride of the Valkyries" began blaring into the tunnel, the enclosed space making it sound almost like a concert hall. The song had been made famous to modern audiences in the movie, *Apocalypse Now*.

He took the *Forss* knife from his pocket and held it in his right hand, then took his Sig Sauer M17 pistol from his side holster and clicked the safety off with a flick of his thumb, holding the gun in his left hand as the power of the song brought a wide smile to his face.

He wished someone was here to film him. It would look epic.

At Level twenty-three, Paul smiled at everyone crowding around the opening. He lifted his arms dramatically, like a rising angel, holding the pistol in his left hand and the knife in his right, music blaring out the building crescendo of the song.

Paul saw Ficks holding his own phone pointed toward Paul, filming him pass by. Paul laughed and said, "Yeah, Ficksie! You send me that video; it's going to be EPIC!"

Ficks grinned. It was the first time Ficks had smiled for as long as Paul could remember.

Then Paul was past the opening. He glanced down the shaft but saw no movement below, so he slowed his ascent to a crawl. Paul needed to give the Vorgroth time to come to him.

Within minutes the lights from the team's flashlights below faded completely away. Paul turned off his helmet light and pulled his night-vision over his right eye. He activated it and the shaft filled with a grainy light. He passed by five more levels, expecting the Vorgroth to reach out and grab him from any of the openings, but each remained empty as he passed by.

Paul felt his tension building and found himself holding his breath when he approached each new level, not knowing where or when the Vorgroth would attack, just knowing it definitely would. He thought the not knowing was worse than an actual attack. It reminded him of an old Jack-in-the-box toy he'd had as a kid. He would slowly turn the little handle on the side of the box, uneven and eerie music playing as he did. He anxiously waited for the top to pop open and the Jack to jump up, but it always seemed to take longer than he expected. And even though he knew it was going to pop up, he jumped every time it did.

Paul approached Level seventeen. He glanced down and was startled to see the Vorgroth only a few levels below him. His heart pounded hard at seeing the creature so close and quickly gaining on him, its arms and legs stretched out to each side of the sixteen-foot-wide shaft.

Paul blinked his eyes, trying to make sense of what he was seeing. It looked like the monster was somehow stretching its limbs as if they were made from rubber, kind of like the Stretch Armstrong action figure Paul had played with as a kid. The Vorgroth must have the ability to transform its body like Bauwen had shown them she could do earlier.

What a weird fucking day this has turned out to be, he thought. If someone had told Paul yesterday that he would find himself in a mine shaft being chased by a fucking Stretch-Armstrong monster, he would have called them a stupid cunt and smacked them a good one. But here he was literally doing that very thing. Life could sure be amusing sometimes.

With that thought, all of the tension melted away from Paul. There was no more waiting for an attack. It was upon him and there was nothing to do now but fight. He aimed his Sig Sauer down and squeezed off a shot. The bullet ricocheted off the thing's head like shooting a BB gun at a road sign.

The Vorgroth—which Paul thought was a stupid fucking name—looked up at him and growled in irritation, then climbed even faster.

Paul increased his speed a little to keep the same distance between the monster and him, but didn't allow himself to go too fast. He wanted to go up the shaft a good long way before he engaged further with the thing. That way, if he was only able to injure it, maybe it would at least fall to its death.

Level thirteen passed by and Paul noticed the darkness of the shaft was no longer absolute. It was night, but the moonlight was just able to penetrate this far down the elevator shaft, the slight angle to the shaft keeping it from fully reaching him.

This should be high enough, he thought.

He reduced the MAD's power and slowed down even more.

The creature growled below him and climbed faster, probably assuming its prey was exhausting itself.

Paul called down, "Well, this is it, big fella. Time to play." Paul knew this was a one-way mission, and he was fine with that. At least he'd take this piece of shit out with him.

When the Vorgroth was only fifteen feet below him, Paul reached up and pulled the MAD's release latch. He immediately dropped in free fall, smiling widely as he did.

The creature tried to swat at Paul but since it was holding onto the tunnel with both its arms, it had to quickly put his arm back to the wall to avoid slipping. It couldn't reach out to him without falling, which was exactly what Paul had hoped would happen.

Paul slammed into the Vorgroth's shoulder and careened sideways, dropping his gun at the same time. He grabbed the Vorgroth's elbow with his left arm and held on, refusing to let go of the *Forse* blade in his right hand.

The Vorgroth turned its head to look at him, its sloping skull at least three times larger than Paul's own head. It lunged forward and snapped its teeth at him, somehow missing Paul by an inch, its teeth cracking together loudly in the air.

Paul chortled. "Good on you for trying, big guy." He put the knife between his own teeth, careful to place the sharpened edge outward to avoid slicing his mouth wide open.

Grunting, Paul swung himself over to the thing's heavily muscled back and wrapped his free arm around its neck. There was no give in the Vorgroth's body; it felt like he was holding onto a concrete statue. He removed the *Forss* knife from his teeth with his right hand and placed the tip to the base of the Vorgroth's corded neck. Then he pushed upward with all of his strength.

Nothing happened. The knife barely scratched the Vorgroth's skin.

"Fuck," Paul said. He had expected the *Forss* blade to slide into the Vorgroth's neck like a hot knife through butter. He should have known it wouldn't be that easy.

Paul couldn't get enough leverage to put more power into his thrust with his one available arm. He grunted and scrambled further up the Vorgroth's back, pulling with all his strength until he managed to wrap his legs around its upper chest. This allowed him to release his left arm.

Paul leaned back, grimacing at the effort of holding onto the creature with just his legs, grabbed the knife handle with both hands and thrust forward and upward with all of his weight and strength. The *Forss* blade slammed into the Vorgroth's neck, just below the base of its skull. Paul stabbed upward about 40 degrees, puncturing the bone with a crack. The blade slid to a stop, its full four inches buried inside the Vorgroth's head.

The Vorgroth jerked from the impact and shrieked in agony. It bucked like a bronco to try and dislodge Paul, roaring in pain and rage.

Paul laughed out loud, then leaned forward to the Vorgroth's right ear and said, "Stings a little huh?"

Reaching forward and using his weight as leverage, Paul began sawing downward at the skull, cutting a longer opening. As he did, the Vorgroth screamed louder. It twisted and bucked harder. Paul twisted the knife and began sawing horizontally until he reckoned the opening was just big enough for what he wanted to do. He reached into his vest pocket, which took three tries as he bounced around on the Vorgroth's back, and pulled out the high-explosive M67 grenade he had placed there before the ascent. When Director Meyers had said they weren't allowed to take any explosives into the mine, the first thing he had done was pack M67 grenades.

Fuck her.

Paul pulled the knife free from the Vorgroth's head. The Vorgroth twisted hard from the pain, and Paul lost his grip on the knife. He leaned back and looked down as it disappeared into the darkness of the elevator shaft. He mentally shrugged; he no longer needing the knife.

Paul pulled the pin from the grenade, released the spoon, and worked the grenade into the open wound, the squishing sound sweet music to his ears. Then he hurriedly took a strap holding five more M67 grenades from his inside vest and threw it around the Vorgroth's neck. Paul yanked at a piece of rope that he had threaded through the pins, pulling them all out at once.

The Vorgroth shrieked and slammed its head

backward, smashing into Paul with the force of a wrecking ball.

Paul's face caved back into his skull like a paper bag. He slipped from the Vorgroth's back and tumbled down the shaft.

In his fading consciousness, Paul heard a shriek from the Vorgroth, then the mother of all explosions.

Paul tried to laugh in triumph, but he had no mouth left.

Then he ceased to exist as the blast blew him apart.

CHAPTER 45

A few minutes earlier, RENN had leaned out into the shaft from the platform on Level twenty-three and craned his head upward, trying to see what was happening with Paul, but his friend was long out of sight. Then Renn looked down the shaft and saw the Vorgroth approaching from five or six levels below. He slowly backed away from the opening and quietly said, "The Vorgroth is approaching. Everyone, remain still. Do not make a sound, move, or look at the Vorgroth no matter what."

The Vorgroth climbed into view. It turned its head and stopped climbing, setting its malevolent gaze upon them.

No one moved or looked directly at it. The Vorgroth stared for almost a half a minute, making a soft, breathy sound deep in its throat. Finally, it looked back up the shaft and continued climbing.

Renn waited thirty seconds, then released his long-held breath when he could be sure the Vorgroth was indeed gone. He had glanced at the Vorgroth from his peripheral vision. After seeing it from so close, he was sure there was no way Paul could do what needed to be done. As good a soldier as Paul was, the Vorgroth was a supranatural killing machine.

Morgan stepped next to him and quietly said, "That is one brave soldier you have up there."

Renn nodded. "Paul is one of the best men I've ever known. He presents as unserious and uncaring, but that man is as selfless as they come."

They stood in silence for a while, the minutes ticking past agonizingly slowly. After a while, they couldn't hear the music any longer. At one point, they heard a single shot ring out, but nothing followed it. A few times, they thought they heard Paul, but he was too far away for them to know for sure. Suddenly, a shriek echoed down to them, filled with pain. Another shriek followed a few moments later, then another.

From behind him, Renn heard Ficks call out, "Paul is definitely giving that motherfucker what for." As soon as Ficks said this, an explosion detonated far above them, bright light filling the shaft.

Renn turned away, blinking as stars filled his eyes. He yelled out, "Everyone, get back!"

They all rushed down the tunnel as the floor shook. Renn heard chunks of rock falling down the shaft. Hell, for all he knew, the entire elevator shaft may be collapsing.

When the last of the rumbling died away, Renn yelled out, "Where did that explosion come from?"

Ficks smiled. "It was Paul. I saw him put a bunch of M67s into his pocket topside before we left the trucks. That crazy motherfucker must have used them on the Vorgroth." Then his eyes clouded when he realized what the explosion meant for Paul.

Renn felt a profound sadness. Paul was dead; of that, he was certain. The Aussie had sacrificed himself for the group.

And he had killed the Vorgroth. Nothing could have survived that blast.

But could they really be sure?

CHAPTER 46

When the dust settled, JOHN helped Claire to her feet. The old woman was struggling, her face drawn. "Are you doing OK, Claire?"

"I'm fine, John. Just getting tired is all. I must say, I am ready to leave this mine."

Andy coughed and wiped dust from his eyes with the inside of his shirt before helping his dad to his feet. They stood together in exhausted silence.

John was drained as well. His body felt twenty years older and fifty pounds heavier than it was. All he wanted to do was lie down and sleep. But they weren't out of danger yet. So, he squared his shoulders and approached Morgan and Renn, who stood peering down the elevator shaft. They glanced at him as he joined them. "Do you think the Vorgroth is dead?" His voice caught. "Do you think Paul…" but he couldn't say it.

Renn shook his head. "Paul is gone."

John solemnly nodded. "He was a good man."

Renn suddenly reached out and grabbed the elevator cables. "Holy shit, the cable is still here! I thought the explosion would have severed it."

Morgan glanced upward. "It is attached far above. The blast may have damaged it, but it is made from three-inch thick, braided steel cable strong enough to lift the massive elevator with tons of ore inside. I think it would take a lot more than that a blast from a grenade to sever it."

"I suppose you're right. We just have to hope none of the levels above have collapsed from the blast."

John had been listening quietly, but now said, "The tunnels were created from much larger explosions than that one. I don't think those grenades would have damaged the tunnels."

Renn shrugged. "I hope you are right, and I guess we will find out soon enough."

John nodded. "We should get going. My group is running out of energy, and we are out of water and food."

Renn said, "We have water and energy bars in our packs." He turned to Sally. "Get everyone to the next exfiltration point on Level twenty-two, then pass out the remaining food and water and have everyone take a quick break." He glanced at his watch. "We only have about two hours until the teams from Thornlandon Holdings arrive. They will most likely leave three teams topside to keep us from escaping from the mine and send the remaining seven teams down to Level thirty-two to start searching for us. They will likely send three of those teams down to Level forty-three to ensure we aren't hiding down there. That leaves four teams chasing us up to the surface. They will take their time since they know there is nowhere for us to go but up, where the other teams will be waiting to kill us. That's what I'd do, at least. It will also take them a bit of time to explore the mining caverns on each level. So, we probably have three to four hours to get to the surface before they catch up with us."

John said, "I hope they won't be able to locate the exit point on the surface."

Renn shook his head. "That information wasn't in our intelligence packet, so I doubt the kill teams will have it either. Maybe the information just isn't available anymore. Let's hope this is the case. But they will likely spread out to cover as much area as possible." There was grumbling from both Renn and Morgan's teams. Renn shrugged. "We will just have to be quiet when we get to the surface, take out anyone we come across, then run like hell."

Renn turned to Tess. "Let's quickly descend the elevator shaft down to Level thirty-two to verify that the Vorgroth is truly dead."

Tess nodded and immediately started strapping into her MAD.

Morgan said, "I am coming with."

Renn nodded. The three of them were soon geared up and ready to descend the shaft. Renn turned to Sally. "We will be back in ten minutes. If we are not back by then, start climbing without us. Got it?"

Sally nodded, then turned to the group. "Alright, let's make our way back to the ladder, then we will take a very short break before we climb the rest of the way out of this mine. John, will you lead the way?"

John turned and said, "Follow me, everyone."

CHAPTER 47

RENN descended the shaft, followed by Morgan and Tess. Dust still rose up the shaft but was clearing out quickly. The shaft acted like an exhaust fan, sucking the dust upward and away from them.

The top of the elevator car appeared below, so he slowed down and called up, "I'm slowing down and will stop in five meters."

Tess and Morgan called down their acknowledgement.

When he was just above the elevator car, Renn stopped.

Morgan came to a stop a foot above him, and Tess the same above Morgan. They were leaning forward to get a good view of the top of the elevator car.

Renn immediately saw the Vorgroth, sprawled as if asleep. The impact of the two-thousand-plus foot drop didn't seem to have caused it much damage.

Taking his rifle from his back, Renn lowered himself until he was able to stand on a free section on the top of the elevator car. He disconnected from the MAD, though he was hesitant to do so. If the Vorgroth was still alive, Renn would not be able to hook back into the MAD in time to escape.

Renn leaned forward, ready to jump back if the Vorgroth made a move. Slowly, as if he were poking a sleeping grizzly bear, Renn nudged the Vorgroth with his boot. It didn't move. Renn knelt and leaned over to get a closer look at its face. He put a hand in front of the Vorgroth's mouth and felt no air movement, nor could Renn see its chest moving.

The Vorgroth's eyes were wide open and still radiated malevolence and rage. But there was no life in them.

Renn breathed a sigh of relief.

The Vorgroth was dead.

At that moment, Morgan touched down next to him, unbuckled from her MAD and knelt next to the Vorgroth. She tried to turn it over, grunting with the effort, but was unable to move it.

Renn joined her, and together, straining as hard as they could, were able to roll it onto its stomach.

They both immediately saw a ragged hole the size of an orange in the back of the Vorgroth's head.

Morgan turned off her night vision, then asked Renn and Tess to do the same. She then turned on her flashlight and aimed the powerful beam into the hole, moving it back and forth as she peered inside. She sat back and whistled, her eyes showing awe. "I think Paul used the *Forss* knife to cut an opening in its skull. Then, he stuffed a grenade inside of its head." She leaned back and said, "Have a look. There is nothing left inside of the skull. The grenade vaporized the brain from the inside. But because the Vorgroth's skin is like steel, its head didn't explode with it."

Renn saw what she meant. The entire inside of its head was blasted clean. The brain matter must have blown right out of the hole in the Vorgroth's head. Renn sat back, then looked around for Paul. Chunks of flesh and blood covered the entire elevator car, but there was nothing that even resembled a human body part.

Renn lowered his head and murmured, "A moment of silence for Paul, please."

Morgan immediately lowered her head, as did Tess, who still hung from the cable a few feet above them.

After a few seconds had passed, Renn lifted his head, and as he did, he saw a glint in the corner of the roof of the elevator. He stepped over the Vorgroth and smiled as he bent down and picked up the *Forss* knife. It had fallen thousands of feet and didn't even have a scratch on it. He removed his own knife and put the *Forss* blade into the empty sheath. He put his own knife into a loop on his vest.

"Alright, let's get back up."

The three of them quickly ascended the shaft and rejoined the rest of the group on Level twenty-three. Renn nodded at their questioning looks and said, "The Vorgroth is dead."

Bauwen fell to her knees and looked up at Renn with disbelieving eyes, "Is it really dead?"

"Yes. Paul killed it."

Bauwen sobbed in relief. "We are finally safe."

Sally looked at her watch and shook her head. "We may be safe from the Vorgroth, but we are still not safe from the Thornlandon Holdings kill teams."

Renn glanced up the ladder. "Alright, let's get going. Tess, you first, followed by the civilians, then the rest of our teams. Now that the Vorgroth is dead, we can move fast without worrying if we will be attacked. Come on, let's get out of this mine."

CHAPTER 48

DEPUTY SHERIFF DANNY MILLER drove his Ford Explorer along Highway 53 North, a few miles outside of Cook, Minnesota.

It was late, just after 2 a.m.

Danny was on night shift. He had recently finished checking on the Onamuni mine site. An unknown caller reported an unusual explosion onsite just before 5 p.m. One of the dayshift deputies had checked it out but was turned away by Onamuni security. Danny thought he might as well stop by, but he had been turned away as well. Since Danny had no right to enter the property without permission, he left without causing a scene.

Onamuni was owned by a foreign investment firm. Most people around the area didn't know much about its parent company, or even what country it was from.

Overall, it had been a quiet shift tonight. Danny slowed his car down briefly when a deer poked its head up from the ditch and was illuminated by Danny's headlights. The animal quickly bounded away in the opposite direction. It was a warm night, still in the low 70s. The hum of his tires on the pavement was comforting and relaxing. Danny felt his eyes close. He jerked his head up when the tires hit the rumble strips on the edge of the road, cursing to himself for almost falling asleep. He glanced quickly in his mirrors, happy no other traffic was out and about. *That's all I need,* he thought. *First week on my own and I almost fall asleep at the wheel.*

Danny checked his mirrors again, slowed down, did a U-turn, and headed back south. He might as well check the Deepstone underground mine center. Sometimes kids met up there late at night to party.

Danny was twenty-three years old. He was tall—just under 6'3" —a bit too thin, with the whisper of a goatee trying to grow on his chin. He had brown eyes, a thin nose, and a ready smile. His size fourteen feet often made him the butt of jokes in high school. Danny grew up in Cook, Minnesota, a town where the entire population could fit into the visitors' bleachers of a college football game. His graduating class only had thirty-five students, and he was still good friends with most of them.

Danny had earned a Bachelor of Science degree in Criminal Justice from Bemidji State University. He had planned to join the FBI, but returned to Cook right after graduation to care for his seventeen-year-old brother, Jeff, when his mother and father died in a car accident. When the Saint Louis County Sheriff department in Virginia, Minnesota had posted an opening for deputy sheriff, he had quickly applied. Danny passed the background investigations, interviews, physical tests, and extensive classroom training. Last week he completed his six-month probationary period. He was now an active deputy sheriff; his assigned areas covered Virginia, Cook, Tower, and everywhere in-between.

A few hours earlier, Danny had responded to a minor accident out by Gheen. A trailer with a fourteen-foot Alumacraft fishing boat detached from its hitch, drifted across its lane, took out a mailbox, rolled into the ditch, and flipped twice. When Danny arrived a few minutes later, the boat owner sat on the edge of the ditch, staring at his now destroyed boat, fishing gear scattered everywhere. But the guy had found his stringer of four walleye, which he held onto protectively.

Old Mrs. Koskii had called about a broken window, which she claimed had been smashed by a bear. Mrs. Koskii was 92 years old and lived alone a few miles outside of Cook. She called the sheriff's office at least once a month to report some minor issue. The other sheriffs often made unpleasant jokes about her and complained when they had to respond to her calls. But Danny didn't mind. He got the feeling the old woman just wanted someone to visit with. He took his time with her and usually left her house with a paper plate loaded with homemade cookies or bars.

Just an hour ago, Danny responded to a disturbing the peace call at one of the Lake Vermillion resorts. Some drunk assholes had been playing loud music and whooping and hollering. When the onsite manager asked them to quiet down, the drunks turned the music louder, cursed, and threw empty beer cans at him. One of the cans had been unopened, and hit the manager in the forehead, almost knocking the poor man out. Danny had called a paramedic to the scene, then arrested a guy named Darryl, along with two other males. The back seat of Danny's Ford Explorer still smelled of stale beer after taking them to the station.

Danny had his windows down as he drove, trying to get the smell of beer out of the car. He relished the warmth because autumn would arrive all too soon, and shortly thereafter, winter. Danny definitely wasn't ready for winter yet.

Caught up in his thoughts, Danny almost missed the Deepstone mine entrance. He braked hard after glancing in his rearview mirror to make sure no cars were behind him. He was able to slow down in time to make the turn onto the gravel road that led to the Deepstone parking lot.

As Danny came around the last curve, he slowed to a stop. Police tape hung across the parking lot entrance. An FBI agent stood in front of it, glaring at him in the lights from his vehicle. She was tall, black, and beautiful.

FBI? What the hell was the FBI doing here at two in the morning? Danny wondered to himself. He put the SUV into "Park" and exited the vehicle, surreptitiously glanced around the area. He reached inside the vehicle, grabbed his hat off the passenger seat, put it on his head, then made his way over to the FBI agent. "Evening, agent. What's going on here?"

The FBI agent smiled. "Evening, Sheriff. Nothing serious. Just an investigation into a suspicious blasting incident at the Onamuni mine today. Covering all the bases."

Danny raised his eyebrows. "Really? Why wasn't the sheriff's office called in to help?"

She leaned forward conspiratorially, "I'm just an agent guarding a parking lot. I'm not exactly part of the investigation, if you know what I mean." Her voice was husky and pleasant.

Danny leaned slightly to look over her left shoulder. He didn't see any other agents around. Danny counted five SUVs with blacked-out windows in the parking lot. They didn't have any FBI markings on them. This didn't necessarily raise Danny's suspicions, as the FBI almost always used unmarked vehicles. But the vehicles did not have government plates, which he thought was strange. Danny also noticed that John Lukkinen's old Subaru was still in the lot. Seven other vehicles were also parked nearby. Danny had been to Deepstone quite a few times during his training on day shift, enough to recognize three of the cars belonged to Tracy, Carl, and Jim. But he had never seen the other four cars before. Besides, the lot should have been empty at 2:00 in the morning. Something strange was going on here.

Danny studied the agent, memorizing her features, clothing, and weapons without giving away what he was doing. He tilted his head and said, "I don't see any other agents around. And why are the employees' cars still here?"

The FBI agent shrugged, "The tourists were all sent away. The agents are interviewing a few of the mine employees in the ticketing office."

Danny knew this couldn't be true. Why would they be questioning John and his team in the middle of the night? The mine tours closed ten hours ago. He needed to call this in but didn't want to tip off the agent. Danny smiled amiably and said, "Ah huh. Makes sense. Alright, agent. Let the sheriff's department know if you need any help." He tipped his hat slightly, then walked back to his Ford Explorer. Danny casually backed up and turned around, then slowly drove away. He glanced in his rearview mirror. The agent stared at his vehicle as he drove away.

Once he was back on the road, Danny exhaled loudly. He had studied FBI tactics in numerous training courses. Nothing about that scene even remotely resembled standard FBI protocol. FBI agents rarely performed guard duty at a scene, they always called in local police for that work. And why were there so many vehicles in the lot? Why would they need so many agents here at Deepstone if they were just investigating leads for something that happened at Onamuni?

Danny grabbed his radio and called in, "Dispatch. This is Deputy Danny Miller."

A male voice replied, "Copy, Deputy Miller."

"I just stopped by the Deepstone mine in Angora Township. There are five FBI vehicles there and the place is cordoned off. I spoke to a single FBI agent on the scene. She said they were investigating an accident or something at Onamuni mine. Can you verify any of this?"

"Hold on, Deputy Miller."

Danny drove a couple miles further, then pulled over to the side of the road to wait. Five minutes passed when a vehicle approached, its headlights off. Danny flicked his lights on and off, the standard sign to let someone know their lights were off, but he was ignored. As it passed, Danny was startled to see a line of SUVs, all with their lights off. He counted ten of them and they looked identical to the six he'd seen already parked in the Deepstone lot. The windows were blacked out so he couldn't get a glimpse of anyone inside.

He watched them in his side-mirror until they

disappeared into the dark.

"What the hell?" he said out loud, to no one in particular.

CHAPTER 49

DIRECTOR JUDITH MEYERS had just taken her first bite of a cold hamburger that had been sitting on her desk for over an hour when her desk phone beeped three times. She had ordered the food from the 24-hour company cafeteria and was only now getting a chance to eat it. The three beeps indicated the call was a redirect from the St. Louis County, Minnesota sheriff office.

Thornlandon Holdings' IT department had been monitoring all law enforcement communications in northern Minnesota. They had recently intercepted a call between the sheriff's office in Virginia and one of their local deputies, Danny Miller. The young deputy had been nosing around and reported suspicious FBI activity at Deepstone. Thornlandon Holdings' IT team had set up a redirect from the sheriff's office to Director Meyers' phone if they tried to contact the FBI office to confirm the activities at Deepstone.

Director Meyers spit out her bite of food and picked up the phone, speaking harshly. "Assistant Executive Director Harper speaking." Jasmin Harper was the actual Assistant Executive Director of the Minneapolis FBI field office, a woman about Judith Meyers' age with a reputation for being less-than-friendly. Director Meyers had Harper's file in front of her, and had listened to a recording of her voice, which she now emulated.

A deep, male voice replied, "Assistant Executive Director Harper, this is Chief Deputy Sheriff Leonidas of the St. Louis County Sheriff's Office, in Virginia. I was wondering if I could ask you a couple of questions about some FBI activity going on up here in this area?"

Judith let out a loud sigh. "Make it quick, Sheriff Leonidas. I only have two minutes."

Sheriff Leonidas said, "Of course. Do you have an FBI action currently taking place at the Deepstone mine in Angora?"

"Yes, we do. It is a minor action relating to an explosion at the Onamuni mine. We suspect it might be a targeted attack. We've been seeing a bit of chatter from eco-terrorists on the Dark Web ever since the Onamuni mine opened up. You know, the basics: threats of violence, protests, that type of thing. Since Deepstone is only three miles from the Onamuni site, we felt it prudent to interview the employees there. We did not want to alarm anyone, so we kept this operation small and quiet. That is why we did not inform your office. We expect to complete the operation within forty-eight hours."

"Would you like our assistance?"

Director Meyers made her voice sound more reasonable, "No, Sheriff Leonidas, that will not be necessary. But you can help us by ensuring all law enforcement stays away from the Deepstone and Onamuni mines for the next forty-eight hours as we complete our investigation. We will share the results with you."

There was silence on the line for a few seconds, then Sheriff Leonidas said, "Of course. Consider it done."

"Thank you, Chief Deputy Sheriff Leonidas. Now, I must go. Thank you for calling." Director Meyers placed the phone back in the cradle before he could ask anything more.

She was just about to take another bite of her hamburger when her phone beeped again. She sighed and picked it up, "Yes?"

Senator Young's charming voice said, "Hello, Judith. How are you doing tonight?"

Director Meyers rolled her eyes. He was the last person she wanted to speak with right now. But she forced an easy demeanor and replied, "I'm fine, Senator. How may I help you?"

"I just wanted to let you know I am resigning from the Board of Thornlandon Holdings."

Director Meyers' heartbeat quickened. Senator Young would not easily give up such a lucrative position. Money and power were all he cared about. She causally asked, "Oh? And why would you do that?"

"I have an election coming up in 2026. You know opposition researchers: they won't stop digging until they find dirt on me. I do not wish to have my involvement on the Thornlandon Holdings board come to light. And if it does, my financials must remain clean, especially if Thornlandon Holdings' stock shoots up after your recent multi-trillion-dollar discovery becomes public knowledge. I may face investigations of insider trading and fraud, especially when it shows that I joined the board and bought stock just before the discovery."

"I understand. You are a smart man. If that is truly your wish, Senator, I will draw up the paperwork to accept your resignation from the board. But I must remind you, the NDA you signed remains in effect even if you are not a board member. You cannot disclose any information about Thornlandon Holdings to anyone."

Senator Young chuckled good-naturedly. "Judith, it is in both of our interests for me to keep my lips sealed. I am selling my shares as we speak. You will never hear from me again, which I am sure your assistant, Helen, will be happy to hear."

Director Meyers smiled. "I'm sure Helen likes you very much. Thank you for contacting me directly. You will receive the resignation paperwork within the hour. Goodbye, Senator Young."

"Thank you. I wish you all the best, Judith "

Director Meyers replaced the phone in the cradle, her mind racing. Something was going on with the senator. She did not trust that man in any way. While his excuses made logical sense, it wasn't in his nature to give up on anything, much less the potential for billions of dollars in profit. She called out, "Helen, come in here."

Her door opened immediately, and Helen walked briskly over to her desk, her heels clicking on the floor.

"Did you listen into that phone call?"

"Of course, Director Meyers."

"What should we do about the senator?"

Helen immediately said, "I suspect he is the one

who sent the text to Renn earlier, warning him of our plan. But since we cannot prove it, and we cannot seem to do anything *to* the senator right now, we must continue monitoring his activities."

Director Meyers leaned back, then scowled at her uneaten hamburger. She pushed it off her desk into the waste basket, her appetite gone. "We still haven't been able to hack into his phone?"

Helen shook her head. "We have our best working on it, but so far, no success. We are not sure how he has such a sophisticated security setup, but we will crack it."

Director Meyers swore, then closed her eyes to think. *The senator was just too powerful, and she didn't believe him when he said she would never hear from him again. Too much was riding on keeping the discovery beneath Deepstone a secret until they gained full control the mine—and disposed of the witnesses currently down there.* She opened her eyes and glared at Helen. "We can't let the senator go to the press or start a congressional investigation. He may blow the whistle on us just to shoot to the top of the next presidential ticket."

Helen's mouth creased into something almost resembling a smile. "Are you saying what I think you are saying?"

Lacing her fingers behind her head, Director Meyers looked up at the ceiling, thinking quickly through the situation. She lowered her gaze to Helen. "Yes. Make it look like an accident. This has to be completely clean."

Helen nodded. "I will send in Kala. Senator Young will be dead within weeks. Even the deepest investigations will show it was just an accident."

"Let me know when it is done."

Helen nodded and left the office, her mobile phone already at her ear.

Director Meyers felt her stomach rumble, her appetite suddenly back. She thought of calling for a freshly made hamburger but decided she didn't want to wait. She leaned to her side and fished the cold burger from her waste basket. She removed a yellow sticky note from the bun, then took a large bite.

For the first time in days, she felt like they had a good plan. By tomorrow, they would sign the paperwork for the mine and surrounding 600-acre property. Once they removed all witnesses, including the senator, they could bring all the resources of Thornlandon Holdings to the mine. Nothing could stop them.

CHAPTER 50

MONIQUE watched the young deputy sheriff drive away, glad she had been able to get rid of him. He was young, nice, and innocent. She didn't want him anywhere nearby for what was to come. Glancing at her smart watch, which was connected to her phone, she read the encrypted texts from the approaching teams. They would arrive in less than ten minutes.

She had waited as long as she could, hoping her team would exfiltrate the mine with the civilians and SafeWell team. Sally and Karl had come up three hours earlier and taken Tess, Terryl, and Gwen back down to fight an ostensibly unkillable creature called a Vorgroth, something she still had difficulty accepting was true. Since then, no one else had come out of the mine. Monique must now follow Sally's orders and exfiltrate the area. There was nothing more she could do for her team.

Glancing around the area in the lingering light of

the recent full moon, Monique listened carefully to make sure no advance team had entered the area. Confident she was still alone, she ran into the woods and made her way to the edge of the Deepstone parking lot entrance from Hwy 1. She looked both ways and listened but didn't see or hear any approaching cars. Crossing the road was the most dangerous part of her escape. Thornlandon Holdings' teams always approached a nighttime target site with their headlights off, using their night vision to drive.

An hour earlier, Monique had driven one of the SUVs a mile east down Hwy 1, turned down a small dirt road, and driven a quarter of a mile until she found an unused overgrown track that led into the woods. She pulled in, parked the vehicle, and jogged back to Deepstone.

Now, Monique took a quick breath and dashed across the blacktop road. She dropped down into the ditch, then crawled her way through the long grass until she got to the tree line. She had only taken a few steps into the woods when she heard the sound of vehicle tires approaching in the distance. Monique immediately crouched down behind a large Norway pine tree. As she had anticipated, she didn't see any headlights. The vehicles stopped about a half mile away. She knew the standard operating procedures. Between four and six black-clad snipers would exit the rear vehicle and melt into the tree line on the opposite side of the road. They would approach the mine site silently from the woods, spread out, and when they had her, Tess, Gwen, and Terryl in their sights, they would count down from three and shoot in unison, killing her team instantly. The vehicles would remain in the same location for eight minutes, then slowly approach the Deepstone entrance directly across from her.

Monique melted into the woods and began her long trek toward where she had hidden the SUV. As she did, she sent a prayer to her friends.

May God help them.

CHAPTER 51

DEPUTY SHERIFF DANNY MILLER'S radio squawked, "Deputy Miller, do you copy?"

"Yes, go ahead."

"Are you sure you saw FBI at Deepstone?"

"Well, the agent was wearing FBI clothing, but I didn't request any identification. I also saw ten more SUVs pass me about an hour ago heading toward Deepstone, all of them identical to the five I reported parked in the Deepstone lot. Oddly, they passed me with their headlights off."

There was silence, then a different voice came on. "Deputy Miller, this is Chief Deputy Sheriff Leonidas. Did you say the ten SUVs had their headlights turned off?"

Deputy Danny Miller was startled to hear his boss's voice so late at night. For the Chief Deputy Sheriff to come down to the station in the middle of the night, it must mean there was something very serious happening. Danny nodded, even though he was on the radio, and said, "Yes, sir. Pretty suspicious, if you ask me."

Leonidas murmured, "Indeed. Very strange." He spoke loudly and clearly, "Stay where you are. We are sending twenty vehicles your way. They will arrive within an hour. Are you still parked along Hwy 1?"

Danny felt a thrill course through his body, in spite of himself. "Yes, Chief. I am parked on the side of the Hwy 1, three miles west of Deepstone. I will wait here. Oh, and Chief?"

"Yes Deputy Miller?"

"I have a bad feeling about this whole thing. I suggest you bring heavy weaponry, as well. Just in case."

Leonidas paused for a few seconds, then came back with, "I trust your gut and will act accordingly, Deputy Miller."

Danny started his Explorer and pulled a U-turn to park on the other side of the road, facing Deepstone. He would be ready to go when his back-up arrived.

CHAPTER 52

JOHN reached the ladder leading up to Level eight and cracked his back, satisfied by the sound. He stepped over to Claire, Andy, Ethan, Jim, Tammy, and Carl, who huddled together in the tunnel not far away from the alcove where the ladder was. "How are you all doing?"

Claire sat down and put her back to the wall, her face pale.

They had been making their way up through the levels of the mine at a quick pace, now that Renn's and Morgan's teams were helping to scout out the location of the ladders leading up to each new level. They had climbed fourteen levels since the Vorgroth had been killed. Up on these higher levels of the mine, the ladders were regularly staggered about five hundred feet apart. John figured the mining company had alternated the entrance and exit point locations according to a plan or blueprint. But as the mine had gone deeper into the earth, they may have created the ladder access points with less intention, merely putting them wherever it had been convenient to access the other levels.

Even though they hadn't had to travel very far between access points, the fast pace had taken its toll on Claire. She was in her nineties, after all. Even John, who considered himself pretty fit, was having a difficult time keeping up the agonizing pace. He stepped closer to Morgan and Renn, who seemed to have formed an instant bond as they settled into co-commander roles for the mission. John spoke quietly to them, "I don't think Claire is going to make it up many more levels."

They both glanced back to see Claire slumped against the wall, her face white, her breathing hard. Renn swore softly. "We need to keep moving. The other kill teams must be getting close to this level by now. I sent Ficks ahead and told him to find a way out to the surface. I expect to see him back soon. I also sent Millie back down a few levels to watch our six. If she sees any sign of the kill teams, she will warn us. So far, we've been lucky, but we can't remain stationary for very much longer."

Morgan nodded. "I'll have Jack carry her. Claire can't weigh more than ninety pounds. Jack can climb each ladder with her strapped to his back and holding on to his neck." She softly whistled and both Jack and Karen turned to look. Morgan motioned for Jack to join her.

He quickly made his way over to her.

"Jack, would you carry Claire from here on out? If you get tired, you can switch with another member of Renn's team. But we need to keep moving fast and she won't make it on her own."

Jack nodded. "Affirmative. I'll hook up a harness

for her right now." He turned and with Karen's help, they emptied Jack's large military pack and redistributed the contents to the other team members. Jack then cut holes in the top and bottom of the pack, creating a makeshift harness.

John was impressed. Jack's large pack was the perfect choice, as it was already meant to strap to his back. They were able to get Claire's legs and arms through the holes they had cut so she was sitting inside the pack yet had her arms and legs free. She was kept close to his back and was able to put her arms around him, much like riding on the back of a motorcycle.

John noticed the guilty, slightly ashamed look on Claire's face, so he patted her hand. "You will be fine, Claire. Jack is happy to help you, so don't feel bad. It is for the good of us all that we move quickly."

Claire nodded. "Thank you, John. When we get out of this, you must come by the house and meet my granddaughter, Mia. She is about your age. You two would like each other."

John smiled at her. "When we get out of this mine, I will take you up on that, Claire."

Claire took John's hand in hers and squeezed it with a small smile. "I will hold you to that, John." She let go of John's hand as Jack walked, with her on his back, toward the ladder leading up to Level eight.

Morgan grinned as John watched Jack and Claire walk away. "Looks like you just got a date, John."

John felt his face redden. Then he chuckled. "The funny thing is, I will call her. If Claire's granddaughter is anything like Claire, I could do a lot worse. That woman is in her nineties and is braver than most people I've ever known."

Morgan put a hand on his shoulder. "I agree.

Now, it's time for you to climb."

John went up the ladder, surprised at how he no longer thought twice about climbing a one-hundred-foot ladder through a hole in solid rock deep within the earth. They climbed up five more levels before meeting up with Ficks.

The wiry man pointed up a ladder and spoke to Renn and Morgan. "The way is clear through the final two levels, all the way to the surface. The final hatch opens onto the forest floor about a hundred meters from the mine buildings. I didn't see any sign of the kill teams near the opening, although I suspect they have four or five snipers stationed throughout the woods."

"Ok, good work. So far, we have stayed ahead of the kill teams chasing us, and with any luck, we will be able to slip away quietly when we reach the surface."

Pounding feet approached down the tunnel. Millie raced around the corner and slid to a stop in front of Renn. "They are two levels below us and moving fast."

Renn seemed to have expected this news—or at least wasn't surprised by it. He sternly addressed the group, "Everyone, we need to move more quickly. Millie, stay back as far as you can to monitor the kill teams."

They moved as fast as they could through the tunnel. This passageway, like the previous dozen or so, was wider than the tunnels in the lower levels. John suspected that the deeper the miners went into the earth, the narrower the tunnels would become to ensure they were well supported.

They soon arrived at the alcove with the ladder that went up to Level two and quickly climbed it.

They traversed Levels two and one without stopping and finally reached the ladder leading up to the surface.

John's heart raced. They were so close. How he longed to breathe fresh air again.

Millie rushed forward, her eyes bright and her face flushed. "They are on this level and will reach us in two minutes."

Renn nodded and motioned, "Everyone, up the ladder now. It will be dark outside. Remain silent and move deeper into the forest as you exit the hatch. Be ready for an attack from the kill teams out there, including snipers. Go, go, go!"

Ficks, Greg, Karl, Terryl, Karen, Gwen, and Sally went up first to secure the area, then Jack carried Claire up the ladder. Andy, Ethan, Tammy, Carl, and Jim followed.

That left John, Renn, Morgan, Bauwen, Millie, and Tess still down below.

Renn motioned for John to climb, and he practically flew up the ladder, the exhaustion he had felt just a moment ago now dissipated by a rush of adrenaline at finally reaching the surface.

John climbed through the hatch as gunfire erupted below him. He quickly stepped onto the forest floor. A nearly full moon provided a soft, unearthly glow to the woods. He breathed in deeply. Smelling the earthen aroma of the woods was the most enjoyable experience he thought he had ever had.

Bauwen, Millie, and Tess soon exited the hatch, followed by Morgan.

Renn was last and almost tumbled out of the opening.

Millie quietly lowered the steel hatch and spun the wheel.

351

A voice softly called out from the woods, "John, is that you?"

CHAPTER 53

A half-hour earlier, as DEPUTY SHERIFF DANNY MILLER sat in his vehicle on the side of Hwy 1 waiting for the rest of the backup vehicles to arrive, he got a call on his personal cell phone from Chief Deputy Sheriff Leonidas.

"Miller, this is Leonidas. We have staged at the intersection of Hwy 53 and Hwy 1 about two miles from you. But we have a hell of a complication. I need you to do something for me before we can proceed."

Without hesitating, Danny asked, "What do you need me to do, Chief?"

"I called the Minneapolis FBI office and was told to stand down. Apparently, this is a quiet FBI investigation into the explosion at Onamuni today. They've asked us to keep everyone away from Onamuni and Deepstone for the next forty-eight hours. We are not to approach the Deepstone mine under any circumstances."

Danny felt his blood run cold. "But sir—that was clearly no FBI agent I saw at Deepstone. And those ten SUVs were likely carrying a large force of people. I would stake my career on it. Something is not right here."

"I agree, Deputy. I just received a mysterious call, as well. Someone I do not know, and who did not identify himself, told me there is an emergency at Deepstone that we need to investigate immediately. It appears that someone is trying to keep us away from Deepstone, while someone else is trying to do the opposite. Off the record, I need you to get proof that this is no FBI action. It could be dangerous for you, but if pressed, I can justify it as a lone Deputy just doing his job. Whereas, if I send in twenty vehicles after being ordered to stand down, and it turns out to be a real FBI investigation, we will all be out of jobs by morning. Do not engage. Just report to me what you see."

"Roger that, Chief."

"Oh, and Deputy Miller? You be safe, you hear?"

"Yes, sir. I promise I will."

Danny knew this area well. Not far away was a small grassy field where he and his high school friends had partied a few times. Danny started his Explorer. The moon was bright, so he turned off the headlights. He drove a couple miles, keeping his speed under 30 mph to keep the road noise from his tires to a minimum. Soon he saw the old car tracks leading into the woods to his left. Danny turned off the road and slowly followed the tracks through the wooded area until he came to a small field. He turned his engine off and quietly exited the vehicle, shutting the door with a soft click instead of slamming it. Sound carried in the woods, especially at night.

Danny opened the back of the vehicle and put on his tactical vest. He then grabbed the M16A1 assault rifle from the rack, along with three magazines. Finally, he attached his police camera to his vest and activated it. There was a night vision scope in a case in the back, but he left it. The moon was too bright to use it, anyway. Danny quietly closed the back of the vehicle.

He turned the volume of his radio down as low as it would go, lifted it to his mouth and said, "This is Deputy Miller. I am parked in the old beer-drinking field a quarter of a mile behind Deepstone." Most of the deputies in the Northland knew the high school party places. He continued, "I will approach on foot from here. Going radio silent from here on out."

The soft voice of Chief Deputy Sheriff Leonidas replied, "Roger that."

Danny turned the volume completely off. He moved across the small, grassy field and soon entered the tree line. He found a narrow deer trail and followed it through the trees. An owl hooted in the distance, and another owl responded from the opposite direction. Within five minutes, he could see the lights from Deepstone through the trees. He slowed down, careful where he placed each step. He had been raised in the country and had hunted deer his whole life. He knew how to be quiet in the woods.

Danny was about three-hundred feet from the mine clearing when he heard a soft swish of cloth to his left. He froze, holding his breath as he listened. He slowly turned his head and saw a shadow of a figure crouching next to a tree not more than three feet from him, peering through the scope of a long rifle toward the mine. Deputy Danny Miller shifted his weight slightly and his shoe brushed against a twig on the ground. The sound wasn't much, but it was enough for the figure to spin around toward him and point the rifle right at his face. Danny dove to the ground as the rifle quietly spat twice, the suppressor making a soft hiss. The shots missed him. Danny lunged forward into the figure and tackled the person to the ground.

Danny heard a soft cry. The person struggled briefly, then seemed to weaken until they became still beneath him. Danny pushed himself off the shooter and carefully pulled the black head covering from their face. He gasped. A sharp, jagged branch about an inch in diameter had pierced through the middle of woman's neck, the wound pumping thick blood around the wood. Her eyes stared at him vacantly, opened wide as if in surprise.

Danny sat back on his heels, feeling sick to his stomach. He had just killed someone. Danny had never even gotten into a fight before. He stared at the woman's face, unable to look away from her vacant eyes.

After a few moments, Danny swallowed hard, then leaned forward to examine the body. He rifled through her vest and pants pockets, but found no ID. She didn't even have a driver's license on her. This was no FBI agent. He lifted his radio, turned the volume back on at its lowest setting, and said, "This is Deputy Miller. Do you copy?"

Leonidas immediately replied, "Yes. Do you have anything?"

Danny gave him a short report of what had happened, ending with, "What do you want me to do?"

Before Leonidas could respond, Danny heard a swishing sound. Then, about ten feet away, the leaves on the forest floor rose up to reveal a hatch in the ground. Danny immediately turned his radio off and lowered himself to the ground, worried it was another sniper. He peered through the brush.

A man rose halfway through the opening and looked carefully around. He didn't see Danny, who remained perfectly still.

The man silently climbed out and another person immediately exited the opening, followed by another.

Danny heard automatic gunfire from below the people. The sounds were soft and muffled, obviously equipped with suppressors.

Danny stayed still and silently watched as a steady stream of people climbed quickly out of the hatch and into the clearing. When it looked like everyone was topside, a woman holding an automatic rifle softly closed the hatch and spun a wheel to lock it.

Danny studied the group, a mixture of hardened soldiers and civilians, including a boy of about fourteen and an old woman who must be in her nineties. He knew right away these people were not part of the fake FBI operation.

Then he recognized John Lukkinen.

Danny stood and softly called out, "John, is that you?"

The soldiers immediately raised and pointed their weapons toward Danny.

John spoke up, "He's OK. I know him."

Renn stepped forward and studied Danny closely for a few seconds, then knelt down to study the dead woman at Danny's feet. Renn relaxed slightly and whispered over his shoulder, "He's a real deputy and not part of Thornlandon Holdings." He turned back to Danny and softly said, "Deputy, did you kill this woman?"

Danny nodded, "Yes, sir. She tried to kill me, and when I tackled her, a stick punctured her neck."

Renn glanced down, then looked at him quizzically. "I wouldn't have believed anyone could get close enough to Charlene to kill her. She was one of the best snipers in the unit."

Danny stepped back. "She was with you?"

"Not exactly. She was sent here to kill us. There will be more time later to explain. Right now, we need your help to get away from here."

Danny nodded. "I know a way through the woods back to my vehicle."

Renn turned to the group and quietly said, "Sally, follow the Deputy and get everyone out of here. Millie, Morgan, and I will cover you."

Gunfire suddenly erupted from the direction of the mine, bullets striking trees all around them.

Danny crouched low and turned, raising his weapon. He could not see who was shooting, so he spun around and called out to those around him, "Follow me." Then he took off down the narrow deer trail, not looking back to verify if the group of people were behind him or not.

Within just a few minutes, he arrived at the field where he had parked his Explorer. Danny turned to see the group right behind him. He gestured toward the vehicle. "Quick, get behind the truck." He pulled his radio from the clip at his shoulder and cranked the volume up. Only slightly out of breath he said, "This is Deputy Miller. I located a group of people who exited from the mine via a secret hatch. They are friendlies. We are being chased by whomever was in the ten SUVs. They are firing upon us. I repeat, they are firing at us. They have fully automatic weapons.

They are shooting to kill. I repeat. They are shooting to kill. Over."

Chief Deputy Sheriff Leonidas replied instantly. "We on our way. ETA, two minutes."

"Roger that. Out."

Danny joined the people behind his truck. Within seconds, Renn, Millie, and Morgan emerged from the tree line, walking backward and firing their weapons in short bursts.

Millie suddenly spun around. She had obviously been hit and fell to the ground without even a cry. Neither Renn nor Morgan noticed, concentrating on returning fire.

Danny jumped out from behind the truck and sprinted across the field to the fallen woman. Her left leg had been torn apart by multiple bullet impacts. He bent down and hoisted her up over his shoulder and sprinted back to the vehicle as bullets struck all around him. Not far from the truck, he felt a searing pain in his arm, and then another in his leg. He half-fell to the ground, his strength suddenly gone. He struggled to his feet and staggered forward until he reached the truck. John helped him carefully lower Millie to the ground behind it.

Sally, Karl, and Gwen leaned against the hood of the truck, returning fire. Ficks, and Greg were shooting from around the back of the truck. Karen and Jack were kneeling and returning fire. Tess and Terryl were lying on the ground about ten yards away, carefully taking aim and shooting with their sniper rifles. They all fired into the woods, replacing spent magazines so smoothly that they hardly had to stop firing.

In the distance, Danny heard sirens screaming in the night.

Renn and Morgan arrived out of breath. Suddenly Renn yelled out, "They have an RPG. Get away from the truck! Run toward the woods. Now, now, now!"

Danny scooped up Millie, the pain in his leg and arm almost making him fall back to the ground. He gritted his teeth and straightened up, Millie in his arms, and limped toward the woods as quickly as he could go, following the fleeing figures around him. He made it fifteen strides before he heard a whoosh, followed by a huge explosion. He was thrown forward by the blast and landed hard on top of Millie.

Danny lay on top of Millie for a few seconds, his ears ringing and brain refusing to work. Finally, he forced himself to roll over. Turning his head, Danny saw his Ford Explorer on its side, flames roaring through its twisted metal.

Following the explosion, at least fifteen figures stepped out of the tree line, all firing their weapons.

Millie sat groggily up, unaware of the danger, and Danny pulled her back down to the ground.

They were sitting ducks, with no cover. Bullets struck the ground around Danny. He heard a couple muffled cries as other people were hit. Danny rolled away from Millie and struggled to pull his assault rifle from his back. His thoughts seemed to move in slow motion, but he was finally able to get the rifle into his hands. Danny wiped sweat from his eyes, then leaned forward. Another bullet hit the ground right next to him, but he ignored it as he sighted across the field. He chambered a round, released the safety, and set the rifle to single shot. He let out his breath, even as more bullets impacted the earth around him, one hitting only six inches from his head.

Danny felt a sense of calm as he settled on an approaching figure, lining the sight with the person's head. He suspected they were probably wearing tactical Kevlar armor, so he avoided a center-mass shot. He squeezed the trigger. The soldier's head snapped backward, and they dropped limply to the ground. Danny quickly moved to the next figure, settled his aim once again on the head, and squeezed the trigger. The person fell dead. He quickly followed with two more kills.

The sirens were loud now. Danny's eyes blurred, either from sweat or a concussion, he didn't know. He blinked but couldn't clear his vision.

Then sheriffs' vehicles shrieked as they raced into the field, fanning out before stopping. Officers immediately exited their vehicles, knelt behind their doors, and started firing at the people across the field. A helicopter roared up and shined a spotlight at the enemy soldiers. This was enough for them. The remaining soldiers quickly retreated back into the forest.

Chief Deputy Sheriff Leonidas yelled instructions into his radio, then called out, "SWAT is close. ETA, seven minutes. Deputy Jenkins, take ten cars to the Deepstone entrance and block it. The chopper will support you. Now!" he yelled.

Ten vehicles spun around and roared down the trail back to Hwy 1, and Danny could hear their sirens moving away toward the Deepstone entrance.

Leonidas ran over to Danny and knelt down, concern in his eyes. "Are you injured, Deputy?"

"I took a couple of hits, but I think I am fine."

Renn stepped over and held out his hand to Leonidas. "My name is Renn Holder. Thank you for your help."

Leonidas looked up at Renn, then held out his hand, "Chief Deputy Sheriff Leonidas. Stick around

361

when this is over. I have a lot of questions."

"Of course, Sheriff."

Leonidas picked up his radio. "We need Emergency Medical Services to our location." He replaced the radio and yelled out to three deputies, "We need med kits over here."

The deputies ran to their vehicles, grabbed the kits, and returned. One of them knelt by Danny, but he shook his head and pointed to Millie. "Her first. She is in bad shape."

The deputy nodded and went to work on Millie's wounds.

Lying in a dazed state, Danny heard the SWAT team pass by, including the rumble of a tactical vehicle.

Then his eyes closed, and he passed out.

CHAPTER 54

MORGAN turned her head as four Audi Q7 SUVs, all with blacked-out windows, pulled up to the scene five minutes after the sheriff's team arrived. The sheriff deputy guarding the entrance to the field lifted her rifle as the Audi doors opened and four people exited the vehicles, all dressed casually, as if they were tourists. One man stepped forward and held up an ID badge. Morgan was not surprised to see that it was her boss, Henry Skuggs. The sheriff studied the ID carefully, then nodded and pointed to Chief Deputy Sheriff Leonidas, who was still calling out commands into his radio.

Skuggs strode across the field and stopped next to Leonidas, waiting patiently for him to finish his commands.

Finally, Leonidas put the radio back onto his shoulder mount and faced Skuggs. They briefly spoke. Skuggs showed his badge again and Leonidas pointed across the field, then lifted his radio again and began talking into it.

Skuggs made his way across the grassy area and approached Morgan, who had been helping a medic stop the bleeding in Millie's torn-up leg. Deputy Danny Miller was passed out not far away, another deputy tending to his wounds until the medics arrived. Morgan had been told that Miller had calmly shot four of the kill team's soldiers after he had saved Millie, taking two bullets himself in the process. He was a man she would like to have on the SafeWell team. You never truly knew a person until you saw them in battle. The toughest-looking soldier might run as soon as bullets began flying, while a less physically-impressive soldier may be the one who stays and fights to the end.

Morgan nodded to Skuggs as she held a bandage against one of Millie's wounds while the sheriff wrapped gauze around it. The medics had not yet arrived, so they were doing what they could with the minimal supplies they had. When the sheriff finished wrapping the wound, Morgan stood up. "Thank you, Sheriff." The young woman nodded and returned to her vehicle to put the small medical kit into the trunk.

Morgan turned to Skuggs. "Sir, how did you get here so quickly?"

Grimly looking around at all the damage, Skuggs turned back to Morgan and said, "When I received your MATCOM transmissions, I immediately gathered a small team and came here." He smiled slightly and said, "Drove 140 miles per hour from that little Cook airport. Thankfully, all the police were already here. It would have been a problematic ticket if we had been pulled over." His smile faded as he asked, "Are Jack and Karen alright?"

Morgan motioned with her head toward Jack and Karen who stood near the edge of the field, shielding

Bauwen from prying eyes. They had wrapped
Bauwen in a blanket to hide her unusual skin.

Skuggs squinted. "Is that…?"

"Yes, that is Bauwen behind them. We decided to
keep her out of sight. Can you get her out of here and
back to headquarters? The fewer people who notice
her, the better."

"Of course." He motioned with his hand and the
three SafeWell operatives who had accompanied him
stepped forward. Skuggs motioned with his head
toward the woods. "Bring the cars over there and take
Jack, Karen, and their guest away from here. Quietly.
Bring them to the plane at the airport and get them
back to headquarters immediately. I will charter
another plane later."

The three operatives nodded curtly and
immediately jogged back to two of the Audis and
slowly drove them toward Jack, Karen, and Bauwen.
They had to zigzag around the still-burning pieces of
Danny's SUV.

Morgan walked across the field, followed by
Skuggs. They joined Jack, Karen, and Bauwen just as
the vehicles arrived.

Morgan said, "Jack, Karen, please take Bauwen
back to headquarters. Skuggs and I will follow once
we wrap things up here."

Jack and Karen dipped their heads in
acknowledgement.

Morgan stepped closer to Bauwen. "Would you
please go with them? We need to get you to safety.
Our headquarters is the safest place you could ever
be."

Bauwen looked around with wide, frightened
eyes, cringing from the dozens of people rushing
about the field and the flashing blue and red lights

everywhere. She looked to Morgan and nodded. "I would like to leave this bright and noisy place. Will you be coming with me?"

Morgan placed a hand on Bauwen's shoulder, the first time she had touched her. "I will follow in a short while. This is my boss, Henry Skuggs. Skuggs, meet Bauwen."

Skuggs nodded to Bauwen. "It is a pleasure to meet you."

Bauwen half smiled but didn't respond to his greeting.

Morgan continued, "We need to take care of things here first. I will see you in a day, maybe two."

"Okay. I trust you." Then Bauwen surprised Morgan by stepping forward and hugging her tightly. Bauwen whispered in Morgan's ear, "Thank you. For everything." Then she stepped back.

Smiling, Morgan said, "You are welcome."

Karen opened the Audi's back door, but Bauwen held back, staring at the vehicle with suspicion. "What is this thing?"

Karen smiled, "It is called an SUV. It transports us to places. Don't worry, it is safe."

Bauwen leaned forward to looking into the interior, then slid into the plush back seat.

Karen shut the door. She nodded to Skuggs and Morgan, walked around to the other side, and got into the front seat. A SafeWell agent got behind the wheel.

Jack got into the back seat of the second Audi as the two other agents slid into the front.

Morgan turned to thank Skuggs but saw him standing twenty feet away talking with Leonidas again, who turned to study the two vehicles for a moment before nodding and motioning to his deputies to let them leave the active site.

The two Audi SUVs slowly drove out of the field, down the narrow track, and disappeared from view.

Skuggs made his way back to Morgan. "We have work to do here. Who is that large man over there?"

Morgan turned her head and saw Renn standing next to Tess, who was being worked on by a sheriff with a medical kit. "His name is Renn Holder. He is the leader of the first team sent in by Thornlandon Holdings. They were sent to kill us, but he and his team helped us instead. Without them, we would likely not have escaped from the mine."

Skuggs murmured, "Is that so? Interesting. Thornlandon Holdings will not let these people live."

"Yes, sir. I was thinking that SafeWell may want to increase its employee count."

"That is a capital idea. Now, let's get them all out of here." He strode over to Leonidas and spoke with him for some time. Eventually, Leonidas seemed to agree with whatever Skuggs was saying and gave a curt nod.

Morgan made her way to Renn, who turned to her as she stopped next to him. She looked down and asked, "How is Tess?"

Renn looked back at Tess. She was bleeding, and slightly burned, but she was conscious and feebly trying to bat the sheriff's hand away as he tried to bandage her wounds. "She'll be fine." His positive words didn't match his look of worry, though.

They heard more sirens approaching, and soon four red paramedic trucks entered the field, lights flashing. Twelve paramedics spread out to assess the injured, each carrying large bags filled with medical equipment. Renn called out, "Over here!"

Two of them rushed over and the young deputy who had been trying to help Tess gratefully stepped away, happy to let the medics take over. The medical professionals immediately began working on Tess, so Renn and Morgan stepped back to give them space.

Morgan touched his arm. "Renn, she is in good hands."

"I know. I just hate seeing her like this."

"There is someone you need to meet." She turned and walked slowly toward Skuggs, Renn by her side. Morgan said, "That is my boss. He is the founder of SafeWell. His name is…"

"Henry Skuggs," Renn completed the introduction. "I have heard much about SafeWell and Henry Skuggs. We operate in a small world."

Morgan nodded. "That's right. He has given the go ahead to bring you and your team to our headquarters in New Mexico until things settle down. You will all be safe there."

"But for how long? We can't stay there forever."

Morgan didn't have an answer for that, so she stayed quiet.

Skuggs turned toward Morgan and Renn and gave a quick motion toward the other two Audis.

Morgan said, "Come on, let's get your team out of here."

"Thank you. I suspect Thornlandon Holdings will arrive soon, so I appreciate you getting my people to safety. But I need to stay with Tess, Millie, and Ficks. They need immediate hospital care."

Morgan smiled in understanding, and softly said, "Tess, Millie, and Ficks will be flown by helicopter to St. Mary's hospital in Duluth, a Level I trauma center. Skuggs has secured a private wing of the hospital. There will be no record of them being admitted, so Thornlandon Holdings will not find them. The rest of your team with minor or no injuries can fly back to

SafeWell headquarters via our private jet, where the injured will receive excellent medical care."

Renn seemed to relax. "That is good. Thank you. I will stay back with Tess, Millie, and Ficks. They will not be safe in the hospital. I know Thornlandon Holdings. Director Meyers will find where my people are and try to eliminate them."

Morgan silently cursed Thornlandon Holdings, then said. "We will not let that happen. We will post guards at each of their rooms until they are strong enough to be moved."

"Thank you, but I still will not leave them."

Morgan shrugged. "I understand. I will see you back at SafeWell headquarters in a few days, then."

Renn held his hand out. "It's a date."

Morgan slapped his hand away, cocked her head and looked at him sideways as she turned. "We'll see about that."

Renn grinned as she walked away.

CHAPTER 55

JOHN absently watched the police and paramedics rushing around the field, securing the area and loading the wounded into ambulances. He was so tired that he wanted nothing more than to close his eyes and let sleep take him. Instead, he took a deep breath and rubbed his eyes, which didn't seem to help. Numerous flashlights bobbed through the woods as the various law enforcement agencies searched the area. John had not heard any gunfire for at least half an hour, so he assumed that either the police and SWAT had defeated the kill teams from Thornlandon Holdings, or they had escaped.

Dawn was beginning to light up the eastern horizon, turning the black sky a deep, dark blue. John sat on the grassy ground, a blanket around his shoulders. Near him sat Tammy, Carl and Jim. And not far away, Ethan, Andy, and Claire huddled closely together, blankets around their shoulders shielding them from the cool air. Although it had been hot yesterday, the temperature had dropped to the low fifties overnight.

John rubbed his eyes again. He was more tired than he remembered ever having been in his life. One of the paramedics told him it was 5:28 a.m. He and his group had been trapped down in the mine for over twelve hours, but it had felt like days. He couldn't believe they had made it safely back to the surface. *Not all of us did, though*, John thought. Milton, Fiona, Ben, and Larry had not made it out alive. And eight soldiers from Renn's team had been killed, as well. He shivered at the thought of just how close they had all come to dying down there.

Andy stood up and approached him. The teenager's eyes showed a depth of sorrow that no child should know. Andy sat down by John. He didn't say a word. He was obviously struggling.

John put an arm around the boy's shoulder. "Are you alright, Andy?"

"I honestly don't know, Mr. John. I…I…," and then he started to cry. Andy turned and buried his face against John's shoulder. Tears fell freely down his cheeks as he quietly sobbed.

John wrapped his other arm around Andy and held him close.

Andy cried on his shoulder for a short while longer. When he quieted, John loosened his hug and Andy pulled away, wiping tears and snot on his sleeve, looking embarrassed. "I'm sorry, Mr. John. I feel so empty inside. I just can't believe my dad is dead. And Mr. Milton. And all the rest."

"Don't apologize for your feelings, Andy. Ever. What you went through down there is more than most people ever deal with in their whole lives." John leaned closer and quietly and fiercely said, "Your dad was a good man. The best." John touched Andy's chest with a finger and said, "He will always be right here, inside of your heart."

John then touched Andy's forehead, "And your dad will always be with you here, in your thoughts and memories. You will always remember the thousands of little moments you and he had together. Larry's strength will always be there inside of you, guiding you through good times and bad."

Andy started crying again. But now he wasn't ashamed of his tears. He looked into John's eyes and said, "Thank you, Mr. John. I will never forget you, either. Not for as long as I live."

John smiled, tears welling up in his own eyes. "Nor I, you, Andy. One day, we will all get together and reminisce about your dad and catch up on each other's lives. I look forward to hearing about the great things you will achieve in your life. You have a bright future."

"We're really going to see each other again? Promise?"

"Of course."

Sniffling, Andy nodded. "I would like that. I would like that a lot." He pushed himself to his feet, then leaned down to hug John one last time before turning and walking over to sit next to Ethan. He put an arm around his son and smiled at John, mouthing the words, "Thank you."

John sat for almost another hour before they were all brought back to the sheriff's headquarters in Virginia to give their official statements. Their vehicles were also brought back to headquarters, ready when their ordeal was finally over.

It wasn't until nine in the morning that John finally parked his Subaru on the street in front of his house on 5th Street. As he got out of the car and walked up his sidewalk, John stopped. He closed his eyes and tilted his face up to the bright sun above him, feeling the warmth on his face. It felt like weeks since he had left the house to go to work, even though it had only been the previous morning. As John stood there, he knew his life would never be the same again. Whether that was good or bad, he did not yet know.

John took a deep breath, then lowered his head, opened his eyes, and walked the rest of the way to his front door. He unlocked it, kicked off his shoes in the entryway, climbed the stairs, and collapsed on his bed.

There would be no Netflix before bed today.

CHAPTER 56

RENN entered a large room on the top floor of the FBI headquarters in Washington D.C. A long, steel and glass table ran the length of the room. Ten plush, black chairs lined the room, five on each side, all occupied except for one.

A month had passed since the events at Deepstone. Renn had been busy. His life had changed, and for the better. He was an employee of SafeWell, and he loved his new job.

Now, he was finally at FBI headquarters for the closure of the investigation of the events at Deepstone. He dreaded seeing Director Judith Meyers and Helen Polson in person. He wasn't frightened of them; it was just going to be difficult to look at their smug faces without smashing his fist into them, especially since Renn had no doubts how this investigation was going to end.

Chief Deputy Sheriff Leonidas rose from one of the chairs and nodded to Renn before sitting back down next to Assistant Executive Director Harper of the Minneapolis FBI office.

A Black woman of about sixty stepped forward, smartly dressed in a grey, bespoke suit. She held out her hand, her expression warm. "Renn Holder. I am Associate Deputy Director Jameson of the Washington D.C. FBI office. Please, have a seat."

Renn shook the director's hand, then walked over to Morgan, smiling slightly at her as he sat down. To the right of Morgan sat Henry Skuggs, CEO of SafeWell, whom Renn acknowledged with a nod. Renn's smile faded when he glanced across the table. Director Meyers of Thornlandon Holdings sat directly opposite him, flanked by Helen Polson and three Thornlandon Holdings lawyers in power suits.

Director Meyers glared at him, her dark eyes seeming to wish him death.

Associate Deputy Director Jameson remained standing. "Thank you all for coming. This meeting will be short and to the point. We have completed our investigation into the events that took place at the Deepstone underground mine on August the 14th and 15th, 2025. We have reviewed all of the evidence. We have interviewed all the witnesses."

Renn calmly folded his hands and placed them on the tabletop. He never stopped staring into Director Meyers' eyes while the investigation was being summarized.

Her eyes remained cold and lidded.

Associate Deputy Director Jameson continued, "The Deepstone mine was attacked by an unidentified group of people. There were multiple deaths, although the total is unconfirmed. Four civilians died of natural causes."

Morgan cursed quietly at that last statement.

Associate Deputy Director Jameson glanced down at Morgan, her expression briefly sympathetic before she said, "Since Deepstone is no longer owned by the State of Minnesota and is now owned by Thornlandon Holdings, the FBI will not investigate further." Associate Deputy Director Jameson stared icily at Director Meyers for a moment, then said, "Director Meyers has pledged the company's full support in finding the perpetrators, but we have no more evidence to follow, and no legal right to further investigate the mining property."

Associate Deputy Director Jameson glowered down at Director Meyers. "To clarify: No judge has agreed to grant us a search warrant for the Deepstone mine. The FBI's hands are tied."

Renn had met with Skuggs at SafeWell and learned that Skuggs had received incriminating evidence against Director Meyers and Thornlandon Holdings the day after Renn and the others had escaped from Deepstone. Skuggs had used that information to help the FBI build a case against Thornlandon Holdings, but someone at a very high level in the government had ordered a federal judge to throw the evidence out. Skuggs suspected it might even have been someone in the inner circle of the President of the United States, but he had no proof.

Glancing down at some notes, Associate Deputy Director Jameson looked over at Renn. "Renn Holder. As a former employee of Thornlandon Holdings, and at the behest of SafeWell CEO Henry Skuggs, you and your team are cleared of any wrongdoing. But your testimony against Thornlandon Holdings has been thrown out, as it has been determined that your statements are prejudicial since it was argued you are a disgruntled former employee of Thornlandon

Holdings. From this point forward, you shall have no further contact with Thornlandon Holdings as a company, nor with any employee of said company. You shall not speak to any media organization about Thornlandon Holdings. Nor shall you communicate anything of a pejorative nature about Thornlandon Holdings in public, including verbally, or via social media. Do you agree?"

Renn coolly said, "I accept and agree to your conditions." He had known this was going to happen. Thornlandon Holdings was too powerful. It had too many influential connections in Washington to be held accountable for any of their actions in Deepstone.

Helen Polson smiled sweetly at Renn from across the table.

Associate Deputy Director Jameson turned to Skuggs and Morgan. "Henry Skuggs and Morgan Fischer of SafeWell. The company known as SafeWell, including you and its employees, are also bound by the same agreement. Do you agree?"

Skuggs shrugged. "SafeWell and its employees will abide by the conditions." He looked bored, as if he had better things to do with his time.

Morgan simply said, "Yes," her tone clipped and tinged with anger.

Associate Deputy Director Jameson turned to the Thornlandon Holdings side of the table. Her eyes grew cold and lidded. "Director Judith Meyers of Thornlandon Holdings. The company known as Thornlandon Holdings, including you and its employees, will have no further contact with SafeWell, its employees, including Mr. Holder and the former employees of Thornlandon Holdings who were in Deepstone on August the 14th and 15th,

2025. Nor shall you communicate anything of a pejorative nature about any of the aforementioned entities or people in public, including verbally, or via social media. Do you agree?"

Renn chuckled upon seeing the dark look that crossed Judith Meyers' face. He knew from experience that Director Meyers did not like to be told what she could or could not do.

Renn felt for Associate Deputy Director Jameson. She had obviously been forced into whatever decisions had been made here, and she clearly didn't like it.

Judith Meyers gave a curt nod of agreement.

Associate Deputy Director Jameson raised an eyebrow and said, "I require your verbal consent, Ms. Meyers."

Director Meyers glared at Associate Deputy Director Jameson for not using her official title. She looked as if she were not going to respond.

Helen leaned sideways and whispered something out of the corner of her mouth.

Director Judith Meyers sat still for a moment longer, then coldly said, "I agree."

Associate Deputy Director Jameson closed her folder, a raised eyebrow indicating she was almost disappointed by Director Meyers' capitulation. "Alright. You have all signed the agreements. They will be filed when this meeting is adjourned. You and the companies for which you work are all legally bound by the agreements you signed, both civilly and criminally, and you will each be held liable for any break of said agreements. This meeting is adjourned, and this case is closed." Associate Deputy Director Jameson turned and left the room, her heels clicking loudly on the marble floor. She was followed by

Assistant Executive Director Harper of the Minneapolis FBI office.

Renn glanced at Director Meyers, but the woman ignored him as she stood and stormed out of the room. Helen Polson glanced once at Renn as she pushed her chair back before following after her boss. Their lawyers leaned their heads together and chatted briefly to each other, then quickly stood and exited the room as well.

Renn, Morgan, Skuggs, and Chief Deputy Sheriff Leonidas sat in silence for a few seconds, alone now in the room.

Leonidas stood and looked down at the three of them. "I was there that night. I saw what happened. It grates my nerves that those people got off without so much as a reprimand."

Skuggs shrugged. "It is the way of our world, my friend. The powerful never seem to face any consequences."

Leonidas walked to the door, glanced once back at them, then left the room.

"Well, that was fun," Morgan said under her breath as she stood up.

Renn stood as well. "Even though this is all over, we will have to keep our ears to the ground. Judith Meyers is not one to leave any loose ends unattended. The agreements signed here today will not stop her from coming for us."

Skuggs said, "Renn, we have our best people watching Thornlandon Holdings. We will know if they make a move on us."

Renn knew Skuggs was not a man to be messed with. Unlike Director Judith Meyers, though, he was an honest man who treated his people like family. Renn had done his homework on Skuggs and liked what he had found.

"Thank you, Mr. Skuggs."

The man rolled his eyes. "Please, cut out the 'Mr.' crap. Call me Skuggs."

Renn smiled, liking Skuggs even more.

Skuggs motioned with his head, "Now, let's get out of here. I hate Washington D.C."

As they walked out of the FBI building, Renn thought back to his first official meeting with Skuggs at a hotel in Duluth, three days after the events at Deepstone. Skuggs and Morgan had flown back to Minnesota after spending a couple of days with Bauwen at the SafeWell headquarters in New Mexico.

Skuggs called and asked Renn to stop by his room to discuss a few things.

Renn agreed to leave the hospital only when the two SafeWell guards assured him that Tess, Ficks, and Millie would be safe. When Renn knocked on the hotel room door, he was surprised when Morgan opened it. He grinned. "Morgan! You're here, too?"

She laughed. "Of course, Renn. I wanted to come back and check in on Tess, Ficks, and Millie." She stepped aside, "Come in."

Renn entered.

Morgan quickly checked the hallway before shutting the door.

Skuggs sat on an oversized sofa, legs crossed, a cup of coffee in his hand.

"Please, take a seat, Renn. Coffee?"

"No thank you. I've had more hospital coffee than any human should be legally allowed to drink."

Skuggs smiled, then said, "I hear that Tess and Ficks will be alright, and Millie's leg will eventually heal, although she has a lot of rehab work in her future. You have good people, Renn."

"Thank you, sir. They are the best."

Renn stood at attention.

Skuggs sighed. "Please stop that shit and grab a chair."

Relaxing a bit, Renn sat down.

Morgan settled into the chair next to him.

Skuggs set his coffee cup on the side table. He steepled his fingers to his chin, studying Renn. Then he lowered his hands and said, "I have done a full background check on you, Renn. Or should I call you, Tayen Lapahie?"

Renn had suspected his past would not remain a secret to Skuggs. He nodded. "Yes, sir. My real name is Tayen. I was given a new identity by Thornlandon Holdings after they recruited me." He was silent for a few seconds, then whispered, "I killed three men outside of a bar." Those killings weighed heavily on Renn. Not a day went by that he didn't wish he could go back and change things. The three men had actually jumped Renn outside of a bar and tried to kill him. Renn had killed them with their own weapons.

Morgan glanced back and forth between Renn and Skuggs, surprise showing on her face. This was obviously something Skuggs had not shared with her.

Skuggs nodded. "Did you know that whole fight had been arranged by Thornlandon Holdings?"

Renn froze. *Thornlandon Holdings had set up the fight?*

As if reading his thoughts, Skuggs said, "Helen Polson wanted to recruit you, but Director Judith Meyers wanted to test you first. So, Helen set up the fight to prove to Judith that you were just who they needed to lead their military teams. Those men who jumped you were Thornlandon Holdings agents."

Renn felt a deep-burning anger well up inside him. He had killed three people just because Director Meyers wanted to test him.

Skuggs put up a hand, seeing Renn's anger. "Easy, Renn. I understand your anger. But there are better ways to get even with Thornlandon Holdings than through whatever you are thinking of doing right now."

Renn studied Skuggs. "What do you mean?"

Skuggs smiled. "Well, for starters, we can discuss your job offer with SafeWell."

Renn glanced at Morgan, who smiled at him.

"Sir, I will be honored to discuss this with you. But I need to talk about it with my team first."

Skuggs shrugged. "I don't see why. They have already conditionally accepted our offers of employment, pending your approval. They won't commit until you do. They are loyal to you, Renn."

"You've already talked to my team?"

Morgan chuckled and said, "Renn, for once, you are one step behind everyone!"

Renn smiled hesitantly. "I guess so. But who will be the team leader? Me, or Morgan?"

Skuggs had rolled his eyes and said, "We have enough teams for you both to lead. Now come on, Renn. What will it be?"

Renn didn't have to consider the offer very long. He had gotten to know Morgan, Karen, and Jack and had seen them in action. They were good people. He held out his hand. "I accept. Thank you, Skuggs."

Skuggs shook his hand. "Welcome aboard, Renn."

Renn turned serious. "I would like Tess, Ficks, and Millie brought to a private hospital with armed guards. They are not safe from Thornlandon Holdings where they are now."

"Already taken care of," Skuggs had said. "They have been cleared by their doctors to be moved. We will airlift them to our headquarters in New Mexico this afternoon. We have a full medical facility onsite with the best doctors and staff money can buy."

Renn already liked his new employer. "Thank you, Skuggs. I am going back to the hospital and will stay there until they are moved."

"Of course."

Renn stood up. "I look forward to working with you and Morgan." He turned and left the room.

Skuggs had made good on his word. Renn's team had been safely transported to the SafeWell headquarters and were receiving the best medical care possible.

Renn and his team had been living in the barracks at SafeWell headquarters for the past month, though "barracks" was not really appropriate to describe the luxurious accommodations they were given. They all got suites, each one at least 300-square-feet in size; they were basically small apartments. Millie, Ficks, and Tess were rehabbing well from their injuries. The other members of his team who had not been injured in Deepstone, or who sustained only minor injuries, quickly assimilated into the SafeWell culture.

At Morgan's request, Skuggs also recruited Deputy Danny Miller. The young man accepted employment on the condition that his seventeen-year-old brother Jeff could join him at SafeWell. Jeff exhibited promise with computers and was training as a specialist. He would complete his senior year of high school at the facility.

When Danny Miller and Jeff first arrived at SafeWell, Danny was still in a wheelchair because of his gunshot wounds. Renn wheeled him into the reception room. They were greeted by Morgan, Gwen, and other members of SafeWell. Danny's injuries had looked worse than they were, the bullets passing through flesh without hitting any bones. He had multiple surgeries and couldn't yet walk without assistance.

A door opened and Sally wheeled Millie, still lying in her hospital bed, into reception. Her leg was in a large cast and elevated, her face still showed residual bruising. Her injuries had been serious, requiring multiple surgeries.

Sally stopped the bed next to Danny.

Millie smiled at him, then motioned for Danny to stand.

Danny, blushing slightly, awkwardly pushed himself up. He stood on one leg, unsure what to do.

Without a word, Millie reached up and pulled Danny down to her. She cupped his face and gave him a deep kiss. It lasted for over a minute, and cheers erupted from the half-dozen people in the room.

When Millie finally broke the kiss, Danny stood up, completely dazed with a silly smile stretching across his face.

CHAPTER 57

A cold wind jolted RENN out of his thoughts as he, Morgan, and Skuggs exited the FBI headquarters. Autumn had arrived, and with it, the cold temperatures that Washington D.C. was known for.

Skuggs jogged to a black limo idling by the curb. Monique opened the right rear door for him.

When Renn and Morgan reached the car, Monique opened the left rear door for them. Morgan slid in first, and as Renn slid into the car, Monique smiled at him before she shut the door against the wind.

Renn had been relieved to find Monique after she had escaped from Deepstone. It took two weeks, but he had finally been able to make contact with her. They arranged a pickup, taking every precaution against a possible trap by Thornlandon Holdings. Monique was then brought to New Mexico. After a debrief, she was hired by SafeWell.

Safely in the limo, Morgan and Renn looked at each other awkwardly for a few seconds.

Renn found himself thinking of their date last week, and the long kiss they had shared after. Today was the first time they had seen each other since. Morgan, Jack, and Karen had spent the past week in the Amazon jungle of southern Venezuela rescuing a missing pharmaceutical team.

Renn and his team were not yet cleared for SafeWell missions. They were still learning the intricacies of performing various types of rescues. They had to master caving, both above ground and underwater. They trained in multiple climbing scenarios in every climate and weather condition. The list of skills Renn and his team had to master seemed unending. At one point three weeks ago, exhausted and irritated after twelve straight hours of training, Renn had snapped at Morgan when she chided him for looking so tired.

Morgan's eyes flashed and she told him to buck up and stop complaining.

Renn replied hotly, "Yeah, easy for you to say. I don't see you guys training fifteen hours a day."

Morgan rolled her eyes. "Renn, it took me six months before I was allowed on my first mission. And even now, we train for hours a day during our off time. Skuggs' number one directive is safety first. This isn't Thornlandon Holdings where you shoot hostiles for the company. We save people in the worst conditions and situations imaginable."

Renn glared at her for a moment, then grinned sheepishly. "I'm being an ass, aren't I?"

"Yeah, you kind of are." Morgan glared at him until she grinned too.

Coming out of his thoughts, Renn was keenly

aware of Morgan's body next to him in the car.

Skuggs sat opposite them in the limo, reading from a folder, lost in his own thoughts.

Renn whispered to Morgan, "Can I see you again soon?"

Morgan glanced over at Skuggs, then whispered, "Come find me tonight back at headquarters."

Renn felt happier than he had in years.

The limo raced away from the curb, heading to SafeWell's private hanger at Andrews Air Force Base. They were wheels up within minutes of arriving there and Renn leaned back in the plush leather seat of the private jet. He was asleep in moments. As a military operative, he rarely passed up a chance to get some sleep.

When they arrived back at SafeWell headquarters four and a half hours later, Renn first stopped in to see Ficks, who had been shot in the arm. The damage was substantial, but he had already had three operations to repair it, and the doctors felt he would regain full use of his arm.

Ficks nearly smiled when Renn entered the room. They chatted quietly for a few minutes, then Ficks picked up his phone and pressed a few keys. He held the phone out to Renn, who took it.

"Press Play."

Renn did as asked, and a video started playing. It was dark and pixelated, but Renn could still make out the image of Paul rising up the elevator shaft, arms raised like an avenging angel, a silly smile on his face as "Ride of the Valkyries" blared from his phone. Paul rose quickly past Ficks. He filmed the dark shaft for a few moments, then the image jerked to the side and the video clicked off.

Renn handed the phone back to Ficks, his eyes

damp.

Ficks was quiet for a few seconds, holding the phone against his chest. He let out a breath and looked up at Renn. "I was never able to send Paul a copy of this video like he asked for. I miss that Aussie bastard."

"Me too, Ficks. He saved us all."

Ficks didn't say anything more. He just turned his head against his pillow and stared out the window.

Renn stood up and left the room.

Next, he stopped by Millie's room. She was all smiles. She had taken seven bullets to her left leg as they fought Thornlandon Holdings' forces in the field. The doctors at St. Mary's hospital in Duluth had recommended amputating her leg, but Skuggs had refused. He had transported Millie to the medical facilities in SafeWell headquarters instead. Then he had flown in three surgeons: one from Paris, one from the Netherlands, and one from New York, each of them the best in their fields of reconstructive surgery. They had performed seven surgeries over the next thirty days. While Millie would likely require a few more surgeries, she had a good chance of walking normally again. But it would take up to a year of physical therapy to make that happen.

Renn reached over and took Millie's hand as he sat on the side of her bed. They chatted briefly about nothing important. Then Renn asked, "Now, what's this I hear about you and Deputy Danny?"

Millie hit his arm. Hard. "That is my business. Not yours." She looked away from him as if angry, then a small smile creased her mouth. After a few moments, she said, "Danny is...nice."

"Nice?"

Millie's eyes flashed playfully. "Yeah. He isn't an

asshole like you."

Renn nodded. "Good for him. No one should be like me," he agreed dryly.

Millie continued as if she hadn't heard him. "He saved my life, you know. Before anyone on our team even moved, Danny ran across that field against a dozen enemies. He picked me up and carried me back to safety, taking two bullets in the process. Then, as if that wasn't enough, he got me away from the SUV before those bastards fired the RPG at it. Not many people could or would have done what he did. And you know what he said to me yesterday?"

"What?"

She smiled. "He apologized for giving me a black eye when he landed on me after the explosion. He apologized! I mean, who does that?"

Renn smiled. "I guess Danny does. He's a good kid."

Millie punched his arm again. "He is only seven years younger than me."

"Ouch! Alright; he's a good *man*."

As if on cue, Danny hobbled into the room using crutches. He grinned at Renn, and they shook hands. Then he turned to Millie, his smile growing wider. Danny visited Millie every day, often spending hours in her room.

Renn leaned down and hugged Millie. "Get some rest. I will see you tomorrow." He left the room. As he closed the door, he heard Millie softly say, "Renn's gone. Come lay next to me."

Smiling happily, Renn crossed the hallway to Tess's room and knocked.

Her voice called out, "Come in."

Renn opened the door and stepped into the room. Tess lay in her bed. The extensive bruising that had once covered most of her face had now faded to yellow and brown. She had been hit hard by the explosive force of the RPG striking Danny's SUV. Despite her slow and painful recovery, Tess smiled at Renn.

Before he could say anything, she said, "I'm tired of my Ducati Panigale. You should buy me a yellow MV Agusta Superveloce. I think I would like that."

Renn smiled. "Now why would I do that?"

Tess shrugged. "Because I deserve one."

"You do, do you?" Renn's smile vanished as he looked at her bruised face. He leaned forward. "The bike will be waiting for you when you get out of this room."

"Oh Jesus. I was just having a bit of fun with you. Don't get all mushy on me, Renn."

"Don't worry, that'll never happen." He leaned forward and said, "I'll tell you what. I will buy you the bike when you can hit a spinning card from 800 yards again."

Tess smiled. "Really? But that's too easy. How about a thousand yards this time?"

"Deal," Renn said.

"But you better put the order for the MV Agusta in now. It can take up to six months to get one in yellow. Oh. And they aren't cheap, either."

Renn kissed her forehead. "I will order it today."

Tess became serious. "Renn? We barely made it out of that mine. I felt helpless down there against the Vorgroth. I don't want to ever feel helpless again."

"You are now part of SafeWell. Your missions will be to help people. No more monsters."

When Tess didn't respond, Renn stood straight and said, "Get some rest."

She looked up at him as if she were going to say

something, but she just nodded instead.
Renn left the room.

CHAPTER 58

MORGAN knocked and entered the spacious room after she heard a voice say, "Enter."

Bauwen sat with her legs curled beneath her in a comfortable chair watching a movie on a large-screen TV. She glanced up at Morgan and smiled, then pointed to the TV. "This TV is wonderful. It is seventy inches measured diagonally and is made using quantum dot technology. I just read about it yesterday. I am watching a movie about a ship called the Titanic. It has just hit an iceberg, which is a huge chunk of ice that floats in the ocean. Did you know that ninety percent of an iceberg is submerged under the water? And did you also know that the Atlantic Ocean is 41,105,000 square miles in size? A square mile is 27,878,400 square feet. Can you imagine such vast amounts of water? I want to see the ocean one day. I bet it is wonderful. Oh, this movie is about a poor, young man named Jack. He is in love with a rich woman named Rose. It is a wonderful story. I wonder if they will live happily ever after. I saw a movie on something called 'The Hallmark Channel,' and at the end of the movie it said, '*They lived happily ever after*.'" Bauwen smiled. "I like that idea."

Bauwen wore a sleeveless, flowered dress. The skin of her arms changed to match the color and pattern of the chair. Morgan stared transfixed, then looked up at Bauwen. "Are you comfortable? Can I get you anything?"

"No, I am fine." She picked up the remote and scanned it for a moment before pressing the "Pause" button with her index finger. Then she turned to Morgan, her face suddenly serious. "I want to thank you and Henry Skuggs for getting me away from Deepstone and bringing me here."

Morgan sat down in a chair next to Bauwen. "You are welcome. We have a lot of land here. I hope you have gotten a chance to get out and explore it. But please be careful and wear a full set of clothes so you don't get sunburned. Also, there are snakes and scorpions out there that can harm you." Morgan didn't know if the sun would burn Bauwen's skin or not, or if venom could harm her. It was better to be safe.

Bauwen smiled. "Oh yes, Silas told me all about the dangers of your world."

Silas was her educator. He was a former professor of engineering and physics who now worked for SafeWell designing new tools for their rescue efforts. He had been selected to help Bauwen acclimate to her new world above ground. Silas had briefed Skuggs, Morgan, and Renn after just three days of working with Bauwen, exclaiming with wonder about how her mind was so much more advanced than theirs. He seemed awestruck as he exclaimed how Bauwen innately understood everything that he taught her. She picked up languages and mathematics as if they were downloaded to her brain, like they would on a computer.

Bauwen consumed books at an incredible pace. She not only understood everything she read, but she remembered every word. Silas surmised that within just a few months Bauwen would know more than anyone at SafeWell. He had stopped his report at that point and looked at them all with an almost fevered expression, before saying, "I think Bauwen is the next evolution of our species."

Yesterday, Morgan, Renn, and Skuggs had watched Bauwen and Silas during one of their sessions from behind a two-way glass partition.

Bauwen and Silas sat facing each other in the comfortable interview room, the decor inspired by the American Southwest. Rough-textured sandstone walls were painted in shades of rust, terracotta, and green. A large, colorful rug covered the middle of the Spanish tiled floor. Bauwen's legs were curled beneath her on a large sofa and she held a pillow in her lap. She appeared relaxed and happy.

Bauwen casually asked, "Do you know the myth of Atlantis, Silas?"

Silas smiled, saying, "Of course. Everyone knows the story of Atlantis. They were supposedly an advanced civilization that prospered many thousands of years ago. They were punished by the Gods, who sunk their island empire beneath the sea, never to be seen again."

Bauwen smiled slightly, her eyes suddenly focused sharply on him. "That is the myth that my people created long ago. It is funny that it still exists and hasn't changed much since that time."

Silas narrowed his eyes and sat forward, "What do you mean?"

Uncurling her legs, Bauwen repositioned the pillow on her lap, then folded her hands on the soft fabric and cocked her head slightly as if waiting for Silas to figure it out.

A few seconds passed. Silas turned to glance at the two-way glass for a moment before refocusing on Bauwen. "Are you saying your people are from Atlantis? That you are an Atlantean?"

Bauwen shook her head negatively. "No, that is not entirely correct. My people are called Altheans. We lived on the surface for thousands of years before humans even learned speech. We taught humans about language, agriculture, and tools. We lived in peace with them for many thousands of years until the humans eventually became dangerous to us." Bauwen stopped here and turned to look at the two-way glass. "Skuggs, Morgan, Renn, why don't you join us. I know you will have questions."

Morgan turned to Skuggs and Renn and gave a wry smile, not surprised that Bauwen knew they were behind the glass. The three of them entered the room, grabbed some metal folding chairs from a closet, and sat down.

Bauwen waited until they were situated before continuing the story. "You see, humans mostly saw us as gods at first. But over the millennia they grew suspicious of us. They started to blame us for their misfortunes, their pain, and their weaknesses. This animosity grew until a human warlord came to power. He gathered an army of tens of thousands to attack our island city. We could have destroyed them with our advanced technology, but we chose not to.

Instead, we set into motion our plan to leave the surface world. You see, we are a long-lived people and had been studying humans for millennia. Our scientists concluded that our time remaining on the surface world was finite. The humans would continue to breed and expand across the world in search of more land and resources, eventually reaching a point where they would become powerful enough to destroy us. So, we sunk our cities into the ocean, erasing all evidence that we ever existed. We knew that within a few thousand years, humans would think of us as nothing more than myth."

Bauwen saw the looks of disbelief on their faces and continued with her story. "We had been mining *Forss* for tens of thousands of years after discovering it gave us extremely long life and the ability to control the molecular structure of our bodies. Our scientists had located a vast deposit of *Forss* in an underground cavern system 46,000 feet beneath the surface. This massive underground cavern runs from what you now call Minnesota to the other side of what you call the Hudson Bay. We created an entrance deep under the water of Hudson Bay and had formed a small mining colony in this underground world."

Silas interrupted Bauwen, "After about 5000 feet, the temperature of the earth's crust increases the deeper you go. At 46,000 feet the temperature must be…"

Bauwen completed his sentence, "Between 350- and 400-degrees Fahrenheit. Yes, you are correct. But this is a unique underground area that includes a large amount of *Forss*, which as I have explained already, is a heavy metal that is almost 100% unaffected by heat. The high *Forss* levels in the rock reflect heat and keep the temperature at a steady 100 degrees Fahrenheit. When our leaders decided to leave the surface entirely, this underground world made the perfect home for us all. With our advanced technologies, we created an entire ecosystem down below, complete with agriculture, water, fresh air, light sources, and unlimited power for our cities. We have been living down there for more than 9000 years now."

Morgan leaned forward and took a deep breath; she'd almost forgotten to breathe as she listened to Bauwen's history. Finally she asked, "What about the Vorgroth?"

Bauwen cast her eyes down briefly before looking at Morgan. "The Vorgroth is our greatest shame. You see, they inhabited the underground world long before we arrived. When we made our way down to this world, the Vorgroth immediately attacked us. We had been unable to reason with them. They had no language, and their only purpose seemed to be to kill us. So, we fought against them for years, losing many of our people in the process. We were finally able to build a great wall that stretched over two miles up to the roof of our underground complex. We drove them back until we were able to seal them off forever. That is, until I discovered a rift in the wall. I monitored it until one day it was wide enough for me to enter. I made my way through and came face to face with the same Vorgroth that chased me up to the Deepstone mine in 1962."

Renn nodded sadly. "That sounds similar to what happened to the Indigenous people of North America. Our peoples lived here for thousands of years before we were killed in great numbers by the Europeans and finally forced to live on small reservations."

Bauwen nodded, although troubled. She sat silently for a few moments until she squared her shoulders. "I have read the history of your people, Renn, and yes, it is similar to some extent. As you have seen with your own eyes, the Vorgroth are pure killing machines who can't be reasoned with. But in saying that, we entered their world, just like the Europeans entered North America. The Vorgroth attacked us because we chose to invade their world. It was our fault."

Silas coughed softly to get everyone's attention after the intense discussion. "Bauwen, what you have told us changes the history of humanity in every way. May I…"

Skuggs cut Silas off, "No, Silas. What Bauwen has told us must remain a complete secret. We absolutely cannot let the existence of the Altheans become known."

Silas opened his mouth to argue but Skuggs shook his head. "No, Silas. You know what will happen if their existence becomes known. Every government in the world, both friendly and hostile, will begin fighting over access to Bauwen's world. Wars will break out. And the Altheans will be caught in the middle." He stood up and spread his arms. "In fact, we must make sure that Thornlandon Holdings never gains access to the world below. We must monitor them in every manner possible and prepare ourselves to act on a moment's notice if they regain access to the Altheans' world. No one here will speak of what Bauwen has told us. Not a word." He glared at each one of them until they all nodded, then turned to Bauwen. "Thank you for sharing your history with us, Bauwen. We will do everything we can to protect your people."

Bauwen stood up and to Skuggs' surprise, stepped forward and hugged him tightly.

Coming back out of her thoughts now, Morgan realized Bauwen was looking at her with a raised eyebrow, something she had learned to do from watching TV.

"Are you okay, Morgan?"

"I am. Sorry. I was just thinking about our discussion yesterday." She stood up. "I actually just wanted to stop by to say 'hi.' I'm going to get back to work now. Don't hesitate to call me anytime. You know how to use the phone?"

Bauwen picked up her new iPhone and smiled. "Of course. It is a little thing, but quite amazing. Thank you, Morgan."

Morgan stood up and walked to the door, then turned around. "See you at dinner tonight?"

Nodding excitedly, Bauwen said, "I hear they are making something called tacos. I look forward to trying them."

Morgan smiled and left the room.

CHAPTER 59

JOHN stopped walking when he reached the corner of 3rd Avenue and 2nd Street in Virginia. The local bowling alley was across the street; a two-story building made from yellow bricks with an unassuming door in front. Above it, on the second story, boarded-up windows lined the building. A few small businesses had prospered up there until the mid-1980s. When the owner of the building had passed away, the offices quickly closed down.

Almost three months had passed since John had escaped from Deepstone. Since then, he often woke up in the middle of the night. In the dark, it sometimes took him a few moments to realize he was not still trapped down in the mine. John found that sleeping with a small night light helped. He also found that he spent less time indoors than he used to. He craved the open air of the outdoors. John went out for long walks around Virginia almost every day, rain or shine. Usually, he walked with no destination in mind.

John turned away from the bowling alley. He had bowled there a few times as a kid; not often, but enough to get a strike once in a while.

It was 8:30 a.m., but the sun had only risen an hour earlier. It was late November, and the days had grown dramatically shorter.

After the events in Deepstone, John had been debriefed by the FBI. The agents had asked questions about every minute detail, and John had left nothing out, except for Bauwen and the Vorgroth. Bauwen was whisked away by Morgan's people the night of the escape from the mine, and Morgan had asked everyone from their group to keep her existence a secret. John had been forced to sign an NDA. He had not heard from the FBI again.

The Deepstone mine was now owned by Thornlandon Holdings and was off limits to everyone. John had driven past Deepstone one day a few weeks earlier. A thirty-foot-high concrete wall topped with concertina wire now blocked his view of the mine buildings. A security gate had been installed where the mine entrance had been. It was guarded by a half-dozen armed men and women.

John had angrily pounded his steering wheel as he passed by. He had watched good people die in that mine. He had seen things that defied reality. How could Thornlandon Holdings be allowed to buy Deepstone? Despite the firefight between Thornlandon Holdings forces and the sheriff's department in the field, no arrests had been made. No mention about the events that transpired made the papers. Everything seemed to have been swept under the proverbial rug.

As time went by, John had realized there was

nothing he could do about it.

Morgan visited him last week. Over coffee, they exchanged pleasant chit chat. John asked about Tess, Millie, Ficks, and Danny, remembering how badly they had been injured in the battle. Reassured they were all improving, John asked about Bauwen.

Morgan took his hand and said, "She is safe, John. And she is happy. We are protecting her."

John smiled. "Good, I am glad."

They talked about the little things in their lives for a while longer, then Morgan got up and set her empty coffee cup in the sink. She looked at her watch and said she had to leave. They hugged, and she left.

Last week, he logged into his bank account to check if a bill had gone through and was shocked to see $250,000 had been deposited. He received an email from Morgan a few hours later telling him it was an official payment from SafeWell for his services in the mine. He had replied with a simple, "Thank you."

John met with Tammy, Carl, and Jim one time at the local brunch restaurant by the mall. The conversation didn't stray from the weather, current events, or local sports. No one brought up Deepstone, and they departed as soon as they'd finished their meals. It was clear they would not meet again. It was as if by not seeing each other, they could put the horrors they experienced behind them.

John had gotten a few texts from Andy, who didn't seem too bothered by the events in Deepstone. He texted about a new girlfriend he had named Fran, and how they were going to a concert together. Life seemed good for him and Ethan.

Seemingly out of the blue, Claire had called him bright and early this morning. She asked how he was doing, then invited him to her house for coffee and cake. "Fika," she called it, explaining it was a Swedish tradition. He said he would stop by around 10 a.m. She lived outside of town halfway between Virginia and Hibbing.

Standing on the corner, John glanced at his watch. It was time to get back home and shower, then head to her place. He ambled back to his house, showered, and changed into clean clothes. John climbed into his trusty old Subaru, entered Claire's address into Google Maps, and turned right onto Eight street. It ended in a few blocks. He glanced to his left and marveled at the incredible Thomas Rukavina Memorial Bridge that spanned the Rouchleau mine pit. At 204 feet tall, it was the tallest bridge in Minnesota.

He turned right onto Hwy 53 and soon passed by the old Thunderbird Mall. It had been the busiest mall in the area back in the 1970s. He and his friends had often hung out there, visiting the video game arcade, or eating hot dogs at the Kmart. The mall was still there, but all the old stores were now gone, including Kmart, the Red Owl grocery store, and Herberger's department store.

As John drove south on Hwy 169, he passed by numerous rocky hills that rose up a few hundred feet or more, made from old iron-ore tailings piled high by the mining operations of old. Even through the piles of rock, though, small trees and scraggly bushes grew, as if they didn't know they needed soil to survive.

He passed the Campground Rd turnoff that led to the West Two-Rivers Reservoir Campground eight miles south of Virginia. He'd been there many times over the years. The road ended at the reservoir, leading straight into the water on one side, and back out of the water on the other. They had never bothered to build a bridge over the water. Ever practical, the State turned it into a boat ramp.

John turned left onto County Road 25 and within a few miles, Google Maps told him his destination was just ahead. He turned left onto a narrow gravel driveway and within a hundred feet, he came to a stop at Claire's house. Two cars were parked near the house. John looked in the mirror and grunted at his appearance. He needed a haircut. Oh well. Maybe he would do that tomorrow. Or next week. Next month, at the latest. His appearance didn't seem to matter much to him lately.

Pushing the Subaru's door open with a squeak, John stepped out of the car and as he did, Claire opened the inside door of the house, pushed the screen door open, and stepped out on her small deck, smiling at him. "John, it is so nice to see you! Come in. It is getting cold out, isn't it?"

John smiled in return as he shut his car door and walked across the driveway. As he climbed the steps, he realized he was truly happy to see her.

Claire stepped forward and wrapped him in a tight hug. "I've missed you, John. Thank you for visiting." She looked healthy and strong, and even had a tan.

"I've missed you, too, Claire." He stepped out of the hug and looked at her. "You look great. Are you tanned?"

"Oh, poof on that. The days of me looking great passed forty years ago but thank you for saying so." Her eyes sparkled with good humor. "Tanned? Yes, I suppose I am. I spent the past month in Orlando. I just returned a few days ago. I needed some sun and warm temps." She stepped back and said, "Please, come inside."

John entered the house.

Claire shut the door behind him, but John didn't even notice.

A beautiful woman entered the living room from the kitchen saying, "Grandma, the banana bread was done so I took it out of the oven."

The woman took John's breath away. She was tall, only a few inches shorter than John. Her brown hair was shoulder-length, tiny freckles were scattered across her cheeks, and she had the bluest eyes he had ever seen.

She stopped when she saw John standing in the entryway. She looked startled. Then she smiled. It lit up her features and seemed to send a jolt of electricity through him.

John smiled in return. For some reason, he felt like he had known her his whole life, even though he was just meeting her for the first time. He didn't know it at the time but found out later she had felt exactly the same in that moment.

Claire stepped between them and took each of their hands. She smiled. "John, I'd like to introduce you to my granddaughter, Mia. I promised to introduce you to her back in the mine, and I keep my promises."

Claire turned to her granddaughter. "Mia, this is…"

Mia finished Claire's sentence, her voice soft and slightly raspy, as she said, "John."

John and Mia stared into each other's eyes for a few seconds, neither seeming to notice Claire.

Then Mia smiled. "My grandmother has told me all about you. Do you like banana bread?"

CHAPTER 60

SENATOR RONALD YOUNG swung his legs over the side of the bed and stood up. He slipped his feet into cashmere slippers and pulled on the satin robe that lay across the back of the chair by the bed. His wife slept on the other side of the bed, the Ambien she took every night ensuring she'd be out until morning.

His full bladder throbbed as he shuffled to the bathroom. He didn't bother turning on the light, hoping to avoid waking himself up further. He lifted the toilet seat and urine splashed into the water of the bowl, some of it hitting the floor first before he corrected his sleepy aim. Senator Young sighed as the painful throbbing faded away. He finished and flushed the toilet. He washed his hands with cold water, dried them on the towel by the sink, and flicked off the light as he exited the bathroom.

What was that last dream before his bladder had awakened him? Oh yes. It was about one of his aides,

Sandy. She had been naked and touching him all over.

He got an erection just thinking about the dream. His memory of Sandy in the hotel in Pittsburgh last week was even more erotic. What that woman could do with her body. She should have been a contortionist in the circus instead of a senator's aide.

Senator Young forgot all about the dream when he heard a noise out in the hallway. He narrowed his eyes. His heart rate quickened as he strode to the fireplace and lifted a heavy steel poker. The fireplace was gas, but they kept the fireplace tool set for show. Gripping the poker in his hand, Senator Young stepped into the long hall. It ran above the open foyer twenty feet below. He quietly made his way to the landing where the grand staircase led down.

Senator Young thought back to the last phone conversation he had listened to between Director Meyers and Helen Polson on the night that everything had gone down at Deepstone. They had discussed sending an assassin to kill him, someone named Kala.

The next day, he had lost the ability to monitor Director Meyers' and Helen's conversations. The Thornlandon Holdings security team must have discovered their phones were hacked.

Senator Young had tried but been unable to contact his old hacker friend Spencer to verify any of this.

A day later, Spencer had sent a cryptic message to Senator Young's phone that said, "*The darker the night, the brighter the stars.*"

Senator Young had looked it up. It was a quote from *Crime and Punishment* by Fyodor Dostoevsky that meant something like, even in the darkest of times, there is hope. Senator Young knew Spencer had gone dark, disappearing off grid, but his message seemed to mean that Senator Young might soon receive more information about Thornlandon Holdings, perhaps even about the planned assassination attempt against him.

Senator Young had increased his security, adding six more guards outside, and two inside the house. Four bodyguards stayed with him during the day.

Coming out of his thoughts, Senator Young gripped the iron fireplace poker harder in his hands. The house was dark. *Where were his two indoor guards? They should be nearby. Was it them that he had heard? And wasn't there normally a light on over the stairs?* He couldn't remember; he so rarely spent his nights here at the house.

Senator Young turned his head to listen but heard nothing. His senses told him he was not alone, though.

Screw this, he thought. Senator Young turned to go back to his room and call security. As he did, he felt the slightest puff of air against his face. He instantly felt dizzy. Then the hallway began to spin around him. Senator Young gained his balance briefly and shook his head to clear it. He felt another puff of air, just a light touch against his face. He dropped the fireplace poker to the floor and reached out for the railing to stabilize his vertigo, but he couldn't seem to find it.

Senator Young felt a light push against his back. He stumbled forward and his thighs struck something hard. He felt a spinning sensation, then a sense of weightlessness before striking the marble floor headfirst.

Senator Young died instantly.

In the darkness above him, Thornlandon Holdings

assassin, Kala, picked up the fireplace poker and silently glided down the hallway into the master bedroom. She carefully put it back into the stand of other fireplace implements, then stood silently for a few moments, listening to the steady breathing of the woman in bed. Satisfied the senator's wife was still sleeping, Kala re-entered the hallway and made her way to the spare bedroom from which she had entered the house. She glanced at her watch. The guards downstairs would pass through the foyer in three minutes and would discover Senator Young's body.

Kala leaned against the wall and peeked through the window. The manicured lawns of the estate stretched out for acres, visible through her night-vision goggles. Kala stayed motionless for ten seconds, waiting for the next guard to pass by on his standard route.

The man soon appeared from around the side of the house, right on schedule. He walked past her window without even looking up.

Kala waited fifteen seconds, then pushed the window open, climbed through, and hung from the windowsill. She pulled the window shut with one hand, then reached into her pocket and removed a powerful electromagnetic device. She activated the device and moved it slowly across the window frame. The window latch moved with her device until it clicked into place, locking the window from the inside.

Kala put the device back into her pocket, dropped down to a small ledge, then to the ground, landing without a sound. She faded into the darkness of the grounds, moving quickly and invisibly in her black garb. Kala came to the twenty-foot-tall perimeter fence, scaled it, leaped over the top, and landed silently on the other side. She quickly sprinted into the darkness of the woods, then stopped, turned, and removed a small device from another pocket. The device had not only disarmed the alarm, but did it while keeping the logs operating, showing no break in the alarm connection. The security video footage would show nothing. Kala's clothing was designed to absorb light. The cameras literally couldn't see her.

Kala pressed a single button. The perimeter and house alarms rearmed. She turned and faded into the woods as silently as a ghost.

EPILOGUE

In the darkness on Level forty-three of the Deepstone mine, a blinking red light cast a hypnotic shadow against the wall.

In a large topside room within a new, highly secure building built a thousand feet from the elevator shaft, a group of people crowded around a man with a laptop.

DIRECTOR JUDITH MEYERS stood closest to the man at the computer. At her side stood Helen, dressed in her immaculate, expensive suit.

Director Meyers asked, "Are all systems green?"

The man at the laptop nodded and said, "Affirmative."

"Then press the button, Gerry."

Gerry looked around briefly, licked his lips nervously, then raised a finger and pressed the Enter key on his laptop.

The floor of the room shook even though they were 4320 feet above the explosives that had just been triggered down in the cavern on Level forty-three.

Cheers rose up around the room.

Judith Meyers studied the four, 100-inch TVs on the wall in front of her. They showed four live feeds from as many night vision cameras mounted to the walls and ceiling in Level forty-three. Smoke and dust filled the screens. Director Meyers spoke impatiently, "I don't see anything on the cameras yet."

Gerry typed furiously. Two, four-foot-diameter fans down on Level forty-three kicked in and sucked the smoke into the elevator shaft and up to the surface.

The image cleared up.

A night-vision camera positioned on the ceiling, protected by bullet-proof glass, pointed straight down into the opening of a jagged hole in the floor of the cavern, its grainy image glowing eerily.

"Turn on the lights, Gerry."

Gerry typed quickly. Down on Level forty-three, dozens of panels slid back. He typed some more, and the night-vision camera view turned black. Then the lights down below all turned on at once.

Everyone in the room gasped.

Judith Meyers smiled widely, the first time anyone in her employ had ever seen her do so.

In the middle of the cavern, she saw a gaping fissure in the floor, twenty feet across.

The fissure went straight down into the earth.

46,000 feet down.

THE END

The story continues with the second book in
the SafeWell series, releasing in 2027, titled:

DEEPEARTH

A SAFEWELL MISSION: BOOK TWO

LOCATIONS in this book

DEEPSTONE is a fictitious version of a real underground mine in Tower/Soudan Minnesota called: **Tower/Soudan Underground Mine State Park**, located 25 miles from where DEEPSTONE is set in the book. The Tower/Soudan Underground Mine State Park tours are open to the public. Many of the features described in the book are similar to those of the real underground mine tour.

Except for the Vorgroth, of course.

For more information, see
https://www.dnr.state.mn.us/state_parks/park.html?id=spk00285#homepage

Virginia, Minnesota is also a real city. It has a fascinating history filled with many amazing people. The places in Virginia that are described in the book are real, though some names have been changed or left out. The city has many incredible sites to see, including the tallest road bridge in the state of Minnesota.

For more information, see:
https://www.virginiamn.us/

The **Iron Range** is a popular tourist destination in Minnesota. The Iron Range has deep open-pit mines, pristine lakes, and camping options to suit everyone. The Iron Range is also the birthplace of many famous people including Jessica Biel, Bob Dylan, Judy Garland, Chris Pratt, Robert Mondavi, Roger Maris, as well as many players from the 1980 US gold-medal-winning Olympic hockey team. The history of the Iron Range is colorful and fascinating.

For more information, see:
https://www.exploreminnesota.com/profile/iron-range-tourism/2052

About the Author

Dean Lappi was born and raised in Virginia, Minnesota.

He is the author of five novels. All are available on Amazon.

Dean graduated with a Master of Arts degree in English and has worked in a number of industries since then as an Information Developer. He lives with his partner, Erica, who is also his professional book editor. They currently reside in Minnesota with their cat Magnus, whom they rescued while living in Sweden.